Doctor Omega
and the Shadowmen
(Volume 2)

IN THE SAME SERIES

Arnould Galopin. *Doctor Omega*
Jean-Marc & Randy Lofficier (eds.). *Doctor Omega and the Shadowmen (Volume 1)*

Doctor Omega
and the Shadowmen
(Volume 2)

based on the character created by
Arnould Galopin

edited by
Jean-Marc & Randy Lofficier

stories by
**Matthew Baugh, Atom Mudman Bezecny,
David Friend, Martin Gately, Travis Hiltz,
Paul Hugli, Jean-Marc Lofficier, Nigel Malcolm**
and **John Peel.**

A Black Coat Press Book

ISBN 978-1-64932-314-9. First Printing: July 2024. Published
by Black Coat Press, an imprint of Hollywood Comics.com,
LLC, 18321 Ventura Blvd. Suite 915, Tarzana, CA 91356. All
rights reserved. Except for review purposes, no part of this
book may be reproduced or transmitted in any form or by any
means, electronic or mechanical, including photocopying, recording or by any information storage and retrieval system,
without permission in writing from the publisher. The stories
and characters depicted in this anthology are entirely fictional.
Printed in the United States of America.

TABLE OF CONTENTS

Introduction...7

Martin Gately: *The Wolf at the Door of Time*........................11

Travis Hiltz: *What Lurks in Romney Marsh?* 39

Paul Hugli: *As Time Goes By...* 57

Travis Hiltz: *The Next Omega* 77

Travis Hiltz: *All Roads Lead to Mars* 111

Atom Mudman Bezecny: *The Revelation of the Yeti*...........131

John Peel: *Time to Kill*...146

David Friend: *Doctor Omega and the Future Museum*.......167

Matthew Baugh: *The Cubic Displacement of the Soul* 201

Travis Hiltz: *These are the Voyages...* 212

Atom Mudman Bezecny: *Orpheus Omega*...........................237

Jean-Marc Lofficier: *Foiled Again* 249

Nigel Malcolm: *When the Children Leave Home*................253

Travis Hiltz: *The Ghosts of Gascony* 261

Credits and Sources 295

Illustration by J.-M. Breton for the 1906 edition

Introduction

Doctor Omega was created by Arnould Galopin in *Le Docteur Oméga*, a novel first published in France in 1906.

Galopin (1865-1934) is mostly forgotten today; those who remember him are most likely to do so for his juvenile serials such as *Le Tour du Monde de Deux Gosses* [Around The World With Two Kids] (1908) and *Un Aviateur de 15 Ans* [A 15-Year-Old Aviator] (1926).

He was also the author of one of the first French Holmesian pastiches, teaming up an aging Sherlock Holmes and a young Harry Dickson against Jack the Ripper in *L'Homme au Complet Gris* [The Man In Grey] (1910).[1]

Galopin was never a major genre author, nor was he a ground-breaker like H. G. Wells or Jules Verne, but he was an old pro who knew how to spin a yarn and follow a trend. *Le Docteur Oméga*, clearly inspired by Wells, was successful and almost immediately reissued in a series of magazines in 1908 and then reprinted in book form in 1949.

Black Coat Press published an English-language adaptation in 2003 in two editions, one with copies of the original illustrations, the other without.[2]

That adaptation included some minor revisions to the original text, which fell into two categories. The first was some light editing, done to rewrite a number of xenophobic passages—something, sadly, too common at the time—and to smooth over a few particularly clumsy plot points. The second were more cosmetic in nature and intended to pay homage, through revised "technobabble" and visual imagery, not only to *Doctor Who*, but also to other French classics such as Arsène Lupin and Madeline.

---

[1] Black Coat Press, ISBN 978-1-61227-484-3.
[2] ISBNs 978-1-0-9740711-1-4 and 978-0-9740711-0-7.

With *Le Docteur Oméga*, Galopin intended to combine elements from *War of the Worlds* (first published in French in 1900) and *First Men in the Moon* (first published in France in 1901). Stellite is nothing more than cavorite under a different name, and the *Cosmos* is not very different from Cavor's spherical ship. Its shell shape and multi-terrain capabilities were obviously borrowed from Jules Verne.

Galopin's description of Mars is laudably imaginative, but conceptually not very different from what Wells and other French writers had previously imagined. Amongst those were Achille Eyraud, who described the exploration of Venus in *Voyage à Venus* [Voyage to Venus] (1865)[3] and Georges Le Faure & Henry de Graffigny who depicted a journey through the Solar System in *Les Aventures Extraordinaires d'un Savant Russe* [The Extraordinary Adventures of a Russian Scientist Across the Solar System] (1889).[4]

What was, however, unique, was the character of Doctor Omega himself. All its predecessors were eccentrically brilliant scientists, but grounded in the real world. Not so Omega—an unlikely surname to begin with—who remains shrouded in mystery, his background and origins purposefully kept obscure. Why?

One cannot accuse Galopin of lacking in imagination. And from a commercial standpoint, making his main hero a cipher was surely not a good idea. How could a writer as commercially-minded as Galopin make such a beginner's mistake? When Galopin rewrote the novel as a juvenile serial, he had another chance to explain who Omega was, and where he came from, but once again, he chose not to do so.

Another puzzling decision is the *deus ex machina* intervention of the equally mysterious Professor Helvetius at the end of the novel. Helvetius is described as "British," but Gal-

---

[3] Black Coat Press, ISBN 978-1-61227-005-0.
[4] Black Coat Press, ISBNs 978-1-935543-81-8 and 978-1-935543-82-5.

opin tells us nothing about him, certainly not how he could have independently duplicated the secret of manufacturing stellite, enabling him to build a second spacecraft in such a short time. Of all the possible ways of rescuing the characters and returning them to Earth at the end of the novel, this was certainly the clumsiest and the least convincing—unless one simply assumes that there is more to the story of Omega and Helvetius than the author is telling us...

Galopin ended *Le Docteur Oméga* with the promise of further space journeys, but despite this, he never wrote a sequel to it. So we are left with no clues as to why he chose to make Doctor Omega a mystery, and the unlimited potential of his hero (as *Doctor Who* later amply demonstrated) remained sadly untapped. Another French ground-breaking oddity.

Le Docteur Oméga was followed by three more colorful Martian novels, which we heartily recommend: Henri Gayar's *Les Aventures Merveilleuses de Serge Myrandhal sur la Planète Mars* [The Marvelous Adventures of Serge Myrandhal on Mars] (1908),[5] Gustave Le Rouge's *Le Prisonnier de la Planète Mars* [The Vampires of Mars] (1908)[6] and Jean de La Hire's *Le Mystère des XV* [The Nyctalope on Mars] (1911).[7]

Despite a number of superficial and mostly cosmetic resemblance, I do not believe for a minute that the creators of *Doctor Who* had ever heard of *Le Docteur Oméga* which, even in France, had been virtually forgotten by the 1960s. If there is a connection between the two, it is to be found in the writings of Carl Jung, not science fiction.

However, the archetypal nature of Doctor Omega helps explain why he, like Jean de La Hire's Nyctalope or Norbert Sevestre's Sâr Dubnotal, has become one of the favorite French characters used by the contributors to our anthology

[5] Black Coat Press, ISBN 978-1-61227-265-8.

[6] Black Coat Press, ISBN 978-1-934543-30-6.

[7] Black Coat Press, ISBN 978-1-934543-46-7.

Tales of the Shadowmen, devoted to paying homage to often forgotten heroes and villains of French popular fiction.

This second volume of *Doctor Omega and the Shadowmen* collects all of the remaining stories previously published in *Tales of the Shadowmen*, featuring the indomitable Doctor.

Enjoy!

Jean-Marc & Randy Lofficier

British author Martin Gately, who passed away earlier this year, is very much missed amongst the writers who seized upon the eccentric Doctor and spun new yarns about him. This story makes use of another equally odd and enigmatic time traveler, Dr. Moses Nebogipfel, introduced by H. G. Wells in "The Chronic Argonauts" in 1888, which may well have inspired Galopin's creation...

Martin Gately: *The Wolf at the Door of Time*

Doctor Omega eased back on the temporal throttle, bringing the passage of his Space and Time ship—the *Cosmos*—to a virtual stop within the aether. The ship was momentarily buffeted by highly charged energy clouds until the Doctor delicately nudged the controls and the craft moved out of the central turbulence into the gentler time eddies of the gravity foam boundary. Turning slowly in the foam was the object that had first caught his attention in the chronoscope: a derelict time vehicle—an eight-meter cylinder of brass, crystal and ivory, beautifully constructed and only lightly covered with bosonic frost. It had not been lost in the aether for long, perhaps only a few days ship's time, a week at most. The most startling thing about the craft was the ragged hole in its fuselage as if *something* had burst out of it.

The Doctor identified a hatch at the end of the cylinder and maneuvered the *Cosmos* closer until its docking coupler was able to reach out and bring the two ships together. He then reconfigured the environmental controls of the *Cosmos* so that a breathable atmosphere was created and sustained within the derelict. The Doctor donned a fur-lined jacket—it would be cold on the other ship—and grabbed a lantern from the stores. He passed through his own airlock with ease but had to use a sonic wand to open the intransigent frosted hatch into the cylinder. The aged scientist moved carefully into the gloom of the derelict; the cone of illumination from his lantern picked out the empty pilot's chair and sweeping control console with its jewel handled levers and coral toggle switches. Then, in the corner of the chamber, he saw what must once have been a steel cage. The bars of this cage had been bent outwards as easily as if they were pipe-cleaners. The Doctor shuddered involuntarily at the thought of a creature possessed of that level of strength and ferocity and wondered if he had not best return to the *Cosmos* to collect something to use as a weapon. No, the chances were that whatever this creature was it had exited the craft via the ruptured hull some time ago; but that brought its own problems and severe concerns were already starting to coagulate in the back of his mind.

Doctor Omega swept his light over the deck in front of him. Curled up in a fetal position on the floor was a figure in a helmeted environment suit. The suit seemed highly anachronistic: while the derelict itself could easily be the product of a late Victorian age genius experimenter, the almost insectoid suit looked to have been developed by an advanced civilization; at a guess the Arcadian Hegemony of late 42nd century Earth. The Doctor crouched down and put his lantern on the deck, then reached out to rouse the prone figure by shaking his shoulder. The figure stirred suddenly and then aimed at the Doctor what he immediately recognized as a *staseur* energy pistol.

"Go ahead, shoot!" instructed Doctor Omega. "I can assure you that it will have very little effect. The energy weapon suppression field of my ship also envelops yours. Perhaps you would be better served by telling me who you are and how you got into this sorry predicament, eh?"

The man raised the visor of the environment suit helmet and looked squarely at the Doctor.

"My name is Doctor Moses Nebogipfel," he stated flatly. "And all of this has happened to me because I was foolish enough to transport a mesonychid in my time machine."

"Hmm. To say foolish would be putting it rather mildly," admonished Doctor Omega. "In terms of evolutionary biology, that was rather like kicking out the bottom layer of a house of cards and expecting the structure to stay up…"

"I don't know what you mean," said Nebogipfel with a look of genuine puzzlement.

"The mesonychid is a key ancestor for an entire branch of mammalian development. If you removed it from its proper place in space and time before it produced progeny, you will have potentially devastated the ecology of great swathes of the Earth. You understand what the mesonychid is, surely?"

"Yes, it's a colossal and vicious prehistoric wolf," answered Nebogipfel.

The Doctor rubbed his brow and shook his head. Perhaps he had been overly lucky over the years with his choice of companions—such men as Fred, Borel and Tiziraou—it meant that, very unfortunately, he had become unaccustomed to dealing with idiots.

The Doctor shone his lantern on the floor of the cage, noting the massive almost hoof-like paw prints in the compacted foul-smelling excrement. Then he ran the beam over to the gaping tear in the hull.

"The wolf was alive when it went out into the aether?" the old scientist asked.

Nebogipfel merely nodded.

"This is far more serious than I thought," exhaled Doctor Omega.

Later, while Nebogipfel supped hot cocoa from a chipped ceramic mug aboard the *Cosmos,* Doctor Omega piloted the two docked craft towards the Fresnel Tertiary Boundary—the Void equivalent of periscope depth—and deployed the chronoscope. It would allow him to observe the material universe—the 'normal' Euclidean space outside the aether.

Doctor Omega's eyes had been pressed hard against the chronoscope viewer for nearly twenty-five minutes when he gave a snort of triumph and switched on the large flat monitor screen so that Nebogipfel could also see what he had found.

"The wolf has absorbed a phenomenal amount of Feinberg energy and is being hurled forward just above the secondary gravity foam layer. You can see the arc of its path quite clearly. It is as if the beast were a rubber ball thrown very hard in a confined space; so just as the kinetic force propelling the ball would cause it to hit a surface and bounce off, so the valence of the charge will make the mesonychid materialize in space and time. To begin with the materializations will be short, but as the energy dies the beast will manifest in time for longer and longer periods until finally it will come to rest, like a crazily bouncing ball ultimately coming to a stop on a single floor tile," explained the Doctor.

"But it's only a wolf," whined Nebogipfel. "What damage can it really do? Most likely it will be shot by a hunter and that will be the end of it."

"Perhaps that will happen, but we must follow the creature through time and do what we can to mitigate its effect on the continuum. At the moment, I hesitate to use the chronoscope to look into the far future of Earth because I fear what I may see. Let us try to view the wolf's first manifestation. The first temporal arc ends in the year 1577 AD in the village of Bungay in Suffolk, England."

The screen flickered for a moment and then showed a crackly black and white image of a church with a tall, proud spire and cockerel weathervane; then moved in closer, closer until the walls of the church seemed to part to allow a view of the congregation sitting on pews in the middle of their prayers. The pictures from the chronoscope were silent, like ancient newsreel footage, and perhaps that was a blessing when, seconds later, the clergyman's mouth issued forth screams rather than benedictions and the worshippers ran in terror towards the altar away from the dreadful thing wrapped in black lightning that had appeared at the back of the church.

The wolf was as dark as jet and all of its fur stood on end due to the tachyonic static. It was like no wolf that had walked the Earth in tens of millions of years. Its snout and jaws were impossibly elongated, like a creature from a fairy tale picture book. Its cheeks were bulbous and rounded with thick knots of muscle capable of snapping its mandibles together as powerfully as a mantrap. Its teeth were nearly three inches long and looked as if they more properly belonged in the mouth of a crocodile. The eyes blazed, and, though the scanner was only delivering a monochrome image, Doctor Omega knew deep in his soul that they were glowing red—red as hellfire. To these simple folk it must have looked like a hound straight out of Hades.

There was really nothing they could do but watch helplessly as the wolf attacked the people and tore off limbs and heads. The pews were splintered under the beast's hoof-like paws and, most dreadful of all, it grabbed a child in its mouth and shook it to pieces. The beast then pounced on a man and still had his severed leg in its maw when a swirl of inky bubbles lifted the creature away into the void and it was gone from the church as inexplicably as it had arrived.

"That was nauseating, simply horrible," cried Nebogipfel as fat tears ran down his sallow face.

"Horrible, yes—and you are responsible! Why on Earth were you transporting that creature through time? Have you absolutely no sense at all? No sense of the grave responsibility you have as a time traveler not to pollute nor divert the flow of history?"

"I'd travelled to the 42nd Century and settled there for a while; the people there urged me to bring back specimens from the far past for their zoological gardens. There are so few interesting animals left in that time period and they wanted something exciting so I…"

"…Went back to the Eocene and stunned with your *staseur* what with your limited scientific knowledge you mistook for merely some form of primitive hound-like proto-wolf?" interrupted the Doctor. "Transporting animals for profit…hardly original… I have heard of it before to a lesser extent, but nothing as monstrously foolhardy as this."

Nebogipfel looked up at the monitor as if for absolution or inspiration and instead saw that the chronoscope had tracked the end of the next temporal arc; the mesonychid was materializing again.

"It is now 1643," observed Doctor Omega. "Somewhere near the village of Grimpen on Dartmoor. Possibly the circle of Neolithic stones that you see in the background was in some way conducive to the materialization."

Nebogipfel flinched as he attempted to watch the unfolding scene as it was displayed on the screen. A huge, brutal-looking man, dressed in the rich, lace-trimmed finery of a nobleman of the period was viciously attacking a beautiful young maiden out on the bleak vastness of the moors.

The off-white monoliths gleamed dully in the moonlight like a jagged row of broken teeth as the attacker knocked the girl down then tugged and tore at her garments, before finally pulling from his belt a knife and filleting open her bodice to expose heavy, lolling breasts. The man seemed to be salivating uncontrollably as he loomed over her. She clutched at her chest, not through modesty, but from the beginnings of the pain of cardiac arrest.

The picture flickered and Doctor Omega fine-tuned the controls of the chronoscope to restore the image. When the picture came back, it was in garish hues. The girl's lips were blue from cyanosis though her face was a slate grey. The immense rangy lupine form of the mesonychid was advancing now on the nobleman: the black lightning of its previous materialization had resolved itself into a cherry red and gold halo-like glow. The beast looked at up the sky and howled before it leapt and Doctor Omega immediately regretted his fine-tuning. The chronoscope had picked up sound and the howl was the most earsplitting and unnerving thing that he had ever heard. The mesonychid plucked at the throat of the man and long scarlet threads caught between its long teeth. Three men on horseback entered the scene, momentarily blocking the view of the fallen man. One of the men shouted something that might have been "Sir Hugo!" and then they cantered away in terror. The image faded into silvery static.

"You criticize me and yet you have done nothing to save those people!" accused Nebogipfel as he undid the seals of his environment suit and started to extricate himself from it.

"What would you have me do at this stage? You understand so little that I would have to devote most of your life to teaching you the basics of temporal mechanics before we could commence to have an intelligent discussion! You know nothing of the cavitation wave effect I'll wager. You understood my analogy with the bouncing ball so I'll give you another. When I materialize the *Cosmos* in time and space, a harmless wave of energy displaces the molecules that are already there to create a cavity that the ship can occupy. It has no detrimental effect on molecules that are native to any given point in spacetime, but the creature is charged with fantastic amounts of energy from the aether. The wave would give it sufficient impetus to start another temporal arc. Like a billiard ball directly in front of the pocket—it only takes a tiny nudge of kinetic energy to send it down the hole and completely off the table."

"So we can't ever materialize in the same place as the wolf?" asked Nebogipfel.

"Every time we did, we would simply push the beast further on in time. No, we must track it until the energy has dispersed and deal with it then."

"And what of those who are slaughtered by the creature in the interim?"

"I will think on it, but I suspect that there is nothing I can do for them," said the Doctor as he lit his pipe.

Joseph Balsamo approached the hovel in the woods carefully. The stories of man-eating wolves in this locality had greatly unnerved him, but he had a duty to perform and he would not shirk it. A guttural growl from the far side of the structure made him feel as if his stomach were performing somersaults. If he encountered the Beast or one of its progeny now, how would he defend himself? He had been a fool to come here alone and unarmed. The great hound slunk around the side of the hovel and bounded towards him making him cry out with fear. Then as the dog leapt at him there came the embarrassing realization that the creature meant him no harm and was trying to lick his face.

"My dog will not hurt you, sir," said Jean Chastel as he too appeared from inside the hovel's curtained door. The huntsman shouldered his arquebus musket and gave a broad grin as his pet continued to direct its slobbering affections at the stranger.

"Come inside and have some wine, my friend. I can tie Max up outside."

A little while later, Balsamo eased himself onto the rough stool while Chastel poured wine into two old cups.

"I am a novice from the Order of St John of God and I am here on a special mission," explained Balsamo—this was actually a lie, albeit a fairly harmless one. Balsamo had been ejected from the order some time ago, but he could not shake the feeling that the strange dreams he'd had of late were connected with his time with the brotherhood.

"Yes, yes - of course, the ammunition," interjected Chastel.

"*You* know about the ammunition?" asked Balsamo surprised.

"My friend, every clergyman for miles around has travelled here to bless my bullets; either that or sent me the shot they think I should use—most of it doesn't even fit my gun. But I'm glad of the company so you are most welcome here."

"You are truly hunting the Beast alone? Aren't you afraid? They say it has killed over a hundred people..." said Balsamo with genuine admiration.

"I suppose I wouldn't be much of a wolf hunter if I was so very frightened of wolves, but yes, I am more than a little afraid, for I have seen it, more than once, and it is no ordinary wolf. And I don't just mean in size. It is as different from a forest wolf as a lion is from a cat. It does not belong here. Nevertheless, it has rutted and bred with our wolves producing many a tainted offspring. They carry the look of the thing; the

18

length of snout, the heaviness of the paws. Some of these I have already killed. I call them the wolf-mules, for they are barren creatures and neither male nor female. I doubt if they could live a proper lifespan," explained the hunter.

"There is something I must tell you," began Balsamo. "About a month ago, I started to have odd dreams. At first, I ignored them but the man in my dreams became more and more insistent."

"Man?"

"Yes, an old man with long white hair—an untidy lock of hair at the top—wearing a long black coat such as one might wear to a funeral. He wanted me to make something for him; he said that mine was the most sensitive mind in this locality; actually, I think he said time period, and that I already knew something of alchemy and that would help," said Balsamo, once again somewhat embarrassed."

"What did this 'dream man' want you to make?"

"Well, at first, I thought it was a huge hollow cylinder made of silver and filled with cables spun from gold and platinum all inset with crystals and jewels and I asked him how I could build it when the richest man on Earth could not have afforded the riches to put inside it and he explained that the cylinder was something like a bullet and would be no more than an inch or so long. It was impossibly intricate. It nearly drove me to distraction making it because it was so difficult. In the end, he said I should give it to the huntsman Jean Chastel in the forest of Mont Mouchet and that you *must* use it to kill the Beast. He said it is the only way we can be rid of it," and with that Balsamo took the silver cylinder from his pocket and handed it to Chastel.

"It's beautiful, but it is far too large for the barrel of my arquebus," said Chastel and he held the cylinder near the muzzle in order to demonstrate.

The cylinder emitted a sound something like birdsong for a split second before it adjusted its size so that it could easily slip down the barrel.

"The work of the Devil!" exclaimed Chastel.

"I think not. It is not the Devil who wants to destroy the Beast of Gévaudan. Make sure you do use that bullet—I really need to get some proper sleep. Thank you for the wine," said Balsamo as he got up to leave.

Four days later, the mesonychid stepped out of undergrowth in front of Jean Chastel and sat down on the forest path. The creature had learned that musket fire bothered it little more than insect stings and it was totally unafraid. Chastel leveled the arquebus at it and aimed carefully. The immense thing's eyes troubled him; they were a dull dark grayish red, like dying embers. There was an incredible arrogance about the creature that said: "Do your worst!" —like a bruiser in a bar spoiling for a fight who knows that your best punch will only faze him. Chastel gently squeezed the trigger lever on the musket and a liquid silver cage seemed to form around the wolf for a heartbeat, then there was a multi-colored flash of light that somehow reminded the hunter of stained-glass windows and the Beast was gone.

Having seen the miraculous bullet change shape, the huntsman was not entirely surprised at this turn of events. He owed a debt to the strange young alchemist and the white-haired man from his dreams that he would never be able to repay. Now he was left wondering how he could claim the reward on the wolf with no wolf carcass to show. His own ingenuity soon solved this. Two days later he killed a wolf-mule— the largest he had seen—few would question that this was a wolf capable of killing over one hundred men, women and children. The Beast of Gévaudan was gone—gone back to the hellfire from whence it came, for all he cared.

Doctor Omega shook Nebogipfel gently by shoulder to wake him. Nebogipfel sat up in his cot and rubbed his eyes. The Doctor offered him a steaming cup of fresh tea which he gratefully accepted.

"The situation has improved a little while you were sleeping," stated the old man.

"Hmm?" yawned the rather incompetent time traveler.

"The Beast is trapped in a bubble in the aether for the time being. Now I know you understand little of such things and we have no time for long explanations," began the Doctor as if to a cap-wearing dunce. "Essentially, I have equipment aboard the *Cosmos* that can make a precise duplicate of a short stretch of the timestream and by using the power of this craft's engines I can fold a fragment of the universe into an enclosed pocket in which it will repeat itself until it runs out of energy and the bubble collapses. The Beast's reality bubble holds about six days of history from Villers-Cotterets in rural France in the 18th century."

"But that's incredible! Then, this is no mere time machine! You can manipulate and create your own realities... Yet, how did you get the wolf into the bubble?"

"With some minor adaptations of the chronoscope, I was able to cobble together a sort of mental projector and place words, images, commands even, into the mind of a rather brilliant but amoral young man in 1767 and he built for me using his not inconsiderable skills a device that transported the wolf out of normal time using just the odd scraps he scrounged from a local jeweler and the bits and pieces he had on his own alchemy bench."

"Well, this is an enormous relief. So with the whole issue of the wolf resolved you can perhaps assist me in repairing my machine and I can return to my own time period," smiled Nebogipfel nervously.

"Not so fast!" exclaimed the old man. "I only said that the situation had improved, not that it had been sorted out once and for all. Yes, the mesonychid is trapped, but only temporarily. When the bubble breaks down the wolf will arc back into normal spacetime, but its levels of tachyonic energy will be vastly diminished. I doubt if its momentum through time will carry it much beyond the early 20th century."

"How is the wolf's energy being drawn off within the bubble? What is it being expended on?"

"A good question, Nebogipfel. He is granting wishes to another inhabitant of my little pocket universe. A rather self-pitying sabot-maker called Thibault who wants nothing more than an easy yet grandiose life. Each wish reconfigures the reality within the bubble and uses up part of the tachyon charge."

"Why would a wolf be granting wishes?" asked Nebogipfel.

"It thinks it is the Devil," answered the Doctor.

"Oh, no! That really can't be good."

"It is somewhat alarming, but quite useful for our purposes. For a wolf, the mesonychid has a gigantic brain and greater than primate intelligence; but this will not be generally known until the mid-21st century. I am using the psionic projector to exchange thoughts between the wolf and Thibault creating a sort of artificial telepathy between them. Thibault was afraid of the wolf to begin with and asked if it was the Devil. The mesonychid can find no better explanation of its existence and is happy to accept itself as being the Devil."

"Why? Why does a prehistoric wolf have a massive brain? Modern wolves don't have a primate-like intelligence so why should it?"

"I told you it was a key ancestor. Didn't you stop to think what it might be the ancestor of? The mesonychid is the land-based ancestor of all dolphins and whales. Without the presence of this single specimen of mesonychid in the whale lineage, the biological history of the world is re-written. Entire species of whale have simply never existed. Worse still, while you slept I summoned up the courage to direct the chrono-scope to the extreme far future of Earth; to a time when I know the oceans are dry and great pods of sky-whales fly above the planet consuming aerial krill—it is a time I have visited on many occasions—but no longer. The sky-whales have never existed and instead of their deity, Zoomashmarta, the remaining humans worship a titanic bloated wolf; a wolf that eats only human flesh. I saw farms dedicated to breeding humans for it to eat. It has been mutated by its long exposure to the void and grown so large that it dwarfs the sea dwelling whales that it has served to replace," explained the Doctor shuddering.

At this Nebogipfel broke down in sobs and made inarticulate howling noises which the Doctor was not sure whether to categorize as hysterical or merely histrionic.

"Console yourself! With the remedial actions I have taken we can hope that the future I saw will not come to pass. We will now play a waiting game. In a few days, the reality bubble will collapse and the hunt will be on again."

The great wolf walked into Thibault's cottage on its hind legs and dropped the bloody doe carcass onto the floor.

"You wished for meat," said the black wolf. "Well here it is. I did not even have to hunt for it in the forest, I just imagined a deer and the deer appeared in front of me. I like this new world in which I find myself, it is all so easy here."

"I'll be able to sell on this venison to the charcuterie in Laon and make enough money to buy a fine new suit of clothes... I'll be able to woo Agnelette or perhaps a woman of rather higher status. Why should I not set my sights higher now that the Devil himself is my ally?" asked Thibault.

"Why not indeed? Why do you wish for a single mate? All of the women in this realm are yours to take. When I arrive in a new world, every bitch of my kind must submit to me or die. I rip off the heads of cubs that I have not sired and drive away the adult males – that is the best way. For food, I like your species. You are slow runners and your meat is sweet," said the Wolf while Thibault's eyes widened with terror.

"You... you would not eat me?" quaked the little shoemaker.

"No, you I have marked out as special amongst the humans. Our minds are somehow joined and I take pleasure in altering this world to please you. I like the way that your hair changes each time I grant one of your wishes."

23

Thibault had noticed this too. In the broken-looking glass that hung on his cottage wall he inspected his scalp periodically and saw the thick blood red hairs which were sprouting from the center of his parting. To begin with he had been able to cunningly brush his hair so that the strings of scarlet could not be seen. Now it was useless and people were starting to stare or worse to ask him to account for the hairs for they suspected that he was a werewolf. The black wolf had been seen walking away from Thibault's cottage on at least a couple of occasions and the simple folk of the locality had drawn the obvious conclusion that the human occupant of the cottage and the bipedal wolf were one and the same.

"Why do you not walk on all fours like a normal forest wolf?" asked Thibault. "You are making everyone think that I change into a wolf."

"Since our minds joined, I find it easier to walk this way," explained the Devil-wolf. "For a long time, it seemed as if that great body of water—the ocean—called to me. I had urges to run and play in the sea to raise my young there and never leave the dark waters. That desire is dead in me now. I wished instead for a land of plentiful slow-moving prey who cannot defend themselves, who leave their children undefended and sleep soundly at night in weak wooden shelters that I can break down with my heavy paws. I am in that land now, and it is almost perfect; my heart is filled with bliss when I think of the impotence of the human hunters and how their metal projectiles scarcely break my skin."

And so, in the days to come, Thibault's wishes became greater and greater in number, as did the glowing cables of red erupting from his scalp. Thibault became the Lord of Vez— the most powerful nobleman of his region, the master of an impregnable castle guarded by an army of wolves. He was now a giant of a man, a prodigious warrior who exacted the most terrible revenge on those who had tortured him in punishment for his old sideline of being a successful poacher. This night, Thibault and the Devil-wolf stand atop the battlements of the castle and watch the sky together. The sky is slowly opening and beyond it can be seen a howling wild void of dust clouds and swirling star-froth. It feels like the end of the world and it is.

"If this is the final night that will ever be," began Thibault, "then bring me every woman that I have ever desired and I will make love to them all in my bedchamber right now."

"This is the end of everything," said the black wolf. "And my power is fading...go to your bed...I will do my best to bring about your wish."

Thibault went to his room and lit a lamp, then, for want of anything better to do, changed into his night attire. A few minutes later, the door swung open and the exquisite sixteen-year-old Agnelette entered the room, still wearing the simple grey linen cap and country dress that she had on the last time he saw her. He went over to her and removed the little cap allowing the cascade of blond hair to fall to her shoulders. Yet, there was no recognition in her eyes. Her eyes were black and dead. She started to disrobe and her movements were like those of a wind-up automaton. Was this really Agnelette? Thibault drank in the beauty of her form as she tugged off her undergarments. The pink tipped breasts were just as he had seen them in his dreams. Finally, she was naked and something was horribly wrong. In the place where Thibault had always imagined there would be just a downy, feathery triangle of curls there was an impenetrable mass of blood red glowing hairs—each individual hair as thick as an earthworm. It was as if some vile poisonous sea anemone had taken root in the place he desired most of all.

Thibault recoiled in horror at the sight and the door opened again. Now, Madame Magloire—the bailiff's wife whom Thibault had ached with desire for a long time—came in and swiftly divested herself of her clothing. Her limbs were long and sensuous and her bosom two jutting cones of creamy flesh. It was all too much for Thibault to bear, especially when he saw that she too had the great scarlet serpentine fibers, a huge dangling mass of them hanging most of the way down her thighs.

In short order, the delightful little maid Lisette entered and made herself nude, as did her mistress, the Comtesse de Mont-Gobert; and—this last addition was the most physically beautiful of all, for her sinuous shape was truly bewitching—if only her eyes were not dead, if only her pubis was not marred by the angry-looking tendrils. Unable to help himself, he reached out to touch the Comtesse. The red hairs stung his fingers as if they were jellyfish tentacles and when he pulled his hand back it was covered in deep welts. He looked at each of the naked doll-like women in turn; each of them had the same blank face and the same red growth. This was not at all how he had imagined his last night on Earth.

"Wolf! Wolf!" cried out Thibault. "What I wished for is not happening properly. Use your magic again!"

The exhausted wolf crawled into the bed chamber and lay down on the rug.

"The magic has run out, my friend," explained the wolf. "I told you I would do my best, but this is the end of everything."

Thibault threw his arms around the wolf's neck and hugged him. Then Thibault, the castle and the French countryside melted away, and only the wolf was left, tumbling and spinning in the aether.

"This calls for something stronger than tea," smiled Doctor Omega as he opened the little wooden wall cabinet and extracted several bottles of varying sizes and a couple of glasses. "I wonder if the cryogenics unit can spare us some ice for our cocktails."

"Cocktails?" queried Nebogipfel.

"Of course, I always celebrate in style," without further explanation the Doctor added *Dubonnet*, orange bitters and gin to the glasses, then some shards of ice from the cryo-overflow tube, before concluding with French Vermouth. "The reality bubble trap worked very well. Almost all the wolf's energy has been used up. After we have finished our drinks I will deploy the chronoscope for what could very well be the last time."

The two men relaxed and sipped at their delicious cocktails while looking absently out of the porthole at the milky swirls of quantum foam. Suddenly, a white streaking shape with a red and silver trail passed by so close that they could almost have reached out of the porthole and touched it.

"The mesonychid!" shouted Nebogipfel. "And it almost hit us!"

"I don't think so, but let me check that object with the chronoscope just to be sure…"

The old scientist put his eyes to the viewer and swiftly locked the sensors on the departing shape.

"It is a meteorite, an ordinary chondrite to be specific, but highly charged with ionizing radiation from the Void."

"A meteorite?" queried Nebogipfel. "But this isn't ordinary space. How could a something other than a time vehicle enter the aether?"

"It is possible in certain circumstances. There are those that I refer to as the 'discarnate entities.' A few of these, such as Zoomashmarta, have come to dwell within this wormhole. Some are worshipped as gods at different points in the timestream; the points at which their influence is strongest. But if Man knew what little power the gods did wield, he would question the purpose of prayer... These beings sometimes draw things into the void for their own mysterious purposes. To help or hinder mankind as they have judged fit. In this case, I doubt if it is a coincidence. The meteorite is exiting the void in late 1795. That is remarkably near to when the wolf has been manifesting itself in time. Hmmm. A meteorite charged with bosonic particles might cause beneficial mutations. I wonder if someone is trying to give mankind an advantage in the long-term battle against the mesonychid; perhaps even Zoomashmarta himself."

The *Cosmos,* still conjoined with Nebogipfel's ship, which he revealed to Doctor Omega he had rather unimagina-

27

tively christened *The Argo*, continued their gradual progress through the aether, questing for any sign of the termination point of the wolf's latest jaunt through time.

The Doctor allowed Nebogipfel to take a turn at the viewer having taught him how to manipulate the controls. It was over an hour later that the intense gaze of the younger man lighted on a faint energy trail that curved through the roiling foam heading out towards the year 1916. Nebogipfel alerted Doctor Omega straightaway but they were unable to lock the chronoscope onto the wolf's exact position. Their best estimate was that the creature was roving the battlefield of Mons sometime in the late summer of that year.

Captain Yeskes of the Fifth Northumberland Fusiliers awoke in the stench of the muddy charnel pit. Death was all around him. For weeks he had been losing patrols in no-man's land, patrols that had not been victim to either phosgene gas or the German shelling. Now he knew the reason why. The thing that the men had spoken about was real. He had quashed the rumors when he heard them; devised punishment details for those who had even whispered of a monstrous hound that slunk about the great shell holes and abandoned trenches. These were surely stories for children to tell, not grown men fighting for their country. Yet, he had consoled himself that some of these soldiers were little more than boys. Two men had said they had seen the beast up close. They said it was shaped like a massive wolf, almost as big as a dray horse. It had dragged injured soldiers into a gargantuan pit of liquid mud. They called the pit its larder for it was full of dying men and the split human bones that it had opened to sup on the marrow. They said that it must have a human brain because it was more cunning than any ordinary beast. They theorized that it was perhaps some new German weapon. Yeskes put them on a charge and had them flogged. Now, as he lay in the larder pit himself, he wished he'd pulled out the most detailed map he had of the blasted hinterland between the two opposing sets of trenches and got the men to estimate as precisely as they could the position of the beast's pit before directing every single allied artillery piece to fire on it.

The summer sun had hardened most of the battlefield's sucking mud, but not here in the wolf's pit. Yeskes had sunk in almost up to his thighs and he was ever so slowly continuing to sink. He reached for his holster while he still could and pulled out his service revolver. His arm was swollen and painful to move due to the bite he had sustained. The thing had also swiped a heavy paw at his head like a cat playing with a mouse and his forehead was caked with a thick crust of blood. His throat hurt abominably and he was burning up with fever. If the thing came back now it would be tempting to blaze away at it with the revolver—a couple of shots at least—before he turned the gun on himself. He had no intention of being eaten alive.

He sat and waited for the wolf creature to drop back over the rim of the muddy crater and advance on him. He had to stay awake until then. After a while, with his mind drifting back to his childhood he became aware that he was hallucinating. An old man with silvery white hair in a black frock coat was moving down the pit's slopes towards him. Not climbing down, but sort of drifting as if levitating. The old man's hair and white shirt glowed with an unearthly transfiguring light and there was a bluish electric halo about him. Well, thought the injured man, since one legend of no-man's land had proved to be true then why not another? Surely this could only be the Companion in White, the angelic, Christ-like figure who appeared to and sometimes aided dying soldiers?

The "Companion in White" spoke to one of his fellow angels who remained unseen.

"Nebogipfel, there is a man in the crater. Increase the projection energy to hard-light settings. I must help him," the strange vision intoned.

The angel seemed to gain greater substance and settled on the mud to walk about like an ordinary mortal. Captain Yeskes lifted his arms up as if in supplication and the angel reached down and pulled him clear of the quicksand-like drag of the mud with prodigious strength and therefore surprising ease. The angel tore at the rough material of the Captain's battledress jacket exposing the deep and bloody puncture wounds where his arm had been mauled by the wolf. The Companion in White then removed his frock coat and ripped at his own shirtsleeve until he had torn off sufficient material to create an improvised bandage.

"Are you real?" asked Yeskes.

"In the very strictest sense, no. I am a projection beamed to this location from beyond the aether, but that is hardly anything for you to worry about my young friend," said the angel.

"A drink of water...a cigarette?" requested Yeskes through parched lips.

"I very much regret that I can supply neither at this moment, Captain. I must get you out of this pit and back to your own lines."

And with that the angel started to lift up Yeskes. But then after a couple of steps, he set him back down on the earth very gently, then reached for Yeskes's webbing belt and removed the long-bladed bayonet. The mesonychid was padding down the slope softly, stealthily, towards them. Incredibly, it looked somewhat lean and undernourished. The conditions here on the battlefield did not suit it and it had contracted mange thereby losing much of its black fur. This contributed to giving it a canine rather than lupine look, something like a mammoth, freakish lurcher crossed with Fenris of Norse mythology. The angel reached down for his frock coat and then held it in front of him like a matador's cape while still holding the bayonet in his right hand. The wolf glowered at the men with its dull red eyes and then leapt with jaws agape. The Angel sidestepped and jabbed at the wolf's haunches with the bayonet as it flew past in a move that the great bullfighter Juan Belmonte would have envied.

The wolf's momentum carried into the very center of the mud pit and it flopped into the liquid morass. Captain Yeskes looked on expecting the beast to be sucked down into the mire and never seen again. But he had not counted on its fantastic strength, nor its innate, instinctive swimming. The thing originated from a time when no mammals swam, and yet the skill was somehow hard-wired into its brain. It kept its head up and fought against the sucking power of the pit; its limbs rhythmically pounding, unseen, beneath the surface.

Doctor Omega was in a quandary now. His plan to lure the beast into an area of heavy shelling had failed and he now had a responsibility to preserve the life of the young army Captain. But if the wolf bit the time traveler's hard-light simulacrum the bio-electric feedback would short out the sensors attached to his real body aboard the *Cosmos* possibly killing him. If he reverted to a soft-light specular projection or ripped off the sensors he would no longer be able to assist Captain Yeskes. It was an impossible choice. The old man thought nothing of his own safety but if he was slain how might the mesonychid ever be stopped? He barked an order to Nebogipfel to reduce the projector levels to soft-light.

"I can't! There's something wrong with the power controls," shouted Nebogipfel, sounding terrified.

Captain Yeskes watched astonished as the angel jerked and convulsed as if experiencing severe electric shocks. The beast was now only up to its hocks in mud and was edging up towards Omega and Yeskes. Yeskes aimed his Webley revolver squarely at the wolf's head and squeezed off two shots. This weapon was far more powerful than the ancient muskets that the creature had been hunted with in the 18th century, especially at this close range. The bullets pierced its armored hide and thick dark blood spread out over its fur like a wine stain on linen. Shocked and enraged though the wolf was, it neither paused nor retreated. Yeskes checked that there was a third cartridge in the cylinder and then put the barrel to his temple. He shut his eyes, attempted to pull from deep within himself the unequivocal urge to end his own life and failed. The wolf's fetid breath rolled towards him like a hot, sickly cloud. He knew his fate would be to be torn asunder and consumed. A groaning, wheezing sound filled the air. The sound was loud, alarming, slightly unearthly and mixture of a repetitive mechanical grinding fused with something like whale song.

The Captain opened his eyes and saw the wolf fading away; shoved out of the here and now molecule by molecule as the cavitation wave from the combined materialization of the *Cosmos* and the Argo struck it. The Companion in White had disappeared as well. Yeskes looked up and balanced on the edge of the crater was a long ivory colored tube with a blue capsule attached to it. The sight of the ivory tube reminded him that he still needed a cigarette. Shock, dehydration and loss of blood finally caught up with him and his head slumped onto the ground.

"Yes, we need to get the Captain to a hospital," agreed Doctor Omega. "But I have thought the better of returning him to his own lines. We'll take him to a military infirmary in England. If he makes an official report here about the mesonychid the evidence will support its existence and valuable resources will be deployed in looking for it that would be more effectively used elsewhere."

"How much further down the timestream do you think the wolf has gone? It was hardly carrying any charge at all."

"Perhaps only thirty or forty years at most," replied the Doctor. "One more thing, Nebogipfel. I always like to give praise where it is due and your quick thinking in activating the materialization circuits saved my life. The fault in the projection power controls was my responsibility. I have made far too many improvised changes to the electrical systems aboard the *Cosmos* recently."

The two men placed Yeskes onto a cot then headed back to the control room where the Doctor dematerialized the ship in order to shift its position in space.

"As I was saying, I am in your debt Nebogipfel, but your exile on Earth must continue and I must remove from you the ability to travel through time and space until you have properly learned your lesson."

"My exile must continue? What do you mean? I am not in exile?" said Nebogipfel baffled.

"Your supracranial development and ability to cobble together a time vehicle make it quite obvious to me that you and I are of the same race. At some stage, your memory has been partially erased and you have been subjected to hypnotic conditioning. That conditioning is now starting to degrade. Such punishments are commonly handed out by my people to those who meddle in time. The final proof is your name: Moses Nebogipfel. A name that is not a name."

"Quite plainly it is my name! You are going senile, Doctor."

"I think not. It is an anagram, a rather clever anagram, the solution to which almost certainly makes up the hypnotic key words to restore your memory. I must make a note of them."

Doctor Omega looked out of the porthole.

"Ah, we have arrived at the District Voluntary Aid Hospital in Torquay on the English coast. That will do quite nicely. If we bluff our way as medical men we should be able to get Captain Yeskes admitted fairly easily," smiled the Doctor, feeling rather pleased with himself.

Nurse Miller returned to the dimly lit nurses' station at the far end of the ward and sat down at the desk. She quietly rooted around looking for some scrap paper and then started making some notes. Her whispered talk earlier with Captain Yeskes had been fascinating. His recovery was coming along nicely but it was quite obvious that he could not yet differentiate between his fever dreams and the reality of the horror of the trenches. This yarn about a 'hound of death' dragging men to their doom was quite fantastic. It was all so evocative and atmospheric that she determined to use it in one of her stories one day. Yes, she was a budding amateur author but her tastes ran more to crime fiction. Nevertheless, the idea had plenty of mileage in it. She'd fit it in somehow.

"Regarding your exile, I don't think that the 20th century or even the 19th are really very suitable. Too much technological temptation. Otherwise, I'd suggest that rather lovely Italianate village in North Wales near Penrhyndeudraeth," stated the old time traveler.

"Oh no! Not Wales, please… I was in a village there not so very long ago and it really didn't agree with me. Why can't I serve out my exile in the Arcadian Hegemony?"

"In the far future society founded by that renegade starship commander—Captain Strange? I think not since it was doubtless he who was responsible for sending you to get the mesonychid. And don't think I fell for that nonsense about putting the beast in a zoo for people to gawp at. Strange would have wanted it as a biological weapon to use in his grudge match against the Federation! He probably planned to have them cloned by the million," declared the Doctor.

"Captain Strange's wife is rather beautiful. I'm afraid I fell heavily in love with her," confessed Nebogipfel.

"Then you extracted the wolf from the Eocene to curry favor with her? You little fool! She's out of your league…she's made a career of partnering herself with some of the greatest space-heroes and villains of history. She eats men like you for breakfast," chided Omega.

The old man considered for a moment. Where might the best place be for a man who allowed lust for a gorgeous woman to lure him into breaking the laws of time? What could possibly cure him?

"I have it! You will spend the rest of your exile in a monastery that is well known to me. Randgrith Abbey near the Village of Wulnoth in the mid-11th century. You may even come to enjoy monastic life and after ten or fifteen years I will return the *Argo* to you, so make sure you stay in the vicinity. It will materialize for one day only and if you do not claim it, I shall destroy it. If I ever catch you undermining the basic structure of the timestream again…well, let's just say that will be the end of you," warned the Doctor.

The Nyctalope advanced cautiously forward into Kirov Oblast Municipal Park. This part of the city had been totally abandoned to the King Wolf and his brood. The surrounding buildings were empty and lightless. Thick drifts of snow softened the city's hard, man-made edges and the shadows were short under the high full moon. The Nyctalope had been fully briefed on the wolf plague. Never before had so many wolves massed in a single place. Never had they dared to enter and permanently dwell in a city in such large numbers. Two hundred Soviet troops had been sent in to clear the wolves from the city. Only six had returned to the perimeter headquarters. The survivors reported that these were not ordinary wolves. Odd in appearance, ferociously savage and intelligent. They were ruled by a tyrant wolf. The soldiers were strangely diffident in describing the attributes of this King Wolf. It seemed they feared they would not be believed. An officer plied one of the men with vodka until he revealed that the King Wolf was over five meters long and two meters high at the shoulder. Its feet were more like hooves than paws. It was under serious consideration by the Chiefs of Staff to use saturation bombing to destroy the wolf brood. At this point Comrade Frunzoff took personal charge of the problem. He was aware that Leo Saint-Clair—known to some as the Nyctalope because of his ability to see in pitch darkness—was currently visiting Moscow on a temporary assignment from the French Secret Service.

Saint-Clair was more than happy to assist. He had long been concerned at the growing disintegration of relations between East and West. Only a few years before we had all been allies against the Nazi threat; if we continued down this road, then the resulting stand-off had the potential to ultimately destroy the world in an atomic conflagration. Saint-Clair called for special mechanical equipment to be shipped from France to Moscow. The Nyctalope assembled the equipment himself in great secrecy and then travelled with it by road to Kirov.

The Nyctalope wore white snow camouflage ceramic armor with his customary helmet with periscope attachment.

On his back was a powerful battery pack which could be linked to a either a handheld radio transmitter, as it currently was, or to the pommel of short sword which currently hung from a scabbard at his belt. This allowed it to deliver a jolt of electricity powerful enough to fell an elephant. His only other weapon was a MAS-38 sub-machine gun specially adapted to fire electrified bullets. The armored warrior flicked a switch on the radio-transmitter and the four semi-autonomous robotic drones which accompanied him moved forward in unison - these modular drones were the special equipment that had arrived from France and they were armed with high-explosive mortars and automatic shotguns; they also carried infra-red sensors that allowed them to shoot at moving targets even in darkness.

There were times when the Nyctalope regarded his ability to see in the dark as something of a curse. This was perhaps one of those occasions. In a sense, he'd rather not have seen the size of the approaching wolf pack, nor the immensity of the King Wolf. He flicked the red switch on the remote control transmitter and the automatic shot-guns in the drones commenced firing. The King Wolf seemed to hang back, using its servitors as cannon fodder. Though many of the wolves had fallen, the pack was getting too near. The Nyctalope switched two of the drones to mortar firing mode. The heavy crump of the mortars echoed around the park and the air was peppered with bloody fragments of wolf-flesh as the beasts were blasted to smithereens.

Saint-Clair switched all of the drones to mortar mode and ran forward blazing away with the MAS-38. He was almost on the King Wolf now. He stumbled over a dead wolf as he approached but carried on firing, unloading a whole clip directly into the monster's throat. The King Wolf grabbed him by the arm and bit down hard...but the ceramic armor held. The Nyctalope yanked the sword from its scabbard and plunged it into the thing's eye. He fumbled with the power lead, then after half a second discharged enough voltage into its skull to fry its brain. The creature bucked wildly and knocked the Nyctalope high into the air. The drones kept firing on the wolves; they would do so until their ammunition was exhausted.

When the Nyctalope regained his senses, the wolves were all dead and an old man in a black frock coat was bending over the body of the King Wolf, prodding it with a strange buzzing wand.

"What…what are you doing?" asked Saint-Clair.

"I need a sample of its blood, my friend. I must recreate the wolf and put it back in its proper place in time and space…it doesn't belong here," he explained. "There is a lot of human nucleic acid in its gut too. Hmm. I don't think I should get into the business of bringing back the dead—not really my province, eh?"

And with that the strange old man strode off into the snow towards an odd-looking shell-shaped craft which Saint-Clair had not noticed previously.

The Nyctalope trudged wearily out of the park. By the perimeter fence a trio of figures waited for him. A young, balding man with steel- rimmed glasses in the uniform of a Russian army captain (if Saint-Clair judged his epaulette stars correctly). The young captain was just shrugging off his back the twin tanks of a flamethrower and placing them carefully onto the snow; with him was an avuncular man in a raincoat smoking a pipe and a young girl in a white fur coat who could not have been more than twelve. The blond child was armed with a scaled down version of a Degtyarov sub-machine gun and had a red star painted (hopefully rather than tattooed) on her forehead.

"Monsieur? I am Captain Gogol of Army Intelligence. May I offer you my congratulations?"

"Thank you. I take it you are fully aware of my diplomatic status and that no debriefing by Soviet Intelligence is appropriate?" questioned Saint-Clair.

"Of course, Comrade Frunzoff has kept us fully apprised," smiled Gogol.

"What exactly are you three doing here?" asked the Nyctalope. "This is no place to bring a child."

"Hardly. But then Little Oktobriana is not an ordinary child. Along with my friend Avakoum Zahov here, we three are the last line of defense for the Soviet Union. Had you failed…well, it would have been down to us to kill the King Wolf or die trying."

The Nyctalope arched an eyebrow quizzically. The man was deadly serious. And suddenly the Frenchman had the unaccountable feeling that the three of them must have triumphed countless times in similar circumstances to enable Gogol to exude such reckless confidence.

"Come, let us help you recover your equipment," said Zahov. "It will be a walk in the park, eh?"

Nebogipfel sat alone in his monastic cell at Randgrith Abbey. His scalp was still sore from the tonsure he had received and his skin itched from contact with the rough homespun fabric of his habit. Scrunched up in his hand was the page he had stolen from Doctor Omega's notebook. On this slip of paper the old man had written the three simple words he believed would be the key to opening the locks that had been placed by his people in Nebogipfel's mind.

He read them aloud: "Song. Poem. Beliefs."

Long shut synapses commenced to open.

"My God, I know who I am," he whispered.

This first installment in Travis Hiltz's time-hopping saga features various characters looking for Doctor Omega. This story harkens back to the golden age of science fiction, when anything was possible in the intermingled worlds of sf and fantasy. Now, read on as Denis Borel, the Doctor's accidental companion and narrator of the original novel, meets a mild-mannered-by-day Vicar who is anything but at night...

Travis Hiltz: *What Lurks in Romney Marsh?*

Cornwall, 1776

Life is peculiar. One moment, you are a talented, yet underappreciated, violinist on holiday in Normandy; the next, you are invited by an eccentric scientist to travel through space and time, and before you can get used to that experience, you find yourself stranded in the marshlands of Kent, a hundred years before you were born...

Denis Borel frowned.

"A bit too flip," he muttered, tucking a pencil stub into his battered diary and putting it in a coat pocket. "Too flippant by far."

He sighed and looked across the field. The countryside was lush, rolling and green. It had a quiet beauty that could inspire painters or poets, but to Denis, sitting on a stump, it was as oppressive as the dreariest of prisons.

It had been three months since radioactive turbulence had struck Doctor Omega's space-time craft, scattered its crew and left two of them stranded in the small village near Romney Marsh.

Nearly every day since, the young violinist had returned to the place of their arrival in the increasingly desperate hope of finding some hint of rescue, escape, or the whereabouts of his other traveling companions: the diminutive Martian, Tiziraou, or Doctor Omega himself.

Denis sighed again, stood up and trudged back towards the village he had been calling home. His clothes were drab and well-worn, but appropriate to the time period: knee breeches, long coat, waistcoat and blocky black shoes with a buckle on the front. One of the few cheerful things about his exile was that Denis felt he looked quite jaunty in a tri-corner hat.

He soon left the wooded fields and came to the wide dirt road that served as the main thoroughfare for the village of Dymchurch. He strolled past cultivated fields and farmhouses and was soon on the edge of the village itself.

Under other circumstances, Denis would have described Dymchurch as rustic, and even quaint, a loose collection of homes and shops, mostly done in wood or grey stone, with the occasional whitewashed building. Denis trudged along, taking a narrow side lane that lead past a blacksmith's shop. Behind the blacksmith's were an overgrown yard and a small shack with a sagging thatch roof.

Denis pushed through the front door, hung his hat on a crude peg nailed into the wall. The hut consisted of a single room with a wobbly-looking table in the center, a couple of equally unappealing wooden chairs and a rough cot with straw for a mattress. Seated at the table was a burly man with muscular arms and an impressively thick black beard. He was in his shirtsleeves, breeches and a pair of clunky boots that seemed to be held together with twine and wishful thinking. Scattered across the table was a vast collection of odds and ends, and bits of machinery as well as unidentifiable junk that seemed to have no visible use. The bearded man was sorting through this treasure trove, picking out the odd kick-knack and seeing if it fit onto a larger, cylindrical piece of metal with a smoky glass sphere on the top.

"How was the 'great outdoors'?" he rumbled, not looking up from his intent rummaging.

"Frustratingly green and scenic, Fred," Denis muttered, sinking into the other chair and helping himself to a pewter mug on the table. He took a gulp, winced and put the mug back down. "Not a hint, or even a crumb of hope…"

"Denis," Fred grumbled, polishing a greasy bolt with an equally greasy rag, "I am trying to reconstruct a temporal codex amplifier using the few things that came with us when we were flung across the time stream and bits of 18th century technology. That doesn't get any easier when I have to listen to you moping. I don't want to take the time away to throttle you, so I've been tactful and understanding for the last two months, but my patience is nearing an end. So either spit it out, or do something useful, like make dinner."

Denis got up and trudged over to the tiny hearth. He poked at the coals and stirred at a pot of gluey beige gruel. He gave a shudder and put a wedge of cheese and a hunk of bead on a wooden plate and then returned to the table.

"That's just the problem, I think," Denis sighed, sitting back down. "My less than successful attempts to 'do something useful.' You, at least, have the knowledge to try and cobble together some kind of signaling device, while all I can add to our rescue attempts is staring at a field, in the hopes that something happens and a certain gift when it comes to string instruments…"

"Don't sell yourself short, lad," Fred said, helping himself to the hunk of bread. He tore it in half and dunked a piece in his mug. "Your playing at the tavern and giving music lessons to the local children has kept us in pocket money. Kept from starving and gotten us a friendly in with the locals."

"Nice of you to say, but I can't help but feel that things would have gone better if Tiziraou or the Doctor were here…"

"But, they aren't," Fred interrupted, looking up and tossing his rag down on the table. "And we have no idea where or when they are or if they are still aboard the *Cosmos*, or even if they or the ship survived the turbulence. Both the Doctor and the little Martian could have been flung through history and the universe like we were, and be hoping that we will rescue them."

"I just keep hoping they will be able to trace us to the time and place we arrived, but it persists in staying just a field…"

"Well, I may have something that'll help us," Fred said, tossing an object over to the younger man.

It was the charred remnants of a paperback book. The cover was gone and only about a quarter of any given page was legible.

"What is this?" Denis said, gingerly leafing through the ragged stained pages. "It looks like an almanac…?"

"It is. I had it in my workshop, just the right size for keeping one of my workbenches from wobbling. It was one of the bits of flotsam that got flung into the time stream with us." Fred explained, reaching over and taking it back. He leafed through until he found a certain page than handed it back to Denis. "That bit."

"Shooting stars over… Romney Marsh…?" Denis read in a puzzled tone. "There was a comet sighting or meteor crash here…?"

"There will be," Fred corrected. "It won't happen for a couple days, but it may be just what we need."

"How so? What is this 'falling star'?"

"I'm not entirely sure, but while you've been watching that field, I borrowed a telescope from that fellow that runs the tavern, and used those books the vicar loaned you to do a little astronomical research. I'm having a problem finding any trace of our shooting star."

"Is that important?" Denis asked.

"It could be. If it isn't traveling through space…"

"You think the shooting star traveled though time?" Denis interrupted. "Could it be the *Cosmos*?"

"It could be," Fred shrugged. "But, at this point, I'll settle for any rescue…"

"Any rescue? You make it sound like there are a fleet of ships traveling through time out there…?"

"You can't be so naïve to think the Doctor is the only one," Fred grumbled. "You've met his friend from Oxford, as well as that madman, Rotwang. Then there is Doctor Moses Nebogipfel and that Englishman... what was his name...? Anyway, the point is, if our visitor is coming through time, there is no guarantee it's the *Cosmos*. I'll be willing to go with anyone willing to offer us help, or at least get us somewhere with a level of science that gives us a better chance of cobbling together some way to signal the Doctor."

"I'd settle for indoor plumbing, myself," Denis muttered.

"I can't argue that," Fred chuckled. "Anyway, no idea if my guesswork is right, but, if the meteor isn't a rescue ship, we can at least use it to power my temporal codex amplifier and get a signal off."

"What if it's just a meteor?" Denis asked. "You and Doctor Omega are always telling me meteors are just pieces of stone and ice, floating through space?"

"Most of them are, but they also contain elements we can use as a power source, or even just absorb the thermal energy of it traveling through the atmosphere. The important thing is, this shooting star is our best hope in months of getting back to the *Cosmos*."

"What can I do to help?" Denis said, brightly, sitting up straighter in his rickety chair.

"We have a couple days, so I need to make sure the amplifier is going to work. We'll need maps of the area and a small boat..."

"A boat?"

"Look around you, Denis. Chances are the meteor will land in the marsh or just off the coast. To get close enough to it for our needs, we'll need a boat."

"Hmm, true," Denis nodded, sitting back and rubbing his chin thoughtfully. "The vicar loaned me those books; I wager he'd have local maps as well. He knows a great deal about what happens in this village. He'd probably know someone that could loan us a boat."

Denis stood up and began dusting himself off.

"While you work, I'll go stroll over and have a chat with Doctor Syn."

43

The Vicar of Dymchurch's home was plain, but comfortable, a suitable home for a scholarly bachelor. Its only bit of ostentation was the man of the cloth's impressive library. Each room seemed to contain a bookcase.

Doctor Christopher Syn was a tall man, with a high forehead, a prominent, noble nose and piercing blue-grey eyes. It all combined with his usually stoic expression to give Syn an air of authority that reminded Denis of all his most respected teachers. Even at his most relaxed, there was a feeling that the good Doctor was watching you, sizing you up.

"What do I owe the honor of this visit?" Doctor Syn asked, once they were seated and he had sent his sexton to fetch them tea.

"I wanted to return your books," Denis said, retrieving them from a much-abused looking cloth satchel. "They were quite informative. I was also hoping I could impose on your generosity once more."

"I would be a poor vicar to deny the newest members of my flock," Doctor Syn replied, one corner of his mouth going up in a smile. "How can I be of assistance?"

"Well, as you know, my companion and I have accidently found ourselves settled in your fine community…"

"No word from other traveling companion?" Syn asked. "A Professor or Doctor, I believe…?"

"No, nothing yet, but we believe our best bet to be reunited is to stay in one spot, as he is most certainly searching for us. My request in fact involves learning more of our temporarily adopted home."

"I will be happy to offer what assistance I can."

"As you know, I've been enjoying hiking about the area and was wondering you had some local maps I could make use of…perhaps point out some spots of interest?"

"Maps…yes, I do believe I have some…I think in the rectory, I'll have Mipps hunt them down for you."

"If I may impose on your generosity once more, my friend Fred is looking to do some fishing and I was wondering if you knew of anyone in the village that had a small boat we could make use of?'"

"A boat?" Syn asked, with a raised eyebrow.

"Just a small rowboat," Denis said. "We aren't planning to round the Horn, merely a bit of fishing.

"I couldn't say for sure... Mister Mipps, you'd know better than I, anyone in the village with a boat that our new friends could make use of?"

The vicar's sexton was a shorter, gruff-looking man, who, despite his well-groomed clothes, still had an air of someone it was well advised to keep an eye on.

"A small boat...?" Mipps pondered, scratching his chin in need of a shave. "Peters, I believe has one. Hasn't gotten much use out of it since he banged up his leg. He would probably let you gentlemen have it if you tossed a few coppers his way. I could have a word with him, as I have some errands to run."

"That would be most appreciated, Mister Mipps," Denis nodded, finishing off his tea and then standing up. "Thank you both. You've been a great help during this trying time."

"Think nothing of it," Doctor Syn said, standing.

He gestured for Mipps to clear the tea things, as he escorted his guest to the door.

"A word though," the Vicar said, once they had reached the foyer. "You'll want to be cautious on your fishing expedition. While I am not one to indulge in gossip, the stories concerning smuggling in this area are not all fanciful tales. The British navy, as well as the smugglers themselves, I would imagine, take a dark view on any unknown boats that drift into their reach. I would not venture far from the shore."

"Maybe it would be best if we stuck to local streams on our first outing," Denis suggested, retrieving his hat from the rack in the foyer.

"The marsh can be treacherous in its own way," Syn said. "When I find those maps for you, I can point out areas to avoid as well as those to visit."

"More smugglers, or are you speaking of the local legends?" Denis asked, with a smile.

His host smiled in reply, but Denis was disconcerted to notice it did not seem to reach his piercing eyes.

"What stories have they been regaling you with at the tavern?" he asked quietly.

"Oh, the usual sort: ghosts and night creatures. Birds that use their song to lead unwary travelers off the safe paths and there was something about a scarecrow that walks the marsh…fanciful stuff to tell around the fire."

"Hmm," Syn said and nodded, not seeming to share Denis' light-hearted opinion of the tales told about the Romney Marsh. "Well, just exercise caution in your naturalist ramblings."

Denis thanked the Vicar for his help, wished him a good day and strolled back to his ramshackle lodgings, pondering that the Reverend Doctor was a very serious-minded man and probably didn't appreciate Denis' enthusiasm for the stories.

"I suppose a ghostly scarecrow is a bit much," Denis muttered to himself as he walked. "Haunting a field I could see, but why would a scarecrow be in a marsh…?"

Two days passed and, good as his word, Mister Mipps arranged for them to rent Peters rowboat, and even brought along the promised maps. Upon the third day, as the sun was touching the horizon, Fred and Denis were putting the boat into the murky water.

Fred manned the oars, with the cylideral temporal codex amplifier on the bench next to him. Denis sat in the stern, the map laid out on his lap.

"If we follow this stream," Denis said, tracing a path on the map with his finger, "it will lead us deep into the marsh, but after that…?"

He shrugged.

"We may have to haul her over land a bit," Fred grumbled, deep in his beard.

"One thing that I don't understand," Denis said. "Getting close as we can to the place the meteor strikes, aren't we in danger of getting… well, too close? It doesn't do us much good to power up the signaling device if we are moored in the center of a dangerous bull's eye."

"It's a gamble," Fred muttered, craning his head around to scout ahead as he rowed. "Once we have a better idea what the meteor is, we should have time adjust our plan."

Not feeling terribly relieved, Denis sighed and continued to study the map. He shifted, trying to get comfortable on the rough wooden floor of the boat.

"It's a bit of a roundabout trip," he mumbled. "But, I suppose following the stream will let us avoid crossing paths with that navy frigate."

"Yes," Fred nodded, absently. "All we have to worry about is smugglers, quicksand and your ghostly scarecrow."

'Yes," Denis agreed glumly. "And all for the lucky chance of being pulverized by a hunk of stone from outer space. 'Tis a fulfilling and stimulating life, traveling with Doctor Omega."

"It could be worse," Fred suggested. "It could be raining."

The pair meandered their way through the marsh. There were spots where the trees and tall grass crowded up close against the sides of the rowboat. Places where the stream would stretch out, wide and shallow and force the two to get out and carry the boat across the spongy damp ground.

After two hours, they pulled the boat aground on a hummock of land and Denis dug several sandwiches, wrapped in paper, out of his coat pockets. They ate, rested and studied the map.

"It's going to be full dark soon," Fred said, between chews. "Good clear night though. We don't want to use the lantern any more than we have to."

"You really think there are smugglers?" Denis asked. "It's hard to believe, in such a small, quaint village."

Fred shook his head at his companion's naiveté, brushed crumbs out of his beard and got to his feet. They were soon on their way, paddling through the marsh, under a cloudless black sky.

Denis, even during his turn at the oars, couldn't stop from tipping his head back and taking in the vast tapestry of stars overhead. This led him to losing his hat several times and having to pause to fish it out of the water.

The stream eventually merged with the marsh itself and the going got trickier. The muddy water shifted from mere inches to waist-deep with little warning and tree roots protruded from the ground, lurking within the water, ready to catch an oar.

"We're getting close," Fred said, peering at the map and then adjusting several controls on the temporal amplifier.

"It's hard to believe it's going to happen," Denis added. "It's so quiet out here... so peaceful..."

"Almost too quiet," Fred muttered, not looking up from the map.

Denis looked around, noticing that his friend was right, and that the near constant background sounds of nature had hushed. The boat gave a sudden lurch, the bottom scraping against the ground as the prow caught in a thick, snaky tree root that stuck out from a grassy embankment.

"My fault," Denis announced, regaining his balance and adjusting the oars. "There goes my hat again! Sorry, I didn't see us drifting into this little cove... are you all right, Fred?"

"I'm fine," the bearded man grumbled, tucking the map into his coat and shifting so he was kneeling, rather than sitting in the bottom of the boat. "We should be nearly there. Are we stuck?"

"Oh, no," Denis reassured him. "One good push will get us loose. I'm more worried about how shallow it's gotten."

They were moored with the prow wedged into the tree root and the embankment around them formed a makeshift harbor for the little boat.

48

"It should be an open area," Fred said, peering around. "Almost a small pond."

"I'll go have a scout around," Denis said, unsteadily making his way to the prow. He used the roots sticking out of the dirt as steps and grabbed hold of clumps of tall grass to pull himself up.

"Just mind your step," Fred warned. "And don't wander too far. It's easy to get lost."

"I won't be a moment," Denis said, and pushed through the tall grass.

The ground was uneven, but firmer than the rest of the surrounding marsh. It seemed to stretch out for a ways, a sort of peninsula of safe ground. The grass and bushes gave way after several yards for a strand of skeletal trees. Denis walked slowly and cautiously amongst the trees, hoping to find their watery destination without falling into it. He didn't think his hat could survive another dunking. Fred's earlier comment had made him especially aware of how quiet the marsh had become. Even with the full moon, his surroundings were almost oppressively dark and hushed.

Which meant the gently whiney of a horse sounded to his anxious ears like a lion's roar.

Denis bit his lip to keep from yelping in surprise and alarm. He huddled behind a trio of trees grown close together and peered out anxiously. The landscape, which, before, had appeared quiet and full of wonder, was now shadowy, full of menace... The stories told by local tavern dwellers seemed all too plausible.

Denis caught a bit of movement, as a clump of darkness separated itself from a larger shadowy area. He took a second to catch his breath and calm his thoughts. Horses meant riders, and most vengeful spirits were able to get around without the aid of steeds, he surmised.

"Smugglers," Denis muttered, crouching down lower, as he nervously scouted the nearby shadows.

There was no other hint of movement or out of place sound. He crept forward, torn between his need to find their destination and wanting to avoid any smugglers. Getting down on his belly, he crawled through some bushes to get closer to the source of the noise.

It was a horse, black as the night; its bridle and saddle were also black, so, at first glance, Denis thought it wore neither. The animal shook its head and gave a snort.

Denis' forehead wrinkled in thought and he had the sudden, fearful realization that the only place its rider could be was right behind him.

Quickly looking over his shoulder, while praying his was wrong, Denis was startled to see the figure standing behind him.

The figure of a scarecrow.

Dressed all in ragged black, its eerie white cloth face seemed to glow.

Its arms were stretched out and its head cocked slightly to one side, giving the impression that it had been hung on a pole, and there the entire time Denis had been crawling through the undergrowth.

Denis slowly, anxiously got to his feet and leaned in to peer at the strange figure.

"Have ye not been warned?" it rasped, in a gravely sing song. "After dark, any soul that dwells within the marsh is mine!"

Denis flinched back, bumping against one of the trees he had recently used for a hiding spot.

"I didn't… we just wanted… uh… to go home!"

The scarecrow took a step forward, one long black clad arm reaching towards Denis. Both man and night creature halted, as a strange warbling sound drifted through the marsh and a ball of light could be seen in the distance, moving towards them.

"How many creatures lurk in this swamp?" Denis muttered, scooting around the tree.

The light grew brighter, the noise shriller; then, a second noise rent the night.

"Denis lad?" it called. "Where are you?"

Fred stepped into the clearing, a lantern held high and the temporal amplifier tucked under one arm. Several lights on it were blinking green and yellow, and it appeared to be the source of the warbling sound.

Denis dashed from the trees and past the mysterious scarecrow to join his companion. He reached Fred, fear and exertion leaving him breathless.

"Th-thank goodness!" he gasped. 'We need... must... go... it'll find us!"

"What are you nattering on about?" Fred asked. "Of course, we have to go. It'll be here in minutes. What will find us?"

"I will," the scarecrow said, stepping into the cone of light formed by the lantern. It held a black flintlock pistol in its gloved hand.

All three stood locked in place, taking in the others and making their own mental calculations concerning what to do next.

The two stranded time travelers' eyes were wide with fear and disbelief, while those of the scarecrow were cold and seemed almost alive, staring directly into the young violinist's and the bearded handyman's souls.

Any plans or further talk were stalled, as the amplifier began to beep and a bright light appeared overhead.

All three looked upwards in amazement. The object arced downwards with a sound like a massive ocean wave rushing towards the shore.

Fred and Denis bolted through the bushes and trees, racing for their boat. They skidded to a halt at the edge and Fred held out the lantern, as they looked for where they had moored it.

Finding it, Fred handed Denis the lantern and scrambled down the steep embankment. Once in the boat, he adjusted the temporal amplifier. Denis shifted the lantern and was about to begin his descent when a gloved hand with a grip like iron clamped onto his shoulder. He turned his head and found himself inches away from the ghastly face of the scarecrow.

"What have you summoned?" he demanded in an angry growl. "What is that thing?"

"I... don't know," Denis stammered desperately. "We don't think it's a danger... are just... uh... trying to... trying... so desperately to go home!"

Denis' mind reeled, thoughts colliding, as he tried to muddle through all that was happening around him: the need to hurry if they were to have any hope of using the "meteor" to end their exile, the observation that this scarecrow may not be a supernatural being at all and that he seemed more concerned with protection, rather than frightening off, and the realization that he kept referring to the space-time vessel *Cosmos* as "home."

Something in either Denis' tone or expression reached the scarecrow and he released his grip and nodded to the young violinist.

"Do what you must," the scarecrow said. "I shall keep the British away."

Puzzled, Denis looked past the scarecrow and saw several other forms moving among the nearby trees. A trio all dressed in dark colors.

"Go," the scarecrow said. "Before I come to my senses."

Denis, still confused, nodded in reply turned and stumbled down the embankment, landing in an ungraceful heap in the boat. It rocked dangerously for a moment, but Fred, already at the oars was able to wrestle it back into balance.

Once Denis was in, Fred started vigorously rowing away from the little cove and toward the increasingly brighter light.

"He let you go?" Fred asked, intently.

"For some reason," Denis said, struggling to sit up. "He is willing to trust us. If this doesn't work, and the meteor causes any damage, I have a feeling we are in a great deal of danger..."

"Take the oars," Fred snapped, getting up.

He adjusted the cylindrical device, which was now blinking like a set of erratic Christmas lights. Wincing after his tumble, Denis struggled to keep the boat moving, Fred stood in the prow and held the temporal amplifier out, adjusting switches as it beeped and flickered. The light from the approaching object grew brighter and the rush of its descent louder.

Denis winced at the roar, too timid to look upwards and see how close it was. The light was soon bright enough to read by and as it moved closer it appeared almost like the boat was caught in a spotlight.

"Um… Fred…?" he asked, nervously. Then had to shout to be heard. "We seem to be right below the meteor! Isn't that ill-advised if it's just a meteor?"

Fred's answer was drowned out. The bearded man looked up and Denis' last clear view of his friend before the light grew painfully bright was Fred driving towards him. Fred tackled the younger man. The duo lay, huddled in the bottom of the boat while the light and sound swirled around them in a maddening maelstrom.

Minutes passed, then the two men, coming to the realization that they had not been crushed to death by a hunk of rock from the stratosphere, raised their heads.

The meteor was a perfect sphere, with a surface like polished marble. It shone like a light bulb: a light bulb large enough to house a family of four. It hovered several feet above the boat. Getting to his feet, Fred bumped his head against the underside.

Awkwardly and with much haste, they moved the boat till was no longer beneath it, but floating several feet away.

"What is it…?" Denis breathed, wide-eyed.

"No idea," Fred replied, in an equally hushed tone. "There was something similar looking in this village on an island, but not that big…!"

Suddenly, a line formed on the surface of the sphere. It traced across until it was an oval. The shape slid away, revealing an opening in the sphere. There was a light inside, not as bright as the exterior and a figure stepped into the opening.

"I thought I'd find you here," it said.

"Denis!" Fred exclaimed. "It's… It looks like…!"

"Me!" Denis added. "How'd I get there?"

It was indeed Denis Borel standing in the opening, but an older Denis, sporting a thin beard, streaked with grey. He was dressed in a frock coat, waistcoat and trousers of blue. Just past his right shoulder, the younger Denis could make out a second figure, a young woman in a skintight bodysuit.

Older Denis kneeled down and offered his hand to his younger self.

"You need to pay attention," he said. "From here, it's going to get complicated…"

Younger Denis, still feeling a bit shell shocked, stood up to basically shake hands with himself.

Their hands were mere inches apart when the boat rocked and the water around it began to bubble and steam. Leaning over the edge, Fred and Denis could see a light, shining up from the depths of the murky water. Even before they could puzzle over these strange events, a half dozen forms burst through the surface of the marsh water and began to lurch towards the small rowboat.

They were naked with skin red and shiny, like lobsters. They had malevolent, humanish features: snub noses, tiny holes for ears, a black gash mouth and eyes that were no more than orbs of black. They sputtered and screeched as they reached for the boat's occupants with stubby red fingers.

"Lectroids!" the older Denis exclaimed, clutching the edge of the opening in the sphere. "We arrived too late!"

He and the young woman behind him ducked back into the interior of the glowing sphere.

Fred and Denis both grabbed up an oar with the intent of fighting off the strange beings. Denis made a clumsy swing and a red Lectroid grabbed the oar and snapped it like a twig. Fred hit his target and knocked one of the aliens back.

"Grab the lantern!" Fred yelled as he swung again.

As the half dozen creatures were about to climb into the rowboat, a voice rang out across the marsh.

"Denis!" it shouted. "Take shelter!"

The young violinist dove to the bottom of the boat, grabbing hold of Fred's waistcoat and dragging him down, seconds before a volley of shots echoed across the muddy pond.

Anxiously, Denis peered up and saw the Scarecrow and a trio of other men or creatures, each dressed in ragged dark colors and each bearing either the face of a monstrous bird or scarecrow. They held a variety of flintlock pistols and rifles and were all firing intently at the vicious red creatures.

The Lectroids screeched and growled, as the Scarecrow's followers placed their shots with deadly accuracy. The duo in the rowboat got back up just in time to see the dead and dying Lectroids sink into the marsh.

"Um...thank you," Denis said, with a wave towards the mysterious band on the embankment.

"There are more than enough unearthly creatures in Romany marsh," the Scarecrow declared, making a salute with his pistol before melting back into the night.

"Dear me," Older Denis announced, reappearing in the doorway. He and the young woman held bulky, white plastic pistols. "Well, that's sorted, I suppose, but we still have work to do."

"What is going on?" Denis asked.

"The radioactive turbulence striking the *Cosmos* was no accident," Older Denis explained, "but rather an attack. The Lectroids are attempting to enter this dimension in several spots in the time stream. Miss Bauer recruited me to help her find Doctor Omega..."

"We can talk on the way," the young woman snapped. "Two of the dimensional entry points have been dealt with, but that still leaves two more and we still haven't found Doctor Omega. All aboard!"

With that she ducked back inside.

"She's actually quite a charming young woman," Older Denis said, holding a hand out to the men in the boat. "But, she has a point. *Allons-y!*"

Fred and Younger Denis awkwardly climbed from the unsteady boat to the floating sphere.

"Talk about 'Be careful what you wish for'," Fred grumbled.

"Nice hat, by the way," Older Denis said, as he pulled his younger counterpart aboard. "Looks quite jaunty."

In the late and much regretted Paul Hugli's tale, we find Doctor Omega trying to recover his ship lost during the turmoil of World War II. The mysterious Doctor visits the most famous Café Américain of all and challenges the might of the Nazi empire in Egypt...

Paul Hugli: *As Time Goes By...*

Casablanca, Morocco, 1942

> *"With a burning spear and a* horse of air, *to the wilderness I wander."* Tom Brown's Song

The bluish-gray nimbus of the contraband Lucky cigarette haze drifted lazily, circling endlessly, blurring the ruggedly handsome features of the smoker, marred only by a scar on his lower lip. Absently, he took a sip of gin as he studied the man seated before his desk. He was giving him a song-and-dance story, but Rick wasn't buying it. *Not that it matter*, he thought, *Rick Blaine sticks his neck out for no one*. Still he agreed to listen to *this* Frenchman as a favor to Ferrari. Never a good idea. Even in the best of times.

The melody of an old standard by *Bobby Rose and the Rosettas* drifted into the room from Sam and his piano outside, in the gaming area of Rick's *Café Américain*, and Blaine tried to filter it out as he continue to study the man before him. He was elderly, tall and willowy, with long whitish hair, slicked back save for an errant shock of hair which played about his brow. Even in Casablanca's humidity, the man was decked out in black velvet frock coat, scarf (decorated in a motif of whorls and vortexes), dark pants, and highly polished black shoes. In his lap was a triangular fur hat, his agile long fingers absently stroking it as if it were a kitten.

Doctor Omega was, himself, studying the American dressed in a white dinner jacket and black tie. He desperately wanted to trust him. He knew from the histodiscs that Blaine had run guns to the Ethiopians in 1935, and in the next year, fought on the Loyalists side in Spain. Yet, the Doctor couldn't fess up and say: *I was traveling through the aether when, suddenly, there was a breach in the* mufkuzt *collector... Ah, no that would never do...* At the moment Omega had only a faint idea where his craft, the *Cosmos*, was; in fact, that was the reason he was here in the office of the owner of this café.

"I don't see how I can help you, Doctor," Blaine said, calmly firing up another Lucky. "I have no influence here. I'm just an ordinary saloon owner who came here for the waters. And stayed."

"I am not seeking special treatment, young man."

"And you will receive none. Not here. Not from the Vichy French or the Nazis. Major Strasser will see to that."

"I only require an exit visa."

"You require a *letter-of-transit*, and Captain Renault doesn't just hand them out to anybody." Blaine crushed out his cigarette in the overflowing ash tray. "Nor do you have the legs."

"Excuse me?"

"Never mind. I can't..." Blaine began, then suddenly stopped, bolting to his feet. "It can't be..."

The Doctor didn't understand. All he heard was Sam crooning: "*...you must remember this...*"

"Of all the gin joints..." Blaine mumbled as he hurried out of the office.

When he returned to his office, an hour later, he discovered that Doctor Omega had gone--not that he had actually thought about him in the interval. He hurried to his desk and unlocked his bottom right drawer, withdrawing two documents, two transit visas which could not be revoked.

Relieved, he sank into his chair. He had to find a better hiding place for the visas. A piano interlude from Sam filtered into the room, giving Rick Blaine an idea...

Converted Krupp Factory on the Danube, Black Forest,
South-West Germany

The elderly man was stoic in his wood-frame wheel-chair, the burnt scar on his forehead itching and throbbing; but he resisted the temptation to scratch it, having gotten use to the irritation during the past three years. In fact, he had survived many trials and tribulations in the past decade: the actions of *that* masked vigilante had been just a minor set-back.

Rolling across the room, he stopped at a long display table, and studied the object nestled on a cushion of red velvet, within a exquisitely carved cedar box: a broken wooden shaft with a twenty-inch long blacken iron spear point split vertically, with an iron Crucifixion Nail placed in the divide, and held together by weathered leather straps; with the neck of the spear wrapped in gold and silver bands.

It was the object of myth... of legend ... of *Destiny*!

According to the Gospel of John, a crucified man could not remain hanging during the Jewish Passover, so the order was given to break the legs of Jesus, to hasten his death due to apoplectic trauma. But when a soldier was about to carry out the order, he had found the self-proclaimed Christ already dead. To verify this fact, the soldier's spear had pierced the side of Jesus, which had spouted water and blood.

For the rest of the story, one had to refer to non-Canonized sources, such as the *Apocrypha*. They claimed that that soldier was aged and almost completely blind; that the blood and water spouting from Christ's wound had sprayed his eyes, restoring his sight, cleansing his sins. He, in turn, had lovingly proclaimed Christ's divinity; and, with spear in hand, he preached the Good Word along the dusty roads of the Roman Empire for the next 28 years. But the Romans weren't buying what this ex-soldier was preaching. He was tortured, his teeth removed, then his tongue, and, lastly, he lost his head. This dutiful Angel of the Gospel was named Longinus , and his spear, or lance, became known as *Longinus' Lance* or the *Holy Lance* or, more appropriately, the *Spear of Destiny*.

The Spear had been said to have passed through many hands since the be-heading of Longinus, including those of the Third Century C.E. co-ruler of the Holy Roman Empire, Maximianus Herculius, whose daughter, Fausta, married the world's first "Christian" emperor, Constantine. At the First Ecumenical Council of the Church, in Nicaea, to iron-out biblical canon, the Spear was ever-present, representing the conquest of Christianity over paganism and, more notably, the Jews.

It then passed through many and powerful hands, including Emperor Theodosius; Visigoth King Alaric; Justinian I; Charlemagne; Henry I, First King of the distinctly Pan-Germanic State and, to Hitler, the First Reich; his son, Otto I, and so on, down to Henry IV, whose daughter's grandson, King Frederick I, carried it into the Third Crusade. Then history lost it for 150 years, until Charles IV found it, and it passed through five centuries of subsequent monarchs. When Napoleon came looking for it, the Spear was hidden in Vienna. Though it had lost some of its mythical aura, replaced in medieval times by the Holy Grail, it still resonated with the Nazis trying to build a "Thousand Year Reich" around their "Black Camelot" at Himmler's Dahlem Castle, with the Fuhrer as King Arthur, the SS as the Knights of the Round Table, and the Holy Lance as Excalibur.

The Spear had been "liberated" from Austria in 1939, along with the Crown Jewels of the Holy Roman Empire, and hidden in a bunker beneath Nuremberg Castle, after temporary storage in the Kohn Bank's vault. Then, the RAF began bombing Germany in the Summer of 1940... So, Major Liebel of the SS would arrive soon to take possession of the Spear, to be re-united with the Crown Jewels in the re-enforced bunker.

Before joining the Nazi party and becoming leader of the SS in 1929, the *Reichfuhrer* Heinrich Himmler had been a fertilizer salesman. And with all of the nonsense he believed in, such as the Ark of the Covenant, the Holy Grail, Atlantis, and endless other fantasies, he appeared to still be in the bullshit business! But all this meant nothing to the old man... it was all mystical nonsense to him. He was a man of science, not a believer in fairy tales. And, as expected, this man of science found nothing extra-ordinary about the Spear, whether metal-lically, spiritually, magically, or metaphysically. It was an or-dinary iron spear or lance point. Period. Of course, his report would be filled with pseudo-scientific arcana to justify the *Reichfuhrer*'s Black Sun cult, and its research branch, the *Deutsche Ahnenerbe* (the German Ancestral Heritage Re-search and Teaching Society), whose ranking members wore specially created uniforms, ceremonial daggers, and "Death's Head" signet rings.

The old scientist even snickered at the thought of the signet rings and the mythical nonsense surrounding theirs de-signs: skull and crossbones, and a row of Germanic runes, cre-ated in honor of the great Aryan god of thunder, Thor, who possessed a similar ring to which his warriors sworn alle-giance. The ring was presented to officers after three years of dedicated service, and retired with the death of each owner.

The man who had just entered the old man's lab wore just such a ring, having just become a proud member of the SS Elite. This new recruit into the Himmler's Black Sun was the old man's own son, Frank Drexler.

An ex-cop, the former owner of and chief investigator for the Drexler Protection Agency, in New York City, he had been brave and courageous and honest, until he snapped. It was all due to the meddling of a self-proclaimed vigilante, a man who dressed in a silly get-up of a slouch hat and hunch-back, with fright-wig and fangs, calling himself the Spider. The creature had brought down the last of Frank Drexler's fa-ther's *Ironmen*, and destroyed the old man's misguided dream of using giant robots to cure all the ills of the world. He had even used his cigarette lighter to burn his mark—that of the Spider—on the forehead of Professor Drexler, thinking him dead. But the Professor had lived, and his son had cracked, raving about vigilantes who dressed like spiders, bats, cats, or wrapped themselves in the Red, White and Blue of America, or, the Union Jack colors of Great Britain. This lawlessness was worse than democracy, itself a losing cause. *En masse*, the people were incredibly stupid, believing in equality. Absurd! Only the Master Race, the law and order provided by the Nazi Party, could save humanity *and* the Earth, from themselves.

Drexler's father had befriended Nicola Tesla in the past and knew where the inventor kept his papers, so Frank had raided the Manhattan warehouse, microfilming hundreds of pages among the twelve metal boxes, 35 metal cans, five barrels, and eight trunks: the secrets to rotating magnetic fields, frictionless induction motors, AC polyphase power distribution system, charged particle beam, bladeless turbine, VOTL aircraft, and dozens more blueprints were handed over to a Nazi cell in America. This was in 1939. By 1942, father and son had relocated to Germany. The father was a top scientist, and the son had become a proud member of the SS, in charge of the Nazi's *Wunderwaffle* ["Wonder Weapons"] division. All because of the interference of a madman who called himself the Spider!

"Come, Father," Major Drexler said, "the item from the desert awaits your inspection."

Herr Doktor Drexler, as he was now known, glanced at his personally autographed picture from Marlene Dietrich, smiled, and allowed his son to wheel him from the room, and into Krupp's converted factory floor, where, today, he was overseeing the research being conducted on an object recovered in the Egyptian desert, across the Nile from *Tel el-Amarna*, just south of Hermopolis. The converted factory had many projects in the works—a V-rocket, heavy-water experiments, giant robotic weaponry, etc., but the two Nazi were, at the moment, concentrating on the object occupying the center of the factory: a cylindrical, missile-like craft, thirteen meters long and three meters wide, bolted to the bed of a truck by nine large disc-shaped magnetic hooks. To Doktor Drexler the craft reminded him of something out of Jules Verne's *From the Earth to the Moon*, and, perhaps, it was indeed some sort of space craft. He smiled: *First, Europe. Next... the world. Then... the Moon? The Fuhrer would like that...*

Drexler's jackboots echoed through the open space as he paraded around the artifact, his hands clasped together behind his back, wondering out loud to his father what the vehicle—for surely, it was some type of vehicle—was doing, seemingly abandoned, in the Egyptian desert.

"Perhaps it's from the future... a time machine, like the one H. G. Wells mentioned..."

"Hmmm," Doktor Drexler mumbled. "Perhaps it's a space craft? Yes, it's cylindrical... Shell-shaped... A craft from Mars?"

The two freshly-minted Nazis would have been surprised to learn that both their musings were correct: that craft had, indeed, traveled through the aether, including to and from Mars, and had utilized a temporal bubble to traverse time. For the ship was Doctor Omega's *Cosmos*. Its designer, builder and captain was presently cooling his heels, hidden behind a heap of strange exotic electrical equipment tucked in the corner of the gigantic factory. To his right was Fred, his mechanic. The amiable bearded, hulking assistant was fumbling with a transparent cube, six-inches wide, containing what appeared to be an ionized cloud.

Doctor Omega sighed and grabbed the cube from the gentle giant's hands, and was about to replace it on the worktable, yet, for a moment—just a tiny moment—he felt an eerie, tingling sensation surging through his body, inflaming his every pore. It took most of his will-power to put the cube back in its lead container, its glow dying even before he closed the lid.

"Keep your hands in your pockets," he whispered to Fred.

"Sorry, Doctor."

Doctor Omega then turned his attention back to his ship, watching Drexler and his son pace around the *Cosmos*. If it had wheels, the Nazis would probably have kicked the tires. The two Nazis continued to speculate wildly as they tried to discover an access to the craft's interior.

"Good," the Doctor said. "They are stumped. We need to get my ship back."

But at the moment, that was wishful thinking. The Doctor settled behind a wooden crate and pondered how he and Fred had arrived at their present predicament.

Two Months Before

The *Cosmos* had been in the future, in 1986, researching some space-time anomalies. After taking in a "flicker" entitled *Star Trek IV: The Voyage Home*, and foregoing a second feature starring the latest starlet, Christy Canyon, the Doctor and Fred had boarded their craft and began *their* voyage home… to 1904 Normandy, France. Throwing switches and pulling levers, they shot into the temporal void. Then, suddenly, there had been a *pop* and a release of steam and radiometric gases. Quickly Fred reacted, shutting down the chronotron-flux power, causing the *Cosmos*'s stellite shell to shake violently, threatening to rip the craft apart. They had no choice but to drop out of the aether.

The chronometer read: *May 14, 1942.* They would need a new power supply. And the best source was meteor-impact sites. The substance had been called by many names: *t'cam, res mehit,* and *mufkuzt* and *hydrozite.* It has many properties of *vril* energy. Some believe the meteorites originated from an exploding planet, and since they had traces of solidified krypton gas, some referred to it as *k-metal.* It sometime radiated a non-radiometric green glow, caused by bio-illumination created by microbes attached to it, after it had crashed to Earth.

The substance was quite rare, but it emitted a distinct chronal signature, which the ship's temporal meter had picked up. Following the Doctor's instructions, Fred had set the *Cosmos* down amongst swirling dust and sand, just south of the ruins at el-Ashmunein. In ancient times, the place had been known to the Egyptians as *Khmunu,* and was dominated by the temple of Thoth, god of wisdom and writing. In antiquity, on this primeval hill, the Sun God Ra had created the world out of chaos. The Greek Ptolemy had equated Thoth with their god Hermes and thus dubbed the city… Hermopolis.

Though *mufkuzt* itself wasn't radioactive, the collection and processing of it was. But first they had to find a source. While out of the ship, the Doctor and his companion were caught in a menacing sandstorm, a *simoon*. Fortunately, they had brought a portable electro-shield, which provided them with shelter to outlast the storm. At first, the Doctor regaled Fred with stories of vanishing armies, disappearing in *simoon*s, and how many had dreamed of finding the legendary treasures lost in history; especially a certain Persian expedition during Egypt's 27th Dynasty.

Later, while Fred waited out the storm, dreaming of treasures, the Doctor took the time to get some work done: correcting the errors in Noel Essaillon's *Revue de Mathématiques*, a crippled Frenchman who claimed to understand the mechanics of time-travel. *The fool!*

Once the storm had abated, they had made their way back to the *Cosmos*. But it wasn't there!

"Where is it?" the Doctor pondered.

"It couldn't just get up and move itself? Could it?" asked Fred.

"*E pur si muove*."

"Huh?"

"Never mind," the Doctor replied, not explaining Galileo's alleged response after recanting his heretic, heliocentric theory.

Gigantic, deep tracks in the sand soon told the Doctor the story: the *Cosmos* had been loaded aboard a flat-bed truck and driven north.

"Hmph," was all he said as he pondered the situation. The logical option was to follow the *Cosmos*; the truck's tracks were heavy enough in the sand to make it easy. Perhaps, hire a *dahabiya* and motor up the Nile? But the north was occupied by the so-called "Desert Fox," Field Marshall Erwin Johannes Eugen Rommel, and his Afrika Korps' Panzer Division, based at el Alamein, less than 165 kilometers from the Pyramids. *No*, the Doctor thought, *that would not do*. Since the *Cosmos* was destined, no doubt, for Germany, he and Fred would have to go there.

But how?

When they had first become stranded the Doctor had his chrono-spectrometer with him. It was used to track down non-radiometric decay emissions, indicating the presence of stellite; fortunately, the hand-held device could also detect the quantum-signature wave of the *Cosmos'* leaking Chronotron-Flux generator. Yet, there was still one problem: the signature wave could only be picked up within a relatively small distance radius.

The Doctor was pondering these facts, and a thousand more, when Fred asked:

"Now what?"

"Well, the French Foreign Legion have a motto: *Marche ou crève.*"

"*Oui.*"

In the near distance, they saw—if it wasn't a mirage— three men on camels, with three donkeys in tow. They were Bedouins, dressed in *kaftans* and *khafiyas* tied with twisted *agabs*. They looked like extras from some T.E. Lawrence epic or, perhaps, the Three Wise Men, though they didn't seem to be laden with frankincense, myrrh and gold.

"*Habib,*" the Doctor intoned as the trio neared.

"*Aleman? Inglizi?*" the oldest of the trio asked.

"*Merci, Monsieur,* but we're French!" the Doctor replied, slightly peeved at being taken for German, let alone English!

"*Allah yisallimak, habib,*" replied the older of the trio, seemingly satisfied. He introduced himself as Mohammed, and his companions as Mustafa and Daoud.

"*Allah isabbekhum bilkheir,*" the Doctor replied in kind, introducing himself and Fred. After some discussion and bartering, and a fist-full of *baksheesh*, the two Frenchmen were given robes and *khafiyas* to wear, and a donkey each. And thus, they set out across the Libyan Desert.

Skirting Rommel's forces, which controlled most of Northern Egypt and Libya, they proceeded north-westward, through the Bahariya and Faiyum Oases, up to the Siwah Oasis. It seemed to take forever, and Fred kept inquiring when they would arrive at their destination. Mohammed replied softly each time with: *bokra.* That is, *tomorrow.* Anything could happen—*tomorrow.* Plus the Bedouins kept calling Omega *hakim,* even after he constantly told them he was, indeed, a doctor but not a physician.

At the Siwah Oasis, they rested for a day. Doctor Omega and Fred explored the famous site, best known for the Temple of Ammon, which, in 332 B.C.E., had been visited by Alexander the Great. Alexander had asked three questions of the Oracle, and though no one knew what the questions or answers were, the Macedonian King seemed satisfied that he was, indeed, divine and had a special relationship with Ammon, perhaps even that the god was his father and not Philip. According to Arrianof Nicomeda, Alexander "put his questions to the Oracle and received the answers his soul desired." Then again, it was said that Alexander had made it across the Libyan Desert on the guidance of the cawing of ravens and, according to Ptolemy, the advice of two talking snakes.

Here the Bedouins and the Frenchmen parted way. After more *baksheesh* exchanged hands the Doctor and Fred had acquired two camels, date wine, dates, water and other supplies. They set out westward. With the swaying of the camels, Fred came down with a bad case of motion-sickness, discovering why the creatures were referred to as "ships of the desert."

A week later, Doctor Omega and Fred reached Tripoli, former headquarters of the Barbary States. The term *Barbary* was derived from the *barbarians,* who occupied Northern Africa after the fall of the Roman Empire. Now, another band of "barbarians" ruled the region: the "Huns" via their Fascist lackeys, Mussolini's Italy.

In Tripoli, the Doctor, via more *baksheesh* and some mesmerism, managed to get himself and Fred on a plane. Unfortunately, they could only make it as far as *ad-Dar al-Bayda*, better known as Casablanca.

There, discreetly, Doctor Omega asked around, and the answers had landed him in the office of Rick Blaine at the latter's *Café Américain*. But he got nowhere fast—he had to try something else. The opportunity came when Blaine stormed out of his office after mumbling: "Of all the gin joints…"

The Doctor glanced around, decided he was alone, and shrugged. He went around Blaine's desk, picked the lock on the bottom right-hand drawer and, finding an unfolded letter-of-transit, he laid it out on the desk. From his jacket, he removed an electronic device about the size of a deck of Chesterfields—a *facsimilulator*—and photographed the document. Later, when alone, save for Fred, the Doctor pressed a button on the side of the machine and, with a slight hum, the device unfolded itself twice, before quadrupling and octupling its size, creating a flat-bed printer. With the press of a couple more buttons, the Doctor created two perfect letters-of-transit to Lisbon. After forging the official signature, he and Fred were ready to seek out the *Cosmos*.

From Lisbon, the Doctor and Fred, with help from the French Underground, smuggled themselves into war-torn Germany, through the Black Forest, to the old Krupp's factory on the Danube. Then, with the aid of mesmerism, the Doctor managed to get Fred and himself inside factory.

Now, as they watched the Drexlers ponder the wonderments of the space-time ship, the Doctor's eyes fell upon the means of their deliverance. Its schematics and operation manual were sitting on an abandon workbench. He snatched up the data and quickly scanned it, nodding here and there, with an occasional "*hmmm*" to accent his thoughts. Satisfied that he understood the mechanism—which wasn't that difficult for him—, the Doctor set down the manual, and whispered to Fred:

"Let's go."

"Where?"

"There, my man!"

The Doctor pointed to a twenty-foot-tall mechanical man standing against the far wall. Its arms hung from ponderous shoulders. A helmet-like head had a glass-plate for eyes, and a mouth full of teeth like a steam-shovel. Its joints were steel plates overhanging flexible rubber. Its chest was embossed with a giant swastika.

"According to the schematics, it's one of Drexler's *Ironmen.*"

"Huh?"

"A back-up plan in case things turn badly for the Nazis. They plan to bury these *Ironmen*, to be awakened when the Fatherland has regrouped."

"Ah, sleeper agents?"

"Yes."

"I don't think I want to be around when one of these Sleepers awakens."

"Well, that is exactly what we are going to do."

"Wait a minute…"

"Shhhh…."

Stealthily, they inched their way along, behind stacked crates, towards the robot. A quick look told the Doctor that the Nazis were still thrashing out the design of the *Cosmos,* pondering how to get into the damn thing. Satisfied, he began climbing up the metal ladder attached to the concrete wall next to the *Ironman*, reluctantly followed by Fred.

The Doctor pushed a button on the side of the robot's head, just under the "jaw" line, and saw the tempered-glass face-plate rose with an audible hiss. He and Fred scrambled inside, with the Doctor commandeering the only control chair, forcing Fred to stand behind him, amongst a cornucopia of wires, vacuum tubes, levers and switches. The Doctor then made a quick survey of the control panels before starting to push buttons, pull levers, and switch switches.

The *Ironman*'s hydrogen/nitrogen power furnace fired up. The Doctor discovered that the robot had been updated since the prototypes had wrecked New York three years before. Unfortunately, the racket drew the attention of the Nazis and their flunkies. Drexler drew his Luger and pointed it at the awakened "Sleeper" and yelled:

"Fire!"

His men complied. Shells from Lugers and sub-machine guns pelted the *Ironman*, but to no effect against the tempered steel/titanium alloyed body,

As the Doctor became more familiar and comfortable with the controls, the *Ironman* jerked and creaked and took a practice step forward, then another, and another, until it moved like a well-oiled machine. Bullet ricocheted off its metal body, not even leaving a dent, though becoming a danger to the Nazis goons. They were killing themselves with the ricochets.

Despite the chaos, Drexler continued to demand action!

A robotic hand came down and snatched up the Nazi in its claw, raising the struggling SS agent, until he was facing the thermo-glass faceplate of the *Ironman*. He beat his fists against the metallic fingers gripping him, while screaming obscene insults.

Tired of the madman's ravings the Doctor casually flung him aside, sending him crashing into a group of stormtroopers, who tumbled like so many bowling pins. The Doctor then pulled a lever and, with a hum, the potential energy charge stored into the face plate became accessible. The *Ironman*'s eyes glowed, before unleashing a Teslan particle beam, creating a disruptive gash in the floor, and sending chunks of concrete flying into the air, falling back on the Nazis, burying them under the debris.

Next, the Doctor had the robot look upward as he charged the polyphase electronic generator. Suddenly, the entire face-plate of the *Ironman* began to glow as the energy potential built up, ionizing the air, causing it to crackle. A concentrated blast erupted forth from the machine, melting through the ceiling like a hot knife through butter. To finish the job, the Doctor instructed the robot's hands to reach up and grab the sagging girders. With a metallic groan, the girders pulled free, sending steel and concrete crashing down on the Drexlers and their horde.

Turning his attention to the *Cosmos*, the Doctor commanded the mechanical hands to slither under the belly of the ship. With a groan, the giant robot lifted the ship, snapping the circular magnetic braces with had held it to the flat-bed, leaving the top crescent-shaped halves of the braces still attached the hull.

Quickly, the Doctor and Fred slid down the robot's arm and landed feet-first on the flat-bed of the truck, just beneath the spot where the robot had the *Cosmos* suspended. After taking his key from his jacket pocket, the Doctor pushed a button on the ship's underbelly, activating the lock to the ventral hatch.

It irised open.

Fred boosted the Doctor through the hatch, then followed him, securing the door as Omega rushed to sit in front of the control panel, turning dials and pulling levers.

Within a whirlwind of dust, the *Cosmos* began to lift, rising slowly before picking up speed and attitude. Once they cleared the hole in the ceiling created by the *Ironman*'s rampage, the ship tilted up, and, with the pull of two more levers, shot skywards like a rocket.

They had just shot out of Earth's atmosphere when the *Cosmos*'s stellite hull began to violently shake and rattle—space began to warp around the ship. The Chronotron-Flux power-drive was still ruptured, and threatened to burst through the quick-fix mending job Fred had done earlier—the breach that had caused their present predicament in the first place.

"Fred," Omega yelled, sweat pouring down his brow, "the Tesla-Flux Compensator is... is, er, well... over-compensating for the added weight. We need to lose what's left of those magnetic locks."

He tossed a few more switches, and Fred pulled more levers as the *Cosmos* traversed billions of possible time-lines. Popping out of the aether five years in the future, in June

1947, the *Cosmos* shot west across the United States of America.

At last, Doctor Omega was able to gain some control over his ship.

Degaussing the ship's hull caused the nine crescent-shaped metal magnetic anchors to fall away over the Pacific Northwest, where their momentum sent them skipping across the skies, over Mt. Rainer and Mt. Adams, in Washington State. The pilot of a CalAir A-Z, Kenneth Arnold, just a few minutes before 3:00 p.m., at approximately 9200 feet, observed these highly reflected crescent discards. He reported these "half-moon shaped, oval in the front and convex in the rear" objects "flying like a saucer would if you skipped it across water." The newspaper carrying the story dubbed them: *flying saucers*.

With the extra weight now discarded, the *Cosmos* once again shot forward, zooming through the Van Allen belt, rocketing like a speeding fireball into the aether. The Doctor continued fooling with dials, switches and levers, but the temporal rotor was over-reacting, smoking, and unable to maintain the chronal signature bubble and keep the chronotronic flux under control.

"We're losing coherence," Omega shouted. "We still need to repair the time rotor and find additional fuel."

"How about ionizing the dilithium crystals?" Fred exclaimed.

"This isn't a 'flicker,' Fred! This is reality!"

"Then I guess a sling-shot around the Sun is out?"

Doctor Omega ignored him, pulling more levers, tossing more switches in order to effect an emergency landing.

Again they popped out of the aether, right over a source of meteoric *mufkuzt*, according to ship's detectors.

The *Cosmos* descended like a falling leaf, and landed onto the desert sands, kicking up a miniature sandstorm.

The Doctor glanced at the chrono-meter. It read: *May 14, 1357 B.C.E.* The astrogator gave the location: *mid-Egypt, west of the Nile.*

He smiled; time was like the tide—it always returned you to your starting place. Give or take 3300 years!

The area was, however, completely different from what it had been a mere two *relative* months ago. The Temple of Thoth at Khmunu was a glorious sight of magnificent engineering, not the ruins it would become when future generations would label it Hermopolis or el-Ashmunein. But the Doctor and Fred had no time to enjoy any sightseeing; they had work to do if they ever hoped for their own *Voyage Home* back to 1904 France.

Since mining meteoric *mufkuzt* used radiometric elements to process the ore and to refine it, the Doctor and Fred were forced to don special protective overalls, gloves, boots and hoods. From the *Cosmos*, they carried a translucent glob of tempered-glass, three meters in diameter, mounted on a tripod of lead legs. They positioned it carefully over a meteor impact crater. The Doctor adjusted some dials on its base, and, satisfied that the device was working properly, set it on "automatic" so that it could process the ore without their constant supervision. Then, he joined Fred in the *Cosmos* to make repairs to the ship's navigational system.

Unseen by the two time travelers a twelve-year-old native prince, Naphuria, was napping against a pillar dedicated to the God of Wisdom, near the Shrine of Thoth, in the 15th Nome of Kemet, some 240 miles north of Opet—modern-day Thebes. He awoke to the gentle humming of the *mufkuzt* accumulator over the sand hill, and, out of curiosity, wandered towards it as if the sound was beckoning him. And, perhaps, it was.

In the East, the skies began to darken, as if Ra was slowly being devoured by a serpent; but how was that possible? Ra's Solar Barge should be no more than half-way across the skies... The young prince was frightened as more and more of the sun disc disappeared, plunging the land in darkness.

But then he saw it. On the ground before him: *A glowing globe.*

Its eerie light illuminated the darkness of the solar eclipse. Its legs radiated beneath it like out-stretched arms. Set in bas-reliefs on the globe were the symbols of its manufacturer, Sol-Hill Oscillators: a circle with a dot in the center, a half-circle facing up, and a wavy line. The young prince recognized the symbols as the sun, or the deity, a half-loaf of bread, and water: *Creator*, *"T"* and *"N."* Since the Ancient Egyptians used no vowels in their hieroglyphs the young prince interpreted the symbols as *God the Aten*, the non-anthropomorphic, amorphous Solar deity, sometimes favored by his father and mother.

The prince fell to his knees, genuflecting before the globe, mumbling an ancient incantation. Then, daring life itself, the young man reached out his hand and touched the embodiment of the Aten, and, for a full minute, absorbed the gamma radiation caused by the mining process, a transcendental glow engulfing his body. Every hair on his body, including his princely side-lock, stood on end. Then, he was violently repelled, and landed in a daze on his back. Foggy-headed, he crawled away as the light returned to sky—as the eclipse waned and Ra resumed his normal journey across the Heavens.

The effect of this encounter would stay with him for the rest of his life.

An hour later, having finished the repairs on the *Cosmos*, Doctor Omega and Fred re-donned their protective suits, went outside and switched off the accumulator. Between them, they carried it back to their ship. They attached it to the chronogenerator, and replaced the lead shielding.

With everything in place, and the gauges reading normal, Fred tossed a couple switches and pulled a couple levers. The *Cosmos* began to rise. At first, the ship shook and sputtered before humming with electronic proficiency as more levers were pulled. It began to send up a whirlwind of sand dust.

"Where to, Doctor?" Fred said as he checked a couple gauges.

"1904…Home—for the time being" the Doctor replied, with a tear in his eye, writing a few notes on his clipboard as the chronal signature bubble engulfed the *Cosmos*.

And the *Cosmos* left the Ancient Egyptian skies with a "*poof!*"

On the ground, Prince Naphuria watched the space-time ship vanish, and swore an allegiance to this god of the skies. Within two years, his older brother, Tuthmosis V, Crown Prince, High Priest of Ptah, and Overseer of the Prophets of Upper and Lower Egypt, would die in a hunting accident, thus leaving Amenhotep III and Queen Tiye's only surviving son, Naphuria, as Crown Prince and co-regent under his coronation name of Amenhotep IV ("Amen is Satisfied").

During the intervening years, the radiometric effects of the *mufkuzt* accumulator, which the young co-regent, in the darkness of the eclipse, had mistaken for the earthly manifestation of the Aten, had taken their toll, mutating his body: elongating his face, thickening his thighs, reducing his arms to spindles, and making his chest and stomach pendulous.

He married the enigmatic beauty Nefertiti ("The Beauty Has Come") and, in Year Four of their reign, he changed his name to Akhenaten ("Effective Spirit of the Aten") and moved his capitol to the newly-erected Akhataten ("Horizon of the Aten"), the present-day ruins of el-Amarna, across the Nile from where he had first had his Vision of the Aten. Like Ra at Khmunu (Hermopolis), Akhenaten created his city out of the chaos of his times, hoping to bring order to the world. Alas, it was all for naught.

Afterword

> "*Soldiers, from the top of these Pyramids,*
> *forty centuries look down upon you.*"
> Napoleon Bonaparte
> Battle of the Pyramids, 1799

Though Doctor Omega and Fred may well have been the first Frenchmen to visit Egypt, they were not the last.

The Land of the Pharaohs was most notably exploded by Jesuit priest Claude Sicard, who, in 1708, found ten open tombs in the "Place of Truth" (the Valley of the Kings). Then, in the Summer of 1798, under the pretense of stemming the oppressive rule of the *Mamluks*, and to deny the British access to the Red Sea, thus India, Napoleon set sail for Egypt with some 335 ship, including his flag ship, *L'Orient*. Aboard these ships were 40,000 troops, 1200 horses, 171 field guns, and 167 hand-picked scholars, including engineers, surgeons, chemists, botanists, zoologists, and architects, collectively known as the *Commission des Sciences et Arts d'Egypte*.

After the defeat of Napoleon by the British, his scientists were allowed to retain their scientific works, but had to surrender all their finds, including the Rosetta Stone, which became so instrumental in decoding the Ancient Egyptian language, mainly through the efforts of the Frenchman Champollion and his 1924 translation/publication.

Yet, for obvious reasons, the history books are mute about certain events connected to Napoleon and his team.

Alas, that story must wait for another time...

Travis Hiltz returns to his series featuring Doctor Omega who has, somehow, been separated from his companions and is lost in time. Now, we find the Doctor in late 19th century Paris, where his path is going to cross that of Alfred Drious's Parisian Aeronaut (from The Adventures of a Parisian Aeronaut, *an 1856 proto-SF novel)[8] in a tale entitled...*

Travis Hiltz: *The Next Omega*

Paris, 1857

The old man spent all his evenings seated at a small corner table at the corner's café, a pink hatbox tied with twine at his feet, an ordinary cane, and a single glass of red wine at his elbow.

He would just sit there, his wine untouched, a thoughtful, expectant frown on his face. Occasionally, he would nod to one of the other regulars, or merely just scratch his chin absentmindedly as he listened to the swirl of conversations around him. He seemed to always be listening and waiting, but for what, none of the other patrons knew.

On one rare occasion, he actually spoke to the men at the table next to his. They were a trio of workmen, chuckling to themselves over the antics of a local eccentric, a learned savant who would share his wild theories concerning the Moon, the stars and the very universe itself.

They were all a bit stunned when the old man leaned in and rapped a knuckle against the tabletop.

"Whom are you speaking of?" he asked, his stern tone and beaky nose giving him the air of a teacher interrogating a group of unruly students. "The one with the interest in the stars... Doctor... Who did you say?"

"Omega," one of them replied. "Doctor Omega."

---

[8] Black Coat Press, ISBN 978-1-61227-067-8.

The old man spent another minute questioning them, then, after getting the address of this local eccentric, promptly tossed some coins upon his table, scooped up his box and cane, and strode out of the tavern door.

Never to be seen again…

The old man strode through the dusk-shaded streets of Paris, his gaze intently focused on the pavement in front of him.

"Doctor *Omega*, is it?" he muttered to himself. "We shall see about that."

A muffled voice issued from the hatbox tucked under his arm.

"Hush," the old man said, patting the box gently.

His shoulders hunched under his traveling cloak, his features determined, he made his way through the narrow, winding streets. As night deepened, the buildings seemed to loom over the old man. Other pedestrians seemed to dart in and out of the deep shadows.

"A Morlock would feel right at home in this neighborhood," the old man sniffed, pulling his cloak tighter around him to ward off the chill.

He came to the house in question. It was a pleasant enough dwelling, quaintly middle class. Not new, but well cared for.

The old man put the box down on the stoop and was about to knock when the door was flung open and a young man came bounding out, promptly tripping over the hatbox.

"Oh, dear," the old man said, helping the younger one to his feet. "My apologies. I was trying to find the gentleman who lives here—Doctor Omega. Is he in?"

"No longer," the young man replied, brushing himself off and getting to his feet. "But, do not despair, for I am he. Doctor Omega, at your service!"

The young man gave a brief bow and when he straightened up, the older man had a moment to study his features.

His face was thin and friendly, framed by collar length black hair, and a neatly trimmed mustache and beard. His smile was open and charming, and his eyes shone with an energy that could easily have been either genius or madness. His long coat, trousers, waistcoat and shoes were all a touch out of fashion and black. The only trace of color was a bone white shirt and an ascot of red with thin black stripes. A monocle, attached to his lapel by a black ribbon swung back and forth like a pendulum.

"I have business this night," Doctor Omega said, moving off to hail a carriage. "If you wish to speak to me, you must be prepared to travel."

The old man watched the younger one with a puzzled expression.

"Please, Monsieur," a voice said from the doorway. A middle-aged woman, her hair going to grey, stepped out of the house. "Please, go with him. Watch over my... Doctor Omega. Keep him safe."

The sorrow came off her like a wave and the old man, nodded and gave her what he hoped was a reassuring smile.

"Of course. I'd no sooner let Doctor Omega come to harm than I would myself," he said, turning to follow the younger man as quickly as his old legs would allow.

He sank into the carriage, and, as it rolled into the night, he patted his forehead with a handkerchief.

"Well, where are we off to?" he asked, as he struggled to catch his breath and hold onto his cane, his handkerchief, and the hatbox.

"There are strange forces at work in the city," the younger man explained, not looking at his fellow traveler, but rather out into the night-shrouded streets of Paris.

"Are there now? Such as?" the old man asked, tucking his handkerchief back into his coat pocket.

"You must understand," Omega said, earnestly, "I do not speak out of some sense of melodrama, but rather because what I am about to tell you about myself, and my current undertaking, will seem fantastic."

"Not at all," the older man said. "You will find that I am not... unfamiliar with Doctor Omega, his reputation and his exploits. Speak freely. I've an inkling that my, er, own predicament may, in some way, be connected to your own."

He sat back, his legs straddling the box on the floor, his expression patiently expectant.

"Very well, I will take you at your word. As you may be aware, I have a quite extraordinary form of transport in my possession, the *Cosmos*, and with it, I have traveled far and wide. I had just returned to Paris, a rather unceremonious arrival, I must admit, due to a bout of... dizziness. Upon arrival, I stumbled out of the *Cosmos* to get my bearings and found myself in the middle of the most bizarre altercation. A trio of figures in black robes were grappling with a gang of street ruffians. I was disoriented and distracted by some odds and ends that had fallen out of the *Cosmos* when I had exited it, and the next thing I knew, I was in the midst of the skirmish, trying to retrieve my belongings and avoid a severe pummeling."

"Curious," the older man murmured thoughtfully stroking his chin. "And then what? You seem unharmed?"

"Through no skill of my own, I must confess," said Omega, smiling. "Tripping over either my own feet or someone else's, I fell and managed to roll underneath a nearby wagon. The local police arrived and, in the ensuing chaos, most of the combatants and I were able to flee the scene. I made my way to... my... um... the house where you found me, in order to continue my investigation..."

"Of...?"

"Originally, what caused the *Cosmos* to crash, but then, I turned my attention to the participants of the altercation I had stumbled into."

"Are the two events connected?" the older man inquired.

"I don't see how they could be," Omega replied with an indulgent shake of his head. "I did not know when I would be arriving, so I could hardly be the target. There seemed to be an... item, an artifact, that both groups sought, and I was an unfortunate witness to their struggle."

He then leaned forward and knocked on the ceiling of the carriage.

"Eugène!" he called. "We will depart here!" He then turned to his companion. "I am afraid the rest of my journey is to be on foot. It is of a clandestine nature. If you wish, you may stay here or I could have the driver…?"

"No, no, you have quite captured my interest, my young… Doctor," said the older man with a tight-lipped smile. "Your mission is quite serious, and if I can be of assistance, I offer my services."

"Very decent of you," Omega smiled, exiting the carriage. "If you want to leave your box…?"

"No," the older man grunted, climbing out of the carriage while trying to juggle both his cane and the hatbox. He faltered and Omega stepped forward to help him, catching the box as it slid from the older man's grip.

"Here you are… did you hear something? It sounded like a woman's voice?"

"Where are we?" the old man asked, regaining his balance and then possession of his box.

"Ah, yes. I was unable to find any sign of my robed assailants, but I was able to track the others, the ruffians."

"And they led you here?" the older man asked, looking about at the rundown buildings around them.

"Yes. I followed one to a local café and overheard he was meeting his employer in that building," Omega explained, pointing towards a drab three-story hotel that had seen better days. "I'm going to scout about and speak to the concierge. Wait here."

Before the older man could protest, Doctor Omega had sprinted away.

"Will you be needing me then, sir?" the driver asked from his perch.

"Perhaps it would be best if you stayed nearby, but found some discreet spot to park… not too far," he instructed.

The carriage rolled down the block, and the old man settled himself in a doorway, pulling his traveling cloak about him. He placed the pink hatbox on the top step, within the alcove, and opened the lid, removing a severed head.

It was made of metal, appearing more sculpted than manufactured. Its features were vaguely feminine. The old man held it up as though he were about to perform the famous soliloquy from *Hamlet.*

He remembered how the robot head had come in his possession. He had acquired it in the future, in the legend-shrouded city of Metropolis.[9]

"I see the boys brought you back a new toy to play with," he had told Fred, picking up the head and peering into its blank, metal eyes. He had tapped it and, amazingly, the eyes had flickered to life.

"The workers musssst…rise up! They are…zzztt… but pu-puppets, dancing on the elite's string…!"

"Hmmm, and what might you become, now that your own strings have been cut, I wonder?" the Doctor had mused, returning the head to the table.

Later, he had christened it Thea.

"So, Thea, what do you think of our young friend?" he asked. "Is he under some delusion—or is he truly me?"

"Match between two entities estimated at only 64 %," the metal head replied in a voice that was a blend of female and mechanical.

"What?" The old man sputtered. "That… that… deluded popinjay is not… I am Doctor Omega, he is some rank imposter!"

"Inquiry concerning your protest," Thea asked. "Subject has knowledge of Doctor Omega. Subject also shows trace evidence of interplanetary travel. This unit must stand by its statement."

"Traces of interplanetary travel… him…? In this day and age… No, it can't be!"

"Again, inquiry?"

---

[9] See "*The Robots of Metropolis*" in our Vol. 1.

"He's too young. I was much older... er... more mature before I even began traveling, and I was never one to sport a beard," Doctor Omega muttered. "His reasoning is spotty concerning this peculiar mystery he's pursuing. There's no earthly way he is a younger version of myself..."

"Perhaps a future version?" Thea suggested. "You have spoken of your people being very long lived and able to change their appearance."

"In only the direst of circumstances," Omega said, setting Thea down on top of the hatbox. "I'm far too careful in my actions for it to happen. This fellow is obviously mentally unbalanced or up to something... I'm just unsure of what... We need to stay with him, until he tips his hand."

"Brainwave scanning, while limited by my condition, shows several similarities to your own mental energies."

"When were you scanning my brain waves?" Doctor Omega asked, testily. "You know I do not condone that sort of... oh, he's returning!"

Looking up at the sound of approaching footsteps, Doctor Omega hastily replaced the robot head in the pink box. He was retying the twine when the younger Omega jogged towards them.

"I... uh... I could use some assistance," he said, in a slightly breathless tone. His eyes darted about, as if he was looking for something, but at the same time unable to remember what it was.

"What is it?" Doctor Omega asked, getting to his feet. "Did you find your ruffian?"

"In a way."

They summoned the carriage, and the driver, Eugène Papillon, a gruff, wire-thin Parisian, joined them, as they made their way to the third floor of the hotel. The trio entered the room, pausing in the doorway to take in the disarray. The furniture had been overturned and papers were scattered all about the room. Some appeared to have been tossed into the fireplace.

"Rather a cheery fire, in any other circumstances," Doctor Omega muttered, strolling into the room and looking around thoughtfully. He set the hatbox upon a desk and distractedly peered at several sheets of paper. "Curious, these are business papers... receipts and the like. Did your suspect strike you as the entrepreneurial sort?"

Young Omega shook his head as he entered the room. He gestured for Eugène to stand guard at the door.

"He was merely a hireling for a larger criminal enterprise," he explained, moving across the room to an ancient, sagging sofa. "It seemed they were abandoning this place and my quarry was left behind to dispose of any evidence."

"So, he's gone," Doctor Omega nodded.

"In a manner of speaking," the younger man said, waving the older one over to the sofa.

There was a space between the back of the sofa and the wall and there, on the dusty floor, was huddled a body. It wore the rough clothes of a workman. His head was twisted at an odd angle, indicating a broken neck.

"I see," said Doctor Omega, kneeling down to examine the body. "Interesting."

"Yes, but hardly helpful," interjected the younger Omega. "I needed information to find out more concerning who he worked for and what they were up to."

"Not a talkative fellow," Doctor Omega muttered. "But, I think he still has something to tell us..."

He brought up a yellowed business card.

"Hmm, the address for this office is near the docks," the younger Omega said. "Not the most reputable of neighborhoods. The card is stained, hard to read... *Maupertuis!* I've heard that name... But from where...?"

"There was a detective...?" the older Omega said, getting to his feet. "Lecoq... or was it that Marple woman...?"

The scruffy carriage driver stood in the doorway, focusing more on the two pacing savants than guarding them against would-be attackers.

"Perhaps you could do your thinking down in the carriage?" he suggested, hopefully. "No dead men might be more conducive…?"

Both Omegas looked up and nodded. The younger tucked the card in his pocket, while the older scooped up the few remaining intact papers and stuffed them into the hatbox. They made their way to the grey, dingy lobby as three black-cloaked figures came flowing out of the shadows.

"Run!" the younger Omega shouted, hooking his arm through Doctor Omega's and bolting for the door. The older man stumbled along, struggling to hold on to his box and cane.

Eugène outpaced the two and quickly leapt into the driver's seat, giving the two Omegas only seconds to fling themselves into the carriage before it raced off.

The cloaked trio ran after them, but soon realized that they could not catch up on foot and leapt into a plain, black carriage parked in a nearby alley.

"They are still after us!" the younger Omega said, sticking his head out the window to keep an eye on their pursuers.

"The cloaks," Doctor Omega muttered, as he was jostled about. "Like those worn by followers of the Ubasti, but was there something…?"

"Faster, Eugène!" the younger Omega instructed." See if we can lose them!"

"Did you notice anything odd about them?" Doctor Omega asked. "I caught a glimpse of one their hands…?"

"Can't say I did," his younger namesake said, sitting back and frantically rummaging through his coat pockets. "Where is…? Ah-ha! This should deal with them!"

He held out a pencil-sized metal tube triumphantly.

"I don't see how that will fend them off."

"Do not doubt the power of the sonic!" the younger Omega said, leaning out the window. He pointed the metal tube at the pursuing carriage, pressed a tiny button and a thin beam of light shown from the end of the tube. A beam that had no seeming effect on the other carriage.

"Imbecile!" Doctor Omega grumbled, pulling the other Omega back into the carriage. "It's a pen light! Really, the idea that I would rely on some sonic knick-knack to extract myself from a difficult situation... farcical, just farcical!"

He began to pat down his own pockets, taking out a small, crumpled, brown paper bag and an equally crumpled envelope. He handed the bag to the younger man and smiled.

"Now, when I say, empty the bag out the carriage window," he instructed. "Understand?"

"I suppose," the other man muttered, peering into the bag. "But these are...?"

"Yes, I'll apologize to my granddaughter later. Now!"

The younger Omega leaned out the window and emptied the bag of metal jacks onto the cobblestone street. Doctor Omega then touched a match to the paper fuse of a thin string of firecrackers and flung them out the other side. The combination of startling noise and the discomfort caused the horses to struggle against the black carriage's driver. After several minutes, they bolted down a side street to escape their torment.

The noise also startled the horses pulling their own carriage, which then galloped forward, adding even more distance between the two carriages.

"Excellent," the younger Omega announced, sitting back. "Now, we can go to..."

"...The *Cosmos*," Doctor Omega snapped. "It is time we obtained some answers. Until I can put my mind to rest about you, I will be unable to concentrate on this... whatever it is you have gotten yourself mixed up in."

The bearded man toyed with the monocle on his lapel as he pondered what the older man had said. After several moments, he nodded and gave the driver the instructions for their new destination.

Several minutes later, they disembarked at the opening of an alleyway. It was wide and moderately clean, with a wooden gate at the far end. The younger Omega opened the gate with a slight flourish.

"Behold," he said. "The *Cosmos*!"

Sitting in the courtyard was a hot air balloon with an oversized basket. The balloon seemed to be only partially inflated and so bobbed limply.

Doctor Omega frowned and his shoulders slumped. Despite his criticism of the other man, he had held onto a sliver of hope that this *faux* Doctor Omega had somehow gained possession of his real space-time ship, the *Cosmos*.

"That?" he sighed, going to sit on a nearby stack of lumber. "That is your *Cosmos*?"

"Yes, it is," Young Omega said, proudly giving the gondola an affectionate pat as he walked past it. "You are not seeing it at its best, but a day's work and I will once again be capable of journeying amongst the planets."

"Oh, do shut up!" Doctor Omega snapped, sulkily.

"I beg your pardon?"

"I have had enough of this!" the older man said, sternly jabbing a finger at the younger. "I am stranded here, in this time, on this world, trying to discover any means of leaving ,or if my traveling companions are even alive, and that task is made increasingly difficult when some... dandified idiot is constantly babbling, while I am trying to think!"

The younger Omega skidded to a halt, a stunned expression on his thin face, before it quickly morphed into indignant anger.

"Oh, that is rich!" he declared, hands on hips, as he scowled down at the aged savant. "I am in the midst of a serious investigation; a man is dead and there are hints of unearthly forces at work in Paris. None of which is made any easier when some doddering old man dogs my heels, going on like a disapproving school lecturer! Who do you think you are?"

"I? I am Doctor Omega! *The* Doctor Omega! Not some playacting adolescent!" the old man glared, "who has no idea what he has stumbled into and insists on playing out some boys' own adventure story."

"Perhaps, if you would attempt to speak to me, instead of enjoying the sound of your own voice so much!"

"Might I make a suggestion?" A muffled voice said from the hatbox.

Both Omega's stopped at peered at it, one thoughtfully, the other in surprise.

"Ah, Thea, pardon me, with everything happening, I forgot about you," Doctor Omega said, opening the box and rummaging amongst the papers. He held up the metal head. "What do you suggest?"

"What is that...?" the younger Omega stammered. the argument forgotten with the appearance of this new marvel. "You have been to other worlds!"

"What...?"Doctor Omega muttered. "Oh, do control yourself. Thea is a product of this world, an automaton, a product of a future technology. Like you, her mind is not entirely her own. I had hoped that traveling with me would help her to break her programming...find her own way in the world...not turning out quite as I had hoped, but I'm sure that once I'm able to reattach her head..."

"I have done preliminary scans of this other individual," she interrupted. "I can attempt more comprehensive scans."

"Really?" Doctor Omega mused frostily. "At what point do you take my word for it?"

He turned the head till it was facing the balloon.

"Do you imagine that craft capable of traversing the time stream? It doesn't look capable of getting off the ground, let alone reaching other worlds. He is no more me than he is the Man in the Moon."

"The Moon...?" the younger Omega muttered, his gaze moving from the robot head to his balloon. "I was... not the Man in the Moon, but rather... how did you know?"

"What?" Doctor Omega asked, peevishly. 'What are you going on about?"

"Spike in brain wave activity," Thea commented. "If his memories have been altered, then perhaps a more delicate approach is required."

"Yes, yes," the older man muttered, tucking the robot's head under his arm as he stood up and went over to the younger.

The younger Omega swayed slightly and rubbed his forehead. He no longer seemed aware of the presence of the old man and the robot. He turned his gaze and footsteps towards the gondola of his balloon. Upon reaching it, he leaned against the edge of the basket and stared up at the deflated balloon without seeming to see it.

"How did I know what, young man?" Doctor Omega asked, coming to stand next to him. His voice was low and soothing. "What about the Moon?"

"I had... um... had just returned... from the Moon, when all this... whatever it is, began," the younger Omega muttered. He seemed to need the support of the gondola to stay on his feet. "Something... happened on the Moon..."

"That could mean something. The Moon is actually not as desolate as Monsieur Verne would have people believe."

"Who...?"

"Never mind," Doctor Omega said, taking the younger man by the arm. "Come, have a seat."

Once he had the dazed young man seated on the lumber pile, Doctor Omega set down Thea's head and took a seat himself. He then began patting his coat pockets, eventually bringing forth another crumpled paper bag.

"Licorice Allsorts?" He offered.

"Are these your granddaughter's as well?"

"No, these are mine. I keep them in my coat, so my granddaughter doesn't take them from me. Now, let me tell you a story: My ship, the *Cosmos*, which is not and has never been a balloon, was traveling through space and time, as it does, and encountered a wave of radioactive turbulence. My traveling companions and I were flung out into the void. Thea and I found ourselves here, in Paris."

He paused and patted the metal head affectionately and then looked up at the younger man, hoping for an expression of realization. Instead he was met with further confusion.

"Yes, well, another indicator that I'm right," Doctor Omega muttered. "If you were me, that would have made perfect sense."

The younger Omega continued to peer at him, dumbfounded.

"As I was saying, it becomes clear that it is no coincidence that, shortly after I began my exile here, you suddenly are racing the streets, believing you are Doctor Omega..."

"But, how can you still deny it?" the younger man protested. "I have the knowledge; I have traveled amongst the... the... um... planets."

"Tell me about some of your journeys, Doctor Omega," the older savant said, his tone taking on a soothing rhythm. "What wonders have you seen?"

"I traveled to the Moon..."

"So you've said. Where else? Mars, the far future, Quinnis in the fourth universe...?"

"No!" the younger Omega exclaimed, his hands clutching at his temples. "This... is... wrong! I am Doctor Omega! I have traversed the vastness of space, yet, all I can recall is my trip to the Moon and... and even that..."

"We are not going to get answers by forcing matters," Doctor Omega said. He poked a finger into the bag of candy and took one out, studying it thoughtfully as he spoke. "Your memories have been tampered with. Who or why, we do not know, but now that we can see the scaffold, we can fill in the gaps and discover what has been built, as it were. The human mind is a wondrous and delicate thing. Answers do us no good if we cause you harm along the way. Tell, me more about this mystery that you've stumbled into, upon your return to Earth...?"

"Yes, of course," the other man nodded, relieved to think of something else. "I was intrigued by what those two groups were fighting over. As you may know, Paris is rife with criminal gangs and shadowy groups that all seem to spend as much time in conflict with each other as they are with the police. While it never occurred to me that the Ubasti would be operating in Paris, until you mentioned them, I did recognize a couple of the street ruffians from... hmmm... I was at the docks...?"

"We can sift through the details later," Doctor Omega reassured him. "What criminal group do they work for?"

"No one in particular," the younger man shrugged. "At the time, they were taking coin from a businessman of questionable reputation, Oscar Maupertuis... he claims a title, Earl was it?"

"Baron," Doctor Omega prompted, quietly. "Baron Maupertuis. I knew the name was familiar to me and while it is an answer of sorts, it leads to more questions. Can you describe the Baron to me?"

"Not well. I don't believe we've met face to face. There was a picture in a newspaper and I saw him from a distance at a gathering at the Louvre. He considers himself quite the patron of the arts, but there have been rumors of him collecting artwork and artifacts through dubious means..."

He paused, catching a glimpse of the older man's impatient frown.

"He is of... um... medium height and a touch overweight, rather impressive set of whiskers, fair-haired and middle-aged, blue eyes and a rather nasty smile. Is that the man you knew?"

"Yes, he had discarded the whiskers for a mustache, but in every other respect, it may be... This is curious and bothersome."

"How so?"

"I encountered the Baron in 1891 and he was still a middle-aged man with a nasty smile," Doctor Omega explained. "I knew then that he was more than a mere schemer... probably for the best Watson decided not to publish..."

"A son perhaps? Following in the fathers' conniving footsteps?"

"No, I suspect there's more to the Baron," Doctor Omega nodded.

"You believe he's... immortal?" the younger Omega asked, helping himself to a piece of candy. "Or does he travel in time, like you claim to?"

"Claim...?" Doctor Omega muttered, frowning.

The younger man got to his feet and began to pace about the yard.

"Now, it begins to make sense, I think," he said, hands clasped behind his back, as he walked.

"What?" Doctor Omega grumbled.

"One of the things that kept me from understanding this mystery, was what were both groups after. Now understanding that we are looking at the cult of Ubasti vying with a criminal with an unnaturally extended lifespan, it suddenly becomes clear what they are after: One of the surviving crystals of Atlantis!"

"One of the what?" Doctor Omega sputtered.

"You see," the younger Omega explained, sitting back down. "There are many legends about the lost city, and many concern artifacts that were scattered across the world when it sank. Many of them speak of the Atlanteans working in crystal, the way we would metal, and creating crystals that were capable of operating... machinery, of a sort, as well as channeling energy for health and longevity. You see? It makes perfect sense! The Ubasti, coming as they do from Atlantis' sister city, Lemuria, would know of the crystals' existence, while if the Baron is prolonging his life through some... unnatural means, would seek them out as well!"

He smiled in triumph at the older man.

"You... buffoon!" Doctor Omega exclaimed in reply.

"What? What did I say?"

"Yes, there are many myths and legends springing from the sinking of Atlantis, most of them were invented by the Atlanteans themselves, to hide and protect their powers and secrets. Which of the numerous Atlantises is the actual, true Atlantis is one of them. Another is, that there are no 'magical crystals' of Atlantis."

"But..." the younger Omega began to protest.

"I am not merely dashing skeptical cold water on your theory. I was there, I know. The crystals are a ruse, a fairy tale to trap the attention of the vain, the desperate and the hopelessly naïve."

The young man sank down onto the lumber pile shoulders slumped, clasping his hands loosely in front of him.

"Well, that, besides being slightly disappointing, makes no sense," the younger Omega muttered. "If the Ubasti know the crystals are just a fairy tale, then why are they involved?"

There was a moment of silence and both Omegas sat up and peered at each other, struck by sudden inspiration.

"Unless they know what it actually is!" the young man breathed.

"They aren't the Ubasti," Doctor Omega said.

The younger Omega sighed, bowed his head and made a vague 'after you' gesture.

"Did you notice anything about the three cultists that pursued us at the hotel?" he asked.

"Besides that they were dressed in black robes and chasing us down the street?"

"Don't be facetious," Doctor Omega chided. "Though, you have brought up an important point: the Ubasti operate in the shadows, in secret, and they chased us down a Paris street in ceremonial robes: hardly the work of a competent secret society. Not to mention brawling with Maupertuis' hired ruffians in the middle of the street…"

"Their skin…!" the younger man interrupted. "I meant to ask about it, but in the confusion of events it slipped my mind. The one that almost grabbed my arm, his skin was… odd. It had a particular reddish coloring, as though he'd suffered a burn or was an American Indian…?"

"Lectroids," Doctor Omega said, in a concerned tone.

"What? Is that what you think they were?"

"No," he replied, pointing past the younger man. "I think that's what they are."

The younger Omega spun and then gaped at the three black-robed figures standing in the alleyway. They pushed back their hoods, revealing bald heads, the color and texture of a boiled lobster shell. Their lips were thin harsh lines, their noses mere slits and cruel black orbs for eyes.

"Ah, Lectroids," the young man nodded, toying anxiously with his lapel ribbon. "Yes, never occurred to me actually... What do we do now?"

He got his answer when Doctor Omega scooped up Thea's head and ran for the balloon. The younger Omega shrugged, grabbed a stout stick, and ran after his older namesake, swinging wildly as the cloaked aliens lunged at them. He caught one Lectroid across the temple and it fell to its knees. The second met the wooden bludgeon head on and cracked it in half.

Doctor Omega stuck out his cane as he hobbled by, tripping up the third. The two men staggered past the Lectroids and fell into the basket of the balloon. The younger Omega flailed about, hitting various levers and dials on the clunky jumble of equipment that took up one corner of the gondola. Doctor Omega frantically struggled to pull in the anchor, while keeping an eye on the quickly recovering and quite angry looking Lectroids. The anchor came loose suddenly striking the older time traveler in the shoulder as it fell into the gondola.

The balloon sluggishly inflated and rose upwards, reaching a height of ten feet by the time the alien trio reached them. They jumped and snarled, their blunt, jagged fingernails leaving gouge trails in the exterior of the basket, but the Lectroids were unable to get a grip and climb up after their quarry.

Doctor Omega fell back, sitting awkwardly on the floor of the basket, struggling to catch his breath.

"That went as well as could have been expected, I suppose," he muttered, wiping his face with his handkerchief. He pulled over the pink hatbox. Thea's head was laying facedown amongst the papers. She was muttering to herself in a tinny, sullen voice.

"I do apologize, my dear," Doctor Omega said, picking her up and brushing her off. He set her down on a trunk and began fishing papers out of the box.

"That should do it," the younger man announced, pulling a long lever on the side of the machinery. "We are at a safe height and, while it is a vaguely ostentatious way of getting about the city, the *Cosmos* will provide us with safe passage to our next destination…whatever that may be. I must confess I find myself even more baffled with each new piece of information we acquire."

He checked some dials and was pleasantly surprised to find a cigar tucked behind one and with a smile, lit it and puffed thoughtfully.

"If you were really me, you'd have a pipe," Doctor Omega muttered, as he looked through the papers they'd found at the hotel.

"Those were Lectroids… Red Lectroids…?" the younger Omega muttered, between puffs. Absently, he adjusted the controls on the clunky device. "Here, in Paris, that isn't right… I think?"

He looked over at the older savant for reassurance. Doctor Omega nodded.

"Sounds like the memory blocks are coming loose," he nodded, thoughtfully. "Interesting. Yet, you are showing none of the dizziness or fear you felt before. Maybe there is more to your *Cosmos* than meets the eye."

"Well, that's good, I suppose, except we can't just float up here forever. We have transport, but no destination."

"Yes, I was thinking about that," Doctor Omega said, waving the paper in his hand. "I think these scraps can give us the means to locate the Baron. Do you have a map amongst all this clutter?"

"Yes, must apologize, wasn't expecting company," the younger Omega said, as he rummaged amongst the scattered bits of luggage and machinery. "Arrived back in Paris and haven't had a quiet moment for housekeeping…ah, here it is!"

"Yet, you acquired rooms?" Doctor Omega said, accepting the rolled-up map. Placing a pince-nez upon his beakish nose, he studied the map, using the scraps of paper to help him identify and then figure out the location of their quarry. After several moments, he frowned in frustration and placed the map on the floor of the gondola. He circled the likely locations with a felt tip marker and placed Thea's head on the map. As he struggled to stand up, he gave the robot an encouraging pat on the head.

"I do believe, if we can locate the Baron, and I don't see the Lectroids having any difficulty tracking us through Paris, then we have a good chance to wrap this whole convoluted business up tonight."

The basket swayed slightly in the breeze, as it drifted over the darkened rooftops of Paris. Doctor Omega gripped the wicker railing to keep his feet.

"You think if we bring both sides together, we can sort out who is up to what and deal with them all?" the younger man asked, joining the Doctor at the rail.

"I think so. Be easier if we knew what this 'magic crystal' actually was," He said with a frown.

"Oh, well, if that will help, then I could retrieve it from its hiding place." The younger Omega smiled at his traveling companion. The older man replied with a look of stunned amazement.

"You know where this thing… artifact… is?"

"Well, yes."

"You've known this entire time?"

"Yes."

"And it never occurred to you to mention this not insignificant fact to me?"

"Yes, you see… um… is it healthy for your knuckles to get that white? Maybe you should let go of your cane?"

"Yes, quite reasonable. You can't steer the balloon to the artifact's location if I knock you senseless," Doctor Omega agreed through gritted teeth.

"Oh, it won't be that difficult," The younger man said, reaching into his inside coat pocket.

"You've had it with you the whole time… Of course, you did," Doctor Omega sighed. "And why was this information kept from me during the course of our investigations?"

"Because for most of 'our investigations,' you've been shouting at me and generally acting like an unstable old lunatic," the younger Omega explained. "I've never seen you before tonight and you show up and treat me like I'm some sort of deluded bumbler…"

"Which we've established you are."

"Perhaps. My memories have been interfered with," the younger man shrugged. "But until we discover some proof that I'm not you, I'm quite content to be Doctor Omega."

"As you should be," Doctor Omega said, reaching up to clutch at his lapels and standing proudly stiff backed. "So, until we get things sorted, I will be generous enough to share my identity, as well as my intellect and deductive skills with you. Now, let's see what's caused all the fuss, shall we?"

The younger Omega handed the object over to the older man. It was a crystal, roughly eight inches long and deep blue in color. It seemed to soak up the moonlight and reflect it back with a faint, warm glow.

"Ah!" Doctor Omega said with a satisfied smile. "It all begins to make a bit of sense."

"It does…?" The younger man asked.

"Yes. This crystal did not come Atlantis," Doctor Omega explained. "It came from Metebelis-Three."

He nodded to himself, before glancing over at his companion and noticing his dumbfounded expression.

"The crystals of Metebelis-Three have the ability to store and channel various forms of energy, including mental," he continued.

"How do you know all of this?" Young Omega asked.

"Because, up until a fortnight ago, this crystal was sitting on my mantelpiece, next to a Tibetan sacred bell… I must get around to returning that to the monastery someday… um, where was I? Ah, yes, the crystal is mine. It was obviously cast out into the time stream at the same time I was, and found its way into the hands of either the Lectroids or the scheming Baron, setting off this struggle to gain it and use it for their own nefarious purposes: Maupertuis for extending his lifespan, but the Lectroids... that bodes badly for Paris, if not the Earth, if they get their claws on it."

"Do we still go ahead with our plan to bring both sides together?" the younger Omega asked. "If we no longer need information...?"

"Letting them fight it out could solve all our problems," Doctor Omega replied. "Besides, I'm still curious as to who Baron Maupertuis is. Thea, have you worked out our destination yet?"

"Yes, Doctor," the robot head replied. Her eyes lit up and twin beams of light shone on a spot on the map. The younger Omega knelt down and picked up both the map and the metal head. He handed Thea to the Doctor and studied the map, looking down at the rooftops of Paris.

"I think if the wind doesn't pick up, we should have no trouble."

He turned a small crank and pulled a lever. The balloon gained a bit of height, as well as changing direction.

Doctor Omega peered up towards the balloon.

"Heat-absorbing fabric... steering device that controls vertical as well as horizontal movement and some of these supplies and other pieces of equipment... You may not be me, my boy, but you are someone with a first-class mind," he said, nodding thoughtfully. "Maybe that's where we need to look to discover who you are and how you arrived to be mixed up in all this? Where were you going when you... unceremoniously landed? You were returning from somewhere, correct?"

"Yes," the younger Omega nodded, adjusting a control dial. "I was returning to... huh... Paris. I'd just completed a... no, I'd attempted... that's odd...?"

He leaned against the basket rail and rubbed at his temples a puzzled frown on his bearded face.

"Just speak as things come to you," Doctor Omega said in a quiet tone. "You were in the balloon, drifting along, just as we are now. Could you see where you were going? Did you travel by night?"

"Yes, but there was a full moon... the Moon!"

The young man turned to face Doctor Omega, a bright smile on his face. He gestured triumphantly.

"The Moon! I told you I had been to the Moon, and I had! That's where I was returning from. It just... it felt... unreal, like a dream..."

"You traveled to the Moon, and yet, when you try and speak of it, it begins to feel unreal to you, like a half-remembered dream," Doctor Omega muttered, stroking his chin thoughtfully. "Of course!"

He smiled at the younger man and patted his arm comfortingly.

"Now, we have answers. You did travel to the Moon, and there, you encountered the Lunian Immortals," he explained.

"Who... wait, yes, there was someone. A tall man in a white robe of some kind... he was... was like a Greek statue..." The man muttered his brow wrinkled in concentration. "But, he said, he was an... angel... or perhaps...?"

"The Lunian Immortals are a race of eternal beings," Doctor Omega explained, in a tone that suggested he was speaking in a university lecture hall rather than the gondola of a hot air balloon. "No one is entirely sure where they originated from, but they settled on your Moon. As I said, they are eternal, not to mention arrogant and insufferably smug in their dealings with other beings. Their claims of being 'God's chosen' are completely unfounded, though it is believed that their visits to Earth are the origin of many cultures' belief in angels and deities."

"They found me when I was drifting towards the Moon!" the young man exclaimed. "They showed me their city... their beautiful, white city and brought me back and showed me all of the Earth..."

"The whole time telling you what a rank, ignorant race humans are, while they sang their own, superior and highly moral praises," Doctor Omega grumbled. "Yes, they do it quite often. They claim it's in order to educate and enlighten 'lesser races.' I believe immortality has driven them, as a race, into a kind of collective boredom and it's all part of an elaborate game they play to while away the millennia. Either way, that is what happened to you."

"They returned me to Earth, believing I was you?"

"No, they returned you to Earth believing that your entire encounter was all a dream," Doctor Omega continued. "Unfortunately, in the trance state they'd put you, your mind was very susceptible to outside influences…"

"And I found the blue crystal! I… um… absorbed the mental energy it had gotten from you!" The young man exclaimed. "So, I'm not an enigmatic traveler in space in time, but I did prove my balloon design worked and that it could carry me beyond the boundaries of Earth's atmosphere and out into space! It works and all those who said 'Gerpré is a dreamer with only his head in the clouds' will have to eat their words!"

"Gerpré…?" Doctor Omega asked. "Is that your name?"

The young man stopped, as though the revelation of his name had come as a big a surprise to himself, as it had to his learned companion.

"Gerpré…?" he breathed. Lingering over the word as though savoring its taste. "Antoine Gerpré…! Gerpré, student, inventor and balloonist extraordinaire!"

"My dear Gerpré," Doctor Omega said, smiling as he took the younger man's hand and shook it. "A pleasure to make your acquaintance!"

"Pleased to meet you, Doctor." Gerpré smiled, giving a short bow. "So, now that we have been properly introduced, let us go make the acquaintance of Baron Maupertuis."

He turned back to the balloon's controls and steered it across the city. Doctor Omega, smiling to himself, picked up

Thea's head and placed it upon the control console, while he sat on a wicker basket.

Soon, they found themselves floating over one of Paris' more upscale neighborhoods. The houses were grander and there was more land separating them.

"There!" Gerpré announced, pointing to a specific roof.

"Are you sure?"

"He is correct," Thea responded.

"Thank you," The young balloonist said to the robot head, as he rummaged through a trunk. He brought out a long length of rope with a grappling hook tied to it. He lowered it over the side, swinging it until it caught the eves of the roof-top. He tugged the rope to make sure it was secure, and then adjusted the controls so the balloon began to descend. Once the balloon had touched down, Gerpré threw another loop of rope over a small nearby chimney to secure the balloon. He then climbed out of the basket. Doctor Omega picked up Thea and then handing the metal head and his cane to the young Parisian, awkwardly climbed out to join him.

"What's our next move?" Gerpré asked, handing the two objects back.

"We need to be sure the Baron is in residence," Doctor Omega said. "And since your balloon is hardly a subtle mode of travel, we must be quick about it."

"Commencing scan," Thea announced, her eyes lighting up. "Detecting unusual life sign."

"Are you sure that's not just the Lectroids?" the older savant asked.

"I am certain," the robot head replied. "The life sign is within the dwelling."

"Well, then," Gerpré said, prying opening an attic window. "Why don't we see if the… lady can lead us to the master of the house?"

The trio climbed in the window and made their way through a cluttered, dusty attic until they found a narrow staircase that led down into the house.

They moved through opulent hallways and rooms, their footsteps muffled by the lush carpeting, as they crept past shadowy furnishings.

"Um…besides the Baron," Gerpré asked in a whisper, "what might we be looking for?"

"Not entirely sure," Doctor Omega replied, holding Thea out in front of him like a lantern. "Maupertuis may be using any number of unorthodox methods to extend his life span, ranging from otherworldly science to more arcane practices. Depending on what he believes the crystal to be…"

The Doctor's explanation trailed off and he came to a halt in front of a large oil painting. He paused and held Thea's head up to shine a light on it. It was a heavy-set man dressed in the fashion of the past century.

"Is that the Baron?" He mused. "Something familiar…especially around the eyes…?"

"I don't mean to be rude, but we need more of a plan than we seem to have at the moment," Gerpré suggested, looking about anxiously. "What should we be looking for? "

"Perhaps," a gruff voice said from out of the shadows, "some artifact that he could use to channel the crystal's energy?"

Both men spun, as a trio stepped into the shafts of moonlight that came in through the windows.

At their head was obviously Baron Maupertuis. His suit was up to date and fashionable. His features were broad and arrogant, his blue eyes burned with a cold hatred. He held a heavy flintlock pistol trained on Doctor Omega. Behind him stood two large men that looked like they'd be more comfortable in dockworkers' garb than the servant's livery that they were currently wearing. One also held a pistol, the other a heavy wooden cane.

"Ah," Doctor Omega frowned.

"Um…?"Gerpré added.

"Unusual biological profile located," Thea said, unnecessarily.

"Doctor Omega," the Baron growled, not lowering his weapon. In fact, his finger tightened on the trigger. "I should have guessed that this... popinjay was your cat's paw and all his foolish antics were merely to lure me out, so once again you could interfere with my plans."

"Have we met?" Doctor Omega asked puzzled. "You seem to have me at a disadvantage."

"You break into my home," Baron Maupertuis grumbled. "And now you want to pretend you don't know me? Have you forgotten our last meeting?"

"Well, I do recall our next meeting, but must say the previous one has slipped my memory," Doctor Omega said. He handed Thea to Gerpré and stepped closer to the Baron and his servants. "There is something familiar about you... humph, no, I'm sorry to say I can't recall..."

"Damn your eyes, you doddering simpleton!" the Baron roared. "I will not...!"

"Eyes...? That's it!" Doctor Omega exclaimed relief at solving a mystery mixed with the knowledge that the answer was not good news. "Ozer, you may change your appearance, but your eyes will always give you away."

"Ozer?" Gerpré asked, in a quiet tone. "Who is he?"

Doctor Omega turned away from the Baron and his men, as though surprised to remember the young balloonist was still there.

"You recall we spoke of the Lunian immortals? Well, the Earth has produced immortals of its own, and there are roughly a dozen of them, all claiming to be the Wandering Jew of legend..."

"Claiming...!" Baron Maupertuis growled.

"The Baron, here, is one of them." Doctor Omega continued in his lecturer's tone, as though he wasn't at gunpoint. "In fact, 'Baron Maupertuis' is but the latest in a long line of false names. He claims to be Ozer, a soldier of Herod's, the very soldier who pierced the side of Christ. You probably have heard the story, it's a quaint, mildly entertaining..."

"You are trying my patience, old man," Ozer snarled, jabbing his pistol into Doctor Omega's back. "I don't know what game you are playing, but if the black brethren do not have the crystal, then I believe I can guess who does!"

Doctor Omega raised his hands at the touch of the gun in a sign of surrender. As he did so, he spun his cane around, catching the immortal across the temple. As Ozer staggered back, he raised his gun hand and the flintlock went off, sending the bullet into the ceiling.

"Quickly!' The Doctor exclaimed, grabbing Gerpré by the arm.

The balloonist nodded and charged past the Baron, creating a path between the two servants with two well-placed shoves. Since he was still clutching the robot head, Gerpré had the appearance of a player in a particularly bizarre game of rugby. They ran down the corridor. Doctor Omega would pause to peek into rooms as they passed, but apparently found nothing to interest him.

At the end of the hallway they came to a broad, carpeted staircase.

"What now?" Gerpré asked, anxiously.

"Down, I think," the savant replied, breathlessly. "Hurry… to the front door!"

"Why not the balloon?" Gerpré asked, before spotting the pursuing servants, and abandoning his question. They stumbled hurriedly down the stairs, arriving ungracefully in the roomy foyer. The two men skidded on the oriental area rug; Doctor Omega came to a halt and adjusted his cravat. Gerpré collided with the heavy, oaken front door.

The time traveler looked around the foyer with a touch of admiration at the décor. Gerpré shook his head and rubbed his bruised shoulder.

"We aren't getting out that way," he muttered, looking around for an escape route or makeshift weapon as he spotted the Baron and his men at the top of the stairs.

Doctor Omega frowned at his partner in crime, and taking off his tiepin fiddled with the lock on the door. He then swung it open wide and peered out into the approaching dawn. He frowned, then licked his finger and held it up to test the wind.

"Hmmm, thought they'd be here by now…disappointing," he muttered, turning back to face Gerpré and the quickly approaching violent trio. "Could you keep them busy for a few moments?"

"Um… I don't… know?" Gerpré muttered, peering doubtfully at the umbrella he found by the door.

"Not you," Doctor Omega said, looking at Thea, who was still in the crock of the young balloonist's arm.

"Affirmative," Thea replied.

As the Baron and his men reached the bottom of the stairs, Gerpré held up the robot head. Thea emitted a bright light and a high-pitched screech that sent the trio rocking back on their heels. While this was going on, Doctor Omega stepped out onto the front steps and taking the blue crystal out of his coat pocket waved it over his head.

"Come out, come out, wherever you are!" he shouted.

He soon spotted the cloaked Lectroids skulking down the street, keeping to the shadows. Spotting Doctor Omega, they broke into a run and raced for the doorway.

Smiling to himself, he ducked back inside, grabbed Gerpré by the coattails and pulled him into a side alcove, as the two groups came bolting forward, Ozer firing, as his henchmen lunged at the black robed forms.

The bullets did no more than cause the aliens to stumble. They then tore off their clocks to keep from tripping on them as they fought.

The Lectroids were dressed in various styles and levels of taste. One was shirtless; another looked like he had just left a wedding, and a third was in fashionable tweeds and a bow-ler. All three wore bulky black belts, strewn with wires and gears.

"Just as I thought," Doctor Omega muttered from his hiding place.

He allowed the combat to continue for several more minutes, the Baron's men taking the worst of the punishment, as the Lectroids were stronger than any earthly opponent. He then stepped up and held the blue crystal up over his head. Closing his eyes, his forehead wrinkled in concentration, the crystal began to glow. The light caught the attention of all of the remaining combatants. One of the Baron's men had had his neck broken and one of the Lectroids took a bullet through the eye and was lying in an ever-widening pool of sludgy black blood.

"Gentlemen!" Doctor Omega shouted, opening his eyes. "I think I know a way to solve this conflict between you!"

With that announcement, he swung his arm and the alien crystal struck a marble pillar, shattering into a thousand blue fragments. A wave of energy rushed out from the remains of the crystal, washing over the foyer and its occupants. The Lectroids' belts began to spark and with a roar a rift opened around them and they were sucked out of the foyer like water down a tub drain.

Ozer dropped his weapon and clutched at his abdomen, grinding his teeth as he fell to his knees.

"That went quite well," Doctor Omega said, dusting off his hands.

Gerpré came staggering out of the alcove, rubbing one of his temples.

"I must say it feels as though I'm the only one occupying my skull," he announced, wincing slightly.

"Just as I planned."

"Ah, I have distinct memories of this," Gerpré said, smiling at his older companion. "I pull off some last-minute bit of improvisation and then discuss it as though I had a grand scheme planned the whole time. Go ahead, it'll be fun to not have to do it myself."

Doctor Omega frowned at the young balloonist, then at the robot head still in Gerpré's hand. The eyes had burnt out and there was a trickle of smoke coming up from the right earpiece. Doctor Omega took Thea from Gerpré and looked it over with a sad, thoughtful smile.

"Poor child," he said. "Once we return to the *Cosmos*, Fred and I will get you fixed up."

He then tucked her damaged head under his arm and turned his attention to the young balloonist and the ailing immortal.

"Now, where was I...?"

"Convincing me that you actually had a plan, I believe," Gerpré reminded him.

"Yes, I was and yes I did," Doctor Omega grumbled. "Now, let's see if there's any lingering trace of my intellect rattling around in your head... what was I up to?"

"Fine, have it your way," The younger man said, gripping his lapels in gentle mockery of his companion. "Once you discovered what both sides were after... the Baron to continue in his wicked immortal ways and the Lectroids in... um... order to... either use the crystal to stay in this dimension or open a rift to bring more of their kind to Earth...?"

"Very good," Doctor Omega said, walking over to the stairs. He sat, exhaling heavily and placed Thea down next to him. Gerpré dodged the remaining henchman, who bolted for the door and ran off into the night, and joined the Doctor on the stairs.

"Should we...?" Gerpré asked, pointing to the doorway.

Doctor Omega waved the idea away.

"We have enough to deal with," he said, nodding towards the prone form of Ozer. "So, knowing what we do, why bring everyone to the same locale?"

"At what point do you stop talking to me like I'm attending your class?" Gerpré asked, with a smile.

"When you show signs of learning something," Doctor Omega replied.

"Fine," Gerpré nodded. "Bringing them here allows you to... um... show them you had the crystal and knew what it truly was...?"

"Never mind," Doctor Omega frowned. "Though, it's re-assuring to know you are back to normal. In order to avoid having Ozer's men or the Lectroids stalking you for the rest of your life, or causing who knows what amount of havoc, we needed to show them that the crystal was beyond their grasp."

"As well as letting them subdue each other," Gerpré suggested, rubbing his bruised shoulder.

"There is that. I was also quite sure I could refocus the crystal's energies in a manner that would render both sides harmless."

"So, you sent the Lectroids back to... no, it's gone. I guess I am just me. The only alien world I seem to have any knowledge of is the Moon."

"Yes, I sent the Lectroids back and with the Baron..."

"What did you do to him?" Gerpré asked. "He looks the same. Is he mortal now?"

"No, I haven't the faintest idea what gave the various Wandering Jews their immortality... something beyond my ability to take away, but I knew about Ozer's method of im-mortality. He would take over other bodies, moving on to the next until it got too sick, old or inconvenient for him to stay. What the crystal's energy did was to trap him in that one. He's still immortal, but he'll have to be happy with the body he's got. He's not going anywhere and apparently it works, as he was still the Baron Maupertuis when I met him, fifty years from now. Might also explain why he acted so unpleasant in 1889. I wondered... now, I know."

"And breaking the crystal and dispelling its energy seems to have allowed me to shake off your memories and remember my own," Gerpré nodded. "Shame that you had to destroy such a pretty item to accomplish it."

"No matter. I suppose I'll go back to Metebelis-Three, someday and fetch another one," Doctor Omega said, getting to his feet. "We should be on our way. Your *Cosmos* is bound to attract attention and I could do with some breakfast. Not to mention needing to see to Thea and figure out how in the world I'm going to find my friends and my own *Cosmos*."

He sighed and shook his head.

"You are more than welcome to stay with my mother and I while you sort that out," Gerpré said, standing up and patting the old time traveler on the shoulder. "And, as to breakfast, I believe I still have some supplies in the balloon. Never did get to unpack it. Now that I think of it, Eugène is probably wondering what became of us."

The two men climbed the stairs, not giving the prone form of Ozer a second thought and made their way back up to the roof.

The sun was coming up and Gerpré climbed into the gondola to check his steering device and prepare for takeoff.

Doctor Omega stood on the roof, Thea's head tucked under his arm, as he looked out across the Paris neighborhood.

I suppose this is home… for now," he sighed.

"Getting maudlin in your old age?" a voice said.

Doctor Omega turned to see a short, stout, bearded man dressed in Victorian tweeds and a cap standing on the rooftop next to him. He held a short metal tube with a row of buttons and appeared to be standing in a doorway in the air.

"Helvetius!" Doctor Omega exclaimed. "What are you…?"

"No time for chit chat," the other space-time traveler interrupted. "Come along, fate of the universe and all that, and I've already wasted too much time away from my studies looking for you."

He reached out, grabbed Omega by the arm and pulled him into the unearthly doorway. Tapping a button on the metal rod, the door closed leaving no trace that it, or even that the two men had been there at all.

"Ready to takeoff," Gerpré said, climbing out of gondola. "Doctor…?"

Gerpré searched the rooftop, then the house and, over the course of the next year, a good portion of Paris.

Finding the mysterious savant became his second obsession. After refining his balloon to continue his travels, he came to believe Doctor Omega had just returned from where or when he'd originally come from, and Gerpré set his mind on finding the old man as well as stepping foot upon the Moon himself and perhaps encountering the Lunian immortals once more.

It took several years of experimentation, research and struggle, but eventually young Gerpré accomplished both goals.

Doctor Omega and his friends have been flung from his ship, the Cosmos, *and into the time-stream. Scattered across history, they have discovered that the strange rifts that are responsible for their predicament have also released the Red Lectroids from their other-dimensional prison. Our heroes have now joined forces with Hexagon Comics' Time Brigade and the peaceful Black Lectroids to deal with the increasingly unstable rifts in space and time and discover what is behind them...*

Travis Hiltz: *All Roads Lead to Mars*

Russia, 1812

It had snowed the day before. By dusk what had once been a field had been trampled and churned into a vast expanse of mud. The occasional broken wagon or discarded corpse littered the ground. There was a feeling of uneasiness amongst the platoon of soldiers gathered on the hill, overlooking the field.

Napoleon's forces were retreating through Russia; the Russian army close behind, to ensure that the French did not change their mind about returning home. Occasionally they would catch up with the French soldiers and provide a brutal reminder of how Russia treated uninvited guests.

Doctor Omega stood on the hill, overlooking the muddy field and its grumbling occupants. He was huddled within his traveling cloak and leaning heavily upon his cane. Gathered around him was a half-dozen mismatched individuals, including his bearded handyman Fred, looking even more like a bear in a borrowed Russian hat and fur coat. On the other side stood two shivering versions of his companion Denis, one middle aged and bearded, the other younger and dressed in the fashion of the mid-1700s, complete with knee breeches and a tricorner hat.

111

Gathered behind the quartet were members of the Time Brigade, guardians of all human history—or perhaps they were from the Time Patrol? Doctor Omega could never remember which was which) and some Black Lectroids, an inter-dimensional race of alien beings. They had been gathered in a hurry and so their uniforms and weapons were a mix of several different eras. The Lectroids merely had an eclectic and otherworldly dress-sense.

"Are you sure this is the right place?" Young Denis asked, shifting anxiously, while trying not to fumble the pink hatbox he had been charged with carrying.

"Or even the correct time?" his older counterpart added. "It wouldn't be the first time you were off by an hour... or a decade..."

"Hush, the both of you," the elderly scientist grumbled, reaching into his coat pocket.

He came out with a sheaf of papers, including a bit of medieval parchment and a napkin from Disneyworld's Crystal Palace restaurant. All were covered in intricate mathematical formula, scribbles and computations.

"You are more than welcome to review my calculations...!"

Both men stepped back, making placating gestures. As they did, two other figures, a blond-haired man in a futuristic red bodysuit, and a tall African-American with dreadlocks, clad in the style of a tourist to the tropics approached Doctor Omega. Neither man seemed bothered by the cold.

"You were correct," the man with the dreadlocks said, in a thick, yet difficult to place accent. "There was a rift incident in Grover Mills."

"We were able to get a tech team there and repair the damage," the man in red added. "Between our team and the Lectroids, we were able to capture most of the Red Lectroids."

"My people have made arrangements in case any of the escapees should attempt to recreate the rift," the African-American man said.

"Thank you, Mr. Spell, John Fibhead," Doctor Omega nodded. "I'm sure that John's people will find allies in New Jersey, and we can focus our energies upon this rift."

He took an ornate, but much abused-looking pocket watch and a pair of opera glasses out of his pocket and spent the next few minutes alternating from studying one to peering through the other.

"Just as I'd calculated," he muttered. "Traces of quantum foam and ionic pulses... Mr. Spell, ready your men!"

He tucked the items back into his coat and pulled his traveling cloak tighter around his ancient body.

"Where?" Jason Spell, the commander of the Time Brigade forces, asked.

"Right to the left of the horse carcass."

The man from the future nodded grimly, and moved off to prepare his troops. John Fibhead gestured to his own people to ready themselves.

Soon, both groups had joined the human troops the Time Brigade had 'recruited' to assist them, upon the field. The two groups formed a pair of crescents, facing the predicted arrival point of the space-time rift.

The first crescent was the Black Lectroids. To human eyes, the aliens appeared as a dozen African-American men dressed for either a tropical vacation or a night at the disco. Each brandished a short tube-shaped device, decorated with lights, wires and what looked to be barnacles. As one, the line of Black Lectroids went down on one knee, allowing the human troops to aim weapons over their heads.

A minute passed and then two; the troops began to fidget and the younger Denis finally lost the fight to not ask any more questions, and had just begun to open his mouth, when he started, wide-eyed and mouth still agape.

A strange sound drifted across the field, a hum that seemed to come on the chill winter wind. It rose and fell as it swirled around the assembled soldiers, aliens and time travelers.

A light joined the sound, no bigger than an apple. It hovered ten feet off the ground. It flickered and pulsed, shrinking and expanding in rhythm to the hum. It flared and the rift tore open, unleashing two-dozen hate-crazed Red Lectroids out onto the Russian soil.

The soldiers from the Time Brigade fired, their weapons, a mix of projectile and energy beam based. The Black Lectroids activated their devices, focusing the tubes' energies on the rift itself.

Up on the hill, both versions of Denis stepped forward, only to be halted by the raised arm and cane of Doctor Omega.

"Steady, my boy, both of you," he said, his gaze not leaving the battle on the field. "We all have a part to play and yours does not involve your questionable fighting prowess."

The battle below was savage, but brief. The Red Lectroids were inhumanly strong and driven by a raw animal need to escape their other-dimensional prison, but even that was no match for the advanced weaponry and strategy of Doctor Omega and his allies.

As the smoke and noise cleared, the quartet on the hill spotted Captain Spencer, an English World War I Tommy, jogging up the hill towards them.

"Excuse me, sir," the soldier said, snapping off a hasty salute at the elderly scientist. "Commander Spell says we've got the lobsters under control and you can go ahead with…whatever you've got planned…"

Doctor Omega nodded curtly and then trudged down the hill, his companions following close behind.

The Time Brigade troops were rounding up the subdued Red Lectroids. Off to the side, they had erected a makeshift field hospital to deal with the few wounded from both sides.

The quartet joined the leader of the Time Brigade forces. They watched as a pair of Black Lectroids embedded two of the tube devices into the ground, on either side of the shrunken rift, connecting the tubes with what looked like strings of Christmas lights and plastic clothespins.

"All set, are we?" Doctor Omega asked, peering intently at the odd set up and then at the swirling hole in the fabric of space. He nodded at the Lectroids work and then gestured for the two Denises to move over to the rift.

"What... us...?" They both asked, skeptically.

"You wanted to help," the white-haired time traveler replied, peevishly. "Now is your opportunity. Each of you stand by one of the tubes... young Denis, hand me the box... Now, John Panther, help them with the contact wires..."

"I'm... uh..." Young Denis stammered. "What is this all about...?"

"Oh dear," Older Denis muttered. "I never listened."

"Gentlemen," Jason Spell said, stepping forward to help set things up. "Your presence here, at the same time, creates a paradox. Any form of time travel causes an energy build up, paradoxes even more so. The two of you, in such close contact, will hopefully generate enough chronal energy to keep the rift stable, while we deal with tracing its source."

"Get all that, did you?" Doctor Omega grumbled. "Or were you too preoccupied with your new hat?

"What...? No, of course not...! We generate... chronic... um... energy." Young Denis stammered.

"So, how did it happen...?" Older Denis started then raised his eyebrows in surprise. "Doctor...you sent that letter that drew me into...all this...!"

"Or will in the future," Doctor Omega nodded, patting at his coat pockets. "Must make a note... Don't want to cause a paradox while causing a paradox..."

"Are you all right, Doctor?" Fred asked. His attempt to lean in and whisper discreetly instead came across as looming over the time traveler and growling.

"Fine, fine," Doctor Omega muttered, waving away the handyman's concerns. "Just a bit tired. Come now, you two, raise them a bit higher and activate the large stub towards the top."

Both men followed the instructions and both tubes suddenly flared to life. The energy swirled and grew thin, like kite strings made of light.

"Hold them up," Doctor Omega commanded, sounding like an exasperated schoolmaster. "Face each other. The streams need to cross…"

"I thought you weren't supposed to do that?" Fred rumbled, nervously.

"Our options are limited," Spell said, quietly. "And despite our occupations, we are running out of time."

The two versions of Denis anxiously reached out with their devices until the swirling streamers of energy entwined above the rift. Then the streams traced around the ragged edge of the rift until they encircled it.

Everyone held his breath as the circle of light pulsed and sparked for several moments, before settling down into what looked like a solid band of light.

"There," Doctor Omega nodded, as though he'd never doubted it for a moment and couldn't understand why all the others had gotten themselves worked up.

He stepped up to the rift and peered thoughtfully at it, tucking his cane under his arm in order to reach out and run a fingertip across the surface of the distortion. The others all flinched back, while the Doctor merely pulled his finger back and studied it, as though he'd merely been checking for dust.

"Just about there," he said, nodding thoughtfully to himself.

"I don't agree that this is the best course of action," Spell said, his tone a mixture of stern and anxious.

"And as you've also said," Doctor Omega grumbled over his shoulder. "We are running out of options and time."

With that, he adjusted his traveling cloak, tightened his grip on his cane and stepped through the rift.

"What did he mean?" Fred grumbled.

"He'll be all right?" Young Denis asked.

"Won't he?" his older self added.

"I hope so," Spell replied. "I was hoping he'd allow someone else to take the risk…"

"What risk?" Fred growled, one of his large, mittened hands clamping onto the Time Brigade leader's shoulder. "What did you two concoct?"

"My people and the Black Lectroids have been tracking down all the rifts," Spell explained, grimly. "We have sealed off all but two, this one and one in 1980s New Jersey. We arranged with the Doctor that, after a certain interval, our operatives at both rift sites would implode the rifts…"

"That would trap the Doctor… wherever the rifts lead to…?!" Young Denis exclaimed.

"If he survives…!" Fred muttered, anxiously.

An uncomfortable silence fell over the group. Each man glanced about; waiting and hoping for someone else to say something reassuring that would brush away the worry over Doctor Omega's possible return.

Somewhere just to the left of reality, Doctor Omega spent a timeless second, every fiber of his being thrumming like one of Denis' violin strings. The white void made his eyes burn with snow blindness and his limbs felt as unsubstantial as smoke.

Wincing with a vertigo that threatened his senses and sanity, Doctor Omega suddenly found himself standing upon a sandy plain, a vast desert that stretched to the horizon.

Kneeling down, he set the hatbox on the ground and took a pinch of reddish sand between his fingers.

"Hmmm, bit heavy in iron oxidants… I wonder…?"

Picking up the hatbox, Doctor Omega trudged up a red sand dune. Once at the top, he saw a black pyramid in the distance.

"Mars…?" he muttered. "Though, it seems a bit different from my last visit…"

There was a rumble and he could feel a vibration through the soles of his shoes. Off in the distance, he watched as a

117

mountain range blew apart and a dozen craggy, black ships arced off into the upper atmosphere.

"Curious," he muttered. "Very curious indeed."

"Who... Who isss there?" a faint voice demanded.

Stumbling in the loose sand, Doctor Omega made his way down the other side of the dune. Lying at the bottom, was sprawled an alien creature, one massive leg twisted at an odd angle and one arm smeared with what appeared to be its own blood.

The alien was large, close to seven feet tall. Its body was encased in a rough green armor or perhaps an organic outer shell. This armor was textured and green, giving it the appearance of some strange blending of man and crocodile. Its head was encased in a helmet like structure with large red eyes that looked more like lenses. Instead of hands, it had over-sized clamps.

Despite his dire condition, this alien had the bearing of a warrior.

Doctor Omega kneeled down next to the alien unsure what was armor and what was skin and so unsure what, if anything, he could do to help.

"You look to be in a bad way," Doctor Omega muttered.

"I... am... dying," the alien told him, his voice coming out as a wet hiss. "But, my life will ensssure...my people will live... we have sssacrificed many lives and our home, but the Setissi... will ssssurvive...!"

"The Setissi...?" Doctor Omega muttered, glancing around at their desert surroundings. "I've met your kind before, long ago, in the depths of the Polar Sea... So, your people eventually came to rule Mars? How curious...?"

He was distracted from his own thoughts, by a soft groan from the Setissi.

"I am sorry I can't do anything to relieve your suffering," the time traveler continued, "but I too am on a mission to save... Well, I guess you could call them my people, and hopefully, my home. You may be able to help... I am unsure how I arrived on Mars, but it seems important that I am here."

"I fear… I… hnn… can be no… help to you, traveler…" the alien gasped faintly before growing silent and still.

Doctor Omega nodded sadly and patted the cold shoulder of the alien warrior.

"A noble fellow. I hope when I next encounter your people it will be as friends."

He stood up, dusting the sand off his hands and pant leg.

"No answers," he muttered. "Only more questions."

With a sigh, he picked up the hatbox and began walking.

He couldn't feel even the slightest breeze, and yet with each step, there was a struggle to move forward, as though he was walking into a strong wind. He closed his eyes, fighting off a wave of dizziness and again felt that thrumming sensation through his entire body and the sensation, as if he was being dragged along, of riding some enormous wave, while something had a hold on the back of his coat.

He blinked and with a feeling like he'd just sneezed, opened his eyes to find that the landscape had changed.

There were still the reddish tones and thin atmosphere of Mars, but the texture of the ground beneath his feet had changed. Also gone was the black pyramid, to be replaced by the ruins of an ancient city.

Doctor Omega shook his head in a mix of confusion and annoyance as he rummaged around in his coat pocket, taking out a handkerchief and dabbing at his forehead.

"Hmmf!" he muttered, tucking his handkerchief away.

Seeing nothing else about, he began trudging towards the ruins.

He was within feet of the ancient structure, when he halted, straining his ears to make sense of a distant noise. He soon recognized it as the sound of combat and was pondering if he wished to continue walking or avoid the whole thing, when the noise stopped as abruptly as if a switch had been thrown.

After several minutes, a man came limping out of the ruins. He was tall, with midnight black hair and a muscular form tanned bronze by the desert sun.

He wore a loincloth-like garment, a sword belt, harness and sandals. In his right hand he held a blood-streaked sword, in his left the over-sized head of a gorilla with snow-white skin and fur.

The swordsman took a few more halting steps then sat down wearily on a block of stone. He stuck his sword, point first, into the sand and casually tossed the severed head aside. He took a water skin off his belt and was drinking deep, when he glanced around and spotted the old man with the cane and the hatbox.

The swordsman got to his feet, dropping the water skin and snatching his weapon out of the sand. He leapt the distance between himself and the time traveler in a single surprising bound.

"Omega...?" The swordsman exclaimed. "Doctor Omega? What are you doing on Barsoom?"

"Barsoom?" Omega muttered. "Curious, I thought I was on Mars...?"

"Barsoom *is* Mars," The swordsman said. "What are you doing here? How...?"

"What are you chattering on about?" Doctor Omega snapped. "How could you know who I am? I have never been to Bassoon..."

"Barsoom."

"...Before in my... Carter...?"

"Yes."

"Colonel Carter!"

"Captain, actually," the Swordsman said, lowering his sword. "But, since leaving Earth, I don't use the title much."

"Captain John Carter," Doctor Omega muttered. "Haven't seen you since that incident, during the war, with the..."

"Yes, yes, I was there," Carter interrupted. "How did you get here? What are you doing here?!"

The two men walked back to the block of stone. Doctor Omega sat down and explained about his and his companions' previous encounters with the rifts and the risky gambit to follow them to their source.

"These Polar Warriors... Setissi.. you mention sound like none of the people of Barsoom," Carter mused, wiping his sword clean, while they talked. "But these rifts... there may be something...?"

"How so?"

"Well, it means something for those of us that have traveled to Barsoom from other worlds," Carter explained. "I thought it was a form of, I guess you'd call it, astral projection, but I've been told that I may have traveled in time or even across dimensions to a Mars very different from the one described by Earth scientists."

He shrugged and re-sheathed his sword.

"Personally, I never cared enough about it to study it further," Carter said, getting to his feet. "This is my home. It's where I belong."

"Yes, yes," Doctor Omega muttered, absently. "I wonder..."

"We can't stay here," Carter interrupted.

"Why not?"

"That," replied the swordsman, gesturing toward the severed head, "will have friends nearby. This may have been his territory, but the noise and smell of blood will make the other apes... curious. I have a flyer in the courtyard. You are welcome to accompany me to Helium. I have a bit of influence there and could put you in touch with the Council of Science."

"That might be best. This whole ordeal has gotten a bit much. I seem to be running hither and yon without much idea of where my destination might be. Feel like I've been blindfolded and given a jigsaw puzzle... Pieces fit, but I can't see the picture... I'm babbling... getting old... I would be grateful for any help you can offer."

John Carter offered a hand to help the savant to his feet. Instead of clasping hands, they passed through each other.

"Oh, bother," Doctor Omega muttered, as the void scooped him up once more.

He was no longer drifting, but rather being tossed about by another-dimensional tempest and the feeling that unseen hands were grabbing and pulling him was even stronger. It was hard to tell if they were trying to pull him out of the swirling, tumbling void or to deeper into the depths.

Reality snapped back into place so abruptly that Doctor Omega stumbled, landing in the red sand on his hands and knees, losing his grip on both his cane and the pink hatbox. While struggling to catch his breath, he also realized that, along the way, he'd also lost his hat.

Shaking his head in weary frustration, the time traveler grabbed hold of his cane and struggled to his feet.

"This is growing tiresome," he muttered, brushing himself off, yet again. "Never going to get this coat clean…"

Still frowning, he glanced up to take in his new surroundings and his eyebrows shot quickly up to the top of his forehead.

The plain was an expanse of rust-colored dirt and gravel. Situated in the center was a clunky six-wheeled vehicle. It resembled a children's toy that had been rendered full-sized. It was an odd collection of devices, thick wires and folded robotic limbs. It had a stout pipe standing mast-like from the front corner, with a white plastic box on the top. It sported a singular red lens. A faint humming coming from it was almost drowned out by a low grinding noise from one of the middle wheels.

"Ah," Doctor Omega mused, a slight smile creeping across his tired features. "A Mars rover… how quaint."

He gathered up his cloak and hatbox and strolled over to the Rover, peering over the various pieces of equipment, appearing more like a perspective buyer than a lost interdimensional traveler. He would nod approvingly at a component or frown at a wiring junction.

After pacing a complete circle around the Rover, Doctor Omega stretched up onto the tips of his toes, reaching up to pat the device with its single red eye. His expression was that of someone encountering a particularly talented and lovable dog.

"Now, why are you loitering around here, hmmm?" he asked, kneeling down to look at the Rover's wheels. On the right side one, he found a fist-sized stone wedged in the inner tread.

He then moved to a boxy device on the Rover's side. A couple moments' study and, after setting his cloak, cane and hatbox on the Rover, flipped open an access panel and delicately poked a finger at the inner workings with a slightly disapproving expression on his face. He took down the hatbox and undid the twine around it. Reaching in, Doctor Omega brought out a robot head. It was made of dull grey metal. Its vaguely female features were scuffed, scratched and smeared with soot and dirt. One earpiece huge on by a strand of wire and one eye flickered with a faint light. Wires trailed from its metal neck.

Doctor Omega took two of these wires and connected them to points in the Rover's panel.

"Poor child," he murmured patting the metal head affectionately. "If we survive sorting out this whole mess, I will see to it that Fred and I patch you up. You have more than earned your place aboard the *Cosmos*, Thea."

Both the Rover and the robot head hummed and her one eye flickered rapidly. Doctor Omega took out his prince-nez and studied a tiny screen nestled amongst the circuits and wiring of the section of the Rover.

"Ah, here we are!" he muttered. "Time stamp gives us the date.... and... ah, yes, planetary coordinates... helpful... yes, quite helpful...."

He rummaged around in his coat pockets, taking out the tiny stub of a pencil and a crumpled grocery list. He scribbled the coordinates down, straightened up, putting away his various knickknacks and retrieved his cloak, cane and hatbox.

"Now, Thea, I think we may be putting pieces together," he said, as he disconnected her head from the Rover. "Still a bit of a jumble, but we are no longer stumbling in the dark... We have found ourselves a tiny candle."

He smiled at the robot head, and then getting no reply shrugged and returned her to the box. He walked back to the middle wheel and reaching down and pried loose the chunk of Martian stone. With a wheezing-groan, the Rover began to roll off across the plain.

"There's my good deed for the day," Doctor Omega said, walking in the opposite direction. He studied the scribbled numbers and glanced up at the sky. After several minutes he reached a bare spot and scratched an 'X' in the dirt with the tip of his cane. He stood on the marked spot, eyes closed, breathing growing rhythmic and deep.

And the void swallowed him up once more.

Doctor Omega kept his eyes closed, and just felt the flow and rhythm of the other-dimensional energy. He felt the surreal touch of invisible hands and this time willed himself to reach out to them... and found himself standing in a rocky valley.

It was early evening and the stars shown dimly overhead. Three figures stood around him.

They were humanoid, but inhumanly tall and inhumanly thin. Their pale skin had a feathery quality to it. Each one held, in their seven-fingered hands, an equally tall and thin metal staff with what looked like a silver lantern on top.

They nodded at him, their features vague and serene and he respectfully returned the greeting.

"Welcome to Malacandra," the lead alien intoned. "We regret the crude and chaotic manner of your summoning."

"I understand. My own efforts have been a bit on the impromptu side," Doctor Omega replied. "If I had known the Seroni were involved, it would have made matters a bit clearer..."

"We come to you, speaking for the Oyarsa," the Sorn continued, "since it is their bent brethren, the exiled Oyarsa of Thulcandra, who has set these events in motion."

"Celestial beings," Doctor Omega grumbled. "Nothing but trouble. How is it that the black sheep of the host of planetary angels is able to wreck this kind of havoc...?"

"In his exile, the bent Oyarsa was drawn to the cosmic maelstrom that lingers about Malacandra," the Sorn said, grimly.

A chrono-synclastic infundibulum!" Doctor Omega breathed. "Of course! A being like an Eldil channeling the infudibulum's energy... I shudder to imagine... Not that I need to, I've been twirled across time and space like a top because of it... That begs the question: why am I the target of this 'fallen angel'? Why have my companions and I been scattered and hunted...?"

"We were sent by the Oyarsa," the Sorn continued, ignoring the question, "to convey you to the site of the Bent One's containment."

"Why isn't the Oyarsa speaking to me directly?" Doctor Omega asked, a trace of testiness creeping into his voice.

"The Oyarsa of Malacandra is locked in struggle, containing not just the Bent Eldil, but the chrono-synclastic infundibulum from causing further damage to the fabric of the Heavens," the Sorn explained.

"Fair enough," Doctor Omega shrugged. "Let's be on our way then."

The Sorn formed a triangle around him and raised their staffs until the lantern-like pieces touched. Light flared in each one and the light passed over Doctor Omega like a dry wind.

"Getting quite irritated with this mode of travel," he muttered rubbing his eyes.

When he opened them, he was standing in his ship, the *Cosmos*.

He gazed in surprise and wonder at his surroundings, like he was seeing them for the first time, as though an absence of several days had wiped all trace of his beloved ship from his memory. During his quest to return to the *Cosmos*, he had come to accept the possibility that he would never see his beloved space-time ship again.

As he looked about at the cluttered mix of Victorian décor and high-tech equipment, a sudden realization swirled about in his brain and a thin, immensely satisfied smile crossed his face.

"Of course," he breathed, hanging his cloak over the back of a wing-backed chair and leaning his cane against the mantelpiece. "It was you all along! You sensed the turbulence caused by traveling too close to the chrono-synclastic infundibulum and jettisoned us into the void! You frustrated the Eldil's plans by plunging into the infundibulum... Truly you are the finest craft to ply the vast sea of stars and time!"

He patted the wall tenderly. "So, let us see if we can pull off one last miracle."

The hatbox tucked under his arm, Doctor Omega made his way down the corridor to bridge of the *Cosmos*. He strode up to the ship's mushroom-shaped console, pausing a moment to nod happily at its vast array of switches, buttons and levers, before placing the hatbox on the floor by his feet.

His ancient fingers were a flurry of movement across the brass and ivory keyboard then pounded a large red button and the lights around the console room flickered and grew dim.

"Come now," Doctor Omega said, glancing upwards. "No point being coy. You know we are going to have this out. The *Cosmos* isn't big enough for the both of us."

In the far corner of the room, a light appeared, a pillar of rainbow light. It pulsed and glimmered.

"Yes, yes, very dramatic," Doctor Omega muttered, "but, we aren't going to accomplish much if all you do is float and sulk."

He opened a small wooden panel on the console and then drew up a glass rod with a metal prong on the end. He kneeled down, took Thea's head out of the hatbox and set it upon the glass rod, fitting the metal prong into her neck hole.

Her eyes lit up, beams of light pouring from them and her mouth sparked. A thin wisp of smoke trickled from her damaged earpiece.

"What would you have me say, man of time?" the Eldil known as the Bent One said, speaking through the robot head. "Would you have me bargain or barter for my freedom? I hold your ship and even as it fights me, I still have the might to slash through the walls of the universe and send the Lectroid hordes into history!"

"Yes, quite fierce, I can see why your brethren would rather wrestle with the infundibulum than deal with you," Doctor Omega said, reaching across the console, and flicking several switches, then adjusting a large dial. "Any other time, I might even sympathize with your plight: exiled by your people and cast out into the void, but I am tired and apparently getting cantankerous in my old age, because being deprived of sleeping in my own bed has left me with little interest in debate or reconciliation."

Doctor Omega straightened up one hand holding his coat's lapel, the other hand resting upon a brass lever.

"Your disruption of the fabric of the universe was so severe that the *Cosmos* felt she should have to sacrifice herself to keep my companions and I safe. You have intruded upon my ship... my home... and then pursued my friends... perhaps due to arrogance, perhaps due to fear. I believe you were right to feel a sliver of fear about this old man and his eccentric little craft. Separated across the gulf of infinity, we have thwarted your schemes... Now, reunited, you do not stand a chance. So you can release your hold over the infundibulum and the *Cosmos*, return to the void and whatever mercy your brethren feel inclined to bestow upon you, or..."

His fingers merely tapped the lever and his smile was fiercely enigmatic.

The pillar of light flickered and pulsed. It seemed caught up in some invisible struggle.

"What are you... doing?" the robot head growled angrily. "You... do... not have... the power...t o..."

"Really?" Doctor Omega mused, absently. "I'm in a ship that can transverse the whole of space and time, which is lodged at the center of one of the most expansive and powerful rifts in the fabric of the universe... I think I have the power to do anything I wish, and you should consider yourself lucky I'm not prone to megalomania or thoughts of violent revenge… Perhaps we'll talk again at a later, or even earlier, date, and I hope you'll have gained some wisdom in that time… Good-bye!"

Doctor Omega pushed the lever forward and the celestial creature began to pulse and flicker violently, the sounds coming from Thea's head becoming evermore incoherent and frantic, till, with a finale tinny screech, the light flared.

When the console room's lighting returned to normal the Doctor and Thea were the sole occupants.

"It would be refreshing," he muttered, adjusting controls with one hand, while scratching his beak of a nose with the other, "if just once, I could encounter a celestial being that didn't act like a spoiled six-year-old. Very undignified."

"Whu-what… where..zzzt… di-di-di-didddddd…?" Thea slurred.

Calm down," Doctor Omega said, gently patting the robot head. "Don't over-tax yourself. You have been through more than any of us in the course of this little escapade. Rest, let the *Cosmos*' computer interface work its magic on your internal circuits."

He pulled out a handkerchief and began walking around the console, dusting as he went.

"It was really very simple," he explained as he shuffled about. "I merely used the Infundibulum to anchor the *Cosmos* in place and was then able to slingshot our unwelcome guest to the far reaches of time. Gave him what he wanted, if you think about it. He should end up back on Earth… just several quintillion centuries in the future. I'm sure subjugating the giant crabs, mutated vampires or whatever he finds there, to his benevolent rule will keep him busy for a good long time. Not a bad bit of work if I do say so myself… hmmm, don't you agree?"

He'd gone full circle around the console and was facing Thea again. Her eyes were dark and a faint hum came from deep within her metallic skull.

Doctor Omega gave her a brief onceover with the dusting cloth, blew his nose and then tucked it back into his pocket.

"Yes, I think a nap would do us both a world of good," he muttered. "But, I suppose, I should let Mr. Spell and the others know that the time stream is as stable as its likely to get and gather up Denis, Fred and... Hmm, I just realized, we never encountered Tiziraou...I wonder what he got up to...?"

Loompaland, in the heart of darkest Africa.

Tiziraou drew his sword and hacked away at the underbrush. The child-size Martian wore a loincloth, a sword belt made from vines and a broad leaf tied to his pumpkin-sized head as a makeshift hat.

A cluster of Oompa-Loompa warriors huddled behind him as he scouted the jungle ahead. Despite his own diminutive size, none of the Oompa-Loompas stood taller than his shoulder. They gripped their crude wooden spears anxiously.

The hunting party had barely escaped from a snozzwangler pack and just discovered the tracks of a poison-tusked hornswoggler.

Tiziraou paused, his eyes darting back and forth, his tiny ears straining to catch any sound that indicated where predators might be lurking. He turned back to the hunting party, held a thin, pale finger to his lips and then pointed in the direction he thought they should go. Holding his breath, the Martian pushed through the undergrowth and stepped into the clearing.

Across the way, a blunt, bullet-shaped craft was parked at an odd angle, wedged between two boulders. Standing by the round metal door, Doctor Omega was stirring a cup of tea, while peering at the *Cosmos'* landing site with disapproval.

Tiziraou gestured for the Oompa-Loompas to wait and he jogged across the clearing to the old scientist.

He reached Doctor Omega and tugged at his pant leg.

"Ah! There you are," the Doctor said, looking down with a faint smile. "Denis will appreciate your hat, I'm sure."

The diminutive alien smiled back up at his friend, glanced back the way he'd come with a thoughtful expression.

He gestured for Doctor Omega to come closer. The time traveler leaned down. Tiziraou muttered, occasionally pointing back to the hunting party.

He told the story how he'd found himself lost in the jungle and after saving an Oompa-Loompa princess from a wild band of white monkeys was taken in by the tribe and made their warlord and that he wished to do something as a 'thank you' to his adopted tribe.

Doctor Omega nodded, as he straightened up.

"I think we can do that," he said, walking back to the door of the *Cosmos*. "Not too much to ask, for them taking you in, while you were stranded here. "

He leaned into the doorway.

"Fred...? Ah, there you are, could you see if we have some cocoa beans in the pantry?" He then turned back to the diminutive alien. "Though, I will warn you, sometimes people take the gift of cocoa the wrong way."

After bestowing the bag of cocoa beans upon the Oompa-Loompas that had taken him in during his time marooned, Tiziraou returned to the *Cosmos* and his true tribe.

*For the uninitiated, "Barton Werper" is the name of the ficti-
tious author of five unauthorized* Tarzan *novels published in
1964-65. Atom Bezecny decided to use him, along with Nora
the Ape-Woman from the eponymous novel by Félicien
Champsaur[10] and the ever-amazing Doctor Omega, for a fanciful African yarn with cosmic consequences...*

Atom Mudman Bezecny: *The Revelation of the Yeti*

Africa, 1966

The dusty Ugandan road was creating a plume of ash-
white smoke as the car bounced along it. Barton Werper
looked at his aged companion, whose face flashed quickly
back and forth between bemused joy and bitter discomfort

"First time in the African heat, eh, Doctor?" Werper
asked.

Doctor Omega raised his head haughtily and sniffed.

"Hardly," he replied. "I've been to worlds much warmer
than this, my boy. Tell me, have you ever basked in a summer
afternoon on Vulcan?"

"Vulcan! You mean the one from that new sci-fi show?"

Werper was still a young man. He resembled his father,
though he was trying to grow one of the stylish mustaches of
the time, and his hair was a bit longer. The show in question
was a fun past-time for him. (He wasn't quite cool enough to
yet say "groovy.")

"No, no, of course not. I meant another planet entirely, in
another time—you couldn't possibly have heard of it. Tell me
again, Warter—er, Barter—what is the name of the man we're
about to meet?"

---

[10] Black Coat Press, ISBN 978-1-61227-403-4.

Werper's arms strained to get the old jalopy around the dawning curve.

"Our guide's name is Robert John Kilgore. In his correspondence, though, he said he preferred to be called Ki-Gor."

"Ha! What a ridiculous name. Truly ridiculous! Like your biographical subject, that Jungle Lord. One of many, I've heard. But the original was yours, I believe?"

"His Lordship is certainly the most famous, but some in India did start out earlier. Someone called Mowgli, for example."

"Yes, that's right, I remember Mowgli... Well, how long until we reach the estate of this, uh, John-Gor?"

"Wrong continent, Doctor! It's Ki-Gor, remember? As for that, we've just arrived!"

Doctor Omega squinted at the small and humble house that sat hunched below the tall and ancient trees. Already, the chipped front door was opening to reveal a handsome muscled man, his hair lightened and flesh tanned by the merciless sun. He was clad only in a loincloth and a leather belt, which carried on it several weapons. His tempered face broke into a smile as he waved to the arrivals.

Werper waved back, then parked the car and stepped out.

Doctor Omega followed him, taking his time to examine the now-tarnished paintwork of the car. It was hardly a *Cosmos*, but there was something appealing about a simple yellow automobile. Maybe someday he'd have to look into finding one like it for himself. But for now Ki-Gor was talking.

"Gentlemen!" Ki-Gor exclaimed. "Hail and welcome. I hope the drive from Kampala was not too much of a hassle."

"I've had worse, Mr. Ki-Gor," Werper said. "And my blood, for all its infamy, is strong. My father, Lieutenant Werper of the Belgian Army, was tough as nails, even if he became sort of a villain in his final days."

"Yes, I have heard of him. Almost as poor of an abuser of the native peoples of this continent as that ivory trader in the Congo. But you've done good work despite him, son. You told some stories that may not have been told before. Getting an audience with his Lordship is a privilege rarely granted."

"I doubt my skill was enough to accurately convey what he told me about what we're seeking on this expedition," Werper said. "Maybe, if I can keep my line of books going, I can do a sequel to follow up the mystery of the Abominable Snowmen that my subject fought."

Doctor Omega seemed distracted as he looked up at the sky. There was nothing in particular to look at, but, in that moment, it was more entertaining than his companions' discussion. Then, Ki-Gor looked at him and raised an eyebrow.

"And why did you volunteer to leave your fabulous ship to journey into the heart of Africa, Doctor?"

"It has been a long time since I have been on safari," the Doctor said with a cheeky grin. "And in any case, I would be very curious to know if the Yeti exists in this part of the world as well. I heard stories about these creatures when I was a guest at a monastery in Tibet. They believed that some varieties of these animals had origins on another world."

"It's still hard for me to imagine other worlds, Doctor," Werper said simply. He turned to Ki-Gor. "Are we ready, Mr. Ki-Gor? I am eager to start as soon as possible."

"Of course. We'll leave in a minute. I just would like to introduce you to the female member of our company."

Doctor Omega's face lit up.

"It's good to have some manner of diversity in our little expedition, hm? I'm eager to meet this woman."

"Here she comes, Doctor. This is Nora, sometimes called the Ape-Woman—the daughter of such, actually, by a purely human man."

Another figure emerged, wearing similar garments to those of Ki-Gor, although much more conservative. From what Werper and the Doctor observed, her body was lined with the same hard muscles that marked Ki-Gor as a product of a world far from their own lives. She was a captivating and beautiful woman in terms of conventional beauty, and seemingly ageless.

Doctor Omega had met Nora, who was the child of an orangutan and a human—or maybe a great ape turned into a human—a long time ago. He also remembered meeting another like her, one Paula Dupree. In each case, the simian parent was something closer to human, rather like the Yeti he sought.

Of course, he also recalled meeting another human-animal hybrid, named Felifax, who was the laboratory-created son of a human and a tiger. Primitive though it may seem to him, he had to admit a certain degree of admiration for the 19th century of this world, for having the means to create such miracles. If indeed this sort of glorified bestiality was something to be admired...

"*Bonjour, Docteur,*" Nora said.

Her voice had retained her French accent, but otherwise did not betray her origins at all—humanity was still clearly dominant in her; it was a compassionate humanity, but also one backed up by that quiet potential for animal brutality.

"Along with Ki-Gor, I'll be your guide into this territory, in search of these man-apes," she continued. "Perhaps then we can find the source of the material the Jungle Lord talked about in the interview he gave you, Mr. Werper. I look forward to working with all of you."

Doctor Omega and Ki-Gor were satisfied with her statement and walked into Ki-Gor's home. As Nora and Werper followed them, the Ape-Woman leaned towards the writer and whispered:

"Even if you did do something of an injustice to his Lordship. Plagiarism and clichés are no way to get through life when dealing with people worthy of respect."

Werper looked down in guilt, remembering that there was a reason why he was here. Personal redemption.

Nora and Ki-Gor had already drawn up maps that would take them to another site, distinct from the lost Egyptian city that Werper had heard about in his interviews, where the Yeti were forced to fight for sport in a savage and blood-soaked arena.

Ki-Gor had found a lost Egyptian civilization, called Memphre. Some said this city was, like many of other "lost" cities found throughout Africa, such as Opar and Kor, one of the colonies of Karkosa (subject to variant spellings). Some said there were even stranger things in the Americas, his wife Helene had told him. It seemed any number of nameless civilizations had left behind lost cities in Mexico.

At the mention of that country, Doctor Omega smiled broadly.

"I don't visit Mexico all too often," he mused, "but when I do, it's always with a great spirit of adventure. It's a place plentiful with vampires, werewolves, robots and mummies. Mr. Werper, you should write about it someday!"

"I just have to worry about satisfying my own curiosity about these Abominable Snowmen before going any further," Werper said. "I couldn't find much more on the winged men of my novels, nor of the silver globe, the serpent-men, and any of that. But getting a lead for this will help me rest assured."

"We're happy to help, if it means another break from boredom," Nora said, with apparent sincerity. "Ki-Gor and I are in an evaporating age for our kind. Soon we'll have to find some sort of retirement."

"Ages rise and fall like waves, my dear child," said the Doctor. "You will always have something to keep you occupied."

"We must still be careful," Nora said. "Our source said that this land is prone to... strangeness."

"Strangeness?" asked the Doctor. "Of what kind?"

"Shifting dimensions. A sense of displacement. It is said to be one of the places of the world that is... soft."

"And some," Ki-Gor added, "claim that vile cults still thrive there, of a kind unseen since the days of Solomon Kane. They worship elder demons."

His voice had such an ominous tone that it troubled Werper and Doctor Omega, who had heard more than a handful of stories about his various adventures, and the terrible places and monsters he'd braved.

Barton Werper was nervous. Ki-Gor and Nora were fighters in their own right, and Doctor Omega could defend himself with his keen mind, but he was just a writer from the Midwest... words wouldn't do anything to stop a fiendish gorilla-man from tearing him to shreds, or a hooded cultist from stepping out and gutting him in the name of some foul, squirming thing from the stars.

He remembered some of the names of the beings Ki-Gor was presumably talking about... Cthulhu, Azathoth, Dagon... Writers far more articulate than he had written about these unknowable deities. His thoughts were so troubling to him that he murmured aloud:

"What does a glorified Sasquatch have to do with the Great Old Ones?"

"Consider another name I heard in Tibet, my boy," said the Doctor. "That of the Tcho-Tcho. They are hairy dwarves, similar to Africa's own *agogwe*... er, I hope I'm pronouncing that correctly... They worship some of those nameless and ghastly things, in their own strange manner."

Then he smiled, almost paternally, in a way that mildly unsettled Werper, who thought he enjoyed showing off his many fields of knowledge way too much.

"There was a family I heard about during a brief time in the Congo, when I was looking into my mother's ancestors," Nora added. "The Jermyns. They, too, worshipped the Great Old Ones and... wait!"

She held her hand up, and, at once she seemed authoritative. She suddenly appeared to take on inhuman features as she sensed danger around them. Even Ki-Gor looked civilized by comparison.

"Where did this fog come from?" Ki-Gor and Nora said, almost at the same time.

The jungle man tried in vain at sniffing the air to pick up olfactory clues.

"It's the wrong temperature for a mist like this," he said.

Werper was regretting Doctor Omega's decision to bar guns from the expedition—there *was* something wrong going on here, and that possibly meant they were close to their quarry, or else something that was viewing *them* as prey.

His eyes flashed to the daggers on Ki-Gor's belt. Nora likewise had a blade. That made him feel a little more comfortable, but that was lost as the Doctor gave a cry of distress.

"Doctor?" Werper said.

As he put his hands on the Doctor's shoulders, the old man shrugged them away.

"I'm quite alright, my boy. Just a mild shock. I had a brief impression of traveling in space—like on my ship."

"Perhaps we *have* moved in space," Ki-Gor murmured. "This fog may be the evidence of some sort of... gateway. It has no reason to be here."

Evidently, he, too, had felt the physical impression of traveling.

"I'd hate to question the map, but maybe we should go back and find another way around?" Nora suggested.

Ki-Gor nodded, and began to lead the way back through the trees.

Werper felt a flinch of disappointment—perhaps walking deeper into the jungle would help expose the source of what was causing the others—though not himself—to experience that sensation of having left Earth. But before he could think it through, Ki-Gor raised his hand.

"I don't think we *can* turn around," he mused grimly.

Doctor Omega gave a small cry as he saw what spread before them. Nora and Barton, however, were stunned into silence.

What had once been a path through the jungle was now a cliff-side. The jungle was far, far below them, stretching out endlessly in a landscape that indicated they were many miles farther from Ki-Gor's residence than they had traveled over the last several hours.

Not even the Doctor knew the name of the place they had found—one of these shifting places that rotates through space, connecting at random sticking points around the globe. Some had once referred to it as the Plateau of Leng.

137

Nora ran a hand through her coarse black hair.

"Dimensional shifts, then," she sighed. "This is my first."

"Scarcely mine, my dear girl," the Doctor said gleefully.

But despite his paternalism and confident experience, his face was a portrait of seriousness.

"We must be very careful from here on... Perhaps we will find our bounty sooner than expected, but we must also keep our wits about us. We will need to get *out*, eventually."

"So you're used to getting lost, then?" Werper said in an exasperated tone. "Maybe you *can* get us out, then, Doctor."

"I'm all too familiar with being called a hopeless navigator, Mr. Werper. And I must say, I am rather tired of it! Hm! In any case, it is Nora and Mr. Ki-Gor who appear to have gotten us lost..."

A flash of anger went across the Ape-Woman's face, but Ki-Gor raised his hand defensively.

"Bickering amongst ourselves like children isn't going to help us. Let's head deeper into this plateau—we *are* stuck on it, for better or worse. But as a last resort—there may yet be resources for us to climb down its face."

Wordlessly, the other three agreed. They retraced their steps once again, and descended into the mist-shrouded alien jungle.

Despite the temperature being so bizarrely mild, Werper was sweating. The same phenomenon that had caused that sensation of displacement was now upon him, pouncing rather than slowly creeping in, like it had done with the others. Occasionally, he would glance to the side and have the fleeting impression of seeing shapes moving around him through the trees, or hearing whispers from the darkness. He couldn't make out what they were saying, but knew that listening to them would only lead to madness.

Eventually, Nora squinted and scurried ahead. Doctor Omega noticed she was studying something.

"Well, now—are those runes on those chipped stones?"

"I believe so, Doctor," Nora said. "It's been awhile since I've read Aklo."

"Aklo, it is, eh?" the Doctor wheezed. "Oh, that cannot be good, that cannot be good at all. Where I come from, that is a language used only by the worshippers of the beings we discussed earlier."

"Then, there is a cult here," Ki-Gor concluded. "And its patron god must be the one known as Yog-Sothoth."

The Doctor's already-pale face drained of its remaining color.

"The Yeti, or Abominable Snowmen," he whispered, "are not just any variety of ape-men. True, some instances are mere hominid gorillas, but others are distinctly less... animal. On Pluto, they are called the Mi-Go. They are the servitors of the one you know as Yog-Sothoth."

Werper then looked up and realized that none of them had noticed how dark it had suddenly become.

Then, they came, chittering from the darkness. Their mushroom-crustacean bodies, scuttling, cheeping, and murmuring in the jungle.

Ki-Gor and Nora drew their knives, while the Doctor raised his hands in what Werper assumed was a gesture of protection. He tried to maneuver so that he was in the center of the triangle they formed, but the ensuing battle was chaos.

Even twelve years past his retirement, Ki-Gor was as spry as any young warrior, and his dagger cut the Mi-Go savagely. Nora had a knife, too, and was screaming in rage, which shook Werper to his very core. Her ancestry was coming out, and she wrestled the Mi-Go despite the slippery ichor that covered their bodies. Some of the creatures were pulped in her grip, while others, she tore chitinous chunks from until they stopped moving.

Doctor Omega calmly approached one of the creatures, which loomed over him, and in a swift movement unbecoming his appearance, lunged forward with a strike at one of the Mi-Go's soft points, shouting "Hai!" This single strike was enough to knock the creature unconscious—if they were conscious to begin with.

The writer's vision began to blur. He felt his legs go weak under him, and he squeezed his eyes shut tight. When he opened them, he was on his knees, but the others had defeated the Fungi from Yuggoth.

Doctor Omega smiled—or Werper thought he smiled—as he offered him a hand up. He then experienced another jarring sensation of being pulled through space as his three companions led him even deeper in the jungle—perhaps assuming he would emerge soon from his altered state. But everything stayed foggy, and Werper was now having trouble remembering if there really was mist, or if this was all just his eyes...

In no time at all, they were deep amongst the high stones of a Cyclopean city, which they could see extended as far as the eye could see.

As Werper slouched against a tree, Doctor Omega took a pair of opera glasses from his jacket and looked out into the city.

"I can see something. It looks like a door. Perhaps it is a spatial portal of some kind. An artifact of the Ancients, no doubt—the same Ancients who built this city."

"It could be our way home," Ki-Gor suggested.

"Yes, but I can see that there is some kind of gathering near the gate. A flock of Mi-Go, led by people. Humans."

"The cult, no doubt," Nora said.

In that moment, they knew what they had to do.

The four sorcerers stood at the gateway that divided the world. Here, in Leng, they could capitalize on the shift in space to complete their quest.

At the head of the trio, grinning at the three others, was Doctor Karswell. Even he didn't remember how he had come by his extended life, especially as the demons he served had become increasingly strange. He had faked death countless times since his days at Lufford Abbey in Warwickshire.

Alongside him were three other masters of the dark arts, who, like him, had had their lives greatly enhanced by the powers of the Outer Gods. They were Madame Palmyre, who worshipped the entity known as Baal; Cristaldi the Mexican warlock, who had once fought Dracula; and an American simply called the Master, who worshipped an unknown god called Manos, until earlier that year, when incidents led to him to join the others.

"Will it be soon, Palmyre?" Karswell asked. "The gate is now charged from our years of work here. The Great Old Ones have treated us well. Now, we may bring forth the presence of Yog-Sothoth."

"His release into this dimension will shatter time itself," the French sorceress replied, her voice smooth and cunning. "Perhaps then I will find my lover again."

"I, for one, do not seek or need redemption," the Master said authoritatively. "What Yog-Sothoth has decreed, so have I done. His limbs of fate will doom this world." The Master spoke often that he believed the Outer Gods were firm believers in the propagation of torture and violence.

"I *do* seek it," Cristaldi interjected. "It may rid me of this insanity that drives my life beyond my control. I do not want to kill the people of the world, but there is a tiny voice in me who makes it sound wonderful." And then he immediately burst into laughter.

Karswell was glad to know they were so close. His eternal life in a timeless world would be spent learning all of the secrets that had been hidden from him by the universe. But suddenly, he remembered something very important.

"The Mi-Go patrol has not yet returned!"

"Yes..." Cristaldi hissed. "I sensed... interlopers. But I forgot they were here until now..."

Karswell slapped the centuries-old man across the face angrily.

"You old dullard! Who are these interlopers?" '

Behind them, the Master and Palmyre gestured at each other to move closer to the gate. They would need to protect it if the Mexican warlock's predictions came true.

But as they did so, all Cristaldi needed to do was point.

"Doctor Karswell—you can ask them yourself."

Karswell whirled around. *No!* he thought. *It's too soon!* But there was nothing that could be done. The athletic woman and the nearly-nude man were already lunging towards them.

"Destroy the invaders!" the British occultist screeched.

Nora was going after Palmyre, having sprinted ahead to the gate. The sorceress's eyes closed though her eyelids still fluttered, and she began to chant an incantation. The Ape-Woman was ready to knock her to the ground.

Karswell and Ki-Gor were at each other's throat. Using a spell, Karswell set his hands blazing with fire, ready to consume the jungle man.

Doctor Omega calmly approached the hunched Cristaldi. Their eyes began to glitter at the prospect of a mutual battle of wits.

And at last, Werper staggered, weaving between Karswell and Cristaldi, across the plaza. He was trying to avoid everyone, but he was suddenly standing toe to toe with the Master.

The Master stared deep into Werper's eyes, but they were blurry as the writer's head continued spinning. The Master then realized that he was not connecting with the man's mind—something was wrong with it, and it was getting worse the closer he got to the gate.

And he *was* getting closer as he approached the Master. He was about to *attack* him...

That's when the Master experienced his first punch to the face. Bullets were nothing to him, because he would just send them into a parallel world as they traveled towards him. A fist, though, was attached to a larger mass, and it was simply harder for the person on the end of it to be pulled into another dimension. He went flying backward and his head slammed against the gate.

Werper, sweating heavily, screamed from fear.

That scream caused Karswell to look up, as he was in the process of being pinned to the ground by Ki-Gor. The Jungle Man was about to pinch his neck in a way that would render him unconscious, but before he went down, Karswell was able to cry out:

"That boy is beating the Master!"

The Doctor had been attempting to hypnotize Cristaldi, just as the Master had tried to enslave Werper. When he heard Karswell's statement, he looked up to examine Werper's target. During this time, Cristaldi cackled and waved the heavy gnarled stick he leaned on. Energy suddenly swirled around Doctor Omega, forming bars, and soon solidifying into metal.

The Doctor was now sealed in an iron cage, and the others could hear his loud protestations.

Nora looked up as her twisting pull had thrown down one of the Mi-Go that Palmyre had called up. She saw that the sorceress was bolting, but even with her bestial strength, she could not get the fungoid creatures away from her in time to stop her. She was running towards the gate. As she went through it, Nora observed that the image flickered and became that of another world. The gate was randomly changing its destination across various planes of reality. How this would aid Yog-Sothoth, she did not know. She couldn't think hard about it while tearing apart these "Abominable Snowmen."

Barton Werper was lunging towards the Master again, and grabbed him by the hair. Before anyone noticed, he shoved the cultist's head through the portal. He had no idea what he was doing—the world was just a bunch of churning colors to him, set to the music of endless Aklo chanting.

The gate flashed again. Doctor Omega flinched as the man in the black robe was suddenly *sans* his head—his neck sheared by the shift in dimensions.

"Oh, Werper, my boy..." the Doctor whispered.

Karswell was unconscious. At last Ki-Gor stood up, even as Cristaldi assessed the situation.

"The woman's animal state has scared away Palmyre," the Mexican Warlock said. "The young man has murdered the Son of the God of Primal Darkness. The English Doctor is unconscious. I do not wish to pursue this conflict anymore. I surrender, and will aid you in a return from this place..."

Ki-Gor and Doctor Omega seemed satisfied with this.

"You will no longer attempt to call forth the Outer Gods, and torment the people of this country?" Ki-Gor asked.

"I swear it. I... have toiled too long in the service of darkness, to rebel against the hateful evil of a monster I once fought. I deserve only exile, trapped forever in these far lands."

In good faith, he dissolved the Doctor's cage. Nora could read souls and had felt a repulsive evil in the other three cultists, but there was no such thing in the aged Cristaldi. She was about to voice this as Werper stood and charged the Warlock.

"Werper, stop! Stop this foolishness at once!" Doctor Omega cried.

He was about to seize Werper himself when Ki-Gor restrained the writer with great efficiency.

"This place has been bad for his mind," the Jungle Man said grimly. "I'm not sure he'll be able to recall the facts of this adventure, much less write about them."

"So he didn't get the closure he sought," Doctor Omega sighed. "Perhaps in time he will recover. But meanwhile, what a waste. What a terrible waste!"

Cristaldi stood as the others approached this portal.

"Go, and take the wicked Karswell with you," he said. "I will use what power I have left to open a gate to return you to the Africa of Earth. Then I can begin my path of relearning the ways of virtuous magic."

Nora nodded in response, and wished the man the luck of his gods.

Using gestures of his hands, Cristaldi slowly pulled an image of the African jungle into view in the oval gateway.

"Go quickly!"

Doctor Omega held Barton Werper by the shoulder, as one last time, Nora led them, with Ki-Gor in between. The Jungle Lord was carrying Doctor Karswell. He turned around and took a last look around him. It had been good to be in a place so close to home, yet still as alien as Memphre. He felt—young again, despite everything.

They rested upon landing. Werper was already calming down, now that he was free from the madness of the Plateau of Leng. The Doctor was silent; Nora and Ki-Gor were exhausted.

The Doctor wondered if Werper's sanity had been forever destroyed, as the young man's mouth stopped foaming, and he slipped into dreams about unfathomable titans of the void. These creatures also dreamed in the darkness of Africa, sleeping but not dead.

The true nature of the Yeti who, in Tibet, were merely abominable creatures of the snows, now stood revealed in that most terrible of their many aspects.

Doctor Omega did not sleep as Nora and the others did— his kin did not need to sleep as often. And he thought about these Yeti, and how he still had just as many questions as young Werper did.

He hoped he would never encounter them again. Not even the *Cosmos* could outrun the tendrils of something like Yog-Sothoth.

Who better than John Peel, one of Doctor Who*'s very best authors, could craft both a locked room mystery and a time travel conundrum? Bob Morane is a long-standing series of French adventure novels created by Henri Vernes in 1953. Several novels feature time travel plots, starting in 1957, when Bob met a Time Patrol from the future, and later pitting him against the diabolical Monsieur Ming, a.k.a. The Yellow Shadow.*

John Peel: *Time to Kill*

Paris, 1960

"I have a dead body on my hands that I can't explain."

Bob Morane looked at his bank manager, André Durand-Mareuil, and merely raised an eyebrow.

His friend Bill Ballantine, on the other hand, whistled loudly. "Crikey! That must be a bit hard to explain to the police," he commented.

"Quiet, Bill," Bob admonished the burly, red-headed Scotsman. "I have a feeling Monsieur Durand-Mareuil is going to fill us in." They were in Bob's apartment on the Quai Voltaire in Paris, and his landlady had served tea just before announcing the banker. Bob offered the banker a cup of tea, but Durand-Mareuil shook his head.

"There really isn't that much to... ah... fill in," he said, sadly. "And Mr. Ballantine is quite right—it is difficult to explain to the police, and to my bank's Board of Governors. They're not at all happy about the matter, I'm afraid."

Bob rather liked Durand-Mareuil—he'd always been very helpful in the past when he had faced urgent needs to raise funds to gallivant all over the world in some of his more extreme cases, and he felt sorry for the man, who clearly hadn't managed to get much sleep.

"Well, why don't you tell us what you can?" he asked.

"You may already have heard some of this," Durand-Mareuil replied slowly. "The victim was Albert Carrigan."

The name was indeed familiar. "The millionaire?"

Bill sat bolt-upright in his chair. "I read something about that in the papers yesterday! He was shot to death in a bank…" He realized what he was saying. "Oh—*your* bank…"

Durand-Mareuil nodded sadly. "My bank. More specifically, inside my security vault."

"I can't see the problem, then," Bill said. "Whoever did it must have been seen by dozens of people."

"Nobody saw him. Nobody *could* have seen him."

Bob had been in plenty of interesting moments during his time in the Military, and even more in his days since, as a kind of freelance adventurer. He could always tell when something interesting was on the cards, and his intuition was signaling strongly now.

"Perhaps you'd care to explain that rather cryptic comment?"

Durand-Mareuil frowned slightly. "I don't think you've ever been in the bank's security vault, have you?"

Bill laughed. "We've never had the kind of money to need to."

"Quite. Well, it's where all of the safety deposit boxes are kept. Many people store jewelry, stocks and bonds, that sort of thing in our boxes. Mr. Carrigan has—*had*—several with us. He would come into the bank once a week, on Wednesday afternoons at two o'clock precisely."

"He'd been in that habit for some time?" Bob asked.

"Oh, indeed—since before my time, in fact, so over five years."

Bill chewed his lip. "Always dangerous to get into predictable habits."

"Quite so," the banker agreed. "Last Wednesday, Mr. Carrigan came into the bank as usual, and, as always, I accompanied him into the vault, along with one of my security guards. Mr. Carrigan and I opened the door to the box he

147

wished to use. The guard and I then left the room, and the guard closed and locked the door."

"Forgive me a moment," Bob said, "but allow me to ask an obvious, if foolish question: there isn't any other way into the vault, I take it?"

Durand-Mareuil shook his head. "Just the one door, which the guard locked. He remained outside the door for thirty minutes. Mr. Carrigan always stayed for precisely that length of time. I returned when the time had elapsed, and we opened the door together. And inside, we discovered the body of Mr. Carrigan. He had been shot once, through the heart, and was quite dead."

"Crikey!" Bill muttered. "That must have been unsettling. Did he shoot himself, then?"

"He couldn't have done, because there was no gun in the room."

Bob hesitated before asking the obvious question. "I don't like to cast doubt on anyone, but how trustworthy is that guard?"

Durand-Mareuil smiled bleakly. "Yes, the police wondered about that, too, obviously. Their initial theory was that my man had opened the vault door, shot Carrigan, and then closed the door again."

"That *is* the logical conclusion," Bob agreed. "But I take it that was also impossible?"

"I'm afraid it was. You see, the security vault is adjacent to the cash vault. Our chief cashier is locked within that vault while the bank was open—there is a barred door, and his desk is immediately behind it. If any money enters or exits the vault, he and the guard have to open that door together. So while he waited for Mr. Carrigan to finish, the guard was seated just outside this door and in the full view of my chief cashier the entire time. Both men insist that the security vault door was not opened again until I returned."

"They could be in cahoots," Bill suggested.

The banker shrugged. "But to what end?" he asked. "The two men do not socialize; they do not even know where the other lives. Both have worked for the bank for more than a decade, and have always been steady, reliable men, otherwise they would not have been in the positions of trust they occupy. Neither of them have any reason to kill Mr. Carrigan."

"Couldn't they have stolen something from the strong box?" Bill asked. "Some fabulous jewel, or something?" He sounded quite excited.

Durand-Mareuil shrugged again. "It is always possible," he agreed. "The bank has no record of what was kept in the box, of course. But as soon as we discovered the body, I telephoned the police. I remained with the guard until they arrived. Before either the guard or the chief cashier were allowed to leave the bank at the end of the day, they were both thoroughly searched." He coughed, embarrassed. "As was I myself, and quite rightly so. The security vault was checked, and the cash vault. Nothing out of place was discovered anywhere. As far as they were able to ascertain, the motive for the murder was not robbery."

Bob smiled widely. "Monsieur Durand-Mareuil, you couldn't keep us out of this now if you tried." He grinned at Bill. "A classic, eh? A locked room mystery. No way for a murder to have been committed, no possible killer."

"And no clues, either, it sounds like." Despite his pessimistic comment, Bill's grin was just as wide as Bob's. "Sounds right up our street."

The banker's relief was evident. He pumped Bob's hand enthusiastically. "Thank you, thank you. Are you able to accompany me right now? The sooner this mystery can be cleared up, the happier my Board of Directors will be."

"I can't guarantee I can solve it," Bob said, "but I think Bill and I can spare some time, eh?"

Bill nodded. "I'll say." He rubbed his large hands together. "I can't wait to take a peek at the scene of the crime." He looked anxiously at Durand-Mareuil. "We *can* see it, can't we?"

"I've already spoken to the police. They have it sealed off for the time being, running fingerprint tests and such like,

149

but they have agreed to allow you access as representatives of the bank. You will, of course, be recompensed for your time."

Bob smiled. "I think this mystery in itself is going to be payment enough," he said.

"But we accept your generous offer," Bill added, hastily. "Er—it *will* be generous, won't it?"

"Quite so."

"Jolly good."

The bank was just around the corner, so it didn't take them long to walk there. The main floor was conducting business as usual, though there were a couple of policemen watching over things. The handful of customers in the bank were trying not to be caught staring at the officers. The policemen nodded politely to the manager as he led Bob and Bill toward the stairs that led down toward the basement vaults.

As he did so, Bob had a curious sensation that he was being watched. He'd learned never to ignore his instincts, so he glanced around. One of the customers as the central table, standing with a deposit slip in his hand, was looking directly at him. He was an elderly man, with long, white hair (and an errant curl giving him a slightly wild look), carrying a gnarled walking stick under one arm. Bob had never seen him before. He frowned. The man didn't seem to be bothered to be caught staring, and inclined his head slightly in acknowledgment before bending to fill out the form.

Odd. But probably not relevant to their case.

The bank was one of those grand old buildings, filled with artistic flourishes. There were chandeliers on the main floor, and pedestals with fresh flowers. The stairs leading down were wide and marble-covered. There was a bank guard stationed at the head of the stairs, clearly to ensure nobody without official cause got to descend, but he knew Durand-Mareuil, naturally, and stood politely aside for them.

Bob looked carefully around as they walked down. At the foot of the stairs, there was a small area illuminated by another ornate chandelier. Directly in front of them was the cash vault. The barred door was of steel, some six feet tall and about eight across. It looked quite impressive. Behind it, he could see the chief cashier's desk—an ornate wooden affair, with ball and claw legs. The man himself was seated at it now; he was a fiftyish, greying man with the look of a goblin. He was clearly trying to get his work done and ignore two more policemen stationed in the hall.

Outside that door was a small desk and a chair. The bank's security guard was seated there, trying to look uninvolved, though he was clearly uncomfortable. Bob could see that Durand-Mareuil's comments had been entirely accurate: the two men would have been in full view of one another the entire time Carrigan had been in the vault. Unless they were working together, then it was impossible for either they or any other person to have entered the vault to kill the millionaire.

Bob finally turned his attention to the security vault itself. At the moment, the vault door was wide open, but it was a standard door, some six-inch-thick metal. Nobody could have shot Carrigan through the door, and nobody could possibly have opened it without being seen. All that was left was to enter the vault and look around to see if they could find anything that the police might have missed.

"Who is the officer in charge of this case?" Bob asked.

"Need you ask?" came a familiar voice from inside the room. "A case that is inexplicable and potentially career-damaging if I fail to solve it? Who else would they give it to?"

Bob's face broke into a broad grin as he walked into the vault and shook his old friend by the hand. "Commissaire Maigret!" he said, delightedly. "I don't know why they bothered to consult with me. I'm sure you must have the case completely solved by now!"

Maigret grunted. He had his pipe firmly clenched between his teeth though it wasn't lit. "Oh, I have it all solved, my friend," he agreed. "Except for who did it, and how."

Bob knew Maigret's methods of old. "Don't tell me that you don't have a suspect already."

Maigret shrugged. "Indeed I do—the dead man's nephew, Donald Carrigan. He's absolutely the perfect suspect: he likes the high life, he gambles on cards that he plays very badly, and is in a large amount of debt. He stands to inherit millions from his uncle's death."

"And yet?" Bob prompted.

"And yet, he has an unshakable alibi," Maigret said sadly. "At the precise time of the murder, he was losing money at baccarat in the casino at Royale-les-Eaux. There were dozens of witnesses to this fact. He was quite certainly not in Paris at the time of the killing, and, in fact, will not arrive back here until later today—accompanied by Janvier."

"I see your problem," Bob murmured.

"And I am afraid I see yours." Maigret waved his hand about the room. "Feel free to search for clues. If you uncover any, I would be most grateful, because my men and I have found nothing of significance."

"What about the bullet?" Bob asked. "Did you recover that?"

"Yes," the Commissioner said. He took his pipe out of his mouth, looked at it, saw that it was empty, and then replaced it. "Like everything else in this case, it is a puzzle. It is of no known manufacture, and has a rather unique set of patterning on it. It was fired by no gun either I, or anyone in my department, can identify." He shrugged. "As if there were not enough problems with this case."

Bob glanced about the room. It was about twenty feet by sixteen, and the ceiling was about ten-feet-high. There was a table and single chair, closer to the left-hand wall than the right, but no other furniture. The room was illuminated by another of those omnipresent chandeliers—rather brightly, in fact. Three of the walls were lined, floor to ceiling, with small doors that each had two key holes, and behind which the owners' safety deposit boxes resided. The fourth wall contained only the large security door. The walls either side of it were bare.

"Let's eliminate the absurd first," Bob suggested. He tapped the bare wall. "I take it that there's no possibility of a hidden panel behind this?"

Maigret looked over at Durand-Mareuil, who shook his head. "The walls consist only of two inches of covering over four-inch steel."

"I really didn't imagine that there were secret passages, but it's as well to be certain." Bob shook his head. "There doesn't seem to be any other way into this room."

"What about the ventilation system?" Bill asked, cheerily. "In the movies, people are always crawling about them."

Maigret smiled dourly and pointed with the stem of his pipe at a rather small grille set in the ceiling about six inches in from the wall. "It's six inches across. Feel free to try and fit inside it." He eyed the burly Scot with a faint smile.

"OK—not that way, then." Bill thought for a moment. "But what about the gun? *That* would be less than six inches long. If the killer had somehow rigged a gun with a remote-control device so he could place it in the vent and then fire it…" He looked rather pleased with this suggestion.

"Well," Maigret admitted, "that's certainly an idea that had never occurred to the police." He didn't look impressed, however. "The problem with that idea, my friend, is that the vent is *behind* the table where Mr. Carrigan sat, and he was shot from the front. Horizontally, not vertically. The gun must have been placed about…" He walked to the right-hand end of the room and stood in one corner. "Roughly here." He used the stem of his pipe to demonstrate. "Just at the level of a man standing here, holding a gun."

Bob scowled. "I've run into some pretty rum things in my time," he said slowly. "And I can think of only one solution that *might* answer all of the problems." He gave a slight laugh. "The only trouble is that it's even more absurd than the crime—at least on first glance."

"And what is that?" Maigret raised an eyebrow.

"That there really was a man standing there with a gun—but nobody could see him."

"An invisible man, you mean?"

Bob shrugged. "I know it sounds impossible, but, well, Bill and I have witnessed any number of things I'd have thought were impossible. Technology seems to be advancing so swiftly these days…"

"I agree, it sounds foolish, but let us consider it," Maigret said. "Let us postulate the existence of an invisible man…"

"With an invisible gun," Bill said, helpfully.

"As you say, with an invisible gun. He walks through the bank unseen and down into the vault area. When Monsieur Durand-Mareuil here opens the door, he somehow manages to slip inside and waits in the corner. When he is alone with Carrigan, he shoots the victim and then waits for the vault door to be opened and slips out again. Unseen the entire time."

The bank manager shook his head. "Even granting such a silly idea," he glanced apologetically at Bob "we would have *felt* someone brush past us, for the door is not large, and was closed behind us when we entered. I had to open it again when I left, and closed it immediately behind me."

Bob sighed. "Well, it was just a thought." He shrugged. "In that case, I'll admit that I'm completely baffled for the moment." He saw Durand-Mareuil's face fall. "Cheer up, sir! I'm only baffled for the moment. Ideas often come to me later. If you're quite done here, Bill, what say we go back home and think for a while? It's about lunch time, as my stomach is reminding me."

Bill, never averse to the idea of food, nodded his agreement, and they said their goodbyes. As they trudged up the stairs to the bank lobby, Bill turned to Bob. "So, what do you make of this?" he asked.

"Nothing, as yet," Bob admitted. "It seems to have no possible solution. But since we know that Carrigan *was* murdered, then obviously there must be an explanation of some sort. We simply haven't seen it yet."

They emerged onto the main floor of the bank. As they headed toward the exit, a figure moved to intercept them. Bob glanced at him, and realized it was the elderly gentleman who had been looking at him earlier. He held up his stick to block Bob's path.

"Please excuse my imposing myself upon you, Commandant Morane," the man said, politely. "If you would be so kind, I would appreciate the opportunity to speak with you."

Bob shrugged. The man seemed harmless enough, but he clearly had something on his mind. "By all means," he agreed.

"It's about the case that you're on," the stranger said.

And now Bob had him pegged: a retired gentleman with too much time on his hands who read the papers and fancied himself an armchair detective. "I think you'd better leave that to the professionals," he suggested, as kindly as he could—and, he had to admit, a trifle hypocritically, since he himself was hardly a professional.

"Advice you'd do well to take yourself," the man replied, testily. "Believe me, Commandant, this is outside the normal order of things."

"Look," Bob said, in a gentle manner, "I'm sure that you're very good at solving locked room mysteries in detective stories..."

"Your *locked room* isn't locked," the stranger snapped. "You've just come from there yourself."

"It's not locked *now*," Bob agreed, "but it was locked two days ago."

"A room is only ever locked in three dimensions," the man stated. "There are more—you live in four."

Bob smiled. "Don't you?"

"I dislike being confined." The old man reached into his pocket and pulled out a business card which he handed across.

Bob glanced at it. It bore only two words: DOCTOR OMEGA. "No phone number?"

"I am not reachable by phone. I... travel extensively." The old man touched the card. "If you need to contact me, tap the card against any piece of metal—the message will reach me wherever I am."

"Are you an inventor... Doctor Omega?"

"I am much more than that, young man." The old man straightened himself to his full height. "Now, if you wish to solve this case, all you need do is to meet me in the vault next Wednesday, shortly before two p.m."

"And then you'll explain everything?" Bob said, smiling.

"I shall do much better than that," Doctor Omega retorted. "You shall witness the murder taking place." His eyes twinkled as he added: "I suggest you bring a camcorder to record it for evidence."

"A what?" Bill asked.

Doctor Omega considered. "Oh dear—what's the day again?"

"Friday," Bill replied.

"No, no—I meant the *year*."

Bill laughed. "You don't know? It's 1960."

"Ah, quite so, quite so." He tapped Bill's chest with his walking stick. "Then I suggest you bring one of those Super-8 film devices." He inclined his head. "Good day, gentlemen."

"You're not going to tell us your theory?" Bill asked him.

"Theory? I have no *theory*, Commandant—just the truth. And there would be no point in my attempting to explain *that* until you have seen what will happen on Wednesday next. Until then." He spun about and marched from the bank.

"Well," Bill said, laughing, "I don't know how you do it, Bob, but you do manage to attract the weird ones."

"I'm not so sure he's crazy, Bill," Bob said slowly. "One thing he said makes a strange kind of sense."

"Well, you're ahead of me, then," Bill confessed. "I thought he was just rambling—a senile old man. Means well, but…" He tapped his temple. "Not all there."

Bob sympathized with his friend's view, but shook his head. "It's that business about us living in four dimensions, and the door being locked only in three…"

"So?"

"Don't tell me you've forgotten about our little adventure with Professor Hunter's time machine!"

156

Bill shuddered. "How could I ever forget that? Being chased by dinosaurs…" His eyes widened. "You mean he's suggesting that somebody used a time machine to go back and kill Carrigan?"

"Something like that, I imagine. Though there isn't enough room inside that vault for one of Hunter's machines to fit. And I can't imagine anyone simply sitting still when a time machine appeared and a man climbed out—and Carrigan was killed sitting at that table…" Bob shook his head. "And there's something else…"

"What?"

"Doctor Omega, as he calls himself, knew my name and my rank. We haven't mentioned the latter to anyone. And he obviously knew we've had experience with time travel. How could he possibly have known all that?" He couldn't make sense of it himself—yet. "I have a strong feeling that we're going to run into the good Doctor again—probably on Wednesday…"

Over the next several days, Bob and Bill had plenty to occupy their time. Bob tried to puzzle through the facts of the case, but got nowhere. More than once, he'd picked up the business card Doctor Omega had given him and then, sighing, put it down again. On the Monday morning, he'd called in at the prefecture de police to see Maigret and ask about the case.

The Commissioner shook his head. "I'm afraid we know no more than we did on Friday. I did meet with the nephew…" He lit his pipe and took a few puffs. "Every instinct I have tells me that he is the guilty man, and yet he has thirty-seven witnesses who saw him at the moment of the killing and who can testify to that in court."

"Could he have hired an assassin to shoot his uncle?" Bill suggested.

"Of course—anyone might have. But we still have that same problem—*how* did anyone kill Mr. Carrigan in a locked room?" He gave Bob a weary smile. "I am almost ready to believe in your invisible man, my friend."

157

Bob gave a short laugh. "And I am about ready to believe in something even more fantastic," he admitted. He told the detective about his meeting with Doctor Omega, which made Maigret sit up.

"That would explain this, then," he said.

Reaching into the basket of papers on his desk, he extracted an envelope. From it he took another of Omega's business cards, and a brief note, which he handed across to Bob. It read:

Please be so kind as to meet me in the bank security deposit vault shortly before two p.m. on Wednesday. Commandant Morane and Mr. Ballantine will be present.

"Sure of himself, isn't he?" Bill remarked.

Bob smiled. "I think he's relying on our curiosity, Bill. But he's right—I wouldn't miss this for the world."

Bill scowled. "Do you really think he can deliver what he promised?"

"We'll know in two days," Bob answered.

On the Wednesday, Bob and Bill arrived at the bank at one thirty. Durand-Mareuil was in the lobby, pacing nervously, when they arrived and hurried to meet them.

"Monsieur Morane! Thank goodness you are here! Such goings-on in a respectable bank!"

"Steady on," Bob said. "What do you mean?"

"The police are here again, and have asked me to keep the general public out of the vault for the next hour or so. And there's a strange old man prowling about—he's one of our customers, to be sure, but he's behaving very oddly. And he seems to want to give orders, too."

So, Doctor Omega was here! Bob clapped the bank manager on the shoulder. "Whatever the Doctor told you, I suggest you do. Bill and I are going down to the vault now also, so we'll keep an eye on everything."

Durand-Mareuil looked like he was going to erupt again, so Bob added: "And, relax. With a little luck, we'll have unmasked the killer within the hour, and everything will be able to return to normal. Come on, Bill."

And he hurried down the stairs before the nervous man could protest again.

He could see why Durand-Mareuil was so nervous—there were about a dozen uniformed gendarmes in the basement. Several of them were carrying chairs into the security vault. The others allowed Bob and Bill to pass after checking their credentials.

Inside the vault they found Maigret directing the traffic, with Doctor Omega standing in the background.

"What's going on?" Bob asked.

"Your friend here," Maigret said, pointing at the Doctor with his pipe stem, "says we have to simply observe. In that event, I aim to be comfortable and not simply stand about waiting." Once the four chairs he had required were in place, he waved off the gendarmes. "You two stay here," he directed. "The rest of you, upstairs, and give us some room."

When the room was clearer, he flopped into one of the chairs. "That's better." He glanced up at Doctor Omega. "Now, are you going to explain any of this?"

The old man shook his head. "Not quite yet, my good man—I fear that you would not believe my tale. Once you have seen what is to happen—what *has* happened—ah, *then* I promise to explain everything."

"Now, just a minute," Bill began to protest, but Bob held his arm.

"Let him have his minute, Bill. If he can explain this mystery, I think he's deserved it."

Doctor Omega beamed. "Thank you, my young friend. Now, did you bring your movie camera?"

Bill unslung the bag he was carrying over one shoulder. "It's right here, Doc."

"Good, good. Now, if you set it up here and aim it in this direction…" Then he glared. "And don't call me *Doc*." He indicated a place behind the chair set at the table. He watched as

Bill took out a folding tripod and extended it to take the cine camera. "Right! How much film is in there?"

"About twenty minutes."

"Then do not start recording until our killer approaches the table," the Doctor instructed. "Until then, we shall simply wait."

"I'm glad I thought of the chairs," Maigret muttered. He nodded to the one beside him, and Bob sat down also. Bill joined them once he'd finished setting up his camera. Maigret gestured to the fourth chair. "And you, Doctor?"

"Not for me, no. I shall sit here." He settled himself in the chair at the table. "Where our unfortunate victim sat exactly one week ago."

"That's a bit morbid," Bill muttered.

"Now," Doctor Omega said, firmly, "whatever happens, I wish to assure you that I am perfectly safe. Do not interfere with what you are about to witness, any of you. This must play through precisely as it happens."

Bob felt his excitement rising. He had no idea what was to happen—though the Doctor clearly did—but he sensed that it was the final event in a chain forged a while back. It was for moments like this that he lived for—the excitement, the uncertainty, the mystery...

They didn't have long to wait. At five minutes past the hour, there was a noise in the outer hall, and then a man stepped into the vault. He stopped dead as he saw everyone present. Maigret gave a smile. "Donald Carrigan," he said, softly. Bob raised an eyebrow—the prime, impossible suspect.

"What is this?" Carrigan asked the vault guard, who had accompanied him. "I must be alone in here." He held up the small case he was clutching. "That is my right! Clear these men out of here!"

Doctor Omega turned to regard him. There was a faint smile on his lips. "I am sorry, Mr. Carrigan. If you are uncomfortable with an audience, perhaps you would care to come back later?"

"Yes. No. Yes." Carrigan the younger stood stock-still. He was starting to sweat. "Get out, all of you! I must be alone!"

"Mr. Ballantine," Doctor Omega called, and gestured at the camera. Bill hopped up and started it going.

Maigret stood slowly up. "I am Commissaire Maigret," he said. "I am afraid you cannot order me to go anywhere." He sat firmly down again. "I stay."

Bob grinned. "I've nothing better to do this afternoon."

Carrigan was sweating profusely now, and clutching his case tightly. "No," he moaned. "No—I *must* be alone."

"That is not going to happen," Doctor Omega stated. He glanced at his watch. "You have only three more minutes—you had better get busy…"

The young man was moving in a very jerky fashion, like some reluctant puppet being drawn by unyielding strings. He walked, shaking, to the other side of the table, where he placed the case with trembling hands. He was sweating a stream now, and his eyes were wild and terrified. It took him three attempts to open the clasp on the case, and his hands trembled as he drew out an odd-looking gun. The part he clasped looked like a normal pistol, but attached to the barrel was a bulky tube-like structure that looked like an over-fed silencer. There were pulsing lights on it, tinier than any Bob had ever seen before.

Carrigan raised the pistol and pointed it directly at Omega's heart.

Bob gave a cry and jumped to his feet, but the old man's hand slashed out. "Stay!" he commanded. "Remember what I told you! I assure you, I am in no danger."

Shaking horribly now, Carrigan was forced to use his other hand to steady his grip on the pistol. Then, with a wild cry of terror, he fired.

Bob was terrified for a second, expecting to see Doctor Omega to collapse, dead. Instead, absolutely nothing happened. There was no sign of a bullet, and the old man was obviously totally unharmed. It made absolutely no sense.

With another cry, Carrigan dropped the strange pistol to the floor. "You fiend!" he hissed. His hand, no longer shaking, thrust into the case, and he pulled out a second pistol, this one a normal-looking Luger. He raised it and pointed it at Doctor Omega. "I don't know how you did that…" he began.

Bob saw the look of fear on the Doctor's face and realized that this was obviously not part of the old man's plan. He sprang forward and delivered a forceful blow to Carrigan's stomach. The man gasped, and folded as Bob wrenched the gun from his hand.

"Thank you, my friend," the Doctor said, wiping his brow with a handkerchief. "I must confess, I did not think he would have a second gun."

"Just glad to help," Bob said.

Maigret motioned to his two gendarmes, one of whom grabbed hold of Carrigan, who was still whooping for air. "It's nice to see that my instincts were not wrong," he said. He glanced at Omega. "I have a strong suspicion that I really do not want too clear an explanation for what I have just witnessed."

The Doctor smiled. "Probably not." He indicated the movie camera. "You have film of Mr. Carrigan there firing the gun. It has his fingerprints on it, and your ballistics department will be able to match the bullet to that gun—which has only the one bullet missing, the one that killed his uncle a week ago. I believe he will confess his guilt rather than go to trial, so that should prevent any necessity for a clearer explanation of what happened here." The second gendarme had carefully picked up the gun. Omega pulled on a pair of white calfskin gloves. "Ah—if I might?"

The policeman looked at Maigret, who nodded. Omega took the pistol and unsnapped the odd device on the end of the barrel, and then handed the pistol back to the officer.

"It's probably better that this not be left here," he said, gently.

Maigret nodded. "I have my killer," he said. "I have my evidence. I will sleep better without an explanation." He picked up Bill's camera. "I'll return this to you later," he promised. He nodded, and the gendarmes preceded him, dragging the shaking Carrigan.

Bill turned to Doctor Omega. "Well, may *he* doesn't want an explanation, but I do! What just happened here? And why on Earth did Carrigan fire that gonzo gun with so many witnesses present?"

"The inexorable force of Temporal Destiny," Doctor Omega replied solemnly. Seeing Bill's blank expression, he chuckled. "Invite me home for tea, and I shall explain everything," he promised.

A short while later, the three of them were seated comfortably in the apartment on the Quai Voltaire with a fresh pot of tea and some small cakes, courtesy of the landlady. Bill couldn't keep his calm any longer.

"All right!" he exclaimed. "We have tea! We have cakes! Now may we have an explanation?"

Bob couldn't help laughing at his friend's vexation. "Well, the first thing is that our friend here is obviously a time traveler."

Doctor Omega smiled. "I knew you would deduce that, my boy. Capital! Yes, I am indeed a wanderer through the dimensions."

"A time traveler?" Bill said, looking surprised. "How do you know?"

"From what he said. Don't you remember? He said that *we* travel in four dimensions—not himself. And the fourth dimension is time. And he didn't know the year, or what recording capabilities we had."

"I thought he was just cra…" Bill caught himself in time and shut up.

"Yes, well," the Doctor said, shifting uncomfortably in his chair. "Anyway, onto the explanation I promised you. As a wanderer through the dimensions, I have the capability of detecting other time travelers. My ship arrived here just over a week ago, and my instruments detected a waning temporal

163

field, so I investigated. It was not far from Royale-les-Eaux, and I found a dying man." The old man frowned. "He was a member of a rather... ah... unpleasant organization. There was—or, from your point of view—will be... It's very difficult discussing temporal matters—languages these days aren't formulated to speak of things that haven't yet happened for you, but are in the far past for someone from the distant future... Oh well, in about three hundred years, there will arise a dictator who will make Hitler and Stalin look like amateurs." He paused. "You *do* know about Hitler and Stalin, right?"

"Yes," Bob said, grinning.

"Oh, good. As I say, I sometimes lose track... Well, this dictator-to-be was killed under mysterious circumstances, so this... temporal group decided to send a man to assassinate him. But they did so rather cleverly. The dictator was—as all such men are—paranoid, and was surrounded by bodyguards constantly. The group realized, though, that *after* his death there wouldn't be a guard. So they built a weapon..."

"That gun!" Bill exclaimed.

"Precisely, young man—that gun. It was programmed to shoot a single bullet exactly one week into the past. The idea was that the assassin would arrive one week after the dictator's death and fire the gun, thus killing the man one week earlier."

"But something went wrong, I take it?" Bob interjected.

"Indeed. When the would-be killer arrived, he was set upon by a group of soldiers who stumbled upon him accidentally. The man was shot and mortally wounded before he could perform his task. He did, however, manage to trigger his return device. But that, too, had been damaged by firing, and it malfunctioned, dropping him onto the road near Royale-les-Eaux some ten days ago.

"He was found by Donald Carrigan, who was driving to the casino. Carrigan found the man delirious, and heard this fantastic story about being a time traveler and owning a gun that could fire exactly one week into the past. Now, Mr. Carrigan is an amoral and lazy young man, with no love for anyone but himself. He left the dying man, but took his weapon. Obviously, he then hit upon the plan to murder his uncle.

"He would create a perfect alibi for himself for the time of his uncle's murder. He knew of his uncle's habit of visiting the bank vault every Wednesday at exactly the same time, so there was his chance! All he would have to do was to go to the bank one week after his uncle's murder and fire the gun…"

"And the bullet from it would travel a week back in time and kill his uncle!" Bill said, excitedly.

"Correct." Doctor Omega steepled his fingers and stared over them at his friends. "Unfortunately for him, though, I, too, discovered the time traveler before he died, and also heard his rambling tale. Naturally, I did not know the name of the man who took the gun—merely that someone had, with the intention of using it. Then, I read a few days later of the most mysterious death of Mr. Carrigan and understood immediately. I presented myself at the bank, and the rest you know."

"Except for the most important bit!" Bill exclaimed. "I get that Carrigan the younger came to the bank with the intention of shooting the gun that killed his uncle—but, when he saw us, why didn't he leave? Why did he stay and reveal his own guilt?"

"Because he was an amateur messing about with time!" Doctor Omega explained. "Such matters should be left strictly to the professionals. You see, my boy, time is unforgiving. Albert Carrigan was murdered last Wednesday shortly after two o'clock. The gun that did it *had* to be fired, then, today at precisely the same moment. It was the only thing that could happen. And though young Carrigan struggled mightily against it, the force of temporal destiny drove him to commit the crime—even with all of us present as witnesses. The crime *had* been committed—therefore it *had* to be committed."

"I think you've strained my brain," Bill complained.

Bob smiled. "It is a bit hard to grasp," he agreed. "And it's lucky Carrigan didn't work out how to change the settings on the gun—that would have messed everything up, wouldn't it?"

Doctor Omega chuckled. "It might have," he agreed. "But, as I said, he's a very lazy young man who would much rather steal and kill than work. I knew he wouldn't take the time to attempt to understand the weapon he had."

"Still, it took some nerve to sit in front of that gun while he fired it," Bob commented.

The old man chuckled. "I have faith in the workings of time, my boy. Now, if I might trouble you for another of those excellent little cakes…?"

David Friend makes use of the resemblance between Doctor Omega and Doctor Who to craft a story that throws an entirely different light on one of the Doctor's arch-enemies...

David Friend: *Doctor Omega and the Future Museum*

Paris, 1912

Friedrich Köhler was tense, alert, and listening for footsteps that would signal an instant death. All he heard, as he shuffled through a puddle, was the tinkle of his splashes echoing softly across Montmartre hill. It would happen soon, though. He had sensed someone watching him all evening. Tightening his grubby moleskin coat around himself, he bent a balding head in the direction of the Basilica of Sacré-Coeur and his little apartment.

The door, he discovered with a stab of surprise, was already open and a pale glow reached warningly through the crack. Köhler stiffened. This, he knew instinctively, was it. His thin features set into a look of grim resignation, he stepped inside. A man was lounging contentedly in an armchair, nursing a bottle of Armagnac.

"Don't mind, do you? I was parched. You know what it's like."

Köhler squinted, confused. The stranger had boyish brown hair and a wiry body that was almost lost beneath a double-breasted sack suit, thick Raglan overcoat and striped, sponge bag trousers. He seemed to be in his middle thirties with a thin, pale face that somehow managed to be both convivial and cold, and spoke with an English accent.

"Drink with me!" he demanded and raised the bottle in the air. The little that was left slopped guiltily in the glass. "Actually, do you have anything else? I'm in the mood for a malt, for some reason."

167

"I don't know you," said Köhler stoutly.

The Englishman sneered and shook his head with cynical amusement. "Well, I know all about you, Friedrich Köhler. For one thing, I know that isn't your real name." With a squeak of leather upholstery, he leapt restlessly to his feet. His whole body, it seemed, surged with insuppressible energy. "You aren't German either," he continued, "and you don't usually look this way. The real Köhler worked for the White Star Line and died on the *Titanic*. He was a second cousin to the Duke Gerhard of Württemberg. You wrote to his business secretary in Strasbourg and claimed to be Köhler, impoverished after the disaster, and asked for two thousand marks so that you might recover all you have lost. I intercepted the last of these letters and shall show it to Inspector Juve of the Sûreté, if we can't come to an arrangement of our own. I'll settle for a brandy, if that's all you've got in."

Friedrich Köhler seemed too indignant to even speak. "These—these are lies!" he blustered, trembling now.

"No," said his guest pithily, "you're an ingenious French criminal, a master of disguise, who is loyal to no one. In short, you are Fantômas."

Köhler paused, cautious and thoughtful. "I do have some malt," he allowed. His German accent had now vanished. Turning to the sideboard, he picked up a bottle of whiskey and poured a glass. A keen observer would have noticed how the narrow shoulders had folded confidently back and he was no longer trembling.

"So," said the Englishman, clapping his hands briskly together, "do I have to inform the police?"

The word was like a curt command. Fantômas whirled around and hurled the bottle into the hearth. With a dull rumble, the fire swelled angrily outwards, spitting sparks across the carpet and onto the sheepskin rug. The Englishman made to move, but a forceful shove sent him reeling backwards into the chair, upending it onto the floor.

How had this whippet of man found him? The very fact he had done so was embarrassing. Emasculating, even. Fantômas threw off his bald cap disdainfully, unsheathed his coat and knelt over his guest. A glint of silver, and he was suddenly holding a knife. "Tell me, sir," he growled, "who are you? I want to know what to carve on your grave."

The Englishman stared indulgently up at his host with eyes of dark humor and dangerous intent.

"I'm from the future," he said, and smiled.

Shoreditch, 2005

Jaz delved into the washing basket, pulled out a pair of smart trousers, and wondered if she should hang them. Since the accident, her father barely ever left the house, so it was not as though he would need them. He needed nothing, in fact, from his town council days. Jaz could hear the television from the kitchen window—*Eggheads*, as usual—and knew he was sitting sullenly in front of it.

It wasn't fair. He was still a young man, really. Other people were allowed to wander around and do whatever they liked. She stared absently into the property next door. Their old neighbor, for instance, still had the use of his legs, but what did he do with them? He watered plants and clattered noisily in the semi-abandoned hangar located at the other end of his garden, but nothing of use.

She wouldn't have noticed otherwise, but that hangar of his had been silent for half an hour. Jaz paused, her olive face crimped in confusion. Usually, her neighbor was in there, all day. She tossed a sock back into the basket and drifted curiously to the fence. And that was when she saw him, through the half-opened doorway of the hangar. The old man was lying on the ground, his top half hidden from view.

Jaz moved instinctively. Gripping the fence, she hurled herself upwards and onto the other side. For months, she had dreaded something similar happening to her dad, and now all that tension was uncoiling inside her. She rolled the door aside (it was mounted on rails), stumbled, fell to her knees, and stared into her neighbor's thin, lined face.

"What the devil are you doing?" he barked.

Jaz jolted up with fright and hit the metal door behind her. It clanged hollowly. Looking about her, she realized that this was no ordinary hangar. There were tools, yes, and the windows were stained with grease and soot, and there was a bench packed with complex electronic equipment that emitted a strange hum of power—but in the center of it as occupied by a massive object that looked like a giant cannon shell, except with a door and portholes. The old man had been fiddling busily beneath it, and now she wished she hadn't disturbed him.

"Sorry," she said, suddenly breathless. "I thought you were dead!"

Her neighbor's head tilted towards her and his blue-green eyes flashed with indignation. "It will take more than a leaking carburetor to finish me, young lady."

Jaz was stung. It wasn't *her* fault the old goat was still alive. "This looks like that junk yard down the road," she said, nodding at the mess. "What is it you're doing in here, anyway?"

With a groan of effort, her neighbor leaned forward into a squatting position and Jaz had her first proper look at him. Stringy white hair curled down to his neck and the rest of his head was bare, but for a rebellious thick tuft at the front. His clothes were just as odd. He was wearing a yellow tweed waistcoat, a white-collared shirt with a black ribbon tie and a pair of grey tartan trousers and elasticized boots. Jaz had never seen anyone dress in such a way before. Not even for charity.

"I'm a scientist," he said, stretching painfully upright. He was taller than she had realized and his eyes were wide and angry and glared out of his gaunt face as though she had done something unspeakably foul. "I was just making repairs."

"To what?" asked Jaz, undeterred. "That unexploded V-2 rocket?"

The old man smarted fiercely. "Of course not! I wouldn't have any use for something so primitive. No, this is something of mine." He looked at the young woman with a new awareness, taking in her tip-tilted nose, yellow hoop earrings and untidy ponytail. "I'm Doctor Omega," he said and, interrogatively, "Who are you?"

Jaz was caught off-guard. Snapping out questions was usually something *she* did. "Jaz," she said.

"Like Glenn Miller?"

"No, just one…"

"I gave him his first trombone, you know," said the Doctor with sudden reminiscence. "He was fiddling about with a mandolin when I met him."

Jaz frowned bemusedly. The old man was clearly nuts. "Hold on, if this thing of yours needed repairs, it must've worked at some point," she reasoned, "and yet, I haven't seen it before. How did you get it inside in here?"

The Doctor snorted derisively. "You wouldn't have *seen* it," he said. "Humans aren't very observant. I've learned *that* much from being here."

"Being where?"

Perhaps, she wondered, he was from another country. Jaz had always wanted to go abroad—like Greece, or the Gulf of Honduras—but the only time she could book foreign holidays was at the travel agency where she worked and even that was for other people.

"Hopefully, I should be able to take off very soon," he was saying now.

For Jaz, the conversation was unraveling out of all comprehension. "Take off?" she said. "You mean—it can go places, then? Like a plane, or a helicopter?"

"Oh yes, but not in the way that a place or a helicopter can."

"But it could get us to town?"

His pale face creased with amusement and pride. She seemed to have calmed him a little. "It could take us a lot further than that, my dear," he assured her. "Most ships do."

"Ships?"

"That travel through time and space," he said, as though it were obvious.

Jaz lifted her hands. "I'm standing in a garden shed," she said, "which contains a spaceship?"

"Yes."

"*This*," she emphasized, pointing at the shell-like contraption, "is a ship?"

The old man seemed to take her incredulous tone as a personal affront. "Yes, and it is *mine*."

Jaz knew she should humor him. There was something, however, in his manner—that certainty, those incredulous, mocking eyes, the implication that it was *she* who was being ridiculous—which made her deeply irritated. Jasmine Driscoll could be patient and compassionate, and usually was, right up until the moment when she felt her intelligence was being underestimated.

"Explain how it works," she demanded and, even to her, this sounded like a playground dare.

The Doctor accepted this seriously. "Mainly, on Bernoulli's equation but, if you ask me, none of the Bernoulli boys really understood mathematics, though they could get a bit tetchy if you pointed it out to them." He leaned towards the door of the shell and opened it wide, inviting her to get inside. "It would be better if I showed you," he said pragmatically. "Explanations can be dull."

She went inside; he followed her, closing the door behind them. The lower floor of the craft was divided into two rooms, one that led to the engines, and the other a store room.

"The bridge is up there," he said, pointing to a metal ladder bolted to the wall.

Jaz went up. The middle floor was divided into three rooms, each connected to the central column by a small door. She kept climbing and reached the top floor which was clearly the bridge.

There were three chairs bolted to the floor, and six portholes. The middle chair was the pilot's chair. It sat in front of a steering wheel and a console with mysterious, yet simplistic devices that looked as if they'd been pulled out from a Lego box—or a primitive art exhibit.

The Doctor sat in the pilot's chair and, with a single flick of a switch activated one of these mysterious devices. He then looked at her with curious expectation.

"Where would you like to go?" he inquired.

Jaz smiled, confused. "Where would I like to go?"

"Hmm." He seemed to consider this a reasonable offer. "We don't have to leave Shoreditch at all, but we could go somewhere else, if you'd like. Disneyland; the time of Boadicea; Disneyland in the time of Boadicea. Perhaps even Greece or the Gulf of Honduras."

He cocked a knowing eyebrow and Jaz wondered if he was joking, but something in his thin, stern face told her that he wasn't. He seemed to believe everything he had said. With a stir of nerves, she tried to remember whether she had mentioned her travel ambitions. She hadn't, of course. And yet, somehow, he knew of them already.

"All right, then," she relented, like an exhausted parent agreeing to play another game with a child. "Let's travel through time and space."

"Excellent!"

"I'd like to see Paris," she added, still humoring him.

"Priam's son, you mean?" The old man's mouth crimped contemplatively. "Well, I'll warn you, it gets rather bloody. Last time I was there, I almost got shot with an arrow!"

Jaz shook her head briskly and her ponytail danced. "I mean Paris, the city of lights, in present times."

The Doctor shrugged. It made little difference to him. He took hold of a long, white lever and yanked it down with a stiffening squeak. Quite suddenly, Jaz heard something from outside. Somebody's lawn mower? An electric saw? Whatever it was, it seemed to be getting louder too, like a dozen air compressor pipes that were broken and blasting and out of control. She felt a primitive desire to run.

"What's going on?" she shouted.

"The engine, my dear," the Doctor called back unconcernedly.

Jaz gripped her seat's armrest. Suddenly, she wanted to get off this strange contraption. Through the portholes the interior of the hangar had gone, replaced by twirling clouds of light made of ever-changing colored stuff—a kaleidoscopic tunnel made of pure—something.

With a heavy metal thud, the craft was suddenly still. The noise had stopped as well. Jaz felt herself swaying unsteadily in her chair.

Someone was speaking. A male voice, but not her dad's. It was older, colder, and without the concern. Jaz opened her eyes blearily. The strange little scientist was looking at her with a detached interest, as one might stare into a glass tank at a rare breed of tropical fish.

"I've met a fair few humans," he said, "and most have been cynical, unimaginative and irrationally stubborn beings. You're... slightly less so."

Jaz heard the words, but she wasn't ready to untangle them. "Thanks?" she said, not quite knowing whether this was a compliment or not.

The Doctor nodded pompously, as though he himself were receiving praise. "We're here, by the way," he added inconsequentially.

They were certainly somewhere else. Jaz did not know how she was so sure, but it was a firm, frank conviction unlike any other she had ever felt. Whistling tunelessly and without spirit, the old man went down the ladder, moved towards the door and flung it casually open. Jaz followed him, tottering forward, realizing with relief that she could still walk. At this point, she wasn't taking anything for granted.

The hangar, the garden, of course, were no longer there. Instead, a bright artificial light was beckoning them onwards. Jaz paused, unsure whether to leave or not. Finally, after a moment to prepare herself—and, indeed, after many years of wanting desperately to see something other than her local high street and the pale glow of a computer screen—she smiled.

"Well," she said, "I've a feeling we're not in Shoreditch anymore."

Anywhen

The doors opened, music blared, and the Englishman spun on the spot flamboyantly. He had always enjoyed showing off and, in his view, the best thing to show off was power. The big, loud, obvious kind that nobody could deny and everyone could envy. He strutted forward like the whole world was his own private dance floor—shameless, assured and drunk on funk. With an energetic bound, he slid across the console room and towards a vending machine.

"This song's about me!" he crowed. "I'm getting back to where I once belonged!"

Fantômas was standing off to the side, dressed resplendently in a black dinner suit and shirt, his mask draped over his hands. Despite changing into his own clothes, however, he did not feel the control he usually did. All this talk of the coming days and sailing boats to the stars—it was the sort of thing written by Jules Verne or H. G. Wells. And such strange, clattering noise, too. He gave his host a cold stare and the music was reluctantly terminated.

"That," said the Englishman with critical emphasis, "is the greatest band in history. Seriously, you have no taste."

The thief, however, wasn't in the mood for such discussions. "How did you know about the letters?"

"We're still on that?" the Englishman complained. "You end up writing a memoir and I read it. Simple."

"And this...?"

"It's a machine that can reach the sky above and the times ahead. Sorted?" The Englishman turned to the console and began tapping the keyboard keenly. "I've always had difficulty driving these things. I could do with a SatNav, really."

None of this made sense to Fantômas. "It can go places?"

His pilot paused at the keyboard. "Well, yeah," he said, "but not in the way a hansom can."

"But it could get us to town?"

The Englishman laughed. It was a stiff, unmelodious sound and strangely devoid of delight. "It can take us a *little* bit further than that," he said with scorn.

Fantômas decided to focus on matters of which he had some experience. "You want me to steal something for you?"

The Englishman bit his lip hungrily and pulled a lever down hard. A stertorous breathing surrounded them and he punched the air victoriously. "Gets me every time," he enthused, then remembered what his new friend had said. "Stealing. Yes. It shouldn't be difficult for someone like you." He pressed a button and an image sprung up on the monitors above them. It was a photograph of himself beside a thin, blonde woman with delicate features. "In 2007, I am Prime Minister of Great Britain." He bobbed his head, grinning conceitedly. "I know, right? Amazing."

"It certainly is," said Fantômas, but the other did not discern the irony.

"I enslaved the planet, reversed the economy and dismantled the technology. Usual stuff. Now, though, I must focus on bigger things, not on some stupid resistance."

"Resistance?"

"Led by a woman, would you believe? They're bringing hope to the people and are seen as heroes." The future Prime Minister smiled. "But I will put them in their place." He scratched his chin, as though he were used to having a beard there, and began to explain his plan.

It was more than the Frenchman could ever have imagined.

Afterwards, the Prime Minister's face split into a self-satisfied smile. "Come on," he said, taking the lever again, "let's break the speed limit. Live a little." And, with that, there came the crunching, confident chords of *All Right Now.*

Fantômas watched with amusement and awe as they entered into oblivion.

Paris, The Future Museum

It was, to say the least, a surprise.

The rambunctious ride in the craft—which, Jaz had learned, was called the *Cosmos*—could have been simulated somehow, but no such trick could be responsible for this. She stared with methodical concentration at her new surroundings. She had been transported, quite evidently, and in a way which was almost magical. And now, she and the strange old man were standing in an auditorium with a wide linoleum floor, high ceilings and fluorescent lights. Most obviously, there were glass display cases positioned at intervals, though Jaz did not recognize anything that had been placed inside them.

"What is this?" she said with anxious inquiry. "The Louvre?"

The Doctor seemed to enjoy her astonishment. His ashen face had crinkled into a thin smile and he was watching her with paternal indulgence. "Not quite," he said, and pointed to the wall. "Out there are the Catacombs of Paris. An underground graveyard packed with the bones of six million people. Wall to wall skulls and not for the faint-hearted. We're towards the right, beneath the sixteenth arrondissement." He tugged at his lapels grandly. "This, my dear, is the Future Museum."

Jaz looked blank. "What's that?"

She was only asking to be polite. Really, if this was Paris, she wanted to see the Eiffel Tower or the river Seine. What was the point in visiting one of the world's most beautiful cities and spending the entire trip underground? She might as well be trapped in the Channel Tunnel.

The Doctor was disgruntled. "Good gracious me!" he said, his grey brows swerving together like two beetles in a fight. "Isn't it obvious? This museum exhibits artifacts from the future instead of the past." He began moving nimbly between the exhibits. "We jumped the queue, arriving this way, and we haven't had to bother with the gift shop either. All

177

those tea-towels, notebooks, sticks of rock..." He shook his head disapprovingly. "You pay for the name with that sort of thing."

But Jaz wasn't interested in souvenirs. She was staring, dumbstruck, at this most unconventional of museums. "How come I haven't heard of it before?" was the first thing she wanted to know. "You'd think it would be world famous."

She wondered obscurely if this was an insult, but the old scientist seemed to have expected the remark. "Those hinges," he said, lifting a finger to the tall doors, "are fitted with an Automatic Memory Mangle. When you leave, you shall think have seen only *speculative* ideas about the future. You've probably noticed your memory's a bit hazy already."

"Yeah, you're right," said Jaz, and touched her temple dubiously. "I can't... It's weird, but I can't even remember what my dad looks like."

The Doctor nodded, unsurprised. "It's a side effect," he said. "I have it too. This way, whatever invention people see cannot influence the world before it has been invented, therefore preventing paradoxes."

He spoke with such authority that Jaz trusted him implicitly. It was as if she had known him for ages. Almost like a relative. He certainly had a grandfatherly look about him—but then, she supposed, that probably came with getting old. She got the feeling he could be irritable and curmudgeonly, and had been a bit already, but wasn't that the way with all grand-dads?

"This," he said, leading her to a flying car from Aston Airborne, "is what inspired me to start the place. Someone told me how the modern day wasn't what they had expected. I brought this back from the future to show them and, before long, I was putting other things with it too."

Jaz noticed a television mounted on the wall. "Why is there a telly?" she asked. "We have those already."

"Ah, that's a news report announcing the result of the 2071 republican referendum. It shall spell the end of the British monarchy as we know it."

Her expression was caught, somehow, between delight and horror. "Will it hold?"

"In a manner of speaking. After forty-six years, the monarchy will return under the honors system. King- and queenships will be awarded to those who represent Britain in some way internationally, with each incumbent keeping the title for ten years." He suddenly looked quite wistful. "People can get rid of things a little too hastily," he said, "and it isn't long before they want them back again."

Already, Jaz was distracted, scrutinizing a leaflet she had found on the floor. "What's *Death Knell*?"

The Doctor hesitated. "Well, it looks like a metal suitcase, but it's actually a super-weapon," he said carefully. "When it was replaced, it was put on display here, too much controversy."

"I bet," she said, only half-listening. She was looking at another exhibit now and grinned with embarrassment. "A headset," she read from the object label, "which allows two people to share dreams while asleep. A bit racy!"

The Doctor didn't approve of the humor. "Psychic phenomena isn't so unusual. If a person went near his past or future self, the proximity could make their minds entwine, with one asserting itself over the other."

"The way you talk," Jaz said with ironical disbelief, "you could make time-travel boring!"

The old man's mouth set sourly, and she wondered if she had overstepped the mark.

A young voice erupted behind them. "Hey, Mrs. Carnegie," it sneered. "I think you might need this!"

The pair turned to see a short boy of around seven or eight years-old with scrupulously tidy brown hair and designer clothes. A round, middle-aged woman came up beside him. Jaz felt sorry for her. The exhibit was for a "hunger pill" which expanded in the stomach, removing any hunger pangs, and contracted a couple of hours later. It would, she read, threaten weight-loss empires, delight busy business-people

179

and inspire corporations to eliminate lunch breaks among their labor workforces.

"We should keep moving," advised the Doctor. "There's a lot you'll want to see."

Jaz smiled. He seemed to treat these wonders with a sort of weary indifference, as one who lives beside the Statue of Liberty may become bored of the cooing tourists and flashing photographers. Did anything take him unawares? It was certainly not time-and-space machines—those domestic rockets that hurled people across temporal planes and international borders without even touching the sky. Jaz couldn't think of anything weirder than that. Maybe, she speculated, only aliens caught his attention, but did they exist? It was one of the more obvious questions to ask and she was surprised it had only just occurred to her.

"You'd like the Space Room," he said, as though she had already asked him. "It has the first extra-terrestrial ship, discovered by NASA in 2057. Most humans make a fuss of that." He smiled fondly. "Really, you are like dogs barking at your own reflection."

"I'm allowed to be a little impressed," said Jaz coolly. "Weren't you, when you first came here?"

His old face crumpled as he crossed the years. "Back then, there wasn't a museum to be seen," he recalled. "I had to have one built."

Jaz felt a giddy confusion. "Wait," she said, hands flat and fingers splayed in that way she always did when she wanted to get her facts in line. "The museum had to be here for you to have heard of it, but it couldn't be here if you hadn't built it. That's a paradox, surely?"

The Doctor looked amused, like a parent whose child had learned a new word. "No, no. Apparently, I shall live for a while in the early 1980s. Hence, in the past, my future has already happened. I will go on to build the place, but I didn't know that until after I had done it."

She considered this critically. "Sounds a bit... wibbley-wobbley," she concluded. "How long has it been here?"

"The question is," said the Doctor, "how long *will* it be here?"

Jaz made a face. She disliked it when people answered questions with more questions. It was like being criticized and corrected all at once. "Go on, then, how long?"

He was quite lofty about this. "Well, I haven't really checked, but it should be forever. In fact..." He would have continued, but a voice called out from behind him.

"Doctor!"

It belonged to a slim forty-something woman in a blue business suit with blonde hair pulled back into a tight bun. Jaz had the uneasy feeling that she was not to be crossed, but Omega seemed pleased to see her.

"Ah, Liz," he said. "Jasmine, this is Liz Shaw, the curator of the museum. She used to be my assistant, as it were, traveling around."

The woman was serious. "It helped," she recalled wryly, "when it came to my Futurism degree." She eyed Jaz with a curious aspect but, irritatingly, did not speak to her directly. "Your friend, I trust, is from the past, Doctor?"

"2005," he said with a knowing smile. "Still keen for visitors from all eras, Miss Shaw?"

"Temporal diversity is very important," she said stiffly.

The Doctor shook his head with something like disgust. "Political correctness gone mad..."

A radio buzzed. "Excuse me," said Miss Shaw and took it from her pocket. Jaz didn't catch the message, but it was obviously not good news. The curator's face tightened anxiously, like an actor who had forgotten her lines on opening night.

She turned, faltering, to the room at large. "Could I have everyone's attention, please?" she called. "You must all remain in this room until further notice. We are in lock-down."

Doctor Omega was frowning. "What is it, Liz?" he asked, but there was no time to help. No time, it seemed, for anything at all.

With a groan of resignation, the lights above them flickered once before plunging into an empty darkness.

The curator's voice came through coldly. "There's a robbery in progress, Doctor."

Things were going well.

The security guard had been too busy fetching coffee to witness their stylish arrival, and he only noticed something was wrong when his monitor snowballed. Now, the Prime Minister had rerouted all close circuit footage to his ship and was checking to see how many visitors were in the museum.

He had seen the place before—indeed, had life membership and was eligible for free parking and the quarterly magazine—but this was the first time he had tried to rob it, and he felt an almost sensual stir of excitement. A good thief, he had stolen everything from a nerve gas missile to the bodies of living people, but he had trouble accessing vaults—and that was where Fantômas came in.

The criminal himself was at the door and getting restless. "I always act fast," he said with professional pride. The mask cloaked his face—only his eyes were visible—and reached heavily over his neck. "Is our time now?"

"Indeed, it is," said his new partner smoothly. "Let's see if you really are the best cracksman in European history. I shall join you in twenty minutes and help you carry it back here."

The criminal nodded. "And then, Mr. Norman—or whatever your name is—I will expect my letter. You had better not cheat me; I have quite an *appétit* for revenge."

"Oh, I'm aware of that, believe me, though I don't intend to betray you." The Englishman smiled with a sickening sincerity, and Fantômas decided that he must be a politician after all.

The Prime Minister sensed movement on the monitor and turned. The Doctor, he noticed, had slid into view. He had recognized him at once, but only intuitively. It had been many

182

years, and time had certainly changed both their appearances. But then, of course, it changed everything.

"This has just become a little more interesting," he said.

"How?" asked Fantômas. "Who is he?"

"Just an old friend," said the Prime Minister reflectively, and scratched his chin again. "Well, best friend. We even vowed to visit every star in the galaxy together. But you know how it is. You lose touch. Meet new people. Start wars." Brisk again, he tapped at the console busily. "Let's get the security boys back online. Least we can do is give the Doctor half a chance." His fingers finished with a flourish and he turned to Fantômas with new purpose. "The plan is changing slightly."

The thief looked startled. "No!" he protested fiercely. "Who is this... this Doctor, you speak of? Is he a physician? Does he save lives?"

"Sometimes," said the Englishman lightly. "But today he's about to lose a few."

A faint hum, and the back-up generator summoned some light. It wasn't much. Just a few small bulbs glimmering shyly. A birthday cake would have been brighter. But it was better than nothing, Jaz decided, and at least they were able to see one another.

"What now?" she asked. As was usually the case, she was eager to do something, but wasn't sure what that something would be.

Miss Shaw held up her smartphone. "Our cameras are back on now and they just caught this." It was an image of a man in black. "I will run it through the transparency scanner."

Jaz was not sure she could tolerate any more technology. "What's one of them?" she asked, suddenly out of her depth. This, she supposed, was how old people must feel in an age of e-mails, text messages and online banking. Even her dad had struggled with it at first, but he had lately taken to ordering groceries over the internet whenever she couldn't do the late night shop. It was the first sign he was becoming reclusive; something which concerned her still.

"A transparency scanner is a computer software program which scans an image and strips it of fabric, allowing us to see underneath," the Doctor explained. "But it isn't necessary. I recognize the black attire." His flinty eyes tightened distastefully, as though he had just sampled a plate of spoiled fish. "It's Fantômas. A famously ruthless criminal of early twentieth century origin." He harrumphed with frustration. "This is what happens when you hire humans instead of mechonoids as guards."

Miss Shaw was clearly embarrassed. "We do have one, but it's... an exhibit. People stand next to it and get their photograph taken."

With a hiss of static, there came a small, faraway voice of little confidence: "Dr. Shaw? I've tried calling it in, but I can't get through. I don't what happened with the cameras, but he seems to be heading towards the west side of the museum."

The Doctor's brow darkened. "Why would he do that?"

"I'm going to have a look now," the voice added.

"Tony?" said Miss Shaw worriedly, but it was no use. The radio wheezed, and she dropped her arm in defeat.

Jaz had quite forgotten the presence of anyone else, but was rudely reminded of it by the young voice from earlier. "Why are we still waiting?" the boy whined. He sounded as though he were chastising a waiter at a posh restaurant. The middle-aged woman, presumably his nanny, looked like she would rather be anywhere else but beside him.

"I don't know," she answered weakly and, in a poor attempt at optimism, "but I expect we can move on soon."

"Indeed," said the Doctor, overhearing the exchange. "From what I hear, I live to do some remarkable things. Like go fishing and cook an omelet."

Jaz could tell he was trying to distract the little boy, but the mention of food was a bad idea.

"I want an ice cream," he demanded. "I want one now!"

Mrs. Carnegie seemed to summon every ounce of patience she had ever possessed. "Write something in that new book you got," she suggested.

Moodily, the boy pulled out a Future Museum diary and began scribbling, and Jaz luxuriated in a moment of silence.

The Doctor, meanwhile, had turned to the curator with a renewed interest. "So, our man is heading west, hmm? Well, I doubt he's interested in the Domestic Room. It's full of high-dry machines and renewable carpets, and I shouldn't think he wants an anti-gravity nap either. Could he, per chance, be heading for the Military Room?"

"You mean…?"

He shrugged philosophically. "It was bound to happen one day."

"What is it?" asked Jaz, but the pair wouldn't be drawn. She stared at them with injured virtue. She had come across such condescension before. At work, for instance, whenever a snooty customer wanted to book a trip to the Aosta Valley and didn't expect her to know where it was.

The Doctor gave in. "*Death Knell* is in the Military Room," he revealed. "Stupid decision, really."

Behind them, the boy was arguing again and they had to talk louder themselves.

"Oh yes?" said Miss Shaw, sounding like one of those serenely snobbish types in a Barbara Pym novel. "If you remember, the board enjoyed a robust exchange of views, and it was decided to host the exhibit by a vote of seven to five. Besides," she lifted a chin, all poise and stubborn self-belief, "our attendance rose by fourteen per cent in the first calendar year alone."

But Doctor Omega was unfazed by facts, or how vigorously one might massage them. He moved to the door and Jaz joined him, a tingle of anticipation between her shoulders. Looking out, she expected to see Fantômas in his penguin suit with a gun in his grip, but there was nobody there. Just a corridor, like any other. Narrow, long and eerily empty.

Miss Shaw produced a square device with an earbud.

Jaz smiled. "What's that? An iPod?"

"It's a Babble Booster," she said. "Amplifies sound, especially close conversations."

The Doctor took it cheerfully. "I think our young man may like this," he said with oily kindness and turned to offer it to Percy. But the boy wasn't there.

Jaz threw a panicked glance across the auditorium. The woman was missing too.

"Where are they?" she asked, but the Doctor was already alarmed.

He stepped into the corridor, listening intently through the device. Jaz kept behind him—feeling, with frustration, as though she were cowering, but she had to stay close to the wall or risk being seen.

Turning a tight corner, the old man came to an abrupt halt.

Jaz opened her mouth instinctively, but then remembered not to speak. Instead, she followed his gaze and found a figure at their feet.

It was a middle-aged woman with curly hair. Mrs. Carnegie. Jaz fought back the impulse to cry out. The Doctor bent down, pressed his fingers to her pulse. Faint red marks encircled her neck. Someone, it seemed, had squeezed her dead.

With an effort, Jaz lifted her eyes and stared, squinting, down the corridor. All she could see were thick stretches of shadow. She moved forward, listening hard, her ears almost aching with the effort. Perhaps, she wondered, Fantômas had already taken the boy. He might even be dead, and they could tumble over his corpse right now. A restless desperation suddenly seized her and, before she even realized it, Jaz was running. Her footsteps were fast and heavy and she no longer cared about noise. At any moment, she knew, the intruder could curl around the corner and block her path. They might even collide. Despite this, she felt quite removed from the danger. Her concern for the boy—however wretched he was—had somehow numbed any inhibiting fear.

Finally, she halted, hesitant and breathless. If the boy had remained in the corridor, she would have passed him by now. He had to be somewhere else. Jaz ducked into the Culture Room and glanced anxiously around. A light bulb, small and sickly yellow, glimmered weakly from the back. This room, she noticed, had a much homelier design: a couple of bright red sofas and a coffee table with a commemorative coronation mug of King George IX. Facing it, a television was screening *No Kids Allowed*, a popular sitcom from the 2060s, and a tall curtain draped over the wall where the window should have been. The kind of place, perhaps, where a boy might feel safe.

Jaz considered calling out his name, but it was no use. The sound system was playing a new song by The Beatles, created through the technological manipulation of melodies, lyrics and chord progressions from the band's back catalogue, and she couldn't compete. Confidently, knowing her footsteps would not be heard, Jaz peered over exhibits and peeked under tables. She imagined the boy fiddling with a do-it-yourself face-lifting kit or trying to administer a motion-tattoo but, frustratingly, he didn't seem to be anywhere. With this defeat, Jaz felt her chest tighten and, for the first time, realized that she was lost as well.

The song faded and the room fell to silence. Even the television program had finished. She came to a bookcase stacked with post-apocalyptic survival sagas—best-sellers as humanity hoped to outlast a nuclear war—and paused. She had treaded on something. A diary, with the museum's logo embossed across the front. Like the boy's.

Jaz picked it up and flitted through the pages, her anxious eyes scanning the words. Yes, it *was* his; all scribbled notes about the thief and the weapon and the strange old man who was supposed to save them. If he had dropped this, she realized, then he must have been here, and Fantômas must have snatched him. Which meant that the thief was close.

With a rasping whine, the door opened, and she jerked back beside the bookcase. Of course, she didn't move, but she saw something that did. A long, thin shadow, sliding slickly across the floor like a black snake. It was slow in that elegant way of all predators, and merged smoothly into the darkness surrounding it. Jaz had stopped breathing and didn't dare start again. The way things were going, she wouldn't get another chance, anyway. She heard a crunch of glass and the light bulb blinked out. Jaz tensed, and waited to feel hot breath against her face and a blade across her throat.

But it didn't happen. Instead, there was a gentle tapping towards the door and the rustle of clothes as someone passed through it. Fantômas, it seemed, had left.

Though a natural cynic, Jaz felt a stir of hope rise up inside her and sucked in soft air. Maybe, she told herself, it was going to be all right. The thief had been alone, so he couldn't have found the boy yet either. She could continue her own search and find a way out of the museum as well.

Jaz stepped confidently forward and was about to move further when something gripped her arm.

And she gasped.

"I was wondering where you had got to."

A thin torchlight appeared and, behind it, the wizened face of the Doctor.

Jaz started. "Where were you?" she said, noticing the boy beside him, wearing a coat with built-in heating sensors.

"Behind the curtains," said the boy—and, just as casually, "A man in black killed Mrs. Carnegie."

It occurred to Jaz that he may have been in shock. Or maybe he was just callous.

"You dropped this," she said damply, and handed him his book.

"And I was outside," said the Doctor, "though it's just as well I came in here, it's really quite interesting in its own way." He flashed the light idly on something behind Jaz. It was a newspaper, pinned to the wall, with a photograph of armed soldiers strutting through Downing Street.

Jaz noticed it and blanched. "What's this?" she asked, and began reading the article with earnest absorption.

It was dated 2007, and reported that the Prime Minister would order the killing of the American president and no less than ten percent of the world's population. She wondered, disbelievingly, whether this was a practical joke arranged by the staff of the museum. The Doctor, however, was also awed, and she knew it was true.

"There will be a resistance movement," she said with weak hope, but she couldn't even soothe herself. Her insides had twisted savagely with nausea.

The Dark Ages, it seemed, were coming again. A civilization which wasn't even worth the word. Her mind filled with images of people, weak and submissive and constitutionally scared. No democracy, no hope and no escape. She had to do something. She had to help them.

"Come on," said the old scientist quietly. "Things are bleak as it is. I found the security man—or, I should say, his body."

Even more bad news. With a heavy heart, Jaz followed the pair into the corridor. It was silent – though, of course, if the best thief in history was roaming around the place, would he really make that much noise?

She wished they could be in the auditorium again, before this had even happened, and continue staring incredulously at the exhibits. Come to that, she wanted to be back in her garden on Chesterton Road, putting the washing out. It was dull, yes, but refreshingly free of world slavery and time-traveling criminals.

"Why do you have a funny name?" the boy was asking Doctor Omega.

The old man seemed offended. "Why ever not? I chose it in tribute to someone very important."

Jaz waved a hand for silence. "What do we do now?"

"We keep safe," was his simple answer. "By now, Fantômas should've reached the Military Room and may even have accessed the vault. But he shall need to carry it back. It's heavy, so he will walk slowly." A finger pointed eastwards. "That's where the camera caught him. I'm going to block these corridors so he will be trapped between them."

"Blocked?"

"With a solidification spray."

Jaz smiled resignedly. "I'm not even going to ask this time."

The boy, however, was not so proud. "I want to know!" he demanded and, despite the trauma he had so recently endured, did seem interested.

"It's a sort of wall that's made from steam," the Doctor explained, and fished a hand in his pocket. "I snatched some from the Industry Room. Come the 2130s, all the builders will be using this." He revealed a slim, metal can and handed it to the boy. "Point it away from your face."

The boy studied the object cautiously, as one would observe a new bottle of insect repellent. Finally, he lifted it high, squeezed his eyes shut and pressed his finger purposefully on the nozzle. A jet of grey steam charged out of the can, discoloring the air and hanging languidly like a pea soup fog. They watched with playful astonishment as the steam thickened into something stranger and more substantial. It reminded her of a rain-soaked window or a bathroom mirror after she had showered.

The Doctor reached forward. Instead of his fingers passing through and onto the other side, a faint clink was heard, as though he were touching a sheet of glass. He murmured amusement, and tapped out a brief staccato rhythm. It was hard as brick. Jaz smiled at this crotchety old man in a frock coat. Inside, she concluded, he was young in that whimsical, curious and eagerly joyful way that actual children weren't anymore. He was like Alice and Peter Pan and Jim Hawkins, but with a dash of Ebenezer Scrooge and the Wizard of Oz.

"Now, he can't pass," the old scientist declared with the satisfaction of someone who had just put up a shelf. Jaz certainly believed him. It was as though a wall, made entirely of ice, had been erected in the middle of the corridor. He turned towards the other direction, brows swooped determinedly together. "Right, let's head to the next corridor. With any luck, we won't even meet him."

But no sooner had he said this than the old man came to a jerking halt. And listened. Jaz did too, looking back into the gloom. Yes, there *was* something…

The sound of wheels. A trolley, perhaps. The weapon must indeed have been heavy. It was moving, however, with a restless urgency, as though the thief was eager to escape.

Jaz stiffened in anticipation. She could almost feel the rumble beneath her feet, like an oncoming express train hurtling along a track. She glanced at the boy reassuringly. "It will be okay," she said with a confidence she could not feel.

Why did people always say that? Had anyone ever believed it?

With a tap of footsteps and a rustling squeak, the trolley careered through the darkness. It was now uncomfortably close. For a moment, Jaz thought the wall had somehow dissolved and it hadn't stopped Fantômas at all. But then, as something scraped discordantly, it happened. The trolley slammed into the wall, lurched awkwardly to one side, and cast off its briefcase.

Which, as it lay flat on the floor, began to make noises of its own.

The thief paused grimly, heard its ominous hum. Wheels tinkling, he straightened the trolley again and thrust it into the wall. This time, with such force behind it, the wall broke in two and a slab smacked exhaustedly onto the other side.

The darkness seemed thinner now, and Jaz could make out a hand. It reached through the gap and grabbed a greedy hold of the Doctor's collar.

"Leave him!" she shrilled.

The man in black stepped forward, his mask hiding all emotion. Even more disconcertingly, his hand trailed to a pocket. With a clink of cold metal, he pulled out a gun.

The old scientist, however, was unruffled. "Now, look here, young man," he began, but the weapon raised itself towards him. His old eyes flashed indignantly, as if he had just heard a teenager swear. "You won't get anywhere waving that thing around."

191

Jaz couldn't restrain herself. "Yeah, I bet you're nothing without the gun!"

This was not quite true, of course. He had the suitcase, and it was now ringing out a series of slow, assertive chimes.

"That's the *Death Knell*," said the Doctor gravely. "You've triggered it, you fool!" He paused, helpless. "We must find somewhere quiet, where the sound can't kill us. Now!"

Their captor, however, seemed to luxuriate in the sound of Armageddon. Indeed, it had a strangely languid elegance, like church bells in the countryside, evoking a peace it would soon destroy.

The Doctor was forthright. "We're all going to die if we don't move."

"Not all of us," was the bland reply.

Jaz wished she hadn't heard that. "You're going to kill us?" she pursued. "Even the kid?"

Despite the mask, the man's confusion was clear to see. "What kid?"

The other two could have asked themselves the same question. No one, they realized, was lurking behind them. For the second time that day, the boy had vanished.

Jaz felt as though her very soul had been sucked out. The odds of finding the boy and hiding them all in time were precisely none.

But then, impossibly, he was there again—leaping from the side, and the ruins of the wall, brandishing the solidification spray. He aimed it high, pressed it hard, and spurted steam into the man's eyes. Even the mask was no use against it.

The thief stepped back, dazed. But the boy didn't stop there. He pushed himself forward, hands waving, fighting for the gun—which, unfortunately, was too much, as it cracked conclusively through the corridor.

Jaz froze, the breath caught in her throat.

The gunman stiffened. Blood began seeping from his right shoulder, his hand pressed stickily against it. Panting softly and, it seemed, with bitter incredulity, he sank to his knees and onto his side.

Jaz crept closer, cautious but concerned, and fumbled for his pulse.

"What happened?" asked a woman's voice. "What's going on?"

It was Miss Shaw.

"Quickly," instructed Doctor Omega. "Get the boy somewhere quiet."

The curator snatched his hand. "Come on!" she cried.

But the boy was having none of it. He pulled himself free and ran off down the corridor.

Jaz was bent over the body. With a flourish, she pulled off the mask. But the man underneath it was not who she had expected to see.

"What's wrong?" came the Doctor's voice.

She hesitated. "Give me your coat. We need to stop the bleeding."

The Doctor drew level, saw the thief's face.

"Do it!" Jaz commanded. "It doesn't matter who he is."

She wanted to believe this, but it was much too hard. The man lying before them was not the thief they had seen in the image earlier. This, she realized with a cold shock, was their next Prime Minister.

Jaz took the Doctor's coat, pressed it against the wound, and wondered how many breaths he had left. Her mind was reeling. This had been an accident, obviously, but would the court agree? The boy was young and innocent and had fought in self-defense. But then, who knew what laws existed in this place? She wasn't even sure it existed itself. With horror and desperation, Jaz kept on pressing the wound. She should have acted fasted, she realized, tormented. Things should not have ended this way.

The chimes echoed on, but she could barely hear them now. The image of the man's face seemed to have been burned onto her retina, and all she could feel was a cold hand on her shoulder as the Doctor lifted her up.

"We need to get him somewhere too," she said.

"No," said the Doctor gently. "We can't help people like him."

In her weakened state, Jaz didn't question his piety, but allowed herself to be led away. They entered a room where a large, square vault stood grandly in the middle. The chimes were slower now, merging into one another to make a long, weary groan. It was as though a clock was ticking down towards their doom.

The door was ajar and the Doctor pulled it wide. Jaz wasn't expecting to see anyone else and jerked with surprise when she peered inside. A tall man was sitting, hunched, in the vault. He was wearing a sack suit and a Raglan overcoat and, without the mask, was only recognizable from his general height and shape. It was Fantômas, certainly, and he seemed just as anxious as they were.

The Doctor's face was lit with a friendly smile. "May we join you?" he asked politely and, without waiting for an answer, clambered inside. "Glad to meet you at last. I'm afraid we had to hide when you were wandering around the Culture Room earlier."

Jaz pulled the door heavily closed and turned to face Fantômas. She was so weary, by this point, that she couldn't summon the energy to be scared. "That was you?"

"I couldn't find this vault," he admitted despondently. "Once I did, and got that suitcase, my so-called partner insisted we go back separately. I don't think he trusted me with it, as a criminal." The thief smiled weakly, as though only now embarrassed by his profession, despite being its very finest exponent.

"And I'm guessing, to avert our attention, he dressed himself in your clothes while you broke into the vault?"

Fantômas nodded and Jaz, sitting back against the wall, blew out an exhausted sigh. Maybe it was the shock of seeing someone shot, or maybe it was this approximation of a nuclear warning, but Jaz felt weak and her head was heavy. It was like she was five years-old again and had stayed up passed her bedtime. Her mum was always letting her do that. Jaz had thought it was a reward for being a good girl. She later learned it was because her mum could not be bothered to take her upstairs and read her a story. Perhaps she was there again, on the couch, and had fallen asleep in front of the television, and this whole day was a surreal dream.

A hard object hit the roof of the vault and she jerked upright in alarm. She remembered, with something like surprise, that they were still underground. Above them, twenty meters of stone and dirt was being unsettled. Jaz tried to focus on something which didn't involve being trapped in a vault with a notorious criminal and buried under a small rock quarry.

"I hope Liz is all right," the Doctor murmured, ignoring the noise.

Jaz could tell he was worried. "I'm sure she will be," she said, still staring at the ceiling. "After all, she survived her travels with you."

The old man, however, was uneasy. "Just about," he said. "She saw things, you see. Traumatic things. Changed her, really, seeing what becomes of the world, as it would with any human."

Jaz could certainly understand that. She could still see that newspaper now.

"Running this place is how she copes with it," he went on. "She has her own version of the future here."

Jaz looked at him levelly. She had forgotten Fantômas was even there. "And how do *you* cope with it?"

The Doctor suddenly sounded vague. "I'm not sure I do," he confessed. "By helping people, I suppose."

"You always try to do that?"

"I could ask you the same thing," he said with wry amusement. "You care for your father; you tried to help me in the hangar; the boy, too, and that fellow out there. You even want to be a paramedic."

Jaz could have asked him how he knew this, but decided weirder things had happened already.

"I think," he reflected, "we like to feel needed."

"We're certainly needed now," she agreed. "I just wish we knew what it was about."

This spiked the old scientist's interest. "Well, it might have something to do with that political upheaval we read about. I haven't known of it till now, you see. Though how time travel got to be involved, I don't know. Yet."

Outside, the bells had ceased, but the rocks still fell. The vault was half-buried and soil covered the linoleum like carpet. Doctor Omega passed stiffly through the room, somehow managing to avoid being hit. He seemed tired, crestfallen, and Jaz remembered that he had founded the museum. This will not have been his favorite visit. The ceiling rumbled again and the three of them raised their heads with bleak anticipation. It was even more frightening than the chimes.

Jaz searched the corridor. The Prime Minister's recumbent figure was nowhere to be seen. She wondered whether he had found shelter or if the siren had caught him out.

The Doctor appeared behind her. In the lines of his forehead, she read his next few words. "I've found Liz... Miss Shaw," he said quietly. In the distance, there came a crash, as another ceiling fell fatally through. "Her knees were scuffed, as though she had fallen." His voice was hard, unemotional. "She had been made to hear the bells."

"Murder?"

Jaz did not know what to say. The usual platitudes seemed somehow unsuitable. Cracks cut through the ceiling, and the scientist moved off with the purposefulness men had in those old British war films she had watched with her dad. It looked comically absurd, though it really shouldn't have been at all.

"Wait!" she called and, with a bound, drew alongside him. "We need to find the boy."

More rocks dropped, closer now.

"I haven't seen him. He must be somewhere under this mess." Jaz was shocked at his dismissiveness. "All that's bothering me now is my ship."

"Ship?" Jaz echoed. She had forgotten it completely. "What's the matter with it?"

"It's gone." They turned down another corridor, passing rooms of rubble.

"If the boy's gone," she argued, trying to stay calm, "and so is the *Cosmos*, then maybe the two left together."

Reluctantly, the Doctor agreed that this was a possibility. "He may have gone in there to hide," he allowed. "The ship's sensors could have detected him entering and automatically dematerialized."

As he spoke, Jaz realized something. Miss Shaw had been pushed to the ground, but the Prime Minister couldn't have done it. Even if he was still alive, he was too weak. Similarly, Fantômas had been in the vault. Both men, then, had alibis. The only other person...

"This way!" cried Fantômas, gliding ahead, and they followed him through another corridor.

At the corner, they stopped, and a look of surprise came into the old man's eyes.

It was the *Cosmos*.

"How did it get here?" Jaz asked bewilderedly.

But they didn't have time for such questions while the roof was falling asunder.

"Quickly!" instructed Doctor Omega and, as rocks crashed around them, they ran into the ship.

The lights welcomed them warmly. Jaz had never been so pleased to see anything in her whole life. The Doctor got up to the bridge and tapped the dashboard affectionately, as one might pat a dog.

"So, the boy didn't take this ship," said Jaz, relieved. "We were wrong."

The Doctor, however, was looking grim. "Oh, he took it, all right," he said. "Think about it." He turned abruptly and Jaz was reminded of her old headmaster at Coal Hill. "Three people have been killed, and we thought the man in black had done it. The boy even said so. But, if you recall, he had heard

197

me mention Fantômas, and how he was wearing black. He knew, then, just what to say."

Jaz had begun to wonder the same thing. "The boy was responsible," she said, her voice hollow. Out loud, it sounded outrageous. He was, after all, just a boy.

"The siren went off," the Doctor continued, "and he fled in this ship. As you would expect, over time, he ruminated on his crimes, and began to see himself as a ruthless murderer. And so he became one. With no more humanity holding him back, he went on to do even more evil things. Eventually, he became the very man he had killed."

"The Prime Minister?" said Jaz, her mind clouding with doubt. "That's who that boy grows up to be?"

"That isn't the least of it," Omega lamented. "He wanted to keep his power, but needed to defeat a resistance which had been mounted against him. He was also in the room, you will recall, when I mentioned the *Death Knell*."

Despite her own misgivings, things were becoming clearer to Jaz. "He made notes," she said, remembering the boy's boredom, "in that diary of his. I saw them myself."

"Quite. Well, as an adult, and still in possession of this ship, he collected Fantômas and brought him here to steal the weapon to use against the rebels. This spot here is where they landed."

He looked fondly at his home, now it was centuries older than the last time he had seen it.

Jaz turned to Fantômas thoughtfully. "Is this true?"

"I only know that he found me, and he was a most curious man."

"He was indeed," said the Doctor, rubbing his brow sorrowfully. "If it wasn't for the Automatic Memory Mangle, I would have recognized him immediately. You see, he and I grew up together. More often than not, he goes by the name of The Master. We are, I'm afraid, old enemies."

The young woman stared at him in shock. "That's... news," she managed.

"Of course," continued the Doctor, "his younger self left in such a hurry, he hadn't noted in his diary the part where such a person was killed. Nor did he realize the urgency to do so. The instinct to kill, of course, would leave its own mark."

Jaz was earnest. "Earlier, you said how two minds can become one, or something, when you meet your other self. You reckon, then, that the presence of the older Percy could have caused the younger one to adopt the same homicidal tendencies?"

"Certainly I do," said the Doctor, and his voice was one of frustration and regret.

Fantômas joined in. "You mean to say, Doctor, he was murderous, because his older self was murderous, and that was only because his younger self was murderous?"

"Hmm."

"But why push Miss Shaw and force her to hear the siren?"

"To test the weapon. He understood what his older self was up to. And the guard was killed because he was about to search the museum and would have noticed there were two identical ships here. He did the same to his nanny because…"

"Because," finished Jaz heavily, "she wouldn't fetch him an ice cream." She paused, disgusted by such a trivial motive. "I thought, at first, the shot had been accidental, but it couldn't have been."

"It was fate *and* fatal," said the Doctor wryly. "Quite literally, he had himself killed. What we call in time travel a rookie mistake."

Jaz looked away uncomfortably. The old man could be ruthless himself, and it wasn't something she appreciated. She paused again, this time in memory of those who had passed. Despite what that memory widget would do, Jaz didn't think she could forget such an extraordinary day.

It was Fantômas who spoke first. Being a killer himself, he may not even have understood the idea of respectful silences.

199

"Doctor," he said, "can I go home? On this occasion, at least, I have not succeeded in a robbery, which wasn't even my idea."

Jaz did not approve, and she was about to say so, but the Doctor accepted the request without persuasion. Perhaps he suspected how vigorous it might be. "For better or worse," he said, "I try to avoid changing history, and you have a little more of it left to see." He turned to Jaz and his eyes glimmered shrewdly. "And while we're in early twentieth century Paris, we could have a look around ourselves. You always did want to visit the place, and I can get you back home to your father before you even left. What could be better than seeing the City of Light in the Belle Époque, its golden age? With Moulin Rouge, the Ritz Paris and Art Nouveau?"

"Nothing," Jaz agreed but, despite her eagerness to see the place, something was bothering her. "What with everything that's happened here, though, would it be right, do you think? Enjoying ourselves like that?"

The Doctor seemed astonished, and she wondered how a human could be so thoughtless. But then, she realized, she wasn't certain he even *was* human. Few things would surprise her at this point. He looked at her, however, with a delicacy and understanding which seemed to confirm what he had said in the vault. This old man—alien or not—did indeed want to help others. He just hadn't got the hang of it yet.

"The Master tries to ruin lives," he said quietly, "and even ends some to achieve that. The best thing we can do, in response, is live our own."

Jaz nodded philosophically and decided she would light a candle at the nearest church for everyone she had met that day. "Will we have time to visit Notre-Dame?" she asked.

The Doctor smiled. "My dear, with this ship, we have time for everything."

And, with a wheezing, groaning sound, they left the Future Museum behind.

Matthew Baugh presents us with a tale in which The Little Prince weaves a parable of science and faith, logic and emotion, in this little gem appropriately entitled...

Matthew Baugh: *The Cubic Displacement of the Soul*

Asteroid B-612 - October 1890

The professor stared at the smiling blond boy framed against the starry sky and wanted to scream.

"Are you feeling better?" the boy asked. His manner was polite and calm, something the professor found baffling considering the two of them stood on a house-sized chunk of rock that seemed suspended in the depths of space.

"Madness! This is madness!" he whispered.

The boy cocked his head to the side, a gesture the professor thought might mean curiosity.

"The doctor said you might feel like that." He held out a teacup full of a dark, steaming liquid.

The professor took the cup and sniffed at its contents. The odor, something between fresh coffee and wet dog, made him wince.

"What is this?" he demanded.

"Black hellebore tea. The doctor said it would settle your mind and clear your thinking."

"I do not care for the aroma. You said hellebore?" The professor shuffled through his encyclopedic memory. "That's the flower commonly called Christmas rose, I believe, and it is toxic. Are you trying to poison me, child?"

"Poison?" The boy seemed bemused by the question. "Of course not. Here, see?"

He raised the delicate porcelain cup to his mouth and took a long sip. When he lowered it, the professor saw that about a third of the contents were gone.

"It is perfectly safe," the lad said. "You don't have to drink it if you don't want to, but I think it will make you feel better."

The professor took the cup and raised it to his lips. The tea tasted as strange as it smelled, but he drank it without any further reservation. He didn't know much about children, but he knew a great deal about deception, and he was confident the boy hadn't lied. Besides, it would be absurd to stage this elaborate setting just to poison him. The professor knew even more about crime and didn't think this could be a scheme to harm him. No, this boy and the doctor wanted something else, he just hadn't yet figured out what.

To his surprise, the tea helped. His questions didn't vanish, but they shrank to the level of manageable curiosity. The overpowering sense of unreality dwindled to a feeling of irritation. He still didn't understand his situation, but he could accept it.

"That did help," he said. "I suppose I should thank you."

"Thank the doctor," the boy said, beaming. "He was the one who gave me the tea."

"I think he lied to you about its contents. I have a comprehensive knowledge of vegetable toxins."

"The doctor told me it was the same medicine that cured Heracles of his madness."

The professor snorted. "Heracles is a myth. A baseless fantasy for children. In the real world, hellebore has no such medicinal properties."

"Oh, but the doctor didn't get his hellebore from your world. He said it came from Pollux IV."

"Not from my world?"

"Not from your planet," the boy replied. "I think that's the better way to say it."

The professor looked around again. Aside from the boulder on which they stood, there was nothing but black sky dotted with stars. Only one of these stood out, a yellow light several times larger and brighter than anything else.

"The sun?" He whispered.

"It looks smaller from my planet, doesn't it?"

"This can't be another planet!" the professor said. "It's some clever illusion, but that's all. If I just walk away, that will quickly become apparent." Without waiting for a reply, he strode off.

He was back in less than two minutes.

"It doesn't take long to walk around my planet," the boy said.

The professor didn't reply. Turning 90 degrees, he set out toward a different horizon. He did this several times before accepting that he was, in fact, on a tiny planet. It was a pretty world with three tiny volcanoes and an abundance of green plants. None of which made any sense.

"Very well," he said, returning from his sixth circumnavigation. "I admit I am on your planet. I have some questions, but I suppose introductions are in order first. I am Professor James Moriarty, mathematics tutor."

"I'm very pleased to know you, professor." The boy made a graceful bow. "I'm afraid I don't have a proper name. Living alone on my little planet, I've never had much use for one. However, the doctor calls me the Prince, so that will have to do."

"Ah, the doctor. Would that be Doctor Omega?"

"Indeed it would," the Prince said, his smile broadening. "Are you also a friend of his?"

"Not a friend," Moriarty replied. "But I have met him."

Moriarty had come to Paris, looking for an advantage. He didn't know what he wanted, but the detective, Holmes, had grown from nuisance to a real threat, and nothing the professor did could shake him off the trail. Usually, Moriarty would not have turned such outré methods, but his sometime colleague, Nikola, had recommended this place, and Nikola was someone to be respected.

He turned onto the old street; his collar turned against the drizzle that had driven most of the traffic from the roads.

There, between two stone houses, sat the *Bureau d'Echange de Maux*.

"Excuse me, my good fellow."

Moriarty turned toward the voice; a man in what looked to be his eighties stood there, dressed in black cape and astrakhan. His severe expression and shock of unruly white hair gave him the look of a stern schoolmaster.

"Yes?" Moriarty said.

"I see you're headed toward the Bureau."

"What of it?"

"I would not recommend it."

"Frankly, sir, I don't see how it is any of your concern."

"Oh, but it is," the older man said. "In that place, you can trade a good for an evil, but the price is never worth it."

"Again, that is my concern, not yours."

"I have made it my concern to prevent the spread of the sort of evils that are this place's specialty. My name is Doctor Omega; allow me to buy you a brandy and tell you more."

"I see no reason to oblige you. Good day, sir!"

Moriarty turned but had only gone a few steps when the man called out.

"Come, come, Professor Moriarty. You really should listen to me."

He turned slowly, scanning the street as he did. The stranger was alone; he was certain. He was equally sure the man was not Holmes in disguise.

"You know me, sir?"

"I attended a lecture you gave on binomial theorem several years ago. I must say, you are one of the great minds of the century."

Moriarty's mind raced. The fact the man knew him and was aware of the Bureau's dark reputation was a complication. He would have to be eliminated, but it would be best to learn what else he knew first. He forced a smile.

"On second thought, I'd be delighted to have a drink with you."

"So you see, anything you get from that place comes with a terrible consequence," the man—who called himself Doctor Omega—said. "It's a sort of Faustian bargain if you will."

"I don't see any such thing," Moriarty replied. "First, while you have told some harrowing stories of deals others have made at the *Bureau d'Echange de Maux*, you have no evidence that they are true. Even if they are, I see nothing wrong with a bargain like Faust's."

"Nothing wrong in selling your soul to the devil? That seems most peculiar."

"You are an educated man, doctor," Moriarty replied. "You possess an advanced degree, so I will do you the courtesy of assuming you are no fool. Surely, you can appreciate my point of view. First, there is no such thing as a devil. That is a superstitious conceit of humanity with no empirical basis whatsoever."

"Ah, but what I said is metaphorical," Omega said. "Surely, you can see that mortals can assume the traditional role of Satan, tempting us to evil with rich rewards."

"Even so, you depend on intangible, irrational concepts. You must know that evil has no objective existence. It is a quality that we humans give to things for purely arbitrary reasons."

"If the proprietor of the exchange gives you something that will harm you, would you agree to call that 'evil?'"

"I might, but it makes little difference. If this man is Mephistopheles, as you suggest, he is still offering me something of worth in return for my soul. That is to say; he offers something for nothing."

"You do not believe in the soul either, I see," Omega said.

"Of course not," Moriarty snapped. "Why should I believe in something that cannot be seen or touched? The soul is a human invention. Philosophers use it as a way to hide from the reality of death. Clergymen create visions of eternal rewards and punishments that they use to control the gullible."

"I must disagree," Omega said. "The energy that animates all living things is genuine. I have seen it many times in my travels."

"Really?" Moriarty took a sip of his brandy as he wondered if the man was a common lunatic. He had decided mainly against it. Doctor Omega was undoubtedly mad, but there was nothing common about him.

"Tell me, doctor, how might I determine for myself the reality of the soul? What properties does it have that can be measured? Does it have mass? Does it occupy space? If it is real, it must have real properties."

"Oh my, you are a keen one," the doctor said, laughing. "As it happens, one of your country's finest thinkers has established just that. She tells her beloved, 'I love thee to the depth and breadth and height my soul can reach.' Three dimensions, Professor Moriarty. The soul has cubic displacement."

Irritated, Moriarty rose from the table. "Really, doctor, it you're not going to take this topic seriously"

"Tut, tut," Omega said soothingly. "Please forgive my sense of whimsy, but it seems to me that poets and mathematicians have a great deal in common. You each use special language to help people understand things that they cannot see or touch."

"Absurd! Poets deal with fantasies and dreams. Mathematics represents the physical universe."

"You are the author of the *The Dynamics of an Asteroid*, aren't you?"

"I am." The abrupt shift of topic made Moriarty wary.

"A magnificent work," Doctor Omega said. "I daresay you are Britain's foremost authority on the topic."

"I daresay the world's foremost," Moriarty replied dryly.

"Yet you have never touched an asteroid, and never even seen one without a telescope. You know about asteroids, but you do not *know* asteroids."

"You are playing semantic games, doctor."

"No, no. I am very serious when I tell you that I can introduce you to someone who knows asteroids far more intimately than you and can show you things that defy your narrow understanding."

"I would say I've wasted enough of my time here."

He turned to leave and found himself facing a large, muscular man with a pleasant face. Moriarty cursed himself silently for allowing the man to come upon him undetected. The man grabbed the professor, spun him around, and pinned his arms to his sides with hands that seemed as strong as steel clamps.

"Thank you, Fred," Doctor Omega said. "I'm dreadfully sorry for this, professor, but I cannot allow you to go to the *Bureau d'Echange de Maux*. The deal you would make there would destroy not just you, but thousands upon thousands of others."

"Fool! You are both dead men for laying hands on me!" Moriarty said, snarling. "My men are always close at hand. You will not leave this building alive."

"Yes, yes," the doctor said pleasantly. "Ah, there it is."

He produced a silver wand with a red light at the top.

"Just watch the Baltian neuralyzer," he said.

There was a flash of light from the device.

"The next thing I knew, I was on your planet, or rather, your asteroid," Moriarty said. "I have no memory of the passage."

"Well, I am happy for your visit anyway," the Prince said, smiling. "Not many people come to my planet."

"Yes," Moriarty replied, then, "Are you the expert on asteroids that the doctor mentioned to me?"

"I know my planet very well, I suppose," the Prince said. "Would that make me an expert?"

"Perhaps, if only in the mind of that doddering madman."

"But you wrote a book about asteroids. Perhaps you could tell me something about my planet."

"I could, yes. It would take some months of observation, but I could describe its mass, orbit, and rotation down to the smallest degree. I could tell you its density, composition, and a million other facts."

"That would be wonderful!"

"It would take several hundred pages, and would require a level of understanding that even most mathematicians could not grasp."

The Prince thought about that for a moment or two.

"Couldn't you tell me about my planet in some way that would be easier to understand?" he asked. "Perhaps you could draw a picture?"

Moriarty drew himself to his full height.

"Young man, I occasionally make diagrams. I never make drawings."

"That is too bad," the Prince said. "But, could you answer a question I have?"

"What is it?"

"I tend the plants here, and there are always weeds, especially baobab shoots. I have thought that, if I went to Earth and got a sheep, it could eat the weeds for me."

"I am not an authority on sheep," Moriarty said.

"I see. But my question is really about asteroids. If I were to leave and be gone for a long time, would my planet be lonely?"

"A planet is an insensate mass of minerals. It cannot feel lonely. Only living beings have emotions."

"You are saying my planet is not alive?" The Prince seemed shocked by the notion.

"Everyone knows that planetary bodies are not alive," Moriarty said. "The scientific community is in absolute consensus about this. At least, except for George Challenger, and he is a crackpot of the first water."

"I just thought that I would miss my planet, so it made sense that it would also miss me."

"That makes no sense. Then again, there is a great deal about your world that makes no sense. For example, how is there an atmosphere around this rock."

The Prince rubbed his downy chin thoughtfully.

"I suppose that is because, if there were no atmosphere, I would not be able to breathe."

"That is no answer," Moriarty snapped. "Things don't happen just because we need them to. A planet must have sufficient gravity to hold an atmosphere, and for that, it needs sufficient mass. For that matter, why do I feel like I weigh the same here as on Earth? On such a tiny ball, I should be able to leap out into space. What is it that holds me to the ground?"

"I have always assumed that we were held to the planet by love," the Prince said.

Moriarty snorted.

"You sound like Empedocles, or Augustine, or one of those other learned fools of antiquity who thought that gravity was the same as love. It is not!"

"What do you think holds us to the planet," the Prince asked in perfect innocence.

"Something else!" Moriarty's voice had risen almost to a shout. "Some natural, measurable phenomenon!"

Moriarty fell silent, and the Prince watched him quietly for a while. The boy was not frightened, he could tell, but seemed puzzled and a little sad. Finally, he spoke.

"I think I understand why the doctor brought you here," he said. "You don't know my planet."

"I know more about asteroids than anyone on Earth."

"But how can you know someone if you've never met them? How can you ever become friends if you just watch them from far away?"

That caught Moriarty off-guard. He had many associates, some of them he valued highly, but none that he would call friends. His towering intellect had always made human intimacy difficult. He had only encountered one man in his adult life who could talk with him on an equal basis, and that was his deadliest enemy. He had watched Holmes from a distance for several years but had never yet met him face-to-face. What if he did? Was this a chance to know another human being and to be known in return?

"Nonsense," he said, though he kept his voice gentle this time. "I don't see much value in your way of 'knowing' things. My ways are more logical."

"Still, we don't need to agree to be friends," the Prince said. "You are welcome to stay as long as you like."

"Thank you, Your Highness." Moriarty found the offer somehow touching. "I must go, though. I have pressing business back on my planet."

Doctor Omega's ship, the *Cosmos*, arrived several hours later. He didn't try to land, for the vessel was nearly the size of the little planet. Instead, the ship went into a stationary orbit, and Fred lowered a rope ladder, which the professor climbed to the ship.

"How are you, my good professor?" Omega said when he was safely on board.

"Unchanged," Moriarty replied. "I shall need some more of your hellebore tea if you are going to show me more impossibilities, but nothing will sway me from my purpose."

"I'm afraid this calls for something more than hellebore," the doctor said. He raised the silver wand in front of Moriarty's face again.

Professor Moriarty stood on the ancient street in the clear Paris evening, trying to remember how he had come there.

"Professor!"

He turned to see Sebastian Moran running toward him. His lieutenant wore a relieved expression.

"Where have you been?" Moran said, stopping next to him. "We've been looking for you for hours."

"I don't remember," Moriarty replied. He had the vague sense that he had traveled somewhere, met someone. He couldn't capture the details.

"Did you find what you were looking for at the *Bureau d'Echange de Maux*?" Moran asked.

Moriarty looked at where the shop had been. Now the houses that had flanked it stood together, sharing a common wall. It looked like they had existed that way for many centuries. He had the unsettling idea that the Bureau had gotten tired of waiting for him and moved on. He felt angry at himself.

"I was deceived," he said. "There is clearly no such place."

"What do we do now, professor?"

Impossible ideas drifted into his head: traveling the stars, living on an asteroid, becoming a friend of Sherlock Holmes. Angrily, he swept these fantasies from his mind to focus on the practical.

"Back to London," Moriarty said. "I have a murder to arrange."

Travis Hiltz delights us here with a pirate yarn, a genre which, despite the success of the Pirates of the Caribbean *franchise, has not seen much of a revival. Here is an adventure featuring a stellar cast of adventurers cruising the legendary Seven Seas...*

Travis Hiltz: *These are the Voyages...*

1607

The beach was white sand, idyllic; a light breeze ruffled the sea. A long boat had been dragged up, its bow resting on the beach, the stern in the water.

A Moorish sailor, barefoot, clad in a loose linen shirt and knee breeches, lazed in the sun, enjoying the light duty of guarding the boat, while the rest of the landing party trudged inland. He contemplated doing some fishing, but it sounded like too much effort.

"Yusuf ! Yusuf-ben-Moktar!"

The sailor sat up quickly, at the sound of his name, blinking in the sunlight and wondering if he was in trouble.

There were several more shouts and then two men came bursting out of the forest. One wore a tattered soldier's uniform, but it was the uniform of an army that would not exist for several centuries. The other was an older, white-haired gentleman, dressed in a black suit of Edwardian cut and style.

"Yusuf! Get the boat in the water!"

The soldier held one of the older man's arms, helping to propel him along. The duo stumbled frantically down the beach, pursued by what appeared to be a swarm of crawling insects.

Yusuf paused, confused, as the ants seemed to be brandishing swords and were dressed in long coats.

"They're people," he shouted. "Tiny people!"

"Yes, we know!" the older man shouted back. "Push off!"

Their tumbling in was the final push the boat required, and Yusuf quickly clambered aboard, as they drifted away from the beach. The tiny army skidded to a halt, shaking their weapons and fists with angry impotence.

While the older man in black settled on a bench, the soldier gave the sailor a hand vigorously rowing. The white-haired man fished within his coat pockets, pulling out a colored handkerchief and mopping his brow.

"Well, that could have gone better."

The soldier nodded his agreement, peering out at the crystal blue water.

Outside the bay sat a grey, weathered hulk of a frigate. It bore its years with a proud, weary acceptance.

Quickly approaching were two trim vessels of war. In keeping with the army that had pursued the party, the ships resembled children's toys.

As the older man watched the minuscule war ships' attempt to cut off their escape, the flap on his front breast pocket opened and a tiny figure climbed out, perching on his shoulder, to get a clear view.

"My countrymen are a stubborn lot!" he shouted, to be heard over the sound of the waves and the voices of the others in the boat.

Everyone huddled down in the boat, as the small warships began to fire upon them.

Yusuf-ben-Moktar struggled to turn the boat, and the wave caused by the oars threatened to capsize the warships.

The boat made its escape, soon reaching the larger ship, the *Rose Hawk*, while the tiny warships fired pellet-sized cannon balls and shouted in anger. Rope ladders came over the side, and sailors scrambled down, to aid the boats' occupants, and then to secure the boat, before they could sail out of the bay.

The scholar and the soldier leaned on the rail, catching their breath, as well as watching the distant enemy ships.

"That was a wash," the soldier grumbled.

"I feel I bear some share of blame," the tiny swordsman standing on the rail said. "It did not occur to me to warn you that cutting your sandwiches triangularly is a capital crime in Lilliput."

"Yes, yes," the older man muttered, sitting perching on a nearby barrel. "Your assistance was much appreciated."

This trio, appearing so out of place amongst this crew of seventeenth century mariners, were not native to this time period. The gentleman, dressed in Edwardian black, was the eccentric time traveler known as Doctor Omega. His uniformed companion was Lieutenant Marcel Renard, a French soldier from the first world war. Perched upon his shoulder was the Chevalier Shelfin Bundt Arbornoth, a minor noble from the Court of the king of Lilliput. His innate, moral sense and longing for adventure had caused him to side with the travelers over his own people.

A sailor came shuffling up to the trio.

"Captain wishes a word," he said.

Doctor Omega nodded and, leaning heavily on his cane, made his way along the deck.

Private Renard was part of a company of WWI soldiers who had, through the unknowing use of a makeshift time machine, been sent hurtling back to 13th century Spain. After months of carousing and misadventures, most of these "timeslip troopers" had returned to their proper time.[11]

There were, however, complications, and a few had been left behind, while others had been scattered through history during the trip home. Doctor Omega, and his fellow time traveling savant, Professor Helvetius, had been working to correct this situation.

Several of Doctor Omega's traveling companions were working to stabilize the fabric of history, while his handyman, Fred, had been dropped off in 1914 to collect the pieces of the

---

[11] See *Timeslip Troopers*, Black Coat Press, ISBN 978-1-61227-078-4.

troublesome time machine. Doctor Omega had embarked on a mission to collect that last few, lost soldiers. It had proven to be more difficult and bothersome then he'd imagined.

They entered the captain's cabin, a cluttered collection of charts, clothing and knickknacks accumulated during a lifetime spent traversing the seas.

Doctor Omega sank gratefully into a well-cushioned hanging chair and awaited the captain's attention shifting from the chart table to his guests.

Sir Oliver Tressilian, also known as Sakr-el-Babr ("the Hawk of the Seas") was a tall man, tanned from years spent sailing off the Barbary coast, broad at the shoulder, slender at the hip, with hair black as midnight, a black beard, and eyes as fathomless as the sea he navigated.

He tucked his quill back in the ink pot, rubbed at his upper lip, and then glanced up, expectantly at the unusual trio.

"So," he said, with a haughty smile. "Went well, did it?"

Doctor Omega merely harrumphed in reply.

Renard's shoulder twitched and he leaned his head over. He then nodded, stepped forward and held out his arm. Shelfin scurried down, and once standing on the captain's desk, made a leg and presented his sword.

"My service to your fine vessel!" he announced, dramatically.

Sir Oliver gaped for a moment, before regaining his composure and replying with a nod.

"Welcome aboard, Monsieur. I hope you do not mind bunking with these gentlemen," he replied. "Perhaps Renard would be kind enough to show you your new quarters, whilst I have a word with the Doctor?"

The French soldier took the hint and he and the tiny swordsman left.

Doctor Omega leaned on his cane, wearily willing to let the Captain speak first.

"While you were away, your ghost returned," the buccaneer said, sternly.

"She is neither 'mine,' nor a 'ghost,'" Doctor Omega replied, irritably, implying this was a continuation of a disagreement that had been revisited throughout the voyage.

"What is she then?"

"Lotte is... complicated. Did she speak to anyone?"

"Startled the man on the forecastle, so he nearly toppled over the side," Sir Oliver continued. "Then pestered several, others asking if they wanted to play..."

"Yes, yes, but did she pass along a message?" the older man grumbled.

"Of course," the bearded corsair nodded. "After she frightens my crew, she always does. She said, 'my father is coming.'"

Doctor Omega sat back and tapped thoughtfully with a crooked finger at his sharp chin.

"Curious."

"Is that meant to imply good news or ill?"

"If Lotte's father plans to join our quest, he would be a most formable ally," Omega nodded, thoughtfully. "I am curious as to how he would manage to rendezvous with your ship, however..."

"While we are speaking of our travels..."

Sir Oliver leaned forward and drew out a length of parchment from a compartment. He unrolled a map and began weighing down the corners with bits of bric-a-brac from his desk.

"Would you care to share what our next destination might be?"

Doctor Omega leaned over to the map, fishing a pince-nez out of his coat pocket as well as a metal protractor and several scraps of paper. He then spent several minutes, consulting his notes and the map intently. Finally, he took off his pince-nez and used it to point at two spots on the map.

"Here," he said, decisively. "And... here."

The Captain peered at the map for several minutes before looking up at the time traveler.

"That's empty ocean. Both spots."

Omega frowned, took the stub of a pencil from his pocket. With a stern gesture, he marked the two spots.

"One of the islands tends to vigorously avoid any attempt to map it," he said, returning to his chair. "The other is ringed by high cliffs, making it inaccessible to all but the most intrepid explorers."

"You will, of course, have a list of 'conditions' for exploring them, as you did with Lilliput and… what was the other island… Paradise? The one inhabited only by maidens…?"

"Are you indulging in some kind of monkey business, Captain?" Doctor Omega asked. "Or is this a serious objection to our arrangement?"

"No, not at all!" Sir Oliver smiled, sitting back. "I want only two things in this world: enough coin to pay my way and to indulge my longing for what's beyond the horizon, and you have supplied both, amply! Your ways are… odd, to be honest, and knowing you have secrets teases at my mind, but I feel more than content with entering in your employ, Doctor!"

Doctor Omega frowned at the haughty mariner. He'd had a choice of buccaneers, and had picked the 'Seahawk' because he appeared to be the most honorable of a morally challenged lot.

"The first island will be difficult to approach, for it is prone to be surrounded by storms and other strange phenomena," he explained. "The second is rocky, but easily arrived at. In both instances, only Private Renard and I shall be going ashore."

"Of course," Sir Oliver said with a gallant gesture. "I well understand, you not wishing to have any of the crew wandering about the Nameless Isle!"

"How did you know that?" Omega asked, accusingly.

"I'd be a poor sailor, if I hadn't heard a few stories about the strange island '*with the warmest, brightest light one has ever felt*'," the Captain responded.

The two men locked gazes, and Doctor Omega paused, unsure how to proceed. He knew the reputation of Sir Oliver Tressilian as a generally trustworthy adventurer, but any man can be tempted, and the secret of the Nameless Isle was rumored to be enough to tempt the noblest of souls.

"My pardon, the jest was in poor taste," Sir Oliver said, with a rueful grin. "I read the name off one of your scraps of paper. I saw it jotted down. It drew my interest, along with the many exotic dishes served at that place, Lee Ho Fook's."

Remembering that the list of islands to be investigated was written on a takeout menu from the eatery in question, Doctor Omega relaxed slightly. He was unsure of the Captain's intentions, and so settled on a disapproving frown.

"Hummph! Well, if you're done being amusing, I believe I will go rest. How soon do you think we will arrive, at either island?"

Appearing contrite, the pirate leaned forward, tapping at his chin thoughtfully.

"The Nameless Isle should be reached in a matter of days," He said, all business. "Weather holds and your stay there isn't too long, I'd say another seven days to Caspak."

"Satisfactory," Doctor Omega muttered, rising slowly to his feet and hobbling away.

The days passed, the stories of Lilliput and a further sighting of the "ghost girl," along with more mundane chores, kept the crew occupied, until their arrival at the Nameless Isle.

Shelfin was assigned several of the cabin boys to convey him about the ship, as the novelty of being a mode of transportation soon lost its appeal to Private Renard. Never having served in the Lilliputian navy, the tiny swordsman was fascinated with the ship and all aspects of the voyage.

The sea grew wine dark and choppy.

There was no cry of 'Land Ho!', as no one was sure that any land existed with the dense bank of fog the ship approached. Only the fog's lack of movement hinted at anything solid within its mass.

"You still wish to follow your course of action?" Sir Oliver asked, concernedly studying the tempest-tossed water. All joviality had faded from his tone, now that they were within sight of their destination. "At least, someone more skilled at handling a boat…?"

Both Doctor Omega and the French soldier frowned, but for different reasons.

"No," the savant replied. "This is a delicate matter. If you'd please."

Sir Oliver and Omega shared another glance, and then the Captain simply nodded.

Soon, Doctor Omega and Renard were bobbing along. The French soldier was determined to prove his boating skills to the Captain.

The waters surged and it was a struggle to keep the boat on course. It felt to the time-displaced soldier that the water was actively pushing them away from the fog bank and its mysterious contents.

"Pull the oars in," Doctor Omega instructed from the front of the boat.

"What?" Renard protested. "We can't!"

"Do as you're asked!" the older man snapped, glancing over his shoulder.

He then returned his gaze back to the swirling mist, sitting patiently huddled in his traveling cloak. The French soldier, frowning skeptically, pulled in the oars, and sat, anxiously gripping the sides of the rocking boat.

The sea pushed them deeper into the fog, and, in the distance, they could hear breakers, the sound of waves striking land. Unsure how inviting or safe that land was, Renard felt no sense of relief. For all he knew, they were about to be dashed against the rocks. He held tight, bracing for what he was sure was the inevitable crash.

The sea and fog moved about them, like a living thing. Renard could swear, he could see shapes… forms, moving about the boat: almost human, but not quite or maybe more than human, perhaps guiding the boat along. He found himself transfixed, staring into the storm, trying to catch a solid glimpse of their airy entourage, all thoughts of his peril melting away.

He almost fell off his seat when the boat came to a sudden halt, upon a gravelly beach.

As if a switch had been hit, clouds rolled back and the sun shone down.

The two men climbed out of the boat. Renard shaded his eyes with his hand and peered about nervously. Doctor Omega trudged up the beach.

A figure stood, on a slight rise, where the sand met the straggling grass that marked its border.

An older man, clad in the plain robes and skullcap of a hermit scholar. His beard was white as the sand and tumbled down to his chest. Thin, bony hands clutched his wooden staff, as he surveyed the two new arrivals. He made no movement to join them, patiently waiting for the equally aged time traveler to reach him.

"Omega," he said simply.

"Your Grace," Doctor Omega replied, with a respectful nod of his head.

"You are being polite. You seek a favor?"

"I seek, merely the answer to a question," Doctor Omega said. "I hope to locate some soldiers, lost not just on the seas, but in time."

"Ah," the other man said. "That would explain matters. My... servants had come to me, concerned over some ripples in the ether..." He nodded to himself. "So, to answer your question: no, I have had no visitors to my island."

"Well, then..."

"But I am expecting some," the old duke continued. "And your presence and the presence of your vessel are not part of my plans for receiving them..."

He allowed his next command to float in the air between them.

"Yes, I see." Doctor Omega said, with a frown. "We shall be on our way. My best wishes to you and your daughter."

He turned and began to trudge back to his boat.

"Omega."

The time traveler stopped and looked back at Duke Prospero.

"There is a tempest brewing. I shall keep it at bay, as long as time allows, in order that you may reach calmer seas"

"Most appreciated."

The two men exchanged smiles, dry and knowing, before parting.

"Was he of any help?" Renard asked, when Doctor Omega reached the boat.

"Some," the older man said, with a thoughtful nod. "Let us be on our way. We can talk back at the ship."

Once off the beach and into the water, Renard found their return journey much easier than their arrival. The small, weathered boat, glided across the sea and while the fog still hung heavily, it seemed not to impede or confuses their progress.

Days passed, not uneventfully, as they sailed.

It was with a certain relief when they came in sight of the island of Caspak.

Grumbling accompanied the announcement that only the white-haired Doctor and Renard would be going ashore.

The island was a rugged, uninviting lump. The boat scraped across the rocks, as Renard hauled it ashore.

Feeling the weight of his travels, Doctor Omega hobbled up the beach, his eyes intently studying the rocky ground, until he spotted the faint traces of a path.

Renard caught up with him where the beach morphed into equally rocky hills.

"What're we looking for?" he asked, glancing around.

"Traces of your friends," Doctor Omega replied, absently.

He peered about, then stopped, and poked at something on the ground with his cane. Renard kneeled down and plucked it from the dirt.

"It's a button," Renard muttered, holding it against his own uniform jacket. "A uniform button."

Tucking it in his pocket, Renard walked quickly up the path. Doctor Omega struggled to keep up. The landscape remained rocky. This section of the island seemed made of jagged rock and barren hills.

Renard, wandered along, until he spotted a cave.

"Hello…!" he called, tentative, yet hopefully.

He ducked to enter it, his eyes struggling to make out shapes in the darkened chamber.

When finally, Doctor Omega caught up to him, Renard was standing, his gaze locked on what looked to be a pile of rag and bones on the cave floor. The bones were two skeletons and the rags were the remains of their World War One era military uniforms. Scattered about the two skeletons were gold nuggets and gems that sparkled in the faint sunlight.

"Ah," Doctor Omega said, fanning himself with his free hand. "I feared as much. My condolences. Any thought to who they were?"

Renard shook his head, as he kneeled down to examine the remains.

"Might be Duranton," he muttered. "He was tall… and greedy. The other, I dunno…"

He shrugged, resigned. He dusted off his hands, his eyes on the bones. He then took notice of the treasure scattered about.

"Paying Captain Tressilian won't be an issue."

He moved to pick up a coin, but was stopped by Omega pressing the tip of the cane against the coin.

"No," he said, simply. "The treasures of Caspak are not a gift, it is a burden. It is not for us. We found what we came for."

He waved vaguely at the two skeletons. The French soldier nodded, and began gathering up the remains of his comrades.

Back on the beach, they fished out a length of tattered sailcloth from the bottom of the boat and bundled up the skeletons. Doctor Omega sat, leaning on his cane, while Renard kneeled on the rocky beach, tying up the makeshift shroud.

He stood up and shifted the bundle into the boat.

"Um…Doctor…?" he said, peering out at the ocean, while he reached out to tap the older man's arm.

"Yes? What is it?" Doctor Omega asked, wearily, before following his companion's gaze. "Ah!"

There was a ripple in the water, and then a man came striding up out of the surf. He was impressively tall, seven feet if he was an inch, his wide brimmed, peaked hat adding another foot to his height. His ash-colored hair touched his collar, and his beard extended down his chest. His soaked garments and boots were tattered and travel-worn. There was a satchel slung over one shoulder and he held a staff nearly as long, as he was tall.

Renard gaped as the bearded man, shaking the water from his hair and beard, while he strolled over to the boat.

"Omega," he said simply, upon spotting the time traveler. "Walk with me."

With an effort, the Doctor got to his feet and the two strolled along the beach, leaving Renard to sit on the edge of the boat, shaking his head in bafflement.

The journey back to the *Rose Hawk* was silent and subdued. Doctor Omega, brusquely explained that the bearded wanderer, whose name was Isaac, had agreed to join them on their mission, but would be making his own way to the ship.

Captain Tressilian was at the rail to greet them. His attempt at a joyous welcome was cut short upon spotting the grim bundle they returned with.

He performed a brief last rites over the bones and had them stowed in the ship's surgeon's quarters.

"So, you have found some of your wayward soldiers," he said, as he and Doctor Omega strolled about the deck.

"Yes, and I fear we will find the remainder in a similar state," the older scientist mused. "We may have reached an end to our quest. Unless something occurs to change matters…"

His morose pondering were interrupted by shouts from the crew.

The Captain, the Doctor and the soldier joined the crew by the anchor-side rail. They were gathered in a rough semicircle, leaving space for the ghost.

Lotte was the translucent image of a young girl, her dress and hair plain. She danced about the deck in impatient joy, much to the sailor's distress.

"Ah," Doctor Omega nodded in understanding. "I forgot to mention…"

Several of the sailors by the rail shouted and pointed over the side.

Emerging from the water, Isaac Laquedem pulled himself up the coarse anchor rope. He reached the rail.

"Permission to come aboard, Captain?" he asked, blandly.

"Um…granted," Sir Oliver nodded.

Isaac swung a long leg over, and, nodding his greeting to the crew, walked down the deck. As he passed Doctor Omega, he reached into the battered satchel that hung at his hip, and took out a tightly wound scroll, which he handed to the Doctor. He then strolled the length of the ship, his ghostly child following happily along.

Several of the sailors crossed themselves or muttered a prayer under their breath. All eyes were on the Captain and Doctor Omega.

"I… uh… believe there is room for him to bunk with the crew," The corsair muttered, keeping his tone dignified, while his eyes stayed fixed on the new passenger.

"Isaac requires no hammock," Omega explained. "Just be aware that he must… will always be walking. He will attempt to stay out of the crew's way and requires that they do the same."

He then tapped the Captain with his newly acquired scroll, and nodded his head in the direction of his cabin. They were soon joined by Renard and the minuscule swordsman.

Shelfin paced the Captain's table, studying the maps as he walked across them.

"May I ask what occurred on Caspak?" Sir Oliver asked, having regained some of his composure, settled in his chair and a full goblet in his hand. "No treasure, but several passengers, who... er... leave me at a loss for words."

The others all turned in the direction of Doctor Omega. He had unrolled the scroll and was intently reading it, oblivious to his companions' attention.

After several moments, he put down the scroll and took up his tea cup and sipped contemplatively.

"Well?" Renard asked, finally breaking the tense silence. "What does it say?"

"Hmmm, what...?" Omega said, startled from his thoughts. "Oh, yes, it's a message from another time traveler, like myself, an English acquaintance. Apparently, he was contacted by Helvetius and has passed along the results of his own inquiries. It gives us two more islands to search: two very promising, if concerning, locations..."

He passed the scroll to the Captain, who intently studied the navigational instructions.

He put the paper down, frowning.

"Yes, the first is desolate," He nodded. "The second is yet another of your islands that exist where none should be."

The span between islands was no less hazardous or fantastic. There were days spent trapped in a strange sargasso with an even stranger occupant. There was matching wits and swords with pirates: upon the water; pursued by the Dread Pirate Roberts; upon land, a supply run threatened by the equally dreaded Captain Mephisto.

The Rose Hawk plowed the seas, its rigging tight, as all available sail was unfurled. The crew's enthusiasm could be chalked up to their eagerness to make landfall in the hopes that any and all of their unusual passengers would be disembarking.

Isaac's constant walking proved unnerving; the sound of his footfalls, heard, day and night, lead to whispers that he was everything from some unholy golem, to a cursed sorcerer, to his being the fabled Wandering Jew. Any anxiety he caused was slightly offset by his mild, nonthreatening nature and willingness to help with the ship's chores.

He was well suited as a courier to all parts of the ship, as well as exhibiting a strength that was staggering, when he put his hand to weighing the anchor or helping with the rigging. He was often joined on his constant walking by his spectral daughter, as well as Omega and Sir Shelfin; the latter perching upon his shoulder or residing in a pocket.

They soon came in sight of the island of Borgabunda: a lush wooded peninsula.

"If nothing else," Captain Tressilian remarked, as they observed it from the wheel deck. "A good chance to replenish supplies. Yusuf, assemble a few men to join us."

"Us?" Doctor Omega inquired, pointedly.

"Yes, none of your solitary explorations this time. I can make out movement in the trees. Whether beasts, natives or your lost soldiers, you'll have an escort."

"I don't see anything," Renard muttered, peering through a telescope.

"I have a keen eye, Monsieur Renard," Sir Oliver replied, jauntily. "Will tall Isaac be joining us, or will he be making his own way?"

"I believe he'd like some ground under his feet," Doctor Omega said, "and so, will most likely decline taking one of the boats."

The party soon reached the blunt, rocky beach. A guard was left on the boats, and the group soon split: the Captain and his men going in search of helpful landmarks, as well as water and something to fill the ship's larder, while Doctor Omega, Lieutenant Renard and Sir Shelfin walked up the narrow beach, searching for some sign of their time-lost quarry.

The Lilliputian chose to walk for a bit, as he was unlikely to get lost on the empty stretch of beach.

"I don't see any sign of people," Renard muttered, shading his eyes with his hand as he peered about. "No buildings, no farming… not even footprints or a trail…!"

"Calm down," Doctor Omega said, patting him on the arm. "We have just arrived. Enjoy the walk."

"I've found something!" Sir Shelfin yelled, struggling to be heard over the surf.

"It's a footprint!" Renard said, kneeling down. "A hoof print! That must mean people!"

"Or it might just mean horses," Doctor Omega grumbled. "Start using your head! The Traveler's note referenced some time eddies, but nothing specific..."

Chastened, Renard walked along the beach, occasionally, parting the foliage to peer deeper into the woods. Aside from a few more hoof prints, they saw no other sign of habitation. Shelfin rode in Doctor Omegas' coat pocket, while the soldier trailed along, dejectedly.

Soon, Isaac came walking out of the ocean and fell in step with them, wringing out his clothes and beard while he walked.

"No luck?" he asked, quietly.

Renard, holding the wanderers' staff for him, while he dealt with his sopping garments, merely shook his head.

"There must be something here," the bearded man said. "Otherwise, why send us…?"

"The Doctor said something about 'time eddies', whatever those are. Maybe my friends aren't the only time travelers…?"

He glanced at the other man. Isaac chuckled dryly.

"I travel through time the traditional way: one day at a time. I leave the other sort to you and Omega. Your fellow soldiers may not be here, but there is… something. I can smell it on the wind."

They walked, soon losing sight of the ship. The solitude soon weighed heavy, causing the entire quartet to cast questioning glances at the least noise. As the sun crept closer to the horizon, the shadows grew longer and brought more feeling of unease.

"Something *is* out there," Renard muttered, under his breath. "I can feel it."

Isaac merely nodded and took his staff back. Renard moved closer to Doctor Omega, keeping one hand on the butt of his pistol.

"We should start heading back to the boat," he said, in a conversational tone, meant for both his companion and who-ever might be watching them. "The Captain will be missing us."

"Yes, yes," Doctor Omega replied. "I'm sure he will, but I'm more interested in who is following us."

Oblivious to his friends' concern, the time traveler walked up to the edge of the forest and poked at the nearest bush with his cane.

"Come now, enough of this skulking. Introduce your-self."

The result was not quite what he had hoped for, as the shrubbery erupted with a half-dozen, feral creatures. They were shorter than men, ape-like in stance. They had chalk-colored skin, weak chins, and over-sized red-veined eyes. Flaxen hair covered their heads and ran down their backs. They were clad in scraps of rough cloth and bore rudimentary weapons, mostly just sticks.

Isaac stepped in, swinging his staff. He mowed the crea-tures down as if they were wheat before a scythe.

"Morlocks?" Doctor Omega breathed. "They're Mor-locks! How did they get... Oh, Helvetius, you are an idiot!"

"What? What's that?" Renard asked, brandishing his gun, and trying to draw a bead on the attackers.

Isaac seemed in no need of help, so he just stayed on guard. He was prepared to defend the Doctor, if any Morlocks got past the tall man's staff.

Shelfin leapt out of Doctor Omega's pocket, shimmied down his pant leg, raced across the beach, and promptly stabbed the nearest Morlock in the foot.

"Take that, foul miscreant!" he shouted in triumph.

The Morlock hopped about, cradling his injured foot, making himself an easy target, for Isaac's staff.

The creatures were soon routed, two laying sprawled and unconscious on the beach, the rest escaping into the trees.

"Flee, you poltroons!" Shelfin bellowed. "Or taste my blade once more!"

"Well fought, sir," Isaac said, scooping up the tiny swordsman.

He then turned and walked back down the beach. Renard, took Doctor Omega by the arm and steered him along. Unsure if their attackers were gone , he kept his gun in hand.

"What were those... Morlocks, you said?" He asked, keeping one eye on the trees. "Where do I know them from?"

"Hmmm?" Doctor Omega asked, absently. "What? Oh, yes, of course. Helvetius' harebrained attempt to return your comrades home and deal with the damage they caused to the time stream. You, as well as a tribe of Morlocks, were scooped up... Terrible mess... And it would seem that a portion of both parties ended up scattered about... Would explain the time eddies...!"

"I remember that... Sort of," Renard muttered. "Feels like a dream... There was a girl there and some explorer fellow..."

"Yes, yes," Doctor Omega nodded. "You were traveling from the past to the present, and I believe the Morlocks were traveling from far in your future to the past... Never did find out what that was about.... Anyway, the two groups collided and it caused no end of temporal disruptions."

"So, they don't belong here either?" Renard asked. "Should we be gathering them up, as well? Hate to think of anyone, even those repulsive buggers, being stranded."

"No, no," Doctor Omega replied, in absent thought. "I think they are fine right where they are. This explains a bit. I always thought the Yahoos were a lost tribe of Neanderthals, but the answer might be even more intriguing… Helvetius might have known what he was doing, after all… makes a pleasant change..!"

"You lost me quite a ways back," Renard said. "But, once we are safe on the ship, with a mug full of grog, you can explain it to me all over again."

Back at the beach, Captain Tressilian and the sailors were waiting, looking a bit the worse for wear.

"Ah, you encountered the Morlocks too?" Renard said, looking them over.

"A rather unpleasant group of… I have no idea what they were," the Captain replied, perched on the edge of the boat while he attended to a leg wound. "And then, we were almost trampled by some horses!"

"Houyhhnhnms!" Doctor Omega said, brightening. "Well, that confirms my theory!"

"I am so glad someone is enjoying this excursion," Sir Oliver scowled, as he tore a strip from his vest to bind his leg.

"Apparently, the good Doctor has solved some great mystery," Renard explained.

"So, any luck finding your friends?" the Captain asked,

Renard shook his head.

"Well, then, onward!" he exclaimed, clapping him on the shoulder.

A week later saw them reaching their next destination, a fog shrouded island that existed on no map that Sir Oliver could find.

The ship was at anchor, its captain and passengers at the rail, studying the massive fog bank that enshrouded it, listening to distant waves break upon an unseen shore.

"Well, there it is," Sir Oliver said. "I think, hard to tell, even by my keen eye."

"It's there," Doctor Omega said, studying a small device he took from his pocket. "Strong traces of artron energy, as well as some curious traces of radiation… Best make this a short visit."

"I will join you there," Isaac said, stepping over the rail and dropping into the water.

"I'd prefer a boat, myself," Renard remarked.

"I too," the Captain said. "Mister Pitt, see to the boats, if you please."

The trip across was rough. The waves were fierce and once in the bay they encountered a maze of rocky shapes poking up from the sea floor, like talons.

The beach was strewn with shale and stones. There was a steep incline to a sandy area and then dense jungle and imposing mountains.

"Chilly," Doctor Omega said, huddling into his cloak.

Renard nodded and blew into his cupped hands.

"Drag the boats up," Sir Oliver instructed. "Yusuf, you and Mister Pitt, see about gathering some firewood. What now, Doctor?"

"Up, that way, I believe," Doctor Omega said, consulting his device, and then gesturing towards the mountains.

"I cannot say I like the looks of this place," The bearded corsair said. "There is something… wrong about it. Can't quite put my finger on what…"

"Walk cautiously," Isaac advised, after he had walked out of the surf, wrung out his beard, and joined the search party on the beach.

"There are footprints!" Renard announced, and then pointed up the beach. "And that looks like the remains of a fire!"

"Seems we've reached our destination," Doctor Omega said. "I do agree, those hills look forbidding. Let's begin our search along the beach."

The party soon scattered, Sir Oliver directing his men. Isaac continued to trudge, alone, down the beach.

No matter which direction, everyone kept an eye on the distant hills, as an echoing noise was carried on the wind down to them. It was the cries of some beast that none of them could readily identify.

Soon, Doctor Omega, Renard and Sir Shelfin were left alone, save for the sailor left to guard the boats, contemplating their search plan.

"Which way?" the Lieutenant asked.

Doctor Omega ignored him, holding out his scanner.

"These readings are… odd," he muttered.

Still talking to himself, he began walking away from the beach and into the undergrowth.

"Um…?" Renard said, before scooping up his Lilliputian companion and jogging after the time traveler. He caught up with Doctor Omega just in time to get whipped across the face with a branch.

"Could you be a bit more careful?" he sputtered indignantly, as he spit out leaves, only to nearly collide with the white-haired scientist.

Doctor Omega was standing in the middle of the narrow path with his arms raised. Poking out of the surrounding foliage were a half dozen rifle barrels.

"What the hell…?" Renard muttered.

"Marcel?" A voice from the jungle asked. "Is that you?"

"Monoclard?"

"Put your guns down, you idiots! It's Lieutenant Renard! Marcel!"

A crowd of soldiers came scrambling out of the jungle, crowding the narrow path.

Their uniforms were the same as Renard's, though very worn at the knees and elbows. Several sported makeshift bandages and slings. They looked dirty and thoroughly bedraggled.

While Renard shook hands, slapped shoulders and attempted to explain the situation, Doctor Omega stayed to the side, frowning at his scanner.

Shelfin, perched on Renard's shoulder, clung desperately to the fabric of the uniform tunic, to keep from being flung off.

"How did you find us?" Monoclard asked.

"It was a bit of a trip," Renard replied. "Um… It's difficult to explain."

"Did you bring any bread?" Cipriani, a fellow with a scraggily mustache asked.

"How'd you get past the dragons?"

"I'm sorry… The what?" soldier, savant and Lilliputian asked as one.

"Dragons?" Doctor Omega asked, raising his voice to be heard above the din. "What do you mean by dragons? Not all at once! You, with the bandages on your head, speak up?"

"They… uh… they're huge beasts… like big toads or lizards!"

"You mean, dinosaurs?" Renard asked, wide-eyed. "But, they're all dead!"

"There have been exceptions," Doctor Omega said, casually. "But best if we continued this conversation away from here."

He and Renard helped the soldiers gather their meager supplies and aided those whose wounds kept them from being very mobile.

They soon reached the beach and the long boats.

"Pitt, go find the Captain," Renard said, as they helped his comrades into the boats.

The sailor jogged off down the beach, while the others anxiously scanned their surroundings.

"Dinosaurs!" Renard breathed, a bit awestruck, despite all the wonders he'd already witnessed. "Just out there, in the hills!"

"In the hills?" one portly soldier scoffed. "They are the hills!"

To emphasize the point, there was another distant growl and the hills seemed to tremble.

"Earthquake?" Doctor Omega asked, faintly.

"No," Monoclard said, shaking his head. "*It*'s waking up."

With that, the nearest hill opened its eyes.

The creature was huge: long as the locomotive that had originally taken the soldiers to the front, and standing three stories-tall at the shoulder. It was brown with yellow, stubby tusks, and a long, knobby tail. Its back was a spiked carapace.

The creature stomped forward on four legs, lazy from its nap and possibly in search of breakfast.

"Judging by the serrated teeth, not a herbivore," Doctor Omega said. "Curious, as it resembles an ankylosaurus."

"This is not a university lecture hall," Renard pointed out. "We need to get away! Even if *that* doesn't try to eat us, we could still be trampled!"

The soldiers nodded along in vigorous agreement.

"What?" Doctor Omega asked, distractedly. "Yes, yes, of course. Not to worry, it isn't paying the least bit of attention to us."

It was a sound plan—at least until Captain Tressilian and his party came around the curve of the beach, saw the huge beast, and immediately started firing at it with their muskets.

The bullets were no more than insect bites to such a creature, yet enough to get its attention. The enormous long snout turned and beady eyes took in the tiny, scurrying forms. With a snort that shook the trees, it lumbered towards the beach.

"Oh, dear," Doctor Omega said.

The soldiers and sailors used slightly less delicate language. Most of them rushed to the boats, while a couple reloaded and continued to fire.

"What is that thing?" Sir Oliver asked.

He had drawn his cutlass, but it hung loosely at his side, as he had realized its pointlessness.

"No time for explanations," Renard said, addressing Doctor Omega rather than the Captain. "To the ship!"

"That beast could easily chase us back to the *Rose Hawk*," Sir Oliver said, with grim practicality. "Take your foundlings in one boat. We will hold it off, and then follow after."

"They can't do this," Renard said, grabbing Doctor Omega's arm. "Even if we give them our army rifles, that thing will kill them. It's idiocy!"

"I hate to intrude!" Shelfin shouted, from Renard's shoulder, "but, if we lead the beast back to the ship, we could all end up stranded here!"

"I will keep the creature occupied," Isaac said, as he walked past them. "Get everyone away. This is no place for men."

They began to protest, but Doctor Omega silenced them with a glare and a gesture, before following after the tall immortal.

"Are you sure about this?" he asked, eyeing the steadily approaching behemoth.

"You know well that I am invulnerable to any and all earthly threats," Isaac said, a touch sadly.

"Yes, but I am not entirely convinced the inhabitants of this island are of an earthly nature."

"Well then, that should make it interesting," Isaac replied, with a small, sardonic smile. "Till we meet again, Omega."

Doctor Omega stood, watching Isaac Laquedem walk off. He nodded to himself and returned to the boats.

"Well?" the Captain asked.

"Isaac will deal with that thing and give us the time we need to set sail or whatever term you use." he explained. "Once we're away from this island, we should be fine. Well, don't just stand there!"

Soon, the two boats were loaded and the men frantically worked the oars, intently and worriedly, watching the lone figure striding determinedly towards the angry monster.

Back on the beach, Isaac spared the boats a glance and then turned his focus back to the enormous creature. Even at seven foot-tall, he had to crane his neck upwards, as it drew closer.

"Yes, this should be interesting," he said, tucking his hat into his satchel and adjusting his grip on his staff.

Back on the ship, the men scattered. The sailors frantically prepared for departure, while Renard found space for his comrades in the hull.

Sir Shelfin leapt from the soldier to Doctor Omega's shoulder and the odd duo stood at the rail, gazing at the dwindling island, listening to the distant sounds of combat.

By nightfall, the *Rose Hawk* was far from the island and on its way to rendezvous with Professor Helvetius on Villings Island. The white-haired time traveler was seated in a rickety deck chair, allowing himself to nod off, now that his task was near completion. A heavy, tattered volume, full of his scribbles concerning the journey, lay in his lap.

"Aren't you chilly out here?" a voice asked.

"Hmmm? What? No," Omega replied, blinking away his sleepiness. "The sea breeze is quite refreshing... Ah, it's you."

The ghostly form of young Lotte stood at his side.

"And what have you been up to, young lady? Not pestering the crew?"

"No, I just wanted to pass along a message. My father has left the island of monsters."

"None the worse for wear, I hope?" asked the Doctor.

"He wanted me to tell you, his day of rest is approaching and so he won't be rejoining you. He spotted an island that he thought he would pass the day on."

"He has more than earned it. What of you? Playing messenger and frightening sailors is no way for a young lady to spend her time."

The petite specter shrugged.

"Well, I myself have some leisure time," Doctor Omega smiled, sitting up. "Fancy a game of checkers?"

In this tale, Atom Bezecny revisits Orpheus, *a 1950 French film directed by Jean Cocteau and starring Jean Marais. It is the central part of a trilogy, which consists of* The Blood of a Poet *(1930),* Orpheus *(1950), and* The Testament of Orpheus *(1960), all inspired by the ancient myth of Orpheus, and already adapted by Cocteau in an eponymous play in 1926. The film embroiders on the theme of the hero's relationship with Death and takes place at an undetermined time, in neutral contemporary settings with fantastic sequences. Death here is a pale-faced woman played by Maria Casarès, who is accompanied in her works by two motorcyclists, who intervene where she must operate. Her mission orders are transmitted to her by "personal messages" of the style of those used on Radio London during the World War II. If she keeps her aura and her mystery in the world of the living, in the Beyond, she is considered as a mere agent working for a mysterious celestial bureaucracy...*

Atom Mudman Bezecny: *Orpheus Omega*

Orpheus cursed. "That machine of yours has really done it this time, Doctor."

Doctor Omega ran a hand through his slicked-back silvery hair. "I can't understand it," he whispered. "I just can't understand it."

"I know I'm not the first to tell you that you can't control that thing. And when it has the ability to go anywhere, anywhen, that's nothing short of a recipe for disaster."

Omega withheld his usual retort, that he could, in fact, steer the *Cosmos*, but it was just too finicky at times.

His vessel had taken them to a strange place indeed, a place so strange he was at a loss for words. He couldn't recognize the burning ruined city that surrounded him—not from any era in Earth's history, and not from any of the alien worlds he had visited in his travels. This wasn't unusual by itself—

what was truly bizarre was the odd feeling in the air. It was a feeling which he knew it would be foolish to ignore, even though he didn't know what it was.

The man known as Orpheus, as a French poet, was able to find the words that Omega could not.

"This place doesn't seem *real*," he said, in that bitter tone of his. "It feels like how I feel when I'm lost in the rush of writing a poem. It's like this is a place of *ideas*—a domain of the human mind."

The Doctor took a while to answer. "As advanced as my ship may be, I don't believe it possesses the power to enter realms that lack physical substance," he said finally.

"Are you sure about that? When I first started traveling with you, you called your ship a possibility machine. And you've always said it could go *anywhere*. Forgive me, but is it not possible that even metaphorical realms are within its reach?"

The Doctor did not answer. In part, this was because these ruins reminded him of the cities he'd seen destroyed by the multitude of evils that he seemed destined to battle again and again. But beyond that, he had an odd certainty that Orpheus was right. Somehow, the ship *had* taken them in a place which didn't really exist.

That was a contradiction in terms—at least, at first glance. Nonexistent places, the Doctor realized, had to exist in some form, being defined by their nonexistence. The only true nonexistent places were ones that had not yet been defined, not yet thought of, or imagined...

He pulled at his lapels and sniffed. That line of thinking was more in Orpheus' department than his own. He was a scientist, and he knew there had to be a scientific explanation for this mysterious realm, beyond the subjective terms of the mind.

"I suppose if these are questions we want to answer... There's nothing we can do but try to learn what we can of our surroundings," he said.

"Let's be careful," Orpheus replied, gesturing toward the falling flames and burning rubble.

Without a further word, the two travelers set out into the dreary landscape.

The air hung quiet as they walked. Their feet carried them for miles, over the course of what felt like hours. There was no variance in their surroundings. Wherever they went, there found only smashed buildings burning in the night. The ground was blasted and seared, as if with struck with an atomic bomb. The ship's scanner had detected no hazardous radiations, but the Doctor knew he could never be too careful.

"This place reminds me of a strange dream I once had," Orpheus said at last. "I don't know why, because it doesn't resemble the dream at all. I was in a far-off place which I didn't recognize. I watched as lamp-light glittered off the casing and lens of a great telescope. It must have been some sort of observatory. In that place, I was visited by a strange figure, who came to me dressed in the clothes of an 18th century aristocrat—his coat was two hundred years out of style, and he had a powdered wig and tricorn hat. He spoke to me about the nature of imagination, and imagination's relationship with death, and time. He had traveled through time to meet me, past the historical point of his own death. He told me such amazing things about art and poetry, which I'm realizing I can only just now remember..."

"Yes, my memory is tickled too... it must be something in the air. I remember when I wore a tricorn hat, when I looked a little different. Perhaps I was the one in your dream..." The Doctor shook his head. "No, that's ridiculous. That never happened. Least of all because I have never changed. Not since I was..."

"Born?" Orpheus suggested.

"Yes, something like that," the Doctor grumbled back. "There must be answer to what happened to this place. Perhaps somewhere, beyond this city, we can find someone living..."

Orpheus, who was looking behind the Doctor, let out a small gasp. He pointed off in the distance, and Omega whirled around to look at what he'd seen. From the basement of one of the ruined buildings, a figure was emerging. A woman with a pale face, dressed in black, with the bearing of a princess.

Once she came into full view, she stared at the two men. "Back again, Orpheus?" she mused. "And you, Doctor... I did not think it was yet your time."

"My time?" asked Doctor Omega. "Do you know me, young lady?"

"I do... though, like Orpheus here, you probably don't remember me." The dark-dressed woman grinned wickedly. "The mind is a fragile thing. It blocks out everything it fears— and there is nothing it fears more than its own nonexistence. It is therefore difficult to remember one's brushes with Death."

Orpheus at once seemed to understand.

"You claim to be Death, young lady?" Omega scoffed. "Death is not a person. It is a natural phenomenon, without persona or soul."

"Did I say I had a soul? Did I say I was a person? You are curious as ever, Doctor—both in that you desire answers, and in that you're a curiosity yourself. I sense in you the questions which only dead men have the wisdom to ask. But like I said, it is not your time, and you are still living..."

"I know this woman, Doctor," Orpheus said then. "I knew her as the Princess, but she *is* Death. At least, she is Death in a shape you and I can comprehend." He paused a moment, before saying: "Don't you remember, Doctor? I have been dead all this time."

The Doctor shuddered.

"You can't be dead, Orpheus. If you are, how did you come to travel aboard my ship?" the Doctor asked. "What about our journey to Tormance, or our battle with the mad poet Glenarvon—?"

"You intercepted me, on my way to... this place. To the Underworld," Orpheus interrupted. "I died before, but I was allowed to come back. I was returning to Death because the life I went back to was only an illusion. I couldn't look upon my own wife, Eurydice, even though I was reunited with her. And so I have decided now to face my eternal end."

He looked firmly then at the Princess who was Death. "Do you still love me?" he asked.

"In this iteration, perhaps I do," she replied.

"I can accept that," the poet said then, gaining the first hint of hope Omega had seen in him. "Come with us, Doctor. I'm sure a being of your stature won't need to *remain* in the Underworld. You could just visit and leave again, under your own power."

"The Doctor is always welcome in my domain," said the Princess, continuing to smile. Once more, a chill ran down Omega's spine.

And yet, his eternal curiosity—the source of all his glories and failures—tugged at him. The Underworld? That was something he had to see.

Nodding his head slowly, like he was dreaming, the Doctor agreed to the offer.

The Princess led the two travelers back towards the dark from whence she came. At first, it seemed only to be a little enclosure, but soon the darkness within it yawned up and swallowed them. The Doctor realized that they had passed into the ice-cold night of the afterlife. He reached out, seeking something familiar—matter, form, shape, time—but none of them greeted his senses. In moments, he was completely unaware of how far he had traveled into the void, whether it was yards or miles.

But his will was strong. He clutched his fists tight, feeling the cold metal of his signet ring press against the palm and fingers of his left hand. So long as he resisted giving in to this place—whatever that meant in the moment—he could endure and survive.

He realized he was slipping away into Death—dying. But as the Princess herself had said, it was not yet his time. Though he was standing close to Death, he was not yet dead. Now he knew that he had stood many times before next to her, without knowing it. Sometimes, out of the corner of his eye, he had glimpsed her—but only for a moment.

"What purpose can there be in this place?" he inquired. "What could one possibly learn here?"

"There is no purpose in Death," the Princess said, "save to be dead. There is nothing to learn, save for the meaning of nothingness."

This idea horrified Doctor Omega, who had always delighted in the *fullness* of existence. To face emptiness was a terror that he had never before fathomed.

But he would not give in to that terror without challenging it, interrogating it. He sensed *something* within this place, beyond the darkness, and that something called to him. All he had to do was answer the call. His thoughts strained against the void, as if he was locking it in a mind-bending contest. After much struggle, his mental grip triumphed, and he was able to speak his piece.

"I have always believed, at heart, that time is cyclical in nature," the Doctor pronounced. "I believe that Omega is Alpha, that the end is the beginning. Many fixtures within time are as circular as is the timestream that cradles them. Extremes are not opposite each other—they are adjacent. The point of ending and beginning occupy one simultaneous point. This is clearly a world where conventional reality does not exist. And without reality, we are close to these cosmic extremes. Within this nothingness there is... everythingness. And vice versa."

Though he could not see her, Death once more grinned at him.

"Yes, Doctor, we are bodiless here, without substance or matter, and that opens us up to all kinds of infinities. You truly are a wise man, for you know how to walk to Heaven from Hell."

"Doctor...?" Orpheus whispered, from the darkness.

"I will not deny you your final rest, my boy," Omega assured him. "But I wish to see the realm of Life before I leave your company." He gazed at where he thought he'd heard

Death's voice. "That is what that place could be called, correct? If this is the realm of Death?"

"Life, creation, imagination—death, entropy, oppression. These are two sides of the same coin. And yet, I cannot accompany you to the realm of Imagination," the Princess said. "I am bound here. Instead, you must seek another guide."

The Doctor was at the point where he didn't feel like questioning the idea of a "spirit guide," though the urge tugged at him.

Suddenly, he could see in the dark, and became aware that there were now two Orpheuses. But as he gazed upon the second "Orpheus," the Doctor realized that he wasn't Orpheus at all. In fact, he wasn't even human. Instead, he looked to be like some sort of alien—a bestial humanoid, a man sporting features of a bear and a wolf. This Beast seemed embittered by Omega staring at him.

"Are you the one guiding me into Imagination?" the Doctor asked.

"Yes," the Beast growled. "I am a native of that realm—I am something of a spirit of magic."

"Magic?" Omega chuckled. "My dear boy, I am afraid that even with all this, I am still not a believer in magic. What we are experiencing right now may be a different form of reality than that in which I normally reside, but to dismiss the qualities of this world as magic seems overly simplistic."

"You deceive yourself, Monsieur le Docteur. Inside, you are still the child who dreamed of magic and wonder. We all are, no matter how many years or centuries may pass."

The Beast began to walk away, leading Omega and Orpheus away from Death's company.

"When I was a child, I was uneducated. My sense of the universe was vague," the Doctor said.

"And yet, you dreamed of exploring it. Were those dreams not magical?"

The Doctor couldn't say they weren't. While he prided himself on what he had learned as a grownup, everything that he was today was because of the childish giddiness that had thrived in his soul. No matter how hard he tried, that side of him was always stronger than the old man on the outside, who often denied things out of hand from pure stubbornness.

Now, the world around him was lightning, its dark burden releasing from his shoulders. Only then did he realize how afraid he had been, sensing the closeness of Death. In an instant, she was gone, and reality changed again.

They stood in the corridor of a building, which resembled to Omega's eyes a hotel from early 20th century Earth. Doors lined the hallway, and the Beast strode confidently past them, speaking to his guests as he moved.

"This is where magic is alive and well. It's like a studio—artists of the Beyond live within these rooms and create their scenes and situations. But unlike in the real world, here, there are no limits on what they can create."

He opened one of the doors and bid the Doctor and Orpheus to look inside.

Inside was a young man working on a painting of a human figure, whose face he was now detailing. Slowly and meticulously, he shaped the image's mouth. He glanced away for a moment, and to the Doctor and Orpheus' befuddlement and horror, the mouth began to move, as if straining to speak. The artist looked back up at his work and observed this miraculous change. He moved his hand up to the canvas and tried to wipe the mouth away, but instead the pigments transferred to his hand, and the orifice continued to try to speak, as part of his body.

"Here, there is no division between reality and imagination," the Beast said, "just as in Death, there is no division between reality and oppression. Here, creation is reality, and in Death, there is not even the concept of freedom. Creation is the antithesis of Death because Death is Entropy. The Creation of new matter, new energy, with *ideas*, is the antithesis of Entropy's gnawing cancer. Creation is Life within Entropy."

"And yet, these realms are only accessible to the dead," Orpheus said. "To those who have forsaken matter."

Doctor Omega looked at his companion with a sharp look. "What do you mean by that?"

Neither figure answered—instead, the Beast led them further down the hall.

"There is more," he said, opening more doors.

The two travelers observed a man slicing open a woman's eye with a straight razor, and a figure resembling Christ leading a young woman back inside a blood-soaked castle. Other images included strange, impossible deserts, oozing clocks, and spinning wheels of yin-yang light.

"Here, freedom thrives, almost to the point of exhaustion. If you were to gaze downward into this world, you would see more minute fairy-scenes playing out, losing their imaginal qualities as they spiral down into material reality."

"I feel it, Doctor," Orpheus said. "Here, one can do *anything*. That Zone, the one which preceded the Underworld, nearly had the same properties, but *this*..."

He raised his hand, and from the floor of the corridor rose a sphere, pulled from the raw matter of the tile. He moved his fingers, and the sphere became a pyramid, and then an octahedron. This shape then turned into a bundle of roses, which tumbled gently to the floor. Orpheus laughed, delighted by the power in his hands.

"And there are places on Earth where rabbit-holes open into this world," the Beast said. "How they were opened, I know not. But if you wish, Doctor, that is your explanation for magic, on Earth at least. The 'wizards' of the world ventured into places where they could work their will without limits."

"I have heard of such a place in Russia," Orpheus said, "though I have no idea who I heard about it from. They say that a meteor crashed there, or maybe aliens, and created a Zone. And at the center of that Zone is a Room, where one's innermost wishes come true."

"I have never heard of such mysteries in all my travels on Earth," the Doctor confessed.

As he spoke, he felt a strange nausea well up in him—for a moment, it felt like his body was wearing thin. He frowned, but only for a split second. But the Beast had seen the lapse of strength in his eyes.

"You should not be here, Doctor," he said. "Admittedly, in describing these realms, I have been bound to the limits of human language. It is easy to think of this bright place as the realm of Life and that dark void at the home of Death. But both of these places are immaterial. They are outside of that which sustains your form."

"Of course," Omega mused. "How could magic and imagination be bound to physical substance? I suppose then I have been wandering here bodiless, like you, or else, some fluke of nature has allowed my form to endure here. But I cannot stay permanently, I presume?"

"No. If you remain here, you will become a fictional character. In fact, that is one of the less horrible fates that awaits a living man here." The Beast sighed. "There are some apotheoses that mortals, even ones who are nigh-immortal, cannot face in life. There are some stories that don't shine until after their author is dead."

"Hmm, yes... I believe that the only way to live forever is to leave something that people will remember. We become immortal by the good we do, and the lives we change. Even if we reach a point where we cannot recognize ourselves—some fragment of who we once were remains in those who remember us, promising buried hope." The Doctor giggled. "I realize that this atmosphere is toxic to me, sir, but I must confess it has been quite some time since I've enjoyed such enlightening discourse."

"You may not remember this conversation when you leave," the Beast warned.

"Oh, but that doesn't mean it didn't happen." Once more the Doctor tugged at his lapels. He turned to face Orpheus. "My dear boy," he said, "I believe this is where we part ways. This is where you belong. Here, you can capture all human experience in your poetry."

Orpheus laughed. "Even in eternity, my friend, there is not enough time for that."

The Doctor shook his hand and bid him goodbye. This was, for Orpheus, a fine ending. By the time the Doctor turned his back, his shade would have faded away, looking for a room in which to get to work.

Omega turned back to the Beast.

"Will you do me the service of escorting me back to my ship?"

"Through here," the Beast growled, opening one of the hallway doors.

The Doctor peered into the room, and to his surprise, he saw the familiar shape of the *Cosmos* within. He did not question how it came here from the Zone outside the Underworld.

He started to say goodbye to the Beast, but before he could speak the Beast interrupted him. "There is no need to show me good sentiment, Monsieur le Docteur—I am a simple Beast. It is my lot to suffer, until a young maiden sets me free. Over and over again, all throughout history, I am reborn, fated to no kindness but that of my *belle*."

"I will thank you all the same, sir, for what you have done for me. I do not believe in any fate that denies one kindness."

The Beast, for the first time, seemed taken aback. The Doctor was not a young maiden—though maybe once he had been, a very long time ago. Regardless, he had acted outside of the cyclical loop which the Beast considered the primal definition of his life—the entirety of his power.

"Perhaps you do belong here after all, Doctor—you are a creature of magic."

The Doctor did not believe that to be so, but now as he surveyed his ship, he wondered if maybe, somehow, the *Cosmos* had been pulled from this realm. It was, as he once told Orpheus, a possibility machine.

In many ways, the ship was like a poem, or a painting—a window into the infinite.

As he stepped aboard, he realized he wouldn't be leaving this place at all, so long as he had his vessel. And in a sense, that meant he'd always carry with him a part of Orpheus, whom he already missed.

Full disclosure: an earlier and slightly different version of this story was originally published in my Prisoner *fanzine,* Rover *No. 5, in 1980 under the title "Encounter at night"...*

Jean-Marc Lofficier: *Foiled Again*

The Village, 1966

No. 6 was walking on the beach. Far behind him, the Village slept. Even those-who-never-slept, the Supervisors, did not care about his lone escapade into the night. Where could he go?

As he walked on the beach, his face was creased with deep thought-lines, thoughts of escape, of freedom...

Suddenly, he heard a clanking, groaning sound, one that broke through the slow whisper of the waves.

A shell-shaped silhouette cut against the dark horizon. There, in front of him, stood an anachronism, a thing that belonged to a world he had never known. It looked like a huge cannon shell, one that could have been fired by the legendary German *Big Bertha* of World War I; but that "shell" had portholes in it, and a door.

The door opened and an old man got out. He was dressed in old-fashioned, turn of the century clothes and wore shoulder-length white hair with a rebellious lock jutting out of his forehead.

"This is not Normandy," he said, looking around him with displeasure.

"Who are you?" asked No. 6.

"Me? I am usually known as Doctor Omega. May I enquire as to your own identity, sir?"

A few thoughts crossed in No. 6's paranoid mind: Who was this stranger? Could he trust him? Was he with *them*?

But somehow, something in the Doctor's sparkling eyes must have reached the Prisoner's soul, for the man known only as Number 6 smiled back, and not one of his canary-swallowing smiles that he kept for his captors.

He offered his hand in trust and began:

"I used to be called..."

"Wait!" the Doctor interrupted. "There is a. high energy concentration nearby. It is coming closer..."

Rover suddenly burst out of the sea and rolled towards them at great speed, roaring.

"Fascinating," whispered the Doctor, not in the least afraid of the Village's guardian.

"You know what that thing is?" No. 6 asked.

"Oh, yes. But I never met one before on this planet. I never dreamed that you Earthmen were so advanced..."

"Did you say 'planet?' 'Earthmen?'"

"This is all very interesting, my dear fellow, but your watery friend will do us a lot of harm if we don't go back to my ship at once. Come, follow me!"

No. 6 looked at Rover which was almost on them. He had seen what the thing could do before. But... to get into a cannon shell?

He stepped in, just as the Doctor was going to get out again to get him.

Inside the shell, much to his surprise, he found several small rooms and, up a metal ladder, a brightly lit control room with a console, two rows of two chairs, one large round porthole and two smaller ones on each side.

"Where am I?"

"In the *Cosmos*," the Doctor answered matter-of-factly, as if it explained everything. "And just in time, I see."

On the screen, No. 6 could see Rover trying to push against the metal ship—without any success.

"Fascinating," muttered the Doctor again. "Well, enough time lost as it is. Off we go!"

He pulled a lever, pushed a couple of buttons, and several lights started flashing on and off. The beach started fading from the portholes.

"Where do you want to go, my boy?" Doctor Omega asked the Prisoner.

"You mean, we have left the Village?"

"The Village? Oh, that place. Yes, of course. We are now, er, let me see, hmm, slightly off course again, but nothing too serious. You see, I have to go back to 1906 Normandy. It is a fairly urgent matter. I left my friend Monsieur Borel in charge of my house in my absence, and as is his wont, he touched something she shouldn't have and released a Horla..." Then, as an afterthought, he added: "The damn thing has been tormenting a poor man named Simon Cordier. I must do something for him before it's too late..."

No. 6 stopped the man who called himself "Doctor" (but was he really a man?) before he got totally lost in his train of thoughts.

"So you are a time traveler?"

"Well, yes, my boy, wasn't it obvious?"

"And we are going to, er, Normandy in 1906 in that machine of yours?" the Prisoner said, persistent.

"Yes, this 'machine,' as you put it, is extremely reliable."

Suddenly, the lights on the console started blinking. A blue streak appeared on the front porthole.

"What is this, hmm?... A time-leash! Incredible!"

The *Cosmos* slowed to a standstill, then started to shudder. Like a broken stretch band, a quick backward motion snowballed into a frenzied acceleration.

"What's happening, Doctor?" asked No. 6. "Is there something wrong?"

"It is a time-leash! Babelian technology! We're being dragged back through the aether to your Village."

"Can we do anything about it?"

The Doctor started punching out buttons. "Yes, yes, we can escape—but only by disrupting totally our space-time-coordinates," he replied in an irritated tone. "We shall plunge into another galaxy, another universe perhaps. It'll be quite a strain on the *Cosmos*, but I will not submit..."

A firm hand gripped the Doctor's arm as he was inputing the course changes.

"No, it's me they want. Not you. The Village wants its Prisoner back."

"But you *can* escape! Just let me fix the coordinates..."

"Could you return us to Earth? To London in 1966? Or Normandy in 1906?"

"In time, yes. I would have to fix the *Cosmos*, of course, but..."

"Then return me to the Village and go. You have better things to do."

"But you want to be free. I can give you the freedom of the stars. You can roam with me; we will see the wonders of the Universe..."

"No, Doctor, I want freedom, it is true, but I want it to be able to return and destroy the Village and all that it represents. Erase it from the face of the Earth. This is my duty, my sole responsibility, and I cannot be free from i—ever. No, Doctor, I cannot take your freedom."

The Doctor looked deep into the eyes of the Prisoner.

"I understand. So be it."

Then he turned towards the console again.

"Come on, Old Thing, quick!" he said flippantly.

But the look in his eyes was anything but flippant.

It is rather unusual to see characters created by Arthur C. Clarke show up in Tales of the Shadowmen. *But Nigel Malcom rises up to the challenge with...*

Nigel Malcolm: *When the Children Leave Home*

The *Cosmos* shook as Doctor Omega frantically worked the controls. They rode the space storm together. He had suddenly come across some invisible force—something new and unwieldy.

"This storm is too powerful!" said Omega. "I can't get anywhere near Earth-119901125664 before its destruction! Any suggestions?"

He was speaking to Thea, a robotic head mounted on a special resting hook on the console, who was plugged directly into the ship's instruments.

"Gravitational forces are random and currently seven hundred times more powerful that the *Cosmos'* ability to withstand them," the robotic head replied.

Omega finally pulled one last lever and the ship came to a rest.

"That's the best I can do," he said, grumbling. "Aethereal ambit. At least, it'll give us time to get our bearings."

He sat there looking at the controls for a moment, before the penny dropped and he looked at Thea suspiciously.

"What did you mean, gravitational forces are random?"

"Analysis shows that the gravitational forces are fluctuating without consistency," replied Thea.

"But surely, there must be some pattern to it," muttered the Doctor. "We may as well all pack up and go home if we can't rely on the Laws of Physics anymore!"

"There is simply not enough data to discern logical patterns," said Thea.

Doctor Omega paused for a moment and sighed.

"I see," he said more calmly. "I'm sorry, Thea, I shouldn't have snapped at you. Please forgive an old duffer." He then changed the subject. "Let's focus our attention on the planet's surface. Is there anything noteworthy about the destruction of this particular Earth?"

As he asked, he flicked a few switches on the control console. New readings and images flickered in front of them.

"There appears to be a high level of energy, manifesting itself in an aurora of light. Much of it is in a condensed upward motion."

"Hmm… A column of energy," murmured the Doctor, summarizing the robot's description.

He typed a command into the console computer with his bony fingers. Ticker tape rattled out. He tore a strip off, read it, and gasped in horror.

"That energy is… people!"

He checked the readings further, and asked the robot to analyze the energy patterns again. More ticker tape came out. He read the latest printout, and compared it to the first.

"This is extraordinary. It looks like a tree made of human energy. So that's what has become of the human race here, hmm?"

The Doctor considered the instruments in front of him and wondered if he ought to look at a visual image of the phenomenon, or not. He'd seen plenty of horrific sights in his long life, and it probably wouldn't be very long before he saw more. He didn't have to go looking for them.

He turned to Thea.

"Are there any…" he searched for the right word, "…corporeal human beings left?"

"Scans indicate that there is one person. A human being is sending a transmission to an alien spaceship," said Thea.

There was a split second, and then Doctor Omega sprang into action, activating the *Cosmos'* communications unit and tuning it in on the source of the transmission.

"Let's try to eavesdrop," he said.

"Doctor, did you not once tell me that eavesdroppers never hear any good of themselves?" asked Thea.

"Well, yes, yes, but never mind that now," replied the Doctor, irritably.

They picked up, through the crackle and with a bit of fine-tuning, a monologue from the last man on Earth. As he described what was happening around him, Omega and Thea watched as the outer surface of the planet began to fade and dissolve.

With a jolt, the Doctor stood up. Then, he sat down again, looking intently at the controls. Thea could tell that he was working out how to get down to the surface and rescue the last man—whose name they now knew was Jan Rodricks. She had to intervene:

"Please do not disable the hostile action protocols, Doctor. Without them, these forces will rip the *Cosmos* apart, killing you and destroying me. You cannot save Jan Rodricks."

The Doctor clenched his fists in frustration. That frustration turned to horror as he saw on the screen in front of them the Earth's outer layers fade into transparency and vanish, unleashing the inner core. This lit up very brightly before burning out. It, too, disappeared. And then, there was nothing left.

Omega sat back, looking at the emptiness thoughtfully. He put his finger on his upper lip. He became aware that it was rough. He then felt his chin and realized that it had been a long time since he had last shaved. Piloting a space/time vehicle made it easy to lose track of time, ironically enough. It was probably very late at night for his own biological clock.

He suddenly felt a little hungry and thirsty. He got up and walked over to a little side table where there was a decanter with some water and a glass tumbler upside down over the rim. Omega picked up the tumbler and poured out a near glass full of water. The decanter was now empty.

As he drank the lukewarm water, he looked at the blackboard next to it. It had two tallies chalked up on it. One marked *Earths Saved*, and the other *People Rescued*. It reflected a long day of hopping across diverging timelines and dimensions, preventing the end of different Earths and differ-ent people—sometimes rescuing alternate versions of the same individuals.

"Well, I suppose I've mostly succeeded," he said. "Eight Earths and seventy-eight people relocated to new homes. That isn't a bad day's work. What a pity to end the day on a disap-pointing note."

Omega finished his water and put the tumbler down.

"Thea, check our systems while I trace the destination of that signal," he commanded. He swiftly tapped a few keys, and laid in some co-ordinates.

"Valve eight has reached 98% of its lifecycle," said Thea.

"Has it indeed? Hmm. Well, let's give it an excuse to go out in a blaze of glory, shall we?"

He suddenly pulled a lever, and the *Cosmos* spun round and shot off through the juddering remains of the solar system.

"Possibly even back to our own Normandy afterwards for some beef bourguignon and a glass of wine." he added.

Somewhere near Pluto the spaceship was stationary, pointing towards the third planet and observing its disappear-ance. Moments afterwards, the ship turned around in the direc-tion of the Overlords' home world and engaged its stardrive.

On its bridge, chief supervisor Karellen looked thought-fully at the big screen, watching the Sun disappear into the distance. As he looked, he mentally saluted those people of Earth. The rest of the ship's crew knew not to disturb him in these moments. Leaving a race that had successfully ascended to the Overmind was always a time of mixed emotions.

Nothing disturbed Karellen's reverie until he heard the invasive wheezing, groaning sound.

He looked around. The other Overlords on the bridge were glancing anxiously at each other. In one corner of the bridge, its metal grey clashing with the metal green walls, was a spaceship. A bizarre looking thing, like a primitive rocket built by a child.

An old man with a lock of unruly white hair marched out and stood looking at them. He drew himself up to his full height and put his hands on his lapels.

"You're a dashed difficult fellow to keep up with." he said.

Karellen looked at this intruder. He had studied humanoids for long enough to realize that while his bluster was clearly a front; this crazy man was not fazed by the Overlords' devilish appearance. He seemed to take no notice of their horns, tails, red skin, or the fact that they were all much taller than him.

Also, despite his appearance, the intruder was not from Earth. The ship, and the man's demeanor, suggested another race. Maybe one he was familiar with.

"It's all right," said Karellen to the rest of the crew. "Stand down. This person is harmless. Resume your duties."

The bridge crew went back to their assigned tasks. Some immediately. Some hesitantly, as though expecting this intruder might suddenly turn violent.

"My men are harmless and unarmed. Who are you?" Karellen asked.

"I, sir, am Doctor Omega. And who might you be?"

"My name is Karellen."

"And are you responsible for the destruction of this Earth?"

Doctor Omega's question was loaded with anger. Karellen chose his words carefully:

"I am the supervisor of the project to help the human race evolve to the point where it could ascend to join the Overmind."

Omega took a couple of steps forward.

"So that's what you call it, hmm?"

"Did you watch the people of Earth as they ascended?" asked Karellen.

"Yes, I did. That's millions of years of development and growth now up in smoke." That hard edge returned to Omega's voice.

257

Karellen responded calmly.

"On the contrary, it is the conclusion of millions of years of development and growth. It is the next stage in their evolution."

"That is death! Genocide!"

"They are beyond death," said Karellen, before his tone changed to curiosity. "I think I know your race. They made incredible advances in their technology and civilization. They can traverse all of space and time. And yet, like my own race, they cannot evolve any further than they have. Both your people and mine have become stuck at an impasse."

At this, the old man seemed to almost jump in revolt. He took a step back. His body language adopted a more defensive tone.

"Impossible. My people have evolved over billions of years!"

Karellen knew this, of course, but decided to politely ignore it. He continued:

"As a matter of fact, I seem to remember that the Overlords considered coming to your homeworld. They even sent out ships. But the Overmind instructed us to go away and leave you untouched. We assumed it was because either your people didn't need our help, or because you were in no position to even be helped."

Omega drew himself up to his full height again.

"My people do not need your help sir. And to meddle with their affairs would cause some very dire consequences. Not just for us, but for every other planet in the universe. Tell me; what are your plans now? Hmm?"

"We will return to my home planet. From there, I will no doubt get instructions to go to another planet and help their species' progress," said Karellen.

"And how would you like it if your own civilization was 'helped' to join this 'Overmind'?" asked Omega, who was clearly hoping this was a master card to play in the argument.

Karellen sighed.

"I would like that very much," he said sadly. "Doctor, you seem to be afraid of what you see as death. I think that is because you see it as the end. You are a man of science, and I suspect you are also a widely traveled man. Does it not occur to you that something as complex and diverse as the universe—with its measures and counterbalances—could lead to something more than the end? We only see what we can see from our limited perspective. Even you, from your point of view, can only perceive a limited amount." He looked directly at Omega. "The Overmind is not the end. It is the beginning of something else."

The Doctor just stood there. For once, he was lost for words.

"Go home, Doctor Omega," continued Karellen. "Or resume your travels. There is nothing you can do for us. Nor your own people. My race means other races no harm. We are merely helping them."

"Very well," said Omega at last. Then in one last impotent gesture he raised his index finger and added: "But I will be watching you so-called 'Overlords', and if you meddle in the affairs of other planets, then I will step in and meddle with yours! Good day to you, sir!"

He turned round and quickly stepped back into the *Cosmos* before Karellen could respond. Even though the Overlord did not intend to.

A moment later, the *Cosmos* vanished.

Back at his controls, Doctor Omega flew his craft away from the Overlords' spaceship, and steered it back to early 20th century Normandy. His Normandy.

He didn't speak a word to Thea, who just remained perched on the console, looking at him in silence.

With the co-ordinates set, Omega then slumped back in the chair, and rubbed his eyes wearily. He remained slumped as he weakly pulled out a handkerchief and fumbled with his pince-nez, cleaning them.

He looked over at the blackboard, with its *Earths Saved* tally and its *Last People Rescued* tally.

He was so young. He still had so much to learn.

In the last issue of Tales of the Shadowmen*, Travis Hiltz brought to an end the various misadventures and schemes of the time-meddling Rotwang...*

Travis Hiltz: *The Ghosts of Gascony*

Gascony, 1650

Dusk was approaching, as Porthos steered his road-weary horse towards the tavern. It was a humble, rustic, one story structure, sagging with its years of service.

He was a large man, made of equal quantities muscle and fat. His clothes, though covered with the dust of the road, were of fine quality, if not of current fashion.

Removing his wide-brimmed hat, he used it to dust himself off. A ragged, barefoot stable boy came jogging out, and skidded to a halt. He peered up at the new arrival.

"Close your mouth, lad," Porthos admonished, absently brushing at his sleeve. "Unless it is open because you are offering to care for my horse or recommend the fare and drink of this tavern. Otherwise, you'll catch flies."

"Uh...," The boy replied, originally impressed by the size and build of the traveler and now slightly confused by his speech.

With a slight chuckle, Porthos, handed the reins to the lad. He felt a tug on his sleeve.

"Careful, lad, that's Portuguese silk."

The boy cocked his head, indicating the musketeer should follow him. Puzzled, Porthos returned his hat to his head and followed, as the stable boy lead his horse around the back of the tavern.

"Where are we going?" he asked, in as quiet a tone as he could muster. He felt something clandestine was occurring, but was just baffled as to what that thing was.

"Come with me," the boy replied, in a nervous hush.

"Why...?"

"He said to look for the giant with a beard and a hat." the boy replied, looking pointedly upwards at the tall musketeer, his need of a shave and his hat.

Feeling a touch self-conscious, Porthos, removed his hat again, and ran a hand through his hair.

He had come to Gascony to join his comrade, D'Artagnan, at the latter's family castle. He could think of no one else that might wish to rendezvous with him, beside his friend, and was quite puzzled how D'Artagnan could have known that his fool horse would take the wrong road and he'd end up at this rustic hovel.

Shrugging his broad shoulders, Porthos plodded along, too tired and hungry to question further.

The barn behind the tavern was, if anything, even more worn and rundown. If time had weighed heavy on the tavern, it had mistakenly sat upon the barn. Its thatched roof was sagging, and its walls seemed to be struggling to stay straight and upright.

Porthos frowned, concerned that if the cooking was on the same level as the carpentry, his stay was not going to be enjoyable.

He ducked to enter the building, and, after watching the young peasant stabling his horse, the musketeer peered around the shadowy interior. He saw no one else, but spotted a comfortable looking haybale on which to rest, while he waited.

He was brushing dust off his hat and adjusting the plume, when he felt the knife pressed against his throat.

"Who sent you?" a hushed voice asked. "What have you done with Isaac?"

"I had heard much of Gascon hospitality," Porthos sighed. "I must speak to D'Artagnan about his countrymen."

He moved as though to replace his hat and instead swatted his assailant. Sputtering, the knife-wielder stumbled backwards. Porthos turned, grabbed the other by the bel,t and yanked the slim figure up and over.

Balanced on the burly musketeer's knee, pinned by a one-armed bearhug, his assailant dropped the knife and struggled to get free. With his free hand, Porthos patted down his attacker, in search of other weapons or some clue to who his new acquaintance was. Reaching under the attacker's tunic, the musketeer suddenly made a startling discovery.

"My apologizes, Mademoiselle!" Porthos stammered, getting to his feet and dropping the young woman to the dirt floor.

He shuffled his feet, and attempted to straighten up his clothing, appearing like an overly large schoolboy confronted by a stern teacher. He offered a gloved hand to her, keeping his gaze averted.

"Aren't you a modest soul!" she said, accepting the offered hand, which dwarfed and enveloped her own. She got to her feet.

She was slim and petite. Her attire, all repurposed men's wear, was various shades of blue. The outfit had seen some wear and tear. She retrieved her own hat, a near shapeless thing with a grey plume, and stood, hands on slim hips, gazing up at her new acquaintance.

Despite the differences in their heights, she had the air of being the figure of authority in this encounter.

"Do you have a name, my modest mountain?" she asked, with an arched eyebrow.

"Yes... uh... Baron du Vallon de Bracieux de Pierrefonds, at your service, Mademoiselle," he mumbled, with a faint, awkward bow.

"Well, that's a mouthful," she replied, taking a step back and stroking her chin, thoughtfully. "I'm generally less formal with the men who grope me..."

"Porthos," he added, avoiding her flirty gaze.

"And you may call me Orlando," she said, reaching out and patting his muscular arm with her slim, gloved hand. "Please, sit. I promise you; I have no intention of screaming for someone to come and protect my innocence. That ship, as they say, sailed long ago and crashed upon a reef."

Orlando perched on a bale of hay and patted the one next to her. The musketeer, feeling increasingly confused and awkward, joined her.

"I think we have stumbled across each other," the young woman continued, "and are speaking at cross purposes. You seem a gallant sort. Let's sift through this misunderstanding."

Still unsure, Porthos merely nodded.

"Now, why don't I begin," Orlando said, with a disarming smile, and an offered wineskin. "Much like my choice of dress, I live an unorthodox life, as you might have guessed. It is a... very, very long story, which I won't bore you with. The reason I'm in this this charming locale is, I'm on an errand for the... hmmm, we'll come back to that... I was supposed to meet a friend here, and while Isaac is a bit taller than you, there is enough of a passing resemblance for the stable boy to make an honest mistake. You see...?"

Orlando gave a brief smile and a "and there you have it" shrug. Porthos gave a noncommittal nod. He found this strange vagabond of a girl charming, and perplexing. With his fellow musketeers, he had generally been content to trust their judgement and go along with whatever course of action they devised. On his own, he tended to make what seemed to him perfectly reasonable decisions. Many was the time, he would later discover, others did not see the obvious logic of his actions. It was quite puzzling and lead to him to, on rare occasions, doubt his choices.

This was such a moment. He missed his comrades Athos and Aramis. He felt he could trust their counsel. Without even his loyal servant, Mousqueton, to use as a sounding board, he felt adrift. Orlando seemed very self-assured and clear in her purpose, but Porthos was unsure if letting a woman be in charge was a wise course. Taking orders from the Queen was one thing...

"Are you listening?" Orlando asked, peering curiously at her new friend. "Are you falling asleep?"

Portos shook his massive head, took the offered wineskin and came close to draining it, before he handed it back. He nodded his thanks, as he wiped his mouth on the back of his hand.

"I have a comrade in the musketeers," he said, haltingly. "He is a Gascon and invited me to visit his family estate. I'd grown weary and bored over a dispute with one of my neighbors, and so set out."

"And got lost and ended up here, as I was waiting for Isaac," Orlando muttered thoughtfully.

"I?" Porthos rumbled, stroking his mustache. "Lost? I have an uncanny sense of direction! It was that dunderhead, Mousqueton, and that sloth of a horse that got lost. I was the unfortunate victim of their bumbling." He shook his head and helped himself to the wineskin, warming to his subject. "You could drop me in the most remote, barren of lands, blindfolded," he continued, "and I would find my way home. Unfortunately, I nodded off, and placed too much trust in that nag!"

"Yes, yes, who hasn't fallen prey to a treacherous horse," Orlando replied, with mock sympathy, as she took the wineskin back and took a swig to rival that of the massive musketeer's before getting back to her feet. "I do apologize for the misunderstanding. I'll find the stable boy and we can set you upon your way..."

"Now, wait!" Porthos interrupted, also standing up. " I feel I have, er, slightly wronged you and should make amends. You are, no matter how clandestinely, a young maiden..."

"Truly, I am neither of those things," Orlando said, attempting to steer Porthos away from any more long speeches.

"...in need of assistance, and I," Porthos continued, unabashed and barely pausing for breath, "as a musketeer and a gentleman, would be a rogue of the lowest order if I ignored that fact!"

"I am sorry," Orlando said. "What are you saying?"

"You are bereft of your companion. I shall accompany you until this bearded giant of yours arrives, or your task is complete."

He placed one hand upon the hilt of his sword, the other he held out to his new acquaintance.

265

Orlando's dainty hand was swallowed in the musketeer's. Her pale forehead wrinkled in puzzlement. Several heartbeats of thought resulted in a smooth forehead and an impish smile crossed her lips.

"Yes, yes," she drawled. "I think your keen mind and strong sword arm might be just the thing to ensure success, of my... um... quest... well, errand."

With a final shake, she disengaged her hand from Porthos' and turned, heading for the barn door.

"Come along, my mountain!" she called over her shoulder.

"Where?"

"I'm not eating dinner in a barn," Orlando explained, airily. "And I am expecting one more arrival."

The room was large, low-ceilinged; the wood darkened by years of cook fire smoke. Seated at a corner table, his back to the wall, and a wide swath of empty space between him and the rest of the tavern's patrons, sat Orlando's other acquaintance.

The years were etched onto his dour face. His white hair hung to his shoulders. Despite his obvious age, he sat ramrod straight; his dark eyes held a spark that marked him as a lion amongst lambs. He wore the plain, black garments of a puritan, the only difference being the brace of pistols and scabbard at his belt. Like his garments, they showed no ornamentation.

Propped against the tavern wall, by his right arm, was a wooden staff. It was decorated with hieroglyphs and the carved head of a cat.

Orlando went directly to his table and pulled over a stool.

Porthos leaned against the bar, relaxing a bit, as he contemplated the tavern's dinner offerings.

"Who is your friend?" the Puritan asked, with the barest movement of his lips or eyes. "Does he bring word of the Wandering Jew?"

"No, he does not. Events have gotten... interesting," Orlando explained, helping herself to the mug on the table. She pulled a face, upon realizing it was only water.

"Talk sense, changeling," the man muttered.

"There's been no sign or word of Isaac," Orlando replied, losing her glib manner. "If I was of a suspicious nature, I'd suspect he was being deliberately kept from meeting us, but knowing Isaac, he could just have been distracted by a hundred other things. Which means, it is just you and I, Solomon. A strong sword arm and a tendency not to overthink matters could serve us well."

She casually gestured, gaining Porthos attention, and much like the proverbial China shop bull, the large musketeer made his way across the room to join them.

The stool groaned and creaked under his girth, as he arranged his bowl of stew, mug of wine, hunk of bread and eating utensils on the small table. Once his meal was arranged to his satisfaction, he raised his mug.

"To your health and the success of our undertaking," he exclaimed, before draining the mug and waving the buxom serving wench over for a refill.

"Now, what might our undertaking be?" he asked, dipping a hunk of bread in his stew. "How can we help you, Monsieur...?"

"Firstly, by lowering your voice," the Puritan replied.

"He's rude, but Solomon has a point," Orlando nodded, as she helped herself to Porthos' wine. "There are political undertones to our undertaking."

"I am known for my discretion," Porthos rumbled, through a mouthful of bread. "Though, I really have no head for politics."

"As you know, Gascony shares a border with Spain..." Orlando began, quietly.

"Spaniards!" Porthos said, frowning. "A troublesome people. Which is a shame, as I do appreciate their wine and women..."

"Pay attention, my mountain," Orlando chided, gently, reaching up to give Porthos' beard a quick tug. "There have been... incidents of a mysterious nature. Both France and Spain are suspicious of each other, so it is doubtful they could work together to investigate them without exacerbating the whole thing. Everyone aware of these incidents would prefer not to go to war over a ghost story."

"Ghosts?" Porthos asked.

"We'll get to that," Orlando continued. "It was decided it'd be wiser if matters were handled by... free agents, shall we say."

"You are both British," Porthos said.

"Well spotted," Orlando said, with a patronizing smile. "I have, on occasion, been employed as a courier for the Crown, while this gentleman, Solomon Kane, has a very pronounced sense of justice...."

The Puritan's frown deepened, and his hand moved to the hilt of his sword. Orlando paused to glance at her somber companion, and judged he did not appreciate her frivolous tone.

"Kane" Porthos mused, oblivious to the tension between his tablemates. "I have heard that name..."

"I had put out word," Orlando continued, hoping her narrative would not be derailed by either Kane's temper or Porthos' contemplative nature. "Isaac and Solomon agreed to join me."

"What is it that we face?" Porthos asked, eagerly.

"Ghosts?"Porthos mused to himself, once they were on their horses and on their way.

His horse lagged a bit behind the other two. He sounded more thoughtful, than skeptical. His two new traveling companions rode ahead of him.

"I am sure you are bursting to chide me," Orlando said, quietly, glancing back at their new acquaintance.

"No."

"Really?"

"Lord protect me, but I can see your reasoning," the dour adventurer said, his voice low, his gaze straight ahead, his ornate staff across his lap. "Our cause is just, but we are stepping into a potentially explosive political quagmire, and neither of us is known for, er, our diplomatic skills. Having a French musketeer at our side may smooth our path."

"Very good," Orlando nodded, with a smile. "It doesn't hurt that he's a renowned swordsman and built like an oak." They both glanced back at Porthos, still deep in thought. "I admit, he's no Wandering Jew," Orlando shrugged. "But what do they say about beggars and choosers...?"

"We have not been followed," Kane said. "So, whatever we face is ahead of us."

"Most likely," Orlando replied, thoughtfully. "Hard to sift through the tales and discover what is the truth and what is rumor."

"Whatever is happening is no mere subterfuge by a would-be political schemer," added Kane, one hand brushing the runes carved into his staff. "Something... unnatural is in the air."

Orlando lifted her head and gave a sniff. "Yes, it's out there," she nodded, running the tip of her tongue across her upper lip. "I can taste it on the wind. It's... not what I was expecting... smells... almost familiar?"

They rode along in silence for several moments. Kane seemed willing to wait as Orlando pursued her thoughts. She frowned and shrugged.

"It's gone," she concluded. "Too many memories, from too many lifetimes, for one delicate, attractive head to hold, I suppose..."

Kane's frown deepened, as any reference Orlando made to her immortality or ability to change sex caused him to bristle.

While Solomon Kane and Orlando had been occasional, reluctant allies, the Puritan warrior had always harbored the belief that there would come a day that he would be forced to treat Orlando like any other supernatural creature and put his one-time comrade to the sword.

Despite his dedication to his crusade against the wicked forces and creatures that lurked in the ungodly fringes of the world, there were rare instances where he encountered beings who challenged his view, his belief that all such things were evil.

Orlando was frivolous, reckless, and too interested in the pleasures of the flesh, but at the same time, she ...or occasionally he, was a reliable companion. Some small corner of his mind was unsettled at the idea of having to cut Orlando down.

Such thoughts invariably led him to also ponder his own unsure placement in the natural order. Whether through the possession of the ancient *juju* staff, once gifted to him by an African shaman, or decades of exposure to various mystical forces, he had lived long, perhaps too long. Had he become the kind of being he had spent so many years hunting? His flesh and blood had been gifted with energy, vitality and years beyond human ken, but what of his immortal soul?

"Is my attempting to plan strategy interrupting your brooding?" Orlando asked.

"I was pondering the future," the Puritan replied quietly, his eyes straight ahead.

"I suppose, if I reach your advanced years, I'd want to start contemplating my sins too," Orlando mused, dryly. "I would hope that if one of my comrades in arms would pay attention, you would be the one. I suppose that leaves... Where is he going?"

Both riders pulled their horses to a halt and glanced back to see Porthos steering his weary steed towards the side of the dirt road.

"Excuse me?" Orlando called. "My dear Baron, where are you going?"

Porthos halted his horse and dismounted, approaching his fellow travelers, before speaking.

"Be discreet," he chided them, unaware that even hushed, his own voice tended to be booming. "I have said, my holiday in Gascony is a quiet affair."

"Yes, and so far," Orlando mused, "you have been the pinnacle of subtle discretion. My question still stands."

"Which question was that?" Porthos asked, absently, as he glanced about while fanning himself with his hat.

"Where were you going?" Kane asked, in the barely patient tone one uses with an exasperating child.

"There's a track between the trees," Porthos explained, patiently, as though it was perfectly obvious. "You can glimpse a barn from here."

He nodded, as though his point was made, only to notice that his companions were still looking at him expectantly.

"It's growing dark, and I am growing tired," Porthos explained. "And as I have made plain, that horse of mine is a poor navigator. I fear if I were to nod off, the wretched beast would have me in Athens by dawn."

He clamped his hat back on his head and returned to his horse.

"Well," Kane said, dismounting and slinging his staff over his shoulder. "The dunderhead has a point. We have all been on the road for days. Those of us that must deal with... mortal frailty could use some rest."

He took hold of his horse's bridle and followed after the musketeer. Orlando shrugged, sighed, and nudged her horse to join the others.

The barn was grey with age. One corner of the roof was sagging, but its interior was relatively dry and rat-free.

Porthos found a heap of dried straw and sprawled, his saddle bags a makeshift pillow. Solomon Kane perched on an overturned wooden bucket, his back against the wall, his cat-headed staff propped up next to him, as though both were standing guard.

Orlando strolled around the building, taking in the windows and dodgy section of roof, before making herself a nest

271

of straw and wrapping up in her cloak. Despite her disdain for her companion's decision, she soon found her eyelids growing a bit heavy.

"Tell me more about these ghosts," Porthos' voice drifted across the barn like a thrown rock.

"Of course," Orlando sighed, sitting up. "The first rumors of spectral sightings were about a month or so ago. Nothing unusual; dead relatives walking the land; French and Spanish soldiers and knights from bygone times patrolling the roads and lurking in mountain passes. Quite dramatic."

"Interesting," Porthos murmured in drowsy thought. "I would be reluctant to fight women, children or grandsires, but it would be a worthy story if I were to pit my blade against the warriors of a past age... My friends would scarcely believe such a thing!"

"We do not walk this path in order to obtain tales to entertain drunkards and trollops," Kane said, grimly, crossing his arms.

"Speak for yourself," Orlando smiled, wiggling in search of a more comfortable seat upon the dirt floor. "So far, the ghosts have been fairly benign. People are frightened, and no one has been attacked, but it has, as would be expected, made both the French and the Spanish suspicious of each other... What's that noise...?"

"Your audience," Kane said, pulling his own plain, black cloak tighter about him.

Orlando got to her feet. Porthos was sprawled in the hay, his hat over his face, snoring like a cannon.

"Sweet dreams, my mountain."

The sky was dark, with only a few, obstinate stars,forcing their way through the clouds. Porthos shifted, brushed aside his hat, and slowly sat up.

Nature was calling, and the over-sized musketeer fumbled with his sword belt and untangled himself from his cloak as he sleepily trudged across the stable, and then through the yard toward a convenient bush.

His business attended to, Porthos blinked away his grogginess and paused to adjust his sleep-rumpled clothing. Upon looking up, he was startled to see three people standing in the stable yard, looking at him. Two men and a woman, all dressed in the drab clothes of peasant farmers. One of the men had a small hay bale slung over his shoulder; the other held a rough walking staff. They had startled looks, seemingly as surprised to see Porthos as he was at their appearance.

The trio seemed as mundane and plain as any of the workers of Porthos' own estate, except for the fact that they were translucent. He could see the trees behind them clearly. They also seemed to have a faint glow, no brighter than moonlight.

"Um... good evening," Porthos called. "Or perhaps 'good morn'... Hard to judge when it's this cloudy."

He moved to doff his hat, gallantly, only to realize he had left it behind.

"I do not mean to impose. We had no idea someone owned the barn. We'd be more than happy to pay for having a roof over our heads... and perhaps some breakfast?"

He patted at his clothes, before coming up with a coin. He held it up, offering it to the trio.

The ghostly peasants recoiled slightly at the coin. The men moved as if to protect the woman. Instinctively, Porthos' hand went to the hilt of his sword. He then felt a hand on his arm.

"Wait," Solomon Kane said, in a quiet, firm voice. "These phantoms will not be dispelled by a blade."

The Puritan stepped in front of Porthos and held out his cat-headed staff. It seemed almost to hum, like a violin string, as he waved it slowly, back and forth. The carved recesses that served as the cat totem's eyes glinted faintly, as though reflecting the dim starlight of the Gascon night sky.

The frown creases about his face deepened, and Solomon Kane placed one hand upon his own sword hilt. "Something is wrong here," he said, puzzled.

The trio of ghosts moved tentatively toward the two swordsmen, growing fuzzy around the edges and more transparent with each step.

"Back, phantoms!" Porthos commanded, stepping forward, his sword drawn. "You seem to be the spirits of decent, hardworking folk, but that will not spare you from my blade!"

Almost within reach of the duo, the ghosts merely dissipated. Both men felt an odd tingling, as if a brief static charge had passed through them.

Porthos sheathed his sword and smoothed out his mustache.

"Curious," he rumbled, thoughtfully. 'Do ghosts often act like that? I bow to your experience, as I am a novice to such things."

"No, this was... different," the Puritan replied, speaking directly to the bedraggled musketeer, as one would to a peer, rather than to one who is tolerated. "There is something about these apparitions that I do not understand."

"In the stories I was told," Porthos mused, using his fingers to comb his hair. "I was led to believe ghosts were vengeful, angry things... Sometimes sad women... This lot seemed quite... dull... Whoever has heard of ghosts performing chores?"

He began to pace, while he pondered, giving the appearance of a restless bear. Solomon Kane stood, straight and stiff, his arms crossed, his staff tucked, like a cane, under one arm, giving the impression that both man and figurehead, were interested in Porthos' thoughts.

Kane was granite-faced to all outward appearances, stoic to the point of boredom. Yet, he took in every word Porthos uttered, adding it to his own thoughts.

"What in the world are you two up to?" a sleep-rumpled Orlando asked, joining them, her sword, a Japanese katana, held lazily in one hand, its blade nearly dragged in the dirt.

"There were ghosts," Porthos replied, gesturing to where they had been, while sounding like a child caught by a stern parent.

Orlando looked at the two swordsmen, while sheathing her sword and continuing to adjust her clothing. When she glanced at Kane, he merely nodded in response to her unasked question.

Orlando ran her tongue over her teeth, while she absently glanced around the barnyard. "There's something wrong about all this," she muttered. "I can taste it in the air."

The trio stood, wrapped in their own thoughts.

"These ghosts are not just rumor and tall tales," Kane intoned.

"No, they are not," Orlando nodded, crossing her arms in thought.

Porthos peered out at the slowly lightening horizon. "What are our plans for breakfast?" he asked, glancing at his companions. "There are scant resources here. Is there somewhere along the road we might stop?"

They saw to their horses and were soon back on the road. They rode through the day. Fields and farms soon gave way to rocky hills.

Like the landscape, the ghosts they saw also changed. At first, they caught glimpses of spectral farmers and peasants. Soon, they were replaced by shepherds and bandits.

The ghosts continued about their mundane tasks. There were occasional bursts of human drama and surprise. A translucent wolf stalked an equally ghostly boy and his flock.

At one point, Kane and Orlando had to restrain Porthos from racing off to protect a phantom damsel being pursued by a phantasmic enraged suiter with a dagger.

"How are you faring, my mountain?" Orlando asked, coming alongside Porthos. "This, I would imagine, is not the restful holiday in Gascony you envisioned?"

"I am... unsure of my words," he replied ,scratching at his beard in thought. "My years as a musketeer have not been uneventful, but nothing prepared me for... this..." He gestured with a gloved hand at a group of ghostly, ragged children, as they joyfully chased a scrawny dog across the dirt road and into the tall grass. "What can one say?" he continued. "If my three comrades were here, they could articulate the thoughts that swirl about my head. I am known more for my sword arm and my impeccable dress."

"No doubt," Orlando replied dryly. "We appreciate your skills and reassuring company."

"It is a little... disorienting, I suppose," the musketeer continued. "I have never spent much time in spiritual contemplation. Generally, I leave that to Aramis.... But, to see the spirits of the dead with my own eyes! None of them seem particularly vengeful though."

"No, they have been most benign and even a bit dull," Orlando nodded. "Curious that so many should appear, only to go about their previous lives."

"And very few seem to have taken notice of our presence," Solomon Kane added.

"I can see how so many ghosts would frighten away the locals," Orlando mused. "But, if none of them are attacking, or even taking notice of the living, what is behind it all? A manifestation of this size does not just happen. Someone or something had to summon them."

"By design or by accident, then becomes the question," Kane said.

"A question for the morning," Porthos said. "Night is drawing in and I do not trust those clouds."

"True," Orlando frowned, glancing about. "Even if the storm passes us by, I do not relish navigating these, for lack of a better term, roads, in the dark. We need shelter and maybe a wild hare. Our larder is quite barren."

"There is a side trail," Kane said, pointing off to the right. "It leads to a small clearing with a bit of an overhang. We could shelter there for the night."

The ground was rocky, but the surrounding hillside gave the clearing a bit of shelter. Porthos was content to guard the makeshift camp and tend the small campfire, while Kane and Orlando scouted around, in search of a better path through the mountains, grass and boughs for bedding, and something for dinner.

Once they had accomplished all three chores, they returned to the clearing to find Porthos, his back against the rockface, his hands clasped across his stomach and his chin on his chest.

Solomon Kane. frowning in disapproval, sat on a stone, across the fire from the musketeer and began to skin and gut the rabbit he had caught.

"So, now that we have proven to our satisfaction that the ghosts are real, and not rumor or political trickery, what do we do?" Orlando asked, dropping a bundle of grass bedding, and brushing off her hands. "I confess, I find myself puzzled." She folded her cloak, into a cushion, sat down and tugged off her boots.

Kane looked up from his work, his face wooden. A briefly raised grey eyebrow encouraged her to continue speaking.

"This feels... unplanned," Orlando continued, flexing her aching toes. "A summoning this large must have had a human agent behind it, but this has all the earmarks of a novice: something has gotten out of control here."

"And it is causing political unrest," Kane said, not looking up from his preparations for dinner. He now had the rabbit on a skewer, over the fire.

"But upon both sides," Orlando countered. "It may give certain statesmen an excuse to push towards war, but the whole thing still feels clumsy. I can't imagine it's anything more than an accidental side effect."

"There is a trail that connects with a better road, through the mountains," Kane said. "Perhaps if you escort our musketeer towards the massing French forces, we may learn more."

"And you?" Orlando asked.

"Someone should keep an eye on the Spanish."

"You also want to keep turning the skewer," Porthos said, not opening his eyes. "Don't want to scorch the rabbit."

The trio awoke in a foggy pre-dawn, broke camp and made their way in the dim light in search of the promised mountain road.

As they ascended, the ground grew rocky and desolate. Reaching the road, they paused to rest the horses and take the lay of the land. The clouds were huddling together, so the approaching sunrise was dim and uninviting.

"I do not like the looks of that storm," Orlando muttered.

Kane had dismounted and leaned on his staff; his fierce, grey eyes gazed upon the clouds with disapproval.

Porthos rubbed his unshaven chin as he steered his horse down the narrow path and onto the mountain road. He dismounted and squeezed the last few drops out of the wineskin, while he waited for his companions.

The road snaked through the mountain, curving back down to the farmlands, as well as up towards the craggy peaks.

Porthos glanced about, noticing several game trails branching off into the undergrowth and amongst the rocks.

"Well, this is a bit better," Orlando said, looking with approval at the hard packed dirt road and picturesque view of Gascony below. "Though, this is likely the way both sides will move their troops."

Solomon Kane peered at the ground, poking at the faint remains of some footprints with the end of his staff. "Some may have already gone this way," he said, straightening up.

"We need to look for shelter," Porthos said, taking a few steps forward, holding his reins, loosely in his hand. "Those clouds are darkening quite fast. Even the ghosts have gone to get out of the rain."

The other two glanced around, uneasily.

"He is right," Orlando said. "As we moved into the mountains, the ghosts have become fewer. We have not seen one since we got up here... Curious..."

Solomon Kane, idlily dragging his staff in the dirt, walked slowly along until he came alongside Orlando. "Something is moving," he said, his face expressionless. He glanced about, as though there was nothing of interest to see. Kane made a vague gesture, showing Orlando where to look.

As the mountain road curved, there was dense undergrowth and a scattering of thin trees. There was movement there that couldn't be explained away by the wind.

Orlando glanced away, acting as though she was taken in by the view. "Animals?" she asked, under her breath.

Kane shook his head faintly. "They are using the trails," the dour puritan said, matter-of -factly. "It may be a frightened shepherd or a bandit..."

He stopped mid-sentence, as two bulky, metal forms emerged from the underbrush.

"Well," Orlando mused, her hand moving to the hilt of her sword. "I know it will seem out of character if I am the one advising caution..."

"Ho, good sir knights!" Porthos called, dropping his wineskin, drawing his rapier and approaching the two new arrivals. "Hold and state your allegiance!"

He strode up to the armored duo, his sword held casually, but his posture indicated he could bring it into play at any second.

The musketeer paused, an eyebrow raised in curiosity. He did not recognize the style of the newcomers' armor and they sported no design or emblems. They even lacked sword belts.

The armors were bulky. There was no sign that the helmets were a separate piece. Their face plates sported two circles for eyes and a thin slit of a mouth. Their boots were blocky, and Solomon Kane realized they were the source of the odd footprints. Their gauntlets did not have fingers, but resembled large crab claws.

The odd pair moved slowly, lumbering along almost like sleepwalkers, more than soldiers on the trail. They trudged to within a yard or two of Porthos and then halted, as though they were equally confused by this encounter.

"From where do you hail?" Porthos asked. "What king do you serve?"

The armored duo continued to stare blankly at the musketeer.

"I do not wish to be rude," Porthos continued, needing to fill the empty space in the conversation. "But I am upon a mission and cannot allow you to proceed until I have ascertained your intent. My apologies in advance if I have besmirched your good character."

Standing back, Solomon Kane stood, statue still, while Orlando took up a casual stance, her Japanese Katanna resting lightly upon her slim shoulder. Her body language indicated someone watching a mildly interesting stage play.

The armored figures clanked and made vague humming sounds, but otherwise made no response to Porthos interrogation.

"I must warn you," Porthos said, sternly, as though addressing errant children. "If you will not speak in your own defense, I will be forced to treat you as foe, and, much as I am loath to brag, my foes do not fare well."

His rapier moved through the air, with a sharp *swish*, and then he took up an *En Garde* stance.

Slowly, one of the armored figures raised an arm and opened its claw-like hand. In the center of its palm was a metal disk. A thin arc of lightning shot out, and when it touched Porthos' sword, the metal sparked and the burly musketeers' whole body shook.

He wrenched his sword loose, and promptly landed flat on his back in the dirt.

His companions sprang forward. Kane stood before his fallen companion, his staff held out, as he stood on guard. Orlando ran at the duo.

Formulating a plan to fend off these malignant ghosts, Orlando was caught completely off guard, when her sword drew sparks when it came in contact with one of the metal forms. She stumbled, turned, and threw a punch at the other.

There was a loud clanging sound, and Orlando stepped back, wincing and shaking her injured hand. She switched hands, and swung her sword wildly, in the hope of driving the two back. Her blade drew sparks, but there was little force behind her attack, as she had expected the duo to be as gossamer thin as the ghostly peasants they'd encountered.

Orlando was unsure if she should be attempting to dispatch these armored foes, or just drive them back, until she and Kane had a chance to make sense of things.

The two clunky, blank-faced knights backed away. They stood, heads together, silently pondering their options. Then, they ponderously turned and shuffled off, down a side trail.

"Well, that was unexpected," Orlando breathed, blowing on her bruised knuckles. "Are the ghosts manifesting as solid beings, or have we stumbled into a new complication?"

Kane strode forward, his staff held out, pointing to where the mysterious knights had stood. "I do not understand this," he muttered. "It does not make sense."

Orlando nodded, while tracing idlily in the dirt with the point of her sword. "There is something here," she muttered. "I have accumulated too many memories to sort through, over the centuries..."

"Did we win?" Porthos mumbled, struggling to sit up. "I hope you dealt with whichever one of the miscreants struck me from behind."

Kane saw to the horses, while Orlando sheathed her sword and helped the musketeer back to his feet.

"Plans have changed," she explained, dusting him off, while he swayed slightly and fumbled to sheath his rapier. "Those knights were not in the least ghostly."

"They bore no ornamentation that I could identify," Porthos muttered, adjusting his disheveled clothing. "So, someone is clandestinely summoning these ghosts, after all?"

"I think we have to concede that point," Orlando nodded. "But it leaves us at a loose end, as there is nothing about those knights that tells us which power might be behind things... Or even if we are dealing with some third group we had not even considered."

"You are complicating matters," Kane said, squinting into the surrounding foliage. "They do not move fast, and they leave an obvious trail. We will have to leave the horses."

"Good," Porthos said, patting the ancient Puritan's shoulder as he strode past him. "We will hunt the villains to their lair!"

He tromped up the mountain road until he spotted the side trails and poked at the undergrowth with his sword. Kane glanced over at Orlando. He did not speak, but she felt the full effect of his chiding her for inviting the musketeer along. She merely shrugged back, before tethering the horses, near a good-sized patch of grass.

Portos pushed aside some of the brambly shrubs. Solomon Kane and Orlando joined him in studying the ground. Amongst the gravel and stone, were more blocky footprints.

"Do ghosts leave footprints?" Porthos asked.

"No," Orlando said. "Monsters do. As do men."

"Which are we dealing with?" Kane asked, thoughtfully.

Swords drawn; the trio moved down the trail. It was a narrow snake of dirt and stone, widened by the armored duo, so along with footprints there was a great deal of broken branches and trodden grass to indicate the path they should follow. While Porthos wished to take the lead, Orlando felt there should be an attempt at stealth, and convinced him to bring up the rear.

The path wound its way up the mountain; it would occasionally branch off, but nearly all of them petered out, and they would backtrack to the main trail. One side trail brought them to a narrow stretch. It would have been overly generous to describe as a clearing. The three of them, standing shoulder to shoulder, barely fit, and it fronted upon a steep incline of rock.

"There are footprints," Orlando muttered. "But there's really nowhere to go."

"No handholds," Porthos added, thoughtfully peering upwards. "Climbing would be quite difficult."

Kane stood, silently peering at the stone wall. He rested his staff against the rock, pulled off one of his gloves and ran his fingers along the surface of the stone incline.

Pressing his fingers into a recess in the rocky surface, a section of wall slid away, revealing a cave that tunneled back into the mountain.

"Curious," Porthos said, stooping slightly, as he stepped into the cave.

Thin veins of luminescence ran along the ceiling. Porthos brushed his fingers along one strand. "Feels like wire," he muttered.

The tunnel widened gradually, as it went. There was a hum in the air and a distant sound that gave Orlando the thought that someone was mining.

"There's an odor in the air," Kane said. "Reminds me of an alchemist's den."

The tunnel opened up, forming a chamber, like an enormous, overturned bowl. Several of the armored figures lumbered about, moving boxes and strange metal devices. At the far end of the cave sat a featureless, grey cube, the size of a peasants' hut.

The whole place had the makeshift feel of an army camp, littered with bizarre items and figures, that felt like approximations of the familiar. As if it had been built by a child, who had to use whatever toys he had to create the scenario in its imagination.

The trio stood, struggling with their mixed feelings: confusion, and a slight feeling of awe, so they were unaware of two other armored creatures, stationed in alcoves on either side of the entranceway.

One caught Porthos in a bearhug that pinned his arms to his sides. The other grabbed Orlando and Kane, each by an arm, clamping down hard enough that the combination of surprise and pain, caused them to drop sword and staff.

"Don't struggle," Orlando said, out of the corner of her mouth, as she was dragged past Porthos.

Kane scowled at the loss of his staff, but went along, as he too surmised, they were on the verge of receiving some answers.

Making a token struggle, the trio were forcibly escorted across the chamber, closer to the mysterious, grey structure. Amongst the sounds of machinery, they could hear voices.

Coming around the back corner of the cube, was an elderly man and a young woman. The man walked with a pronounced limp. His white hair, flared around his head, like neglected shrubbery. He was clad in a heavy overcoat, over multiple layers of brown and grey. One hand was clad in a glove that was such a tight fit, it could have been painted on.

"Oh, our clever hunters!" he rasped in a heavy German accent. "We do not appreciate unwelcome visitors."

He leaned on the young girl's arm. She had an ethereal quality, like a painting come to life. Her gossamer dress was unseasonably light. She moved with a dancers' grace, and her features, while pleasing to the eye, had a still quality about them, again suggesting a portrait of a young woman.

The old man peered at the trio, accusingly, as he hobbled nearer.

"I should have known that you would eventually track me down here, Omega!" he said, in a sullen snarl. "You could not stand to see me... Wait!"

He looked closer at Solomon Kane, pushing the Puritan's hat back, so his face was no longer in shadow.

"You're not... I don't know you," he said accusingly.

"Nor I you," Kane replied, pulling his hat back in place. "But there is the stench of unnatural arts about this place."

The old man, glanced upwards at Porthos, who looked back with equal curiosity. Their captor dismissed the large musketeer with a vague gesture. He then halted before Orlando.

"You," he muttered, darkly. "You, I know."

"Do you?" Orlando asked. "I am sorry, I don't recall meeting you before."

"Don't be foolish. It hasn't happened yet."

284

"Ah, I'm notorious for arriving early," Orlando nodded, despite her circumstances finding herself more amused than concerned over this strange old man and his metal soldiers.

"Still a frivolous popinjay," he grunted, with a disapproving shake of his head.

"Well, good to know," Orlando said.

"So, you are a warlock?" Porthos asked, puzzled. "Or perhaps, an alchemist? I am afraid I do not know the proper terms..."

"Warlock?" the old man snapped, turning back to Porthos. "I am Rotwang! The finest mind of my era! Master of robotics! I do not play with herbs and spells. I bend the flow of history to my will!"

"Oh, dear," Orlando muttered. "Time travel. I knew there was something in the air that felt familiar."

"Attend me, Hélène," Rotwang said, reaching out to the young woman. "These fools are nothing more than a distraction. Have the Volkites detain them until we are finished."

Supported by the vague dancer, he hobbled away from his captives.

"I truly do not understand what is happening," Porthos said, showing no sign he was bothered by the armored man holding him, as he was too distracted by events.

"For once, we are in agreement," Kane muttered.

"Rotwang is not a mystic," Orlando explained, struggling to tug her arm free, with no success. "He is more of an alchemist, or a scientist. They are almost as much trouble as wizards."

"You've met this Rotwang before?" Kane asked, his posture and tone giving the impression he considered being held captive by a large, armored figure no more than an inconvenience. He was focused on the conversation.

"No, but apparently I will in the future," Orlando explained, tapping at the Volkite's arm. There was a whirl of machinery. "You see... This is the tricky bit. Almost makes me miss Omega. He's better at this sort of thing. Time moves like

285

a river. We move, as the current pushes us, or we are on the shore, watching the river flow by. Some people can travel back and forth on the river, go against the current and go ashore wherever they like."

Porthos merely nodded, accepting the information. He was not an imbecile, but neither was he a deep thinker. He tended to trust those around him to do the thinking, and he did what was required to deal with a given situation.

"Most are merely travelers or dabblers in history. Rotwang seems to fall into the other category: those that meddle, threatening history itself, or too deluded or egomaniacal to realize the damage they are causing."

"His metal... constructs... there does not appear to be any men within this armor... they are mining," Kane said. "Perhaps he needs some mineral or substance in order to continue his traveling?"

"But why does he need ghosts?" Porthos asked, moving his arm in order to scratch his chin, and then remembering his arms were pinned to his sides.

"I don't think he's doing that intentionally," Orlando explained, feeling distinctly uncomfortable in her role as fount of wisdom for the group. "Like when you drop a stone into a pond; if you travel in time, you cause ripples. That's what I think the ghosts are."

"This ragged alchemist is causing a war by accident?" Kane asked.

Orlando shrugged, then grimaced, as the Volkite tightened its grip, thinking she was attempting to escape.

"So, if we stop him, the ghosts will go away and tensions between France and Spain will settle down?" Porthos suggested.

"Likely," Orlando replied, looking about.

"Well, then we must stop him," he said simply.

"Yes, about that..."Orlando said, attempting to move her trapped arm.

After several minutes of thought, Porthos leaned forward, as if taking a deep bow. As he did, he arched his back, rolled his shoulders, and lifted up the Volkite holding him, until its feet no longer touched the ground.

Teeth gritted and his face turning red with the exertion, Porthos took several halting steps and then allowed himself to stumble backwards, so that the metal creature slammed against the stone wall.

He managed to step back and slam back against the stone two more times, before he sank to his knees. When he did, the Volkite tumbled off his back, emitting a wheezing, grinding noise. Its back was a mass of dents and scraps.

While Porthos was struggling with his captor, Solomon Kane reached into his belt, drew one of his flintlock pistols, turned slightly and stuck it in the Volkite's eye, before pulling the trigger. It loosened its grip on the two adventurers as it staggered backwards, a whisp of smoke drifting out from the jagged hole where its eye had been.

"Am I the only one who hadn't formulated an escape plan?" Orlando asked, rubbing her sore arm, before moving to help Porthos back to his feet. The large musketeer accepted the hand thankfully, before straightening and dusting himself off.

"What next?" Porthos asked, looking around.

Kane moved to retrieve their scattered weapons, leaning on his staff, while tucking the swords under his arm.

"That grey block?" he asked, handing his companions their blades.

"Probably how he travels through time," Orlando admitted. "Those... um... wires and pipes, most likely... gather fuel and... I don't know, but if we cut those, it will either stop him, or possibly force him to flee else...when."

"I will deal with the guards," Porthos said, giving his rapier a swish and tossing his hat aside, before marching off. Kane glanced up, from reloading his pistol, and looked a question at Orlando.

"Have you a plan now, changeling?" he asked.

"I do not have any answers," she replied. "I barely have questions."

"Then, let me see what I can do," Kane said.

He tossed her one of his flintlocks, before moving closer to the blocky structure. The Puritan found a sandy patch in the cave floor and stuck the wooden *juju* staff into the dirt. He pulled off his gloves and rested his hands upon the carved headpiece. He closed his eyes and lowered his head, until his brow nearly rested upon his gnarled hands. He might be praying or napping, for all Orlando knew.

"There is an energy here," he murmured. "It is being used for evil. I must see it. I must know."

Orlando stood by, waiting, and ready to defend him.

After several moments, she began to grow antsy, as the remaining Volkites were too occupied with Porthos.

"I'm not letting him have all the fun," she announced, running across the stone chamber.

Unnoticed by her, the hieroglyphs carved down the length of the staff began to glow, with a faint blueish light.

Porthos' shoulder blocked one of the clunky mechanical creatures aside, swung a punch square into the flat, blank face of another and bounded past a third to reach the makeshift collection of metal contraptions, wires and chunks of luminescent blue crystal.

A flurry of swordplay kept them at bay, while the musketeer pondered what to do now that he'd managed to reach his destination. A solid kick sent bits and pieces flying and its hum became a discordant growl.

Feeling metal claws grabbing at his shoulders, Porthos spun, and with his back to the stone wall, fought them off. His rapier was unable to do more than scratch their metal plating.

Orlando leapt and with a wild, downswing, severed one of the Volkites' arms. A side slash stabbed through a second's torso, only for Orlando to then be unable to pull her blade free. She let go of the sword and, pulling out the borrowed flintlock, shot her remaining metal opponent in the knee.

The Volkite toppled like a felled tree, into the other one, and the two performed a bizarre dance, struggling to stay upright. They failed and collapsed in a loud heap, trailing wisps of smoke.

Orlando planted a heel on the fallen Volkite's head and pulled her sword loose. Looking up, she watched Porthos jab his rapier through the mouth of his opponent, grab the Volkite by its blocky head and slam it against the collection of machinery, damaging both.

"Well, that's seen to," Orlando said, with a satisfied smile. "What is that noise?"

Almost drowning out the sounds of the damaged Volkites, was a persistent hum, one that you could feel in one's bones. It sent a tremor through the entire cavern, throwing a rain of dirt and stone down upon the trio.

The grey block structure didn't exactly shake, but for a brief second, it seemed to blur. A door-shaped panel in its blank surface slid aside and Rotwang and Hélène rushed out.

"What have you done?" Rotwang raged, wild-eyed, his odd, gloved hand gripping the edge of the doorway.

"Us?" Orlando asked, glancing from the fallen Volkites to the shattered machinery.

Hélène flowed out of the cube, and danced around Orlando, her eyes wide, her expression blank. She turned back to face Rotwang.

"If they are not interfering with the time cube, who is?" Rotwang snapped, in response to a conversation, only he seemed able to hear.

Everyone turned towards Solomon Kane, who had not moved from where he had planted his ancient staff. Both the carvings and the figurehead's eyes were glowing brightly, and the old man's body trembled.

"Solomon?" Orlando breathed. "What are you up to?"

Kane took a deep breath, raised his head and opened his eyes. All about him, blue light, flowed like water. He wondered if he was standing at the bottom of the ocean, or perhaps on a cloud floating through a clear, spring morning.

He was equally shocked to look down upon his hands and see the gnarled, wrinkled skin, like ancient leather, traced with veins, was gone. They were now the hands of a younger man. A younger Solomon Kane. The hair that drooped past his eyes was no longer stringy and white, but rich ebony.

"What have I done?" he asked, puzzled.

"I was rather wandering that myself," a voice replied.

Standing before him was an old man, dressed all in black. His collar-length white hair was swept back, except for one rebellious lock, and his face was wrinkled and careworn.

"You must be... Omega?" Kane said.

"Doctor," the old man said. "Doctor Omega, if you please. Have we met?"

"Perhaps. I am not sure... Maybe in a dream. Or maybe it hasn't happened yet. I have been told such things are possible."

Doctor Omega nodded, as if what Kane had said was so straightforward that it required no response. He tugged at a ribbon, attached to his lapel and drew out a monocle. He seemed to have forgotten the Puritan wanderer, in his interest in the wooden staff Kane held.

"Now, that's interesting." Doctor Omega muttered, excitedly to himself. "Never thought I'd lay eyes on one of the... My, my, good to know life can still surprise you!"

He straightened up, smiling to himself and twirling his monocle ribbon.

"Well, you have stirred up something, haven't you?" he chuckled.

"Have I?" Kane asked, brow furrowed in puzzlement.

"Oh, dear, yes. Poked your stick into the pond and stirred up the silt and sleeping fish, as it were." Omega nodded. "But, you haven't the faintest idea what I'm talking about, or what you have hold of."

"My staff? It was given to me by..."

"Someone who wanted to see it stir up trouble in the world," the white-haired savant interrupted. "Well, I'm quite busy at the moment, so I can't stand around for whatever story you might want to tell. Who is it you're tangling with, hmmm? Hopefully not Morlocks?"

"He calls himself 'Rotwang," Kane said.

"Oh, dear. Well, he does keep causing this kind of havoc," Omega said, with a slight, sad frown. "You'll have to deal with him. Here's what we'll do..."

He reached out a hand and placed it on top of Kane's. The staff trembled in his grasp, and the hieroglyphs, as well as the stone in Doctor Omega's ring, shifted and glowed with a greenish light.

Omega closed his eyes and muttered under his breath something that sounded equal parts mathematical equation and lullaby.

"That should do it," the Doctor said, pulling his hands away. "Now, things are going to happen quickly, so you need to wake up and get away from... whatever Rotwang is up to. On your way."

He snapped his fingers, quickly and sharply, mere inches from Kane's face, and when the Puritan adventurer opened his eyes, he'd returned to the cavern and his tired, ancient body.

The stone chamber trembled, the air was thick with dust and grit, and his companions were on the other side of the room, standing over the remains of the Volkites, while receiving a harsh lecture from Rotwang.

The large, grey block went in and out of focus, like an image reflected on the surface of a pond and all the scattered shards of crystal now glowed with the same green light from his vision... dream... whatever it had been.

"Orlando! Porthos! To me!" Kane shouted, drawing his flintlock, as he realized he was also drawing the attention of the few remaining Volkites and the blank-featured girl with the wide eyes.

Trusting their comrade, and feeling that the cavern was no longer a safe place to remain, they pushed past Rotwang's metal minions and ran to the Puritan's side, then followed him back the way they had entered.

Kane's pace slacked, and his breathing grew labored. He began to stumble. Porthos sheathed his sword and threw his new friends arm over his broad shoulder, until Kane was no longer sure his boots touched the ground.

Orlando snatched the pistol out of his hand and fired over her shoulder at their lumbering pursuers.

Rotwang's ranting grew harsher and more frantic, as the trembling in the walls and the glow of the crystals increased.

The trio struggled to keep their feet, as the tunnel shook. There was a roar, behind them, like a massive wave, crashing against a beach, and a blast of gritty wind struck, sending them tumbling out of the hidden tunnel and into the brambly undergrowth. The mountain itself seemed to shake, and the air was filled with a strained moaning-growling sound.

Orlando staggered to her feet, spitting out grass, and wiping dirt from her face, with the back of her gloved hand.

"Anyone still alive?" she called, wading through the brush .

Porthos' path was easy to track, and she soon arrived at the small clearing he had made on impact.

"I feel I must still live," he muttered, sitting up and blinking in the sunlight. "As I sincerely doubt death hurts this much. I wish we still had some wine."

Holding Porthos by one muscular arm, Orlando helped him to his feet, and steered him in the direction she believed Kane had fallen. They found his staff, stuck into the trail, as though waiting, expectantly, for its owner. Kane was sitting up, looking bruised and frail.

"How fare you, Solomon Kane?" Porthos asked, crouching down, concerned for his new comrade.

"I live," the Puritan replied. "I merely feel the weight of my many years and the miles I have trod across this wide earth. Perhaps it is time I returned home to rest, and leave these strange secret undertakings to others."

"Yes, find a comfortable chair, a full flagon of wine, and leave this sort of thing to the youngsters," Orlando nodded, as she and Porthos helped the Puritan to his feet and to his staff.

Both men gave her a puzzled glance, but for very different reasons.

They were all pleasantly surprised to find the horses still there, having fed and rested to their hearts' contents, while their owners were galivanting about.

"It has been an adventure, my friends," Porthos said, patting his steed's flank. "But I fear both my good friend, D'Artagnan, and my addle-headed servant will be worried over my lateness. So I should be on my way. If you would care to join me, I plan to stop at the nearest inn or manor house that I find, drink my fill, and restock for my journey."

Kane mounted, nodding his assent.

"Lead on," Orlando said, with a hearty smile. "I must attend one last, brief task and then will rejoin you. I, too, have a powerful thirst and would be amiss to not reward the efforts of my noble comrades."

Unsure what that entailed and to which of them, or both, she was speaking, the swordsmen gave the flirtatious immortal, and then each other, sideways glances and unsure words of farewell, before heading back down the mountain road.

"Come along," Orlando called, once the pair were past the bend in the road and out of sight. "You're wasting daylight, playing shy."

From behind a tree, emerged a ghost, but this one was familiar to Orlando. It was a translucent child, a young girl dressed in fashion, several decades out of date.

"Well, better late than never, I suppose," Orlando said. "Where's Isaac?"

"My father is making his way," the ghost child replied, with a slight frown. "We have been quite busy."

"You've been busy, Lotte? I've postponed a war, shooed away a malicious time traveler, missed breakfast, and have a potential rendezvous with two swordsmen and a serving wench."

Realizing the unearthly child had no idea what she was talking about, Orlando merely smiled, patted Lotte upon the head. and fished something out of her belt.

It was a small shard of crystal from the cave, flickering with a faint light that flowed from blue to green.

"Here, little one. A shiny bauble for your father to add to his collection. I'm going to join my friends. If he can, have Isaac meet me at the tavern. If he cannot, let him know I'm next off to catch a ship to Venice. I have been informed by an acquaintance of mine that there is something lurking in the canals..."

Credits and Sources

The Wolf at the Door of Time

Co-Starring:	**Created by:**
Moses Nebogipfel	H. G. Wells
Joseph Balsamo	Alexandre Dumas
Thibault (The Wolf Leader)	Alexandre Dumas
Agnelette	Alexandre Dumas
Leo Saint-Clair (The Nyctalope)	Jean de La Hire
Captain Gogol	Ian Fleming
Avakoum Zahov	Andrei Gulyashki
Oktobriana	Petr Sadecký
The Wolves:	
The Black Dog of Bungay	*Historical*
The Hound of the Baskervilles	Arthur Conan Doyle
The Beast of Gévaudan	*Historical*
The Hound of Mons	*Historical*
Also Starring:	
Zoomashmarta	Philip José Farmer
Captain Strange of Arcadia	Calvert & Hughes

© 2012, Martin Gately.
Previously published in *Tales of the Shadowmen N°9*, 2012.

What Lurks in Romney Marsh?

Co-Starring:	**Created by:**
Dr. Syn (The Scarecrow)	Russell Thorndyke
Mr. Mipps	Russell Thorndyke
Josie Bauer	Spider Robinson
Also Starring:	
Rotwang	Fritz Lang & Thea Von Harbou
Doctor Nebogipfel	H. G. Wells

The Time Traveler   H. G. Wells

As Time Goes By...

Co-Starring:	Created by:
Rick Blaine	Julius J. Epstein, Philip G. Epstein & Howard Koch
The Drexlers	Norvell W. Page
Also Starring:	
Ferrari	Julius J. Epstein, Philip G. Epstein & Howard Koch
Major Strasser	Julius J. Epstein, Philip G. Epstein & Howard Koch
Sam	Julius J. Epstein, Philip G. Epstein & Howard Koch
The Spider	Harry Steeger
Noël Essaillon	René Barjavel

The Next Omega

Co-Starring:	Created by:
Thea	Thea Von Harbou
Antoine Gerpré (Young Omega)	Alfred Driou
Madame Gerpré	Alfred Driou
Eugène Papillon	Emile Gaboriau
The Cult of Ubasti	Harry Earnshaw,

	R.R. Morgan & Vera Oldham
The Red Lectroids	Earl Mac Rauch
Baron Maupertuis/Ozer	Arthur Conan Doyle
	& Paul Féval

Also Starring:

The Lunian Immortals	Alfred Driou
M. Lecoq	Emile Gaboriau
Miss Marple	Agatha Christie
Dr. John H. Watson	Arthur Conan Doyle

© 2013, Travis Hiltz.
Previously published in *Tales of the Shadowmen N°10*, 2013.

All Roads Lead to Mars

Co-Starring:	**Created by:**
Jason Spell/Time Brigade	Claude Legrand
	& Edmond Ripoll
John ***/Lectroids	Earl Mac Rauch
Captain Spencer	Clive Barker
Setissi/Ice Warriors	Brian Hayles
	and Arnould Galopin
John Carter	Edgar Rice Burroughs
Thea	Thea Von Harbou
Sorns/Seroni	C. S. Lewis
Bent Oyarsa/Eldils	C. S. Lewis
Oompa-Loompas	Roald Dahl

© 2014, Travis Hiltz.
Previously published in *Tales of the Shadowmen N°11*, 2014.

The Revelation of the Yeti

Co-Starring:	**Created by:**
Barton Werper	Peter Scott & Peggy Scott
Ki-Gor	John Peter Drummond
Nora	Félicien Champsaur

The Mi-Go	H. P. Lovecraft
Dr. Karswell	Montague Rhodes James
Madame Palmyre	Renée Dunan
The Master	Hal P. Warren
Cristaldi	Miguel M. Delgado
	& Alfredo Salazar

Also Starring:

Tarzan	Edgar Rice Burroughs
Mowgli	Rudyard Kipling
John-Gor	Robert Moore Williams
Lt. Werper	Edgar Rice Burroughs
Paula Dupree	Ted Fithian, Neil P. Varnick,
	Griffin Jay & Henry Sucher
Felifax	Paul Féval, *fils*
Helene Kilgore	John Peter Drummond
Solomon Kane	Robert E. Howard
Cthulhu	H. P. Lovecraft
Azathoth	H. P. Lovecraft
Dagon	H. P. Lovecraft
Tcho-Tcho	H. P. Lovecraft
The Jermyns	H. P. Lovecraft
Yog-Sothoth	H. P. Lovecraft
Baal	Renée Dunan
Dracula	Bram Stoker
Manos	Hal P. Warren

Previously published in *Tales of the Shadowmen N°12*, 2015.

Time to Kill

Co-Starring:	**Created by:**
Bob Morane	Henri Vernes
Bill Ballantine	Henri Vernes
André Durand-Mareuil	Jean Girault & Louis Sapin
Jules Maigret	Georges Simenon

Also Starring:

Janvier   Georges Simenon
Professor Hunter   Henri Vernes

Doctor Omega and the Future Museum

Co-Starring:	**Created by:**
Fantômas	Pierre Souvestre & Marcel Allain
The Master	Barry Letts, Terrance Dicks & Robert Holmes
Jasmine "Jaz" Driscoll	David Friend
Liz Shaw	Barry Letts, Terrance Dicks & Robert Holmes
Also Starring:	
Inspector Juve	Pierre Souvestre & Marcel Allain
The Mechonoids	Terry Nation

The Cubic Displacement of the Soul

Co-Starring:	**Created by:**
Professor James Moriarty	Arthur Conan Doyle
The Little Prince	Antoine de Saint-Exupéry
Colonel Sebastian Moran	Arthur Conan Doyle
Also Starring:	
Sherlock Holmes	Arthur Conan Doyle
Doctor Nikola	Guy Boothby
Professor George Challenger	Arthur Conan Doyle
Bureau d'Echange de Maux	Lord Dunsany

Previously published in *Tales of the Shadowmen N°17*, 2020.

These are the Voyages...

Co-Starring:	**Created by:**
Yusuf-ben-Moktar	Rafael Sabatini
Marcel Renard	Theo Varlet & André Blandin
Shelfin Bundt Arbornoth	based on Jonathan Swift
Sir Oliver Tressilian	Rafael Sabatini
Duke Prospero	William Shakespeare
Isaac Laquedem	Paul Féval
(The Wandering Jew)	
Lotte	Paul Féval
The Morlocks	H.G. Wells
The Yahoos	Jonathan Swift
Mr. Pitt	Rafael Sabatini
Monoclard	Theo Varlet & Andre Blandin
Cipriani	Theo Varlet & Andre Blandin
Anguirus	Motoyoshi Oda
Also Starring:	
Duranton	Theo Varlet & Andre Blandin
Dread Pirate Roberts	William Goldman
Captain Mephisto	Ronald Davidson
The Time Traveler	H. G. Wells
The Houyhhnms	Jonathan Swift
The Islands:	
Lilliput	Jonathan Swift
Paradise	William Moulton Marston
The Nameless Isle	William Shakespeare / Jeffrey Lieber, J. J. Abrams, Damon Lindelof & Carlton Cruse
Caspak	Edgar Rice Burroughs
Borgabunda	Edward G. Montagne / Jonathan Swift
Monster Island	Toho Studios
Villings	Adolfo Bioy Casares

Orpheus Omega

Starring:	**Created by:**
Orpheus	Jean Cocteau
The Princess (Death)	Jean Cocteau
The Beast	Jean Cocteau
	based on Gabrielle-Suzanne Barbot
	de Villeneuve & Jeanne-Marie
	Leprince de Beaumont

Also Starring:	
Glenarvon	Lady Caroline Lamb
Tormance	David Lindsay
The Zone/The Room	Andrei Tarkovsky
	based on Arkady
	& Boris Strugatski

Foiled Again

Starring:	**Created by:**
No. 6 (The Prisoner)	Patrick McGoohan
	& George Markstein

Also Starring:	
The Horla	Guy de Maupassant
Simon Cordier	Robert E. Kent
	based on Guy de Maupassant
The Village	Patrick McGoohan
	& George Markstein

When the Children Leave Home

Co-Starring:	Created by:
Thea	Thea Von Harbou
Karellen	Arthur C. Clarke
The Overlords	Arthur C. Clarke
Also Starring:	
Jan Rodricks	Arthur C. Clarke
The Overmind	Arthur C. Clarke

© 2022, Nigel Malcom.
Previously published in *Tales of the Shadowmen N°19*, 2022.

The Ghosts of Gascony

Co-Starring:	Created by:
M. du Vallon de Bracieux de Pierrefonds (Porthos)	Alexandre Dumas
Orlando	based on Virginia Wolfe and Alan Moore
Solomon Kane	Robert E. Howard
Rotwang	Fritz Lang & Thea Von Harbou
Hélène	Travis Hiltz based on Thea Von Harbou
The Volkites	Maurice Geraghty & Oliver Drake
Lotte	Paul Féval
Also Starring:	
Isaac Laquedem (The Wandering Jew)	Paul Féval
Athos	Alexandre Dumas
Aramis	Alexandre Dumas
D'Artagnan	Alexandre Dumas
Mousqueton	Alexandre Dumas
The Morlocks	H. G. Wells